It all came as natural as walking to Duny Gene. The hard bounce of the heavy gun in his hands was as intoxicating as the whiskey. He let off a few bursts, blowing bark from trees.

"You got it, kid," Hoadie said, laughing. "I told you, Lester, this little son of a bitch can shoot anything that shoots."

Duny Gene emptied the drum and Lester took the gun. It smelled of burning oil, and the barrel was smoking.

"Don't touch that bitch now, along the barrel," Lester said. "Burn right into you. I think we better let it go at that."

"Yeah, some farmer around here's likely to think the Mexicans has come," Hoadie said.

They fired the pistols again, and two of them felt familiar in Duny Gene's hand. Just like the one his father had brought from the war, he told them.

"Bring it along next time we shoot," Lester said. "We can try all of 'em out."

"One of them big automatics is like all the rest," Hoadie said.

"No they ain't. Each one's a little different. Each one's a little sweetie you got to get acquainted with before she'll come across for you."

Duny Gene liked the way Lester talked. And he had this direct way of looking at people, like he was interested in them.

"Duny Gene, you handle a chopper good," Lester said. "You sure you never shot one before?"

"That's the first one I ever saw."

"I told you," Hoadie said. "Son of a bitch can shoot anything."

Tor Books by Douglas C. Jones

*Forthcoming

DOUGLAS C. JONES

WEEDY ROUGH

A TOM DOHERTY ASSOCIATES BOOK

WEEDY ROUGH

Copyright © 1981 by Kemm, Incorporated

Published by arrangement with Henry Holt and Company, Inc.

A TOR Book
Published by Tom Doherty Associates, Inc.
49 West 24 Street
New York, N.Y. 10010

Cover art by Peter Attard

ISBN: 0-812-58463-5   CAN. ISBN: 0-812-58464-3

Library of Congress Catalog Card Number: 80-28297

First Tor edition: December 1989

Printed in the United States of America

0 9 8 7 6 5 4 3 2 1

Weedy Rough . . .

IT IS AN ACTUAL PLACE, ALTHOUGH THERE
is not much to mark it now except a mountain cross-
roads. It bears no resemblance to the town described
in what follows, although both are situated in the
rugged southern Ozarks. The name is used here because there is some elusive fascination and toughness
about it, like the bark on an old hickory, and it
deserves to be set down someplace. Perhaps this is as
good a place as any.

The story is fiction and the characters are imaginary, even though the spirit is as true to the time and
place as possible. The telling is sometimes done in
the idiom of those who would have peopled Weedy
Rough, and the lot of it is for them, who never
existed, but in a thousand ways and a hundred places
did.

PART ONE

· 1 ·

IT WAS SUMMER. WEEDY ROUGH LAY IN ITS cup of valley, dozing in the heat and dust, the high-reaching ridges on three sides holding out any breeze. In every direction except north was high ground, covered with the deep green foliage of oak and hickory.

The Frisco railroad bisected the town, the rails set on their oak crossties like shining ribbons, winding past the store fronts and finally disappearing in the tunnel at the south end of town.

Harsh sunlight slanted down across the buildings along the west side of the railroad tracks. It gleamed hotly on the rails. No one was in sight at the tie yard, where a log wagon stood with a four-mule team, their heads down, broomtails switching at the flies. No one was on the sidewalk before the bank or the grocery store or beer hall, nor on the east side of the tracks, where the sun beat against the façade of a second line of structures—the drugstore, Schirvy's general store, post office, and barbershop. Everyone had gone to shade. Even the peg-leg man had crawled into the dark shadows cast by the big maple at the north end of the Frisco depot to sleep off a drunk.

Facing onto the street from many windows were the placards, not yet faded, displaying a blue eagle and the motto "NRA, We Do Our Part." The face of

Franklin Delano Roosevelt smiled from a poster tacked to the telephone pole in front of the drugstore.

The sounds of a railroad section crew working on the mainline tracks north of town gave metallic punctuation to the scolding of blue jays in the oaks along the slopes of West Mountain. Other than that, it was quiet except for the occasional faint note of a cowbell from somewhere on the high ground behind the post office.

Afterward, few could recall having seen the big Packard touring car come down the West Mountain road, rolling to a stop before the red brick bank with the creak of mechanical brakes. And only a few saw it roar away, not four minutes later, after the sudden, shattering crash of gunfire. There were three people in the car, bending forward as it leaped along the street, each of them wearing a brown fedora hat and a red bandanna across his face.

As the Packard went past, a dog jumped out from the front of the ice-cream parlor barking hysterically and chasing the car for a few hundred feet north, until it was far away toward the open valley, lost in a cloud of powdery dust.

Olie Merton, the barber, ran from his shop along with two hangers-on, watching the big machine disappear.

"I thought I heard a shotgun," Olie said. "And this sure as hell ain't squirrel season!"

There was a woman screaming in the bank, and a man down in the doorway, a twelve-gauge pumpgun in his hands, a neat puncture in his face, and the back of his head flowing away in a red mush. And through the dirt of the street, a splattering of blood pointed toward the tie yard along the railroad siding.

It's difficult to reconstruct the story of that robbery. To do so one has to reach into the guts and marrow of Weedy Rough during the decade before the depths of the Great Depression. All the town's people felt involved in both. Each of them tried to outdo the others in the telling, throwing in little bits and pieces of what life was like there because they thought it might have had something to do with the final felony. Maybe it did. But like most trials, the one that finally came revealed only so much as was admissible in evidence.

"A good system for law, maybe," said Tooth Snowdon, town philosopher and gravedigger. "But it's damned sorry as social history."

Nobody cared to guess where Tooth had learned such a term as *social history*. It didn't matter, really. What mattered was that this robbery had not been done by some wild Oklahoman like Pretty Boy Floyd, as one would expect in that time and place. It had been done, at least partly, by home people, and a local boy would go to the dock, the state claiming a right to strap him in the electric chair at Tucker State Penitentiary.

If Weedy Roughers didn't know exactly how to explain that robbery, at least they were agreed on where to start. It really began just after the Great War, when Barton Pay came up from Fort Smith with his wife Lydia and son Duny Gene to settle in Weedy Rough and buy timber for the Frisco railroad.

It was mostly a good year, 1919. The boys came home and everybody was proud of them. And glad none had been buried in France, which wasn't surprising since the town had sent only fourteen in the first place. That didn't count the ones from the wild country who had come in to the Frisco depot looking to enlist as soon as they heard there was a war. Come in from the sticks, people said. They were slab-sided, long-jawed men who lived off in the deep hills around Devil's Mountain or Signal Rock.

"Our granddaddies fit the Yankees," one was heard to say. "And our daddies fit the Spaniards."

The citizens were proud of them all, even the ones like Constable Leo Sparks's boy, who never got any farther than Camp McClellan, where he played alto horn in the band and caught a dose of clap. In the barbershop, they said you couldn't expect anything better of city women who collected around army camps, although most of the barbershop bunch were a little unsure about the location of Camp McClellan.

Business was good everywhere. Spirits were high. Even the Volstead Act failed to worry anybody, what with very few people ever drinking store whiskey. They bought what they needed in quart mason jars from one or the other of those same yellow-eyed hillmen whose granddaddies had fought the Yankees. It usually tasted like coal oil, but it hit like the late lamented John L. Sullivan, in his grave only a year.

There was a little bubble of sour stomach in autumn, when the American League White Sox baseball team got into a wrangle with gamblers over who should win the World Series. That passed quickly because before any real news of it reached the hills, people had forgotten the ball diamond and were thinking about basketball.

Barton Pay came to town that fall, a well-proportioned man of twenty-five who looked and acted forty. He had a shock of straight black hair, high cheekbones, and gray eyes. And a contract in his pocket to take over the tie yard and start buying. He came up the mountain from Fort Smith on the evening passenger train, taking a room in the railroad hotel next to the bank until he could find a house.

He finally settled on one owned by Parkins Muller. It overlooked the town from East Mountain and was only a few rods' distance along the ridge from where Parkins's own house stood. It was well overpriced, although fairly large for Weedy Rough. It had three bedrooms and two wells and a long porch that ran across the front, where a person could look south and see the railroad tunnel and straight ahead, the south end of town. The slope was so steep that the front stood two stories high, stilted above the ground, while the back was dug five feet into the hillside. Parkins asked two thousand dollars for it, which Barton Pay didn't quibble about, and it was financed through Parkins's Bank of Weedy Rough.

Barton signed all the necessary papers and sent for his family.

"Barton Pay is going to be a big man in this town," Tooth said. "They say his daddy is a famous lawyer in Fort Smith, and knew old Judge Parker back in the wild days of the Indian Nations."

"I hear the old man was a circuit judge down in Sebastian County for a while," Olie Merton said, sitting in his barber chair and looking out across the street toward the railroad tracks, a toothpick as ever at the corner of his mouth. "Then he got appointed United States attorney. I hear he's retired now. Not that lawyers ever retire. But it seems to me a man with such a daddy would have gone into the law."

"Barton Pay is his own man," Tooth said. "I helped him and his family move into that house on the hill, and I could tell he's his own man. I don't feature him no lawyer anyway."

"He looks a little Indian to me," Leo Sparks said. The constable was sitting in one of a line of chairs along the wall, close enough to see the room's only cuspidor, but far enough away to miss it each time he sent a stream of tobacco juice in that direction.

"Hell, he's got them gray eyes, ain't he?" Joe Sanford said, watching through the window for any likely customers who might go into his ice-cream parlor just across the street.

"Lots of gray-eyed men has Indian blood," Tooth said. "Now, you take that old man Shayburg, who comes into town once a year to get drunk in the tie yard. He's black as a nigger, but he's got them gray eyes. I'd wager you he's Indian as hell."

"Well, I hear old Parkins skinned Mr. Pay for that house," Olie said.

"Parkins is in this world for one thing," Tooth said. "To make money. God dammit, Leo, can't you hit that thing? You're about to make me sick."

The Pays settled into Weedy Rough quickly. They joined the Methodist church and Lydia became one of the prime movers in the Ladies' Aid Society. She presented lectures on the importance of missionary work to the heathen in Darkest Africa. Barton was elected to the board of stewards and he always sat in the front pew at church, by himself, with Lydia and the boy farther back in the congregation. He became a member of the school board. He began to carry the mail as a substitute carrier on one of the long back roads west of town, in the rough country around Devil's Mountain. He was the first rural letter carrier in the hills to try a Model T, instead of a horse.

"You can't get mired down on those roads," he said. "There's too much rock."

He did, though, and sometimes had to have hill folk pull him out with a brace of mules. They never expected any pay in return because he became their friend. He bought them stamps and made sure their kids got a Christmas present, and when one of the old ones was sick he always took them a quart fruit jar full of rich beef stew.

But mostly, Barton was the Frisco timber buyer. The wagons would gather each weekday in his tie yard to unload along the sidings that paralleled the mainline tracks. The boxlike stacks of eight-inch by eight-inch by eight-foot solid-oak crossties would grow, almost engulfing the south end of town before the black crews came up from Fort Smith every two weeks to load them into boxcars for shipment.

Lydia wasn't like her husband. She always kept a distance between herself and the townspeople. She was quick to let anyone know that her kin were from Fort Smith high society, their names appearing regularly in the Sunday edition of the newspaper. Some of the women snickered behind her back, laughing at that social talk, and over the stories Lydia told about her family being founders of some of the best towns in Arkansas when they were involved in riverboat trade in the cotton country down south. She never said anything about her husband's family.

Barton never said anything about his family either, not even about his famous lawyer father. In those days, having Indian blood was almost as bad in some quarters as having leprosy. But he was Indian, no doubt about it.

Old man Pay had married a Cherokee woman in his early years, the only wife he ever had or wanted. It lasted only a short while, until Barton was born and the woman died in the bearing, but few people along the old Nations border didn't know about it. Even Lydia knew, later, when Barton began mooning around her. Those days of courtship came to flower with her passion in the back of a buggy parked one evening under the elms, not two blocks along the street from her family home in the old Belle Grove district of Fort Smith.

There had been some kind of excitement about this young dark-faced man with the gray eyes that she couldn't resist, despite all her background of staunch Methodism, and with forebears who had helped build the state and some of whom even served in the legislature. She had never counted on her lack of self-control being responsible for planting the seed in her that was quarter-blood Cherokee, an event unthinkable, and hence the source of a savage resentment for the rest of her life.

Barton married her, of course, although she was three years his senior, and at that time him in the midst of spinning out his wild days.

Resentment or not, the passion lasted almost five years, and then it was suddenly dead and gone forever. She watched her son grow, the black hair and gray eyes reminding her of her shame each time she looked at him. But she came from stock that had always held a bargain made was a bargain kept. That's when she started worrying about the heathen of the Dark Continent. She joined the Eastern Star—her father having been a Mason—and threw herself into housework. Through it all, she never quite forgave the old man, Barton's father Eben, for having married that damned squaw in the first place. She never forgave her son completely for being Cherokee, nor herself for that moment of weakness in the buggy. She wore resentment like an expensive string of pearls, because there was pride in it as well as bitterness.

By the time the Pays came to Weedy Rough, Lydia was sleeping in her own bed. They were likely the only couple in town who kept that arrangement. By then, too, Barton's drinking and hell raising was behind him, and there had been plenty of that. His days were taken with hard work and his nights with reading. He spent as much time as he could with his son.

Duny Gene was a striking boy. He was built like his mother, stocky and tough. Maybe some of that came from the Cherokee forebears, too. But they said he took after his father, with that black hair and brown skin and those startling smoke-colored eyes looking out of the dark face. Some of the women of the town said he was the handsomest boy they'd ever seen, and always polite like his father, tipping his cap, once he got old enough to wear one.

"That's the cleanest boy I ever seen," Tooth said. "Seems like he never gets dirty or has snot on his face like a normal kid. Clean enough to eat off of. But you can't help liking the little devil."

It was true. There was some of his father's old wildness in him, a streak of mischief popping up regular as Halloween, and even apparent in those first years during the early grades at school—hiding girls' lunches and pretending to snore during recitations.

Barton heard very little of this because Duny Gene was shrewd enough in his minor troublemaking to stop short of anything so flagrant as to produce a note for his parents from some irate teacher, and he never came close to being expelled.

It carried over from the school scene, too: taking bean-flip potshots at horseback riders along the road below the Pay house, or stealing sour balls from Esta Stayborn's store, not because he wanted for candy at home, but just for the hell of it, to see if he could get away with the thing.

None of this was ever bad enough, even when he was suspect, to bring the town constable to Barton's door.

So Barton was proud of his boy, and made no bones about it. By then, still in his prime and with no wife to speak of, he seemed satisfied with his boy and his work. He was a part of the town. He became a fox hunter and a tobacco chewer, and a man who would loan out five dollars when he had it. Hardly a day passed in the barbershop when Barton Pay wasn't mentioned, and always with respect.

One of the things Tooth and the others remembered was the business of the bell.

*   *   *

The year Barton Pay became the most active member of the school board, he learned there was a large brass bell available in Fort Smith, almost for the asking. This prompted the board's opinion that the school could use a nice bell, particularly if it didn't cost anything.

The Weedy Rough school was a single-story frame building that stood on Naulty's Ridge south of town. Nearby was its gymnasium, also constructed of pine lumber and with a dirt floor. Often, the school was destroyed by fire and rebuilt again on the old foundations. The gym was apparently immune to flames because it stood unscathed, until it collapsed of old age. It was remarkable that periodically the school was consumed, whereas the old gym—where the kids enjoyed playing basketball—remained intact.

There was no guarantee that the majesty of a bell would stop the fires, but at least it would add some dignity to an otherwise rather drab public structure.

The bell was out of a Gary, Indiana, foundry that had gone bust. It had been sitting on a Fort Smith siding for over a year, collecting spiders and the leavings of birds. It was available for shipping costs, which were reduced even further by Barton Pay's connection with the railroad. He collected the money by insisting that timber sellers coming into his yard donate a tie or two from each load for the civic endeavor. Within a very short time, Weedy Rough had its school bell, a big one, bought with crossties. The thing became known as Mr. Pay's Bell.

Tooth Snowdon assumed responsibility for moving the bell up the mountainside and building an appropriate belfry. He chose Alvie Haus, the rural letter carrier, as his mule driver because Alvie was known as the best ribbons man in the county before he started handling the mails. They used a pair of big wheel mules and a double span of horses, hitched to the biggest log wagon they could find. Tooth said the bell likely weighed well over a ton.

It was a Sunday afternoon. From the depot to the top of Naulty's Ridge was a long mile, all steep upgrade, and people were lined along the route, clinging to the bluffs and hanging onto sassafras bushes, acting as though it were some kind of patriotic parade. Tooth did his best to make it so, singing in his fine Welsh voice as he and Alvie walked beside the wagon, whipping the team along. The singing stopped when they came abreast of the Pay house, which hung above the road like a cliff swallow's nest. Lydia was watching from the long front porch.

Nobody saw Duny Gene run out into the road until he had scrambled up on the wagon and was trying to straddle the brass monster. Tooth bellowed and Alvie yanked up on the reins, and when the team stopped, already blowing hard, Tooth pulled the boy down and sent him back up the hillside with a slap on the butt. Lydia was screaming, the other spectators were cheering, and one of the mules sat down in his traces.

It took them a good twenty minutes to get the parade started again, and the language was so fearful Lydia disappeared into her house, with her boy in tow by then. At last, the team responded to the abuse and the log wagon groaned upward, past the north end of the railroad tunnel, the Methodist church, and finally along the hogback to the school.

Before the fall semester started that year, the bell was in place in its new belfry at the front of the school. Tooth had almost mashed off three fingers in the process, but he was undaunted. On the first day of school, he stood with Barton beneath the belfry. As they pulled the rope, with kids and a good many townspeople standing well back in case the whole thing collapsed, the behemoth sounded for the first time in those hills. Its great throat sent out a deep, vibrant peal that thundered against the ears. It could be heard south of High Bridge and, when the wind was right, across the woody ridges all the way to Signal Rock, ten miles away. When the giant clapper struck, birds flew from the trees along the high ground, and squirrels scrambled for their dens.

"It sounds fine," Tooth said. "But it scares hell out of the chickens. Now take laying hens. When they get old, their innards sometimes get confused and they'll lay a double-yolk egg. But since that big son of a bitch has been ringing on Naulty's Ridge, I ain't seen a single double out of my coop."

The people were so proud of the bell they rang it on the slightest excuse—on holidays, for funerals, for victory on the basketball court. And from time to time it sounded in the middle of the night when Mr. Harmon Budd, the peg-leg man, was still sober enough to walk up Naulty's Ridge and pull the rope just for fun.

One February—it was 1921—the town was roused to a bitter cold night with the dreaded shout of "Fire," and the tolling of the great bell. Some brave soul was heaving on the rope, even though it was the school that was burning. There was only one well on Naulty's Ridge, and before a bucket brigade could be formed, the fire was beyond stopping.

By the time most of the townspeople had gathered to watch, the structure was an inferno. The belfry was enveloped in fire, and in the bright flames they could see the bell, silent now, a massive black silhouette. Soon, the tower collapsed. Under the red reflection on the billowing cloud of smoke, a great shower of sparks went up, bursting into the black night sky like frenzied fireflies. As the bell struck the ground, it gave off a dull metallic thump and began to roll down the back side of Naulty's Ridge.

People screamed and scattered before the oncoming brass terror as it crashed through brush and small timber. Then, suddenly, it stopped, lodged firmly against the trunk of a large white oak tree about a hundred yards from the still-flaming schoolhouse. As the noise and commotion ceased, a sigh went up from around the circle of people, whether of relief or disappointment, nobody was sure.

By morning, there was nothing left but the smoking ruin, blackened metal folding chairs and desks thrusting up through the charcoal like tar-pit skeletons. The kids were in a state of near hysterical delight, thinking the summer vacation would start three months early. The joy was short-lived. Classes resumed that very day in the churches and the Methodist parsonage, which was empty at the time.

Sitting on the back steps of the parsonage during recess that spring, Duny Gene Pay learned to smoke cigarettes. They were hand-rolled by his closest friend, Hoadie Renkin. Both were nine years old.

After the cold weather let up, they built their new school. But not on the old foundations. Tooth Snowdon said it would be too damned much trouble moving that bell back up the hill, and the board agreed. They built the new one around the bell, where it had come to rest. It meant the end of the white oak tree that had stopped the bell's career downhill, but nobody worried about white oak trees because they all figured there were enough of those to last forever.

Once more, in due time and to the kids' disgust, the great bell was heard across the hills.

Two years later, in the early fall, the school burned again. And again, the people came to watch Mr. Pay's bell bound off down the hill, farther still from the town. And then the rebuilding, where the bell had come to rest.

Putting shingles on the new structure, Tooth paused
on his high perch and wiped the sweat from his long
nose. He wanted a snort of white whiskey, but it was
too much trouble climbing down to fetch it from his
toolbox. He gazed out across the valley toward High
Bridge, south of the railroad tunnel. For as far as he
could see there was wooded wilderness, stretching
away toward the Arkansas River and Fort Smith,
sixty miles away. Not a building nor house nor pigsty
of Weedy Rough was visible from this side of Naulty's
Ridge.

"By God," he said to himself. "This son of a
bitch is edgin' away from us."

It was too much to expect that the new school
would last any longer than the others, and it didn't.
Regular as the clock, it burned to the ground in
February 1925. Only this time when the belfry caved
in, the bell got up enough momentum to crash through
all the undergrowth and small trees, coming to rest
finally at the foot of Naulty's Ridge, in Slicker Creek.

Collectively, the town said, "To hell with it." The
bell was left where it lay in two feet of water, to
collect fine silt and provide a murky green cave for
the minnows and crawdads.

Nobody saw anything prophetic about it at the
time. But years later Olie Merton put the thought to
words.

"We didn't know it then. But that bell was like all
else Barton Pay touched. Good things to start that
went to hell in the end."

And Tooth added, "He deserved better!"

It was strange. The wild country kids, who were
always suspected of setting the fires, kept coming
back to school. They could have stayed away and no
truant officer would have gone into the hills for
them. But they kept coming back, sullen and yellow-

eyed. None of the town kids ever accused them of anything because they were quick to ball a knotty fist. Sticks kids were harder to bark than a hickory tree, and if one was engaged in a scuffle, half a dozen of his kin would suddenly appear, ready to pitch in.

They came, most of them barefooted right through the winter, carrying a tin syrup pail filled with baked sweet potatoes for lunch. Or sometimes, the bucket would be stuffed with wild blackberry cobbler, sour and seedy as discovered sin.

They would grow up as their parents had before them in the woody hills around Signal Rock or Devil's Mountain, living on practically nothing, wearing overalls and flour-sack dresses down to threads, killing squirrels and wild hogs for meat. Growing up dirty and ignorant. Bearing their children in the back room of some clapboard shack, mother on a stained mattress, father the midwife. Avoiding anyone not of their kind.

One such boy was Hoadie Renkin. He wasn't dour, like his brethren. He grinned a lot. But he looked like the rest of the sticks people, skinny as a rake and with pale eyes and a thatch of straw hair. And he had a reputation like the others. When he smiled, kids never knew if he was about to offer them a ripe persimmon or swing at their jaw.

Mostly, Hoadie was different because he liked the town instead of the woods. Sometimes when he came to school on Monday, he wouldn't go home until Friday, sleeping in barns and cow sheds and eating whatever he could beg or borrow from his only town friend, Duny Gene Pay. They were so close it was as if they lived in a world of their own, excluding all other people around them. They made a remarkable pair—the slender, sunburned kid from the sticks, and

Weedy Rough's own Duny Gene, short and heavy and with that Indian hair and gray eyes.

Nobody was ever sure where the rumor started about who set that last school fire. Probably in the barbershop. Some people were saying that maybe the sticks kids were not altogether responsible. Maybe the conflagration that sent Mr. Pay's bell to its rest in Slicker Creek was lighted by Hoadie Renkin and Mr. Pay's own son. But nobody ever had the guts to mention it to Barton Pay.

"Besides," Tooth said. "Iffen he started it, that Renkin kid's the one put him up to it. I never trusted any of them Renkins since three of 'em did this to me one time." With two fingers, he peeled up his lip to expose the gap where four front teeth had once been.

"You had no business sniffin' around one of them Renkin women at that barn dance," Olie Merton said from his barber chair.

"Hell!" Tooth said. "I never got close enough to sniff."

Lydia treated Hoadie like smallpox. When he came near the house, she ran him off, making all sorts of threats they both knew she couldn't carry out.

"You stay away from that hill trash," she told Duny Gene.

"Yes ma'am," the boy said, his eyes flat as gray slate stone, staring at her.

"You hear me, Duny Gene? You stay away from that boy."

"Yes ma'am."

Barton paid it no mind. More and more, all his thoughts seemed to be on buying ties and fox hunting, and now and again taking Duny Gene out on some hill road and the both of them taking turns shooting tin cans with the Army .45 Barton had brought back from the war. They would sit on the running board of the Model T and blast away, Duny Gene having to hold the gun with both hands.

"Best shot I ever saw with a pistol," Barton said. "That boy loves to shoot." And everybody who knew Duny Gene at all was aware that he loved guns, with the same passion most hill boys his age reserved for good-running fox dogs and ice-cream sundaes.

·2·

PARKINS MULLER AND HIS SPINSTER SISTER owned and operated the Bank of Weedy Rough. It was a small enterprise. Hill people had little trust in banks, and even less in Parkins Muller.

Parkins was a small man, always bent forward as though rushing someplace. He had false teeth that rattled when he talked, which he did as little as possible. Everybody had him figured for a mean little bastard.

Sister Veda, two years her brother's junior, with a gray face and pinched lips, was fashioned from the same stone. She had a cast in her left eye that gave her the appearance of a turpentined cat. Girl and woman, she had never entertained a man in bed. Weedy Roughers mistakenly assumed that such a possibility never entered her mind.

The house they lived in overlooked the town from East Mountain, just as Barton Pay's did. In a hill pasture behind, they kept a herd of French alpine goats, most of which had taken on the personality of master and mistress. Anytime Duny Gene Pay and Hoadie Renkin had the opportunity, they pelted the goats with rocks.

Parkins and his money were subjects of continuing speculation in the barbershop. Everyone wondered how much he actually had, but there was never any consensus on it. The fact was, he enjoyed good credit with a couple of Fort Smith banks, and everyone knew that Fort Smith banks did not lend money on faith.

Muller had business interests other than his bank, including some where customers contributed to his wealth without even knowing it. Parkins owned a half-interest in the Muller Mercantile, Weedy Rough's largest grocery and general store. Weekly, without fail, he went over the books and the inventory with his partner, Esta Stayborn, who ran the business. But the Mullers never bought anything in their store. When necessity required, Parkins rode the Frisco to Fayetteville and made his household purchases wholesale, and had the merchandise shipped in care of the Mercantile. This made the waybill a deductible business expense under all the provisions and laws resulting from the odious 1913 constitutional amendment establishing an income tax.

The blacksmith shop and North End Garage were Muller properties, from which he collected rent. He sometimes charged a usurious rate of interest on loans, and twice he brought in a friendly deputy sheriff from Fayetteville to foreclose an overdue mortgage.

And there was Violet Sims. Violet was a plump, rather attractive woman with sienna hair who lived in a house up the slope of West Mountain behind the bank. Parkins Muller owned the house. Violet was in the business of supplying bootleg whiskey to any who wanted a change from white lightning, which she obtained from that same deputy sheriff through Parkins Muller. Parkins shared her profits. Shared, too, the profits of another more lucrative enterprise, supplying the needs of lonely men. And although Parkins was partner in her business, he never bought anything from her store, either.

Each morning, before the southbound passenger train came through, winter and summer alike, Parkins and Miss Veda trooped down the hill from their home, him walking in front and wearing a derby hat cocked over one baleful eye. She always carried a stack of ledger books under one arm. After the day's business, back up the hill they would go, Indian file again, to eat their supper and milk the goats and usually be in bed before the northbound passenger arrived.

They were despised in Weedy Rough, but envied, too, because making a profit was something to be respected. Parkins had always made a profit on anything he tried, and he always had money to lend, provided there was adequate collateral, of course. Some said he was rich because he was stingy. Even after he bought the first Delco generator in town, and later when the electric lines were run into Weedy Rough, lights seldom burned in the Muller household. When they did, it was usually coal-oil lamps.

"Just the kind of people you'd expect to own a bank," Tooth said. "A dried-up old maid and a son of a bitch with no gonads."

People faulted the Mullers almost as much for what they didn't do as for what they did. They never went to church or to pie suppers or dances, and they never appeared at basketball games, a near mortal sin. The only contact with their neighbors came across the counter of the teller's cage, and although they had been in Weedy Rough as long as anyone could remember, they were strangers. Bachelor and spinster sister, living in a cold house that never knew laughter, turned sour as clabber in their loneliness. They didn't even have a radio.

Parkins had always wanted to change it. But he didn't know how. He had never lived any other way.

Wart was a small white dog with a few black spots, of wildly mixed ancestry. Barton Pay bought him from a tie seller who came in with a wagonload of timber and a bitch with nine pups in a box. Barton paid a shiny new quarter for the runt of the litter and named him Wart. He became Duny Gene's constant companion when the boy was around the house, and sometimes when he went afield, so long as an invitation was tendered. Wart seldom went anywhere he wasn't asked.

Like many mongrels, Wart was sharp-eyed and inquisitive, with more intelligence than a lot of people. While he was still a pup, Duny Gene had him retrieving sticks and rocks or anything else thrown. Later came the rolling-over trick and playing dead and jumping into Duny Gene's arms when the boy commanded "Come!"

Wart had an amazing instinct for the human condition. When Barton or Duny Gene was around, he leaped and cavorted and yipped. When Lydia appeared, he sat quietly, smiling at her. And he was sensitive. He didn't enjoy having people watch him eat, and when he felt the urge, he would go to the barn lot, hunker down, and look over his shoulder to ensure that no one was there to watch him make his deposit.

Wart quickly established himself as part of the Pay household. Even Lydia began to appreciate him, especially when Barton was late coming in from a fox hunt and the dog was lying on the front porch, fifteen pounds of protective fury. There was no doubt about his courage. Since maturity, he had never failed to send larger dogs yapping if they strayed into his territory.

"That dog's got to have some terrier in him," Barton said proudly. "He's such a fine little infighter."

The dog cared little for the woods. When his young master went off on forays for squirrel or just exploring among the hills with Hoadie Renkin, and commanded the dog to stay, Wart seemed not to mind. He would retreat to the long front porch and lie down, watching the town below, waiting patiently for Duny Gene's return. He was no hunter, no pointer or retriever. He was nothing. Just a nice little yard dog that seldom barked at night and never messed the rugs because Lydia refused to let him in the house, though sometimes she petted him in the yard when she thought no one was looking.

There was one flaw in his character. He was a marauder, short-range. He tried to fight it, but at least once each day temptation overwhelmed him and he headed for Parkins Muller's goat pasture. He tried to act nonchalant trotting across the backyard and the Pay's barn lot and through the fence to the long sloping field where the goats grazed.

He approached the herd as though he were casting for rabbits, paying no attention to them as they watched him, glass-eyed and stock-still and waiting for him to make his move. When he was near, he charged, sending goats in all directions, bleating, milk-filled udders swaying heavily.

After that one assault, he would return by way of Parkins Muller's outbuildings, looking for guinea hens. If they had not heard the bedlam in the goat pasture and were still about, he scattered them in flurries of gray feathers.

Wart never actually bit any of Parkins Muller's goats, nor harmed a single guinea. But each time after the chase, he would return to the Pay yard like a Comanche war party home from the kill, strutting and grinning. What he could not comprehend was that with each day he multiplied the hatred of a mortal enemy.

Cal Coolidge was president in 1925, but not many Weedy Roughers cared one way or the other. Kids in school knew that Jack Dempsey could whip any man in the world, but they were a little hazy on who was in the White House.

Even so, the outside world had begun to squeeze in on them. There were a number of resort hotels on various ridges around the town, inhabited in summer by what the people called the Texas Trade. From them, Weedy Roughers knew a little about the cosmopolitan life. But now, other external forces were at work that would change the people and their town forever.

On a good night, the radio might pick up Rudy Vallee singing "Betty Co-Ed." A few people had windup Victrolas and they listened to Ruth Etting sing "Shakin' the Blues Away." There was heated discussion in the barbershop about the color of Miss Etting's skin. It never got fistfight-serious, because Olie Merton's gang still leaned toward fiddle and banjo and "Turkey in the Straw."

Storefront windows and billboards on the highway to the county seat displayed smiling young women, their hair cut in a shingle bob, claiming that Coca-Cola was the pause that refreshes, and ruddy-cheeked men vowed they'd walk a mile for a Camel.

"Some of these magazines are downright indecent," Lydia said one evening, thumbing through her *McCall's*. She was glaring at a hosiery advertisement of a fine-looking woman whose bare thighs showed above her stockings under a sheer black slip.

"Since the war, everybody's gone a little crazy," Barton said.

"Such things should be outlawed."

"Well, it's better here than most places. Old ways still hold on hard. New things get second shrift. Reese Walls told me his wife bought a pair of these new golf knickers for his oldest kid. First time the kid wore 'em some boy beat hell out of him."

"That's a fine thing, and a fine way for you to put it. I'd bet it was someone like that no-account Hoadie Renkin."

"That's who it was, all right. Said he never took to bloomers on boys, and tied into Reese's kid and almost broke out all his front teeth."

"Hoadie Renkin and his kind ought to be outlawed, too."

There was an airmail service, but a letter sent from the hills had to go by train all the way to Saint Louis, or even farther, before it got onto an airplane. There were more locally owned automobiles, competing for road space with the mules and horses. Business at North End Garage was brisk, mostly flat tires or maintenance jobs that required nothing more than a little ingenuity and some baling wire.

The Texas Trade had the resorts booming. Local women stared in dismay at the flappers from Dallas with their garters showing below short dresses, but the men didn't seem to mind. There were sports roadsters and downy-cheeked young men who wore baggy pants and white shoes. They sipped grain alcohol needled with essence of juniper and called it gin, and they ate ice cream by the gallon. Joe Sanford sold so many sundaes he had to make special trips to Fayetteville in his new Chevy coupe to pick up fudge and butterscotch. And in the drugstore, there was a run on cherry Cokes.

It was a prosperous summer, turning into a fine autumn.

Catching the exuberance of the rest of the country in that time, a few Weedy Rough men thought it would be a nice idea to form a chapter of the Klan. It was resurgent all over the nation, they'd read in the weekly *Denver Post*. In Weedy Rough, an all-white community, there had never been anything ominous about it. The attraction was for those who enjoyed secret societies and secret handshakes and mumbo jumbo understood only by initiates.

Back in the hills, there were more foxes than anyone could remember, and every night there was a pack of dogs running somewhere. Duny Gene Pay could hear them as he lay in his bed with the windows open, the far, faint quavering sound of the hounds coming to him like the frothy crests of ocean waves, a lacework echo of the fury hidden soundlessly beneath. It was a spine-tingling music.

On Naulty's Ridge, the new sandstone school was almost completed. At Violet Sims's, business was better than it had ever been. For everybody, 1925 was a hell of a year.

Except for Parkins Muller.

The Bank of Weedy Rough did a good business with the Texas Trade. There was always more cash in the safe during summer than at any other time, and why anybody would rob it in the fall after the resort people had left was a mystery. But somebody did.

It was the first bank robbery Weedy Roughers had ever experienced, and they treasured it. The story was printed in the Fayetteville newspaper, with all the details. Reading about their own town brought the same civic pride that Mr. Pay's bell had a few years before.

For Parkins Muller, it was humiliation turning to cold rage. Only Miss Veda knew that after it happened he made a personal vow to whatever God he claimed as his own that no one would ever come into his bank again and take money just by waving a pistol. To everyone else, he seemed the same, going about his business as though nothing had happened, his lips thin and bitter as they always were, good times or bad.

Taken on all counts, the holdup didn't amount to much. Three men rode into town from West Mountain on horseback, walked into the red brick bank building, and rifled the little potbellied safe made in Cincinnati, with goldenrods painted across the front. The loot included a small bundle of greenbacks, a double fistful of silver, a mortgage on Tooth Snowdon's log wagon, a box of shotgun shells, and a paper sack full of rubber bands.

The three men came out of the bank still holding weapons and nobody tried to stop them. Constable Sparks was in Carroll County attending a fox-hunting convention. Besides, no one knew what was happening until it was finished. The bandits mounted their horses and rode back across West Mountain the way they had come, in the direction of Oklahoma.

Horseback robberies were rare by then, but anyone who wanted to go from Weedy Rough to Oklahoma in a hurry still had to use horses. The border was only twenty miles due west, but it was rough country and the roads were nothing but wagon traces that didn't end in Oklahoma anyway.

The loss amounted to about four hundred dollars, not counting the cost of the shotgun shells and the rubber bands. So the safe being cleaned out had little effect, except that Tooth Snowdon figured he would be able to ignore that lien on his wagon, what with no paper to prove a loan had ever been made.

For a few days afterward, the barbershop gang allowed it was out-of-state men, and that they had likely made a beeline for the Cookson Hills, where some hot-bottomed Indian woman was waiting. But nobody knew for sure because none of the Bunch of '25, as they came to be called, was ever caught.

"How'd you know it was a robbery?" Hoadie Renkin asked.

They were sitting on the rock wall that helped hold the Pay yard in place on the hillside, their legs hanging. They were watching the small crab-apple tree where sparrows liked to congregate, holding bean flips and the marble glassies they used for ammunition. So far, they had accounted for one bird. Behind them, Wart sat watching, staying out of it because he had no taste for dead sparrows, but there just the same in case he was needed.

"I told you. We saw their guns," Duny Gene said. "Mother was shelling peas and watching downtown through that side window, like she's always doing, and she said she thought somebody was robbing the bank."

"You got fresh peas this time of year?"

"Tooth Snowdon brought 'em," Duny Gene said, a little impatient because the robbery was the important thing here, not the damned peas.

"It's late for peas."

"Tooth's got this garden patch behind his house, and he waters all summer. From his well. He's got lots of late stuff. So Mother was shelling the peas when she saw these men come out of the bank."

"And that's when you seen 'em?"

"Yeah. I was looking at this new Monkey Ward's catalogue we got, and she said somebody was robbing the bank so I went over and we watched them get on their horses and ride up West Mountain."

"What kinda guns?"

"I dunno. One had a six-shooter, I think, and one had an automatic. Like that one Daddy brought from the war. I don't know what the third guy had."

"How'd you know they was robbers? Maybe they was just goin' out huntin'." Hoadie snickered.

"Aw, God dammit, Hoadie, what'd they be huntin' with pistols? Besides, Mother went to the phone and called the operator and said she thought somebody had robbed the bank, but the operator didn't know. But then she called back in a few minutes and said, yeah, Mother was right. They'd robbed the bank."

"You didn't hear shootin', did you?"

"They didn't do any shootin'," Duny Gene said, exasperated.

"Boy, if I robbed a bank, I'd shoot hell out of it. I'd like to see old man Muller's face when somebody stuck a big pistol at him."

Duny Gene laughed.

"There's one of the little bastards," Hoadie said. With a quick, smooth movement, he brought the bean flip up, stretching back the inner-tube bands. The marble whistled across the slope and clipped through the branches of the crab-apple tree like a bullet. The cock sparrow flew away, then made a quick dip to avoid the next shot that Duny Gene sent after him.

"I almost got him on the wing," Duny Gene said.

They dug glassies from their pockets, positioning them in the bean-flip slings, and watched for the next victim.

"Wonder how it'd feel, robbin' a bank?" Hoadie said.

"One of 'em had an automatic, just like Daddy's. From the war, I guess."

"I wish there was a war now," Hoadie said.

"We're not old enough to be in it if there was."

"Well, then, a war that lasted a little while," Hoadie said, grinning with the thought of it. "Long enough so we could get in it. Go off someplace on the train and have a uniform and a gun. Seein' all them big places. Uncle Amil's always talkin' about the war, all the things he's seen."

"Yeah. Daddy is, too. Like France. He says all the kids drink wine and the people smell like garlic."

"Yeah. Uncle Amil's always talkin' about them French women. Boy, that'd be something, wouldn't it? Doin' the stuff with a French woman."

Doing the stuff with women was all Hoadie ever seemed to think about now, and him barely old enough to understand what it meant. Duny Gene was old enough to think about it, but it wasn't a thing he felt easy talking about. It was forbidden talk, and a little dirty, too. His own thinking sometimes made him ashamed later when he was sitting in church beside his mother. Leviticus Hammel, the Methodist minister, had even preached a sermon about it once. About lust of the flesh, and how it would rot a person's soul. All throughout that morning, Duny Gene had sat squirming and sweating, thinking everyone was looking at him because of what he'd been thinking about some of the older girls in school.

Anything relating to that region of his developing body created unreasoning shyness. Whenever he was in the woods, Duny Gene always turned away when the time came to relieve himself, but Hoadie would do it right out in front of anybody and brag about the size of his root. Such things were intensely personal to Duny Gene, but he had no idea why.

Hoadie's brazen talk sometimes infuriated Duny Gene to the point of combat. He would take an impulse to ball his fists and smash Hoadie's grinning, mocking face. But it always passed quickly, because Hoadie was his best friend. Maybe his only friend.

Besides, those hands of Hoadie's, with the hickory-nut-hard knuckles, were an effective deterrent. Duny Gene had seen his friend fight larger and stronger boys. Hoadie was fast as a black snake with his hands, and when he struck, the flesh along cheekbones and lips had a tendency to split open and gush blood.

Hoadie was finally finished talking about his Uncle Amil and the French women. He was finished with bird shooting, too, and shoved the bean flip into a rear pocket of his bib overalls. He called Wart over, and the dog came, tail whipping.

"You're a worthless dog, you know that," Hoadie said, scratching Wart's ears. "Hey Duny Gene, maybe we could teach him to tree squirrels."

"He's just a yard dog is all," Duny Gene said defensively.

"Well, I gotta get on back out to the place," Hoadie said, slipping down off the wall. "My pap's been raising hell 'cause I ain't helped with any cuttin' lately."

"You can't cut timber and go to school, too."

"That ain't what Pap says," and Hoadie laughed.

"Well, you won't get there before dark. Is your pap cuttin' timber at night now?"

"No. But anyway, your mother's about due home from that Ladies' Aid meetin'. You know what she thinks about catchin' me here."

"You could sleep in the barn. She'd never know the difference. I could bring your supper."

"Naw. I better get on out to the place."

Duny Gene watched Hoadie scramble down the slope to the road and turn uphill toward Naulty's Ridge. He would pass the new school—where he'd chuck a few rocks at the windows if nobody was around—then turn west along Academy Heights and on into the deep hill country of Devil's Mountain. It was an eight-mile walk to the Renkins' place, the route Hoadie would take, cutting away from the roads on the Heights and picking his way straight through the woods.

Duny Gene sent a few more missiles whistling through the branches of the crab-apple tree, although there were no targets there. Then he hopped down from the wall and started to the house, Wart trotting along beside him, looking up with his bright black eyes, waiting for a friendly hand. But Duny Gene was not inclined to dog petting. He felt a little sour, what with Hoadie's casual reception of his big story about seeing the bank robbers.

In the kitchen, he took a dipper of water from one of the buckets standing on the water table beside the homemade sink that Parkins Muller had put in when he built this house. He drank some, and some he spurted from pursed lips toward the sink, missing with most of it. He glanced into the living room, making sure his mother hadn't somehow come in without his seeing her, then went quickly back to his parents' bedroom.

There was a nightstand beside his father's bed, and Duny Gene slipped open the drawer. The big .45 Army Colt was lying there, blue and deadly. He looked at it a long time before touching it, liking the hard shine and the checked butts. Then he lifted it out of the drawer and pressed the release beside the trigger guard. The loaded magazine popped out into his hand, the lead slugs looking like big juicy grubworms in their bright brass cartridge cases.

Duny Gene worked the slide to be sure there wasn't a round in the chamber. He pointed the cocked automatic at one post of the bed and pulled the trigger. There was the metallic thud of the hammer snapping down.

He thought about those men coming out of Parkins

Muller's bank, one of them holding a pistol just like
this one. He worked the slide again, then repeated his
dry shot at the bedpost, making a little explosive
noise with his lips and flipping back the gun as
though it had kicked.

"Any you other sons a bitches want the same?" he
muttered aloud, waving the pistol around, drawing a
bead on one of his mother's hats hanging on a
coat-tree.

He heard his mother when she set foot on the first
step of the front porch. Quickly, he pressed the
magazine back in place, lay the pistol in the nightstand, and closed the drawer. By the time Lydia
came in, he was on the back porch, rubbing Wart's
flanks.

"Did you stack that firewood yet?" Lydia called,
walking through the kitchen, taking off her new Montgomery Ward hat.

"No," he said. All she had to do was look through
the window. Along the back slope, the split-stave
cookstove wood was still lying in a pile near the
barn-lot wall, where it had been thrown down from
the wagon.

"Well, then get at it before supper."

He walked up through the yard, muttering to himself. He picked up one stave, and then a rock. He
threw the rock up, swung at it with the stave like a
ball bat swinging, and slammed the rock toward the
outside privy.

"Get at that wood, Duny Gene," his mother yelled
from the kitchen.

"All right, God dammit," he said aloud, but not
loud enough for her to hear. As he bent to the work,
Wart sat watching, taunting him with that long-tongued
smile.

Barton came home tired, but not too fagged to feel

the tension. Duny Gene sat at the supper table wolfing down his green beans without looking up, not even when Lydia made some remark about Hoadie Renkin.

"He's always nosing around here when I'm gone, I suspect," she said.

And later, when it was almost dark and Duny Gene had gone out to sit on the wall again, Barton went to join him.

"A little late for spatsies, isn't it?"

"I guess so."

"You and your mother have a little tilt?"

"She acts like I'm somebody to kick on," Duny Gene said sullenly.

"Well, she's got a lot on her mind. And she gets lonesome for her own people. She comes from different stock than us, you know."

"She acts like you're somebody to kick on, too."

Barton gazed up at the darkening sky and sighed.

"There's the evening star. That's Venus," he said.

"Yeah, you told me before," Duny Gene said, and whipped a marble down through the empty crabapple tree, clipping off a few small branches.

"Your mother's a good woman," Barton said quietly, still watching the bright planet that hung over West Mountain. "She means a lot to me and to you. Sometimes her nerves get frazzled, but she loves us. We're her family now. I want you to always be gentle with her, because she's a gentlewoman."

"Sometimes she acts like we're dirty red Indians. From another country."

"Well, maybe we are from another country. Different than hers, anyway. Don't let it upset you. Her people were among those who said bad things about your Grandfather Pay, and how he married. It's not easy for her to overcome that. She does a pretty good job, I think."

"She's always harpin' at me about my friends."

"Hoadie Renkin? Well, the Renkins and your mother are a million miles apart. Devil's Mountain and Bell Grove in Fort Smith are a million miles apart, as far apart as places can ever get."

"Fort Smith's the worst place I ever saw."

"I never liked it much either," Barton said, and placed a hand on Duny Gene's shoulder. "Come on inside now. It's getting a little cold. Let's listen to the radio."

·3·

THE BIG CARTONS HAD ARRIVED FROM THE mail-order house, as they always did, just a week before Christmas. Duny Gene and Barton were filling little animal-cracker-sized boxes with the fruit and nuts and candy, packaging the only present most of the children on the mail route would receive. It had happened every year since the Pays arrived in Weedy Rough and was already as much a custom as going to the Methodist church on Christmas Eve, where there was a large tree and small gifts for the town kids, each and every one, even the Baptists. And popcorn balls made with real hill-country molasses, and hard candy that had long loops and swirls like the choker around the neck of some ancient English queen.

There had been a time when Barton played Santa Claus for those affairs at the church. But it never became a tradition. One year he had walked into the

Pay living room in his red suit and false whiskers and scared hell out of Duny Gene, who was still very young then and not accustomed to seeing odd-looking strangers walk into his mother's house. After that, Barton left the Santa Clausing to others. But each year he continued to carry the little gaily-colored boxes on the route when helping Alvie Haus with the Christmas mail.

During the holiday season, when mail was heavy, Alvie and Barton split the route through the back country, each taking half. The route made a wide circle through the hills to the west, toward Oklahoma. On one day, Barton would take the southern half, Alvie the northern, and the next day they would switch. That gave Barton the opportunity to pass his little gifts along to all the children, either two days before Christmas or on Christmas Eve.

Each year was the same. Barton would close the tie yard for a full week—December was a slack time for timber cutters anyway—and devote himself to the post office and the mail. It gave him a festive feeling.

The year Duny Gene turned fourteen was special because Lydia finally consented to his accompanying Barton on the route when the boxes were delivered. Although it was against the law—a mail carrier with a rider—Barton said not to worry about it. They could just consider Duny Gene another substitute carrier, even though he had not taken a civil-service examination. Besides, a postal inspector had never appeared out in the hills anyway, and likely never would.

It was special, too, because Lydia had finally reconciled herself to spending Christmas away from her family. Earlier, they had always gone to Fort Smith for the holidays, but it had been strained. Lydia's family still resented Barton for the fix he had gotten her into in the first place, and Lydia couldn't stand old man Pay, the bile rising in her throat after only a few minutes around him. Barton and Duny Gene had always gone about the whole thing in a dazed kind of bewilderment, feeling bitterness all around them. Barton was aware, too, that in certain quarters he and his son were an embarrassment, having so much Indian blood in their veins.

Both of them enjoyed being with Barton's father, but Lydia refused to allow such meetings without her being there. She always managed to give them a green persimmon taste, acid and lip-puckering. Even Barton had to admit that his father's law office, smelling of old books and sealing wax, and his small house smelling the same way, were not conducive to the holiday spirit. Not that old man Pay was ungrateful for their visits, but with Lydia laying a frost on every meeting he was usually reserved and distant, as though these people who were his only family came from some hostile tribe.

So now, Christmas was being spent in Weedy Rough, with only a polite exchange of gifts through the mail.

"How many walnuts should go in?" Duny Gene asked. He was sitting cross-legged on the floor, his father like him on the other side of the open cartons of candy and fruit and nuts.

"One tangerine, two walnuts, two pecans, two hazelnuts."

Duny Gene held up one of the hazelnuts. "They look like chinkapins."

"A little. Then, fill it up with candy."

"This candy's bigger than last year," Duny Gene said. "It makes the boxes bulge so they almost bust."

"Burst," his mother said. "And don't put so much candy in. It's not good for those children, so much candy. And stop popping those sour balls into your own mouth. You want your teeth to fall out?"

Barton looked across at his son and winked.

The boxes stacked up like so many multicolored bricks, and when that job was finished they were laid in the now empty cartons. Somehow, it always seemed to come out right, with only a few sour balls and a half-dozen tangerines left over. Lydia put these in a large crystal bowl that would serve as a centerpiece for the dining table throughout the holidays.

"Don't let me catch you into these, Duny Gene," Lydia said.

That night was almost as good as Christmas Eve for Duny Gene, anticipating his trip on the route the next day. He lay awake for a long time, listening to his mother and father arguing softly in their bedroom. He didn't catch enough to know what it was about. Then he listened to a dog bark on West Mountain. Sound carried clearly across the valley in the windless, crisp air. As always happened, a second dog took up the call somewhere along Academy Heights, and then another along Naulty's Ridge. Duny Gene tried to identify each one.

There's that setter of Esta Stayborn's, he thought. And the Budd mongrel that never gets fed because the old man is always drunk. Has to catch ground squirrels or steal slop from hogpens. The sound of each one, barking in turn, was like a bell tone running around the rim of ridgeline that surrounded the town on three sides.

Duny Gene heard Wart, up and wakeful and walking back and forth along the length of the front porch. Duny Gene knew he was listening, too. But although he paced up and down until the last of the distant barking faded and was gone, he made no sound except for his soft pads moving nervously along the porch flooring.

Through the house was the heavy scent of cedar from the tree in the living room. He and Barton had gone into the woods and cut the tree only two days before, but Lydia was complaining already that the horrid thing was shedding on her rug. Soon the house would be full of the smell of baking ham and candied sweet potatoes and mince pies, made with real meat and a dash of brandy he knew his father would buy from Violet Sims. Duny Gene was sure that was all Barton ever bought from her.

He thought about Christmas. Mostly it meant the tree and presents and a lot of good things to eat. The story of the child in the manager had somehow never affected him one way or the other.

Barton had given him two dollars for his shopping. All that had been accomplished at Bee Schirvy's little general store next door to the post office. There was a real bone comb for his mother and a pocket-sized whetstone for Barton, still in its bright red-and-white box.

Duny Gene wondered about the long, clumsily wrapped package under the tree, sent to him by his grandfather, Eben Pay. Gifts from that quarter were always good, even exciting. The ones from his mother's family were always dull—mittens or a woolen scarf he never wore.

Someday, he thought, maybe I can get some money of my own, and then I can buy Grandfather Pay a nice present. He had no desire to buy anything for the people in Lydia's family. They were strange and cold and hard-faced, and he didn't like the way they smelled.

And he thought about Maudie Snowdon, Tooth's oldest girl, and wondered what his father would think if he asked for another dollar to buy her a ribbon for her red hair. But he forgot that quickly because he knew he didn't have the guts to come right out and give a gift to some girl. Hoadie and the other boys might make so much fun it would be either a fistfight or dishonor.

He recalled last Valentine's Day, when he'd asked for money to buy his teacher a small heart-shaped red box of chocolates. Only the candy had not gone to a teacher. He had slipped it into Maudie's desk at recess, having carried it to school in his lunch sack. He hadn't added a note that might indicate where it came from, and although Maudie had professed ignorance as to its origin, Duny Gene was sure she knew. At least had a suspicion.

He thought about her hair, just like her father's, flame-colored in the sun, and about her round face that had an apple-pie look, dusted with cinnamon. She had the most perfect teeth he'd ever seen, and he wondered why. She'd never been to a dentist in her life and she ate like most hill people, heavy on the dried beans and meat gravy and corn bread. Duny Gene knew about teeth. Already, he had spent a few horrible moments in the chair of a Fort Smith dentist, where Lydia had rushed him twice when he complained of toothache.

He thought then of Barton and the day he had been in the tie yard talking with timber sellers about a sticks girl who had gotten herself in trouble. The words had been indignant yet sad, and Duny Gene had walked up unnoticed at first, hearing a good deal of it.

When Barton realized his son was there, he looked embarrassed and guided Duny Gene back among the stacks of ties, where they sat on some unloaded posts. Barton took a box of chocolate-covered peanuts from his pocket and handed them to Duny Gene.

"I guess you heard us mention little Clarisa Vandiver," he said.

"She's not very little," Duny Gene said, popping a chocolate-covered peanut into his mouth. "She can whip most of the boys in school."

Barton looked as though he had stomach acid.

"Well, it's time we talked about such things," and he looked away. It was a long time before he continued, Duny Gene chewing the chocolate-covered peanuts all the while, waiting. "I suppose you know what married people do if they want to have a little baby."

"Yeah. Clarisa does it all the time," Duny Gene said. "She'll do it with anybody."

And with a note of panic in his voice, Barton said quickly, "Don't talk about it like that. Boys aren't supposed to do such a thing until they're married to a girl. I hope you . . ."

He had stopped then, and Duny Gene could see his father's mouth working but no words coming out. Finally Barton spoke.

"I've got to get back to work," and he rose quickly and walked away. It was the finish of anything Barton ever said on the subject.

Now, in his bed thinking on it, Duny Gene felt compassion for his father, although he would not have described it that way. I should have told him a long time ago that I've never done it, he thought. But I know all about it. Hoadie took care of that. But I should have told him I know about it, so he wouldn't have to worry on telling me things he thinks are dirty unless they're blessed by some parson.

He went to sleep with Maudie's face in his mind, but his thoughts went no further than kiss stealing or handholding. Anything beyond that with the girl he wanted to marry someday was beyond question. The vessel of Maudie Snowdon's body was sacred, to be violated only at the proper time, blessed by preacher. He knew Barton would be proud of such thinking.

It was a long time before first light when Barton Pay drove the Ford down into Weedy Rough to the post office. Dawn would be later than usual because this was an overcast day, wintry and gray, with the clouds down close against the tops of the ridges, and Barton figured there might be fog on some of the higher mountains along the route.

He felt good. His boy would be with him today, and that would mean someone to talk to besides himself. Not that he disliked being alone when he carried the mail. But this would be a nice change, a Christmas change.

Carrying the mail had strengthened his religion. Spending hours alone in the high wooded country where the trees marched close along all the ridges and water in the valley streams ran cold and clear, the sight of deer and possum and the tracks of wolves in the icy, sandy creek beds, all made for a journey through the wilderness. Not the same kind of wilderness the Old Testament people went into, searching for The Word, with all that sand and blasting sun. But a wilderness just the same.

Barton often thought that he should have been a preacher. It was not an unusual quality in his bloodline. One of his great-grandfathers had been so inclined, but like Barton had kept it to himself until he was finally swept into the Civil War, went off to fight with Lee in Virginia, and returned with all the ardor of any ministry burned out by the fires of Antietam and the Wilderness.

There was no method in it, but the hill country and its people brought Barton closer to preaching, in spirit and in fact. He recognized it, but would not accept it as chance. As he grew older, it seemed to him that all things were predetermined, set on an inexorable course with their conception. He came to feel more and more that whatever happened was the will of God.

Driving down to the post office that morning, Barton shivered in the cold. He thought about his days on the route, in foul weather and good, and about the people who lived out there along the woody ridgelines.

During good weather, Barton had always stopped for lunch at a little backwoods church were there was a graveyard, and a spring where water ran from sandstone outcrops, clear and cold and so pure it had no taste at all. There was a stand of sycamores around the church, spaced out along the hogback ridge, bright and flamboyant there above the somber oaks in the valleys on either side.

It was the very first year he carried the mail. He was riding horseback that day, and coming along the road he saw a group of people around the slab-lumber church building and the graveyard behind. He saw an open hole and a mound of fresh earth, and a long wooden box.

One of the men had come out to the road where Barton stopped, and told him that a farmer was dead, leaving a young widow and a house full of young-uns and little or nothing to eat in the root cellar. Nobody knew why the farmer had died. He just had, the man said.

There were no undertakers in the hills, and no one had money to pay them anyway. So it was always dead in the night, buried in the morning, especially in hot weather.

"Mr. Pay, there ain't nary a soul to say a word over the grave," the man said.

Barton tied the horse to a persimmon tree and walked to the new hole in the ground, the people making a path for him as he came. The women wiped at red eyes and the men stood expressionless, watching with hats in hands, their pale foreheads looking outlandish above the deep tans of their noses and cheeks. Barton stopped and looked at the coffin and slipped off his hat. He stood there a long time, trying to think of a reading from the Scriptures.

"Blessed are the meek," he finally said.

Barton knew the dead man hardly at all. But at the sight of his tearstained widow and the runny-nosed kids clutching her thin legs, he plunged into it as though he were burying a bishop of the Methodist Church. He spoke with great sensitivity, the appeal of hope and grace hidden behind each word. The people began to feel it, and the kids stopped blubbering.

Tooth Snowdon said later that he'd heard Barton preach a few of those burial sermons. After the first one, anytime there was a death on the route, the bereaved family would have no one to say the service except Barton Pay. Tooth said only a reformed heller could talk so good, and that Barton outpreached any Methodist and most Holiness, which was a compliment because the Holiness were ground stompers and bush jumpers.

Well, there'll be no preaching today, Barton thought.

There was a light in the post office, and there he found Alvie Haus and Bee Schirvy, who was postmaster as well as store owner. The southbound passenger with its mailcar was due, and they were waiting, smoking pipes and sitting with feet propped on the front of the Franklin stove.

"Little cool, ain't it?" Alvie said.

"Smells some of snow," Bee said.

"Too early yet for snow, I hope. Maybe all we'll get is the sniff of it," Barton said.

"Where's your candy boxes?" Alvie asked.

"Up at the house. I'll stop and pick 'em up on the way out. Duny Gene's gonna carry them down to the road. He's taking the route with me today."

"He'll be a big help," Alvie said.

"Yeah," Bee said. "Duny Gene's a fine boy."

Barton slipped off his overcoat and stood by the window, looking out into the street. It was growing lighter now, and he saw Parkins Muller and Miss Veda going across the tracks toward the bank. Along the slope of West Mountain, he could see lampshine in windows of various houses. There was a light in Tooth Snowdon's kitchen.

"I've never seen anybody carry on with his kids the way Tooth does," Barton said. "He wools that little boy around like he was a rag doll."

"Tooth always acts that way with his young-uns, until they get to be school age," Bee said.

"Yeah, I heard Tooth say once when that boy gets older, he won't stand to be kissed by anybody but pretty girls. So Tooth figures he's gotta get in a lifetime of hugs in the first few years," Alvie said.

"That's right," Bee said. "Tooth allows that when a kid gets growed, it's too late to hug him, no matter how much you want to."

Well, that's about right, I guess, Barton thought. He tried to remember the last time he'd put his arms around his own son, but he couldn't.

There were five of them standing at the mailbox beside the road. The oldest was about eight, and he stood a little apart from the others, his hands in the bib of his overalls. The two girls wore sack dresses that hung below their knees, and the wind pressed the cloth against their skinny legs. Like the boys, they wore oversized and worn-out men's brogans without any socks. Each of them had a mop of straw-colored hair, and only the oldest boy's showed any sign of ever having been cut, and that with a bowl placed over his head and anything hanging beneath sheared. There was not a pound of fat on all of them together, and the skin of their faces stretched taut across sharp cheekbones and pointed chins.

Painted crudely across the mail box was the single word *Renkin*.

The slope behind the mailbox had been cleared, and some of the hickory and oak stumps were still there. At the crest of the ridge, the roof of the house was barely visible, the handmade shingles looking warped and rotten. Any smoke coming from the sandstone chimney was whipped away by the wind before it became recognizable.

Somewhere beyond the house, hogs were making a great racket in a sty, and from one of the wooded draws there was the harsh calling of crows.

"Them crows found some ole owl to pester," Squib, the smallest boy, said. But the oldest remained aloof, frowning with concentration and watching the road where it first came into view over a nearby ridge.

On the far side of the road, there was another cleared field in the heavy timber, and a few dismal cornstalks there bent crookedly, making a rattling, dry-paper sound as they swayed in the currents of cold air. Everywhere else, there was only the woods, the tree limbs stark and bare, a gray tangle against a gray sky. In all directions, the treetops dipped down and up, down and up, following the contours of the rough terrain. The short stretch of road that ran in front of the mailbox was the only level ground anywhere in view.

They could hear the Ford, laboring up the ridge before cresting only a few yards from where they stood. The younger ones drew back a little, one of the girls trying to hide behind the oak post that supported the box.

"Here he comes," the oldest said gruffly.

The car came over the ridge and the engine throttled down and muttered along the road toward them, and they could see the man driving, his coat collar up and a felt hat pulled down over his ears. And beside him, a boy, considerably older than any of them, wearing a woolen cap. The car creaked to a halt before them, and the man was smiling.

"Well, Audie, how many this year?" Barton Pay asked.

And Audie, the oldest, stood in the cold and licked his lips and counted on his fingers, because although by now he knew that same question would always be asked, he waited until it came to form an answer. The others moved around him, caution lost now, their eyes on him. The little girl behind the mailbox post came out, and her large eyes cut now and again toward the two in the car, shy and apprehensive but somehow defiant.

"Eleven this year, Mr. Pay," Audie finally said. The others began to push and whisper, each having made their calculations, too, and Audie shoved them away angrily and recounted. "No. There's twelve. Countin' the new one. And Granmaw."

Duny Gene passed the little gaily-colored boxes to his father, and Barton in turn handed them down to Audie. They were distributed to the small clutching hands all around, one by one, with Audie finally holding the extras like a stack of firewood in his arms.

"Eat those tangerines soon, now, or they might go bad on you," Barton said.

"Last year, Squib dropped his in the privy and Pap had to fish it out with the rake," one of the little girls blurted.

"Hush up, you," Audie snapped savagely.

"Well, you say Merry Christmas to your pap and ma for me," Barton said.

The Model T lurched off down the road, and the children watched it, holding the Christmas boxes tightly in their hands, the wind flapping their dresses and overalls against knobby bottoms. Then they turned and trooped up the hill to the house, except for Squib and Audie, who watched a moment longer, even after the car was out of sight.

"Is that Jesus?" Squib asked.

Audie snorted. "Hell no! That's Mr. Pay, goofy." But after all the others, even Audie, had disappeared up the slope, Squib stood there, gripping the red and green and yellow animal-cracker box to his belly, looking along the road where the last sound of the Ford had died. Then he muttered aloud: "Hell yes. It is too Jesus!"

Barton was telling about the things he'd seen along this route, and there was a story for each passing ridge and hollow and farmhouse: once, a big red wolf and her twin cubs, drinking in a stream; and the squirrel migration he'd been caught in once, the little grays crossing the road in numbers he'd never seen before, heading someplace west; and the time he'd almost run over a sticks kid who had fallen off his pap's mule and broken an ankle, and Barton had put him in the car and drove him all the way into Weedy Rough to Dr. Barr.

Barton could talk and drive as well as anyone, because he paid almost no attention to the driving part. He simply set a course down the middle of the road and let the Ford do the rest. He made no effort to avoid ruts, chugholes, or logs in the road. If anything got in the way, he ran over it. Especially snakes. He hated snakes and would maneuver the car any way he could to run them down if he caught one in the road.

Duny Gene stared from the car as the thick growth of gray timber slid past. Barton sensed all the fun had gone out of this affair.

"What's the matter?" he asked. "You got a stomachache or something?"

"Why do people have to live out here, like wild hogs?"

"You mean like the Renkins?" Barton asked. "Well, they farm. They do the best they can. But they don't take much out of this land."

"Why'd they ever come out here?"

"Most of 'em like to be off to themselves. And

besides, most of these people, or their daddies or granddaddies, came in here to homestead. There wasn't anybody else on the land because it isn't worth much. So they farm what they can, and hunt and cut timber.''

"I didn't know he had so many kids in his family,'' Duny Gene said.

"Who? Hoadie? Yeah, that's the thing about these people out here. They get a new one every year, and sometimes the new one lives, and sometimes he doesn't. All those you saw are Hoadie's half brothers and sisters. Same father, different mother.''

Barton couldn't believe it, but Duny Gene started crying. Barton had not seen his son cry since he was nursing age, bellowing now and then when he was hungry. No pain or abuse or bruised feelings had ever brought tears, at least that Barton knew of, but there were tears now, even though the boy was turned away to hide them. It frightened Barton a little, his son crying and already old enough to be practicing with the junior basketball team.

Barton reached over and tentatively touched Duny Gene's shoulder, making an elaborate effort not to look at the boy's face.

"It's all right, son,'' he said. "Don't ever be ashamed to feel sorry for a man worse off than yourself.''

"I'm not feeling sorry,'' Duny Gene said harshly, pulling his shoulder away from Barton's hand. He wiped his face violently, and the crying was finished almost before it had begun.

For the first time in his life, Barton began to wonder who this boy was, what might be in his mind behind those slate-gray eyes.

"The clothes those kids had on looked like they came from some rag bag,'' Duny Gene said.

"They wear what they got. And they haven't got much. But I notice Hoadie usually looks all right.''

The Ford bumped along the rutted road and Barton worked the hand throttle as they started up another long ridge. Duny Gene sat with a grim look on his face, watching the scar-rock outcrops along the road.

"He steals that stuff," Duny Gene said finally.

"Oh? He does?" Barton said, trying to sound surprised.

"Yeah, he steals it out of Esta Stayborn's store. He don't steal much. But when his overalls get ragged, he steals a pair."

"Is that all he steals?"

"Some candy bars sometimes, maybe."

"How do you know all this?"

For a time, Duny Gene sat silently. When he spoke again, the anger was gone from his voice.

"He tells me about it."

But Barton thought perhaps there was more to it than that. He thought that maybe Duny Gene had not just heard, but had been a part of it, even helped a little, keeping Esta's attention while Hoadie lifted the merchandise. But he quickly pushed that from his mind, unwilling to face such a thing.

"Well, I suspect Esta knows a good deal about it. But he knows Hoadie's a boy who hasn't got much money. Esta just takes it all as a loss. But that doesn't make it right. Stealing is against the law." And then he added, "And anybody who knows about it and doesn't tell is an accessory, and that's against the law, too."

Duny Gene turned to his father, and the eyes had a flat, dead look.

"What's the law got to do with friends and family?"

"Hoadie Renkin's not family. And even if he was, and though a good friend, the law's the law. Without it, every man could do what he was strong enough and mean enough to do."

"Nothin' he ever did hurt Esta Stayborn."

"The law's the law," Barton repeated.

"Bein' the law don't make it right."

"No, but you don't change it and make it right by acting like a mad dog in the woods, doing whatever you like. If something's not right, then you change it. By a vote, maybe, or maybe a judge in a court case saying a certain thing's not right."

"Who's gonna listen to a court case for Hoadie Renkin?"

"Nobody, if he steals. That's a law no judge is going to say is wrong. It's a crime. The law's the law on that, and it won't change, and hadn't ought to."

"You don't aim to tell on him, do you?"

"No. I said, Esta likely knows all about it anyway. So maybe it's not stealing, just charity for some poor ignorant sticks kid."

"Hoadie's not ignorant," Duny Gene said fiercely.

"He's not smart, either, going around stealing stuff. He'll try that someday with a man who isn't so understanding as Esta and he'll end up in jail."

"He's not ignorant," Duny Gene said stubbornly. "He's as smart as me. Maybe smarter."

"I hope not. He's smart like a fox or a wolf or some other wild thing in the woods."

"He's smart. He's going to make some money someday. He'll turn out to be something besides sticks people. He knows what everybody calls folks who live out here. Sticks people. He'll make plenty of money someday and then he'll tell everybody they can go . . . Well, he'll make some money someday."

"Well, I hope he does," Barton said. He had become uncomfortable with the whole issue, although he wasn't exactly sure why. "Another mailbox just beyond this bend. Ought to be about eight kids, if I remember. These folks out here may not have much else, but they've got kids. We'll stop in a little while and eat that lunch your mother made for us.''

But he suspected Duny Gene wasn't very hungry.

It was a good Christmas in many ways, and in some manner strange. The evening after they had their celebration—at the church and later at home, opening presents and eating Lydia's excellent mince pie—Duny Gene was in Esta Stayborn's store for eggs. Parkins Muller was there, too, watching Duny Gene suspiciously while starting toward the door with a box of groceries under each arm. On sudden impulse, Duny Gene offered to carry one of the boxes.

Parkins glared for a moment, uncertain, his eyes on a level with the boy's. Then he shrugged and Duny Gene took the largest of the boxes, laying the sack of eggs on top.

''I'm obliged,'' Parkins said.

They crossed the tracks in the snow and went up East Mountain road, then along the icy steps that led to Parkins Muller's house, neither of them saying anything, Duny Gene following in Parkins's footsteps.

On the back porch, Duny Gene stopped while Parkins went in to deposit his groceries and returned. He took the box from Duny Gene's hands and placed it on the kitchen table, never offering the hospitality of his home. When he turned back to Duny Gene, he held a quarter in his hand, along with the eggs.

''Naw, that's all right, Mr. Muller,'' Duny Gene said, taking only the brown sack.

''Well, I'm obliged,'' Parkins said. Duny Gene started to turn away but Parkins stopped him with a hand on his coat sleeve. They stood a moment, white clouds of vapor before their faces.

''Duny Gene, I'd like you to stop rockin' my goats,'' Parkins said. ''I know it's mostly sticks kids you run with making that kind of meanness.

You're a good boy, and I wish you'd stop that."

"We don't mean any harm," Duny Gene said.

"I wish you'd stop."

From behind Parkins came Miss Veda's voice, high and glass-hard, as though it would break into shards in the cold air.

"Who's that?"

"It's Barton Pay's boy," Parkins said. "He helped me bring up the grub."

"Tell him to keep that dog of his out of our pasture," she yelled. "And shut that door. You're letting in the cold."

"I'd like you to take this money," Parkins said and offered the two-bit piece again. Duny Gene took it. "And I'd like it if you'd try to keep your dog away from my livestock."

"Yes sir. I'll see about him."

Duny Gene walked away in the darkness, opened the gate into the Muller barn lot, and crossed to the next gate near the Pay barn. As he scuffed through the deep snow, he thought about Parkins's peace offering, growing warm against his hand inside the coat pocket.

Wart came out to meet him, throwing snow in all directions, laughing and tongue out as though it were summer. Duny Gene bent and rubbed the dog's head.

"You dog. You better leave Muller's goats and guineas alone, you hear?"

And it was at least three days before Duny Gene threw another rock in Parkins Muller's pasture.

During that period of his life, important things seemed to happen in winter. Some he recognized, some he didn't. After the night he earned the quarter, he seldom ever recalled the incident. But the winter that came two years later he remembered always, like bittersweet.

·4·

ON THE BACK SIDE OF EAST MOUNTAIN, there had once been a fence row that ran from the crest of the hill down to the federal highway. Nobody could remember the origins of that fence, nor why it had been dismantled finally. But the mark of it remained, where the trees had been cleared, leaving a firebreak and a perfect bobsled run. When the snows came, it got plenty of use.

In the year Duny Gene Pay began practicing with the high school varsity basketball team, the snow was later than usual, nothing until March. It was irritating because Grandfather Pay had sent Duny Gene a wooden sled for Christmas, and the itch to use it was almost unbearable. The thing had runners that looked suspiciously like plow handles, in two sections, so the front end could be steered. The length was just right, and it felt good when Duny Gene lay belly-down on it, his feet hanging off the rear so toes could be used as a drag brake.

Lydia created a fuss over it, saying it was the best way she knew for someone to break his neck against a tree. To keep down the noise about it, Duny Gene decided to get the sled out of sight. He and Hoadie Renkin carried it up East Mountain to find a hiding place a week after Christmas. They had no idea that the sled would lay concealed on the hill for almost three months before they would get the opportunity to use it.

They had to pass through Parkins Muller's pasture on the way, and they did it quickly, pausing only twice to lay the sled aside and throw rocks at the goats.

It was a banner day for Wart, who went along, too, and after the boys had crossed the topside pasture fence and gone into the woods, they could hear him behind them, barking, and putting the goats into a state of frenzy. Later, Wart appeared beside them once more, tongue hanging out and grinning as though he had accomplished something worth their attention.

Before they covered the sled with fallen tree limbs, near the top of the old fenceline, Hoadie took out a long bone-handled clasp knife and they cut their initials into one of the runners. The wood was cured oak, and by the time they were finished Duny Gene had a blister on his hand.

"With our mark on that sled," Hoadie said, "anybody wants to steal it, they'll know who they got to deal with when we catch 'em."

"Nobody's gonna steal it. What good is it, with no snow?"

"Some folks will steal anything," Hoadie said with some authority. "You better let me prick that blister."

"It's all right. Let it alone."

"No, gimme your hand. You gotta get the water out, or you might get blood poison."

"Hell, that's crazy," Duny Gene said, but he allowed Hoadie to hold his hand and cut the bubble of skin with the knife. Not that he thought it necessary, but he didn't want Hoadie thinking he was afraid of the blade. When the operation was done, Hoadie squeezed the water from the blister, spat on it, and rubbed it. It stung only a little.

"Let Wart lick it," Hoadie said. "A dog's tongue cures cuts."

Duny Gene presented the palm of his hand to Wart, and Wart took a few tentative sniffs and licks, then lost interest and trotted off to mark a tree.

"He ain't too bothered with blisters, is he?" Hoadie said. "But a dog will sure'n hell lick a cut. Cure it right up."

They almost forgot about the sled over the next weeks. Duny Gene was sweating and straining each afternoon in the old gym. Being smaller than anyone else on the team, he had to make up for it with aggressiveness. He was what Tooth Snowdon called a fair-to-middlin' guard on defense, with very fast hands. But when it came to throwing the ball through the hoop, he wasn't worth a damn.

Some afternoons, Hoadie came to watch the practice. He sat back in one corner of the stands, chewing homecured tobacco and splattering the walls with juice. He showed no interest in joining the team.

On the days when a few of the high school girls came in to watch their team work, Hoadie made himself conspicuous among them by telling tales about his half brothers' and sisters' hound-dog table manners, or about the time his pap cut off a finger at some little hill sawmill, or if he was feeling unusually brash, he would explain in detail the technique for castrating hogs.

But mostly, Hoadie went home after school that winter. His father needed help in the timber. "Pap's gettin' old," Hoadie told Duny Gene. "His joints is all tight during cold weather and it hurts him to use a cross-cut saw."

Duny Gene remembered the sled that morning in March when he woke to a cold, dark dawn and felt snow on his face when he went to the privy. The day stretched out endlessly as he sat in school, watching through the windows as the big puffy flakes floated down. For that day at least, the mysteries of plane geometry were lost on him.

By afternoon, there was a powdery layer almost a foot deep, and more falling when Duny Gene and Hoadie went to East Mountain. It took a few runs to pack the snow along the old fenceline, and then it became slick as ice, the fresh snow making it faster each time they went down.

They rode together, Hoadie lying on the bottom and trying to steer, and Duny Gene on top with his toes raking the ground behind when they came to the highway and tried to turn left onto the deserted road. Usually, they missed the turn and skated off into the timber, throwing snow in all directions.

At first, Wart ran along beside them, barking. But as the slope grew slicker along the firebreak, he sensed that trying to keep up with the sled was futile. The rest of the day he spent sitting at the top of the hill, watching. Once, he slipped back into Parkins Muller's pasture and assaulted the goats.

It was Saturday, and the snow was melting on the hilltops, but still deep in the valley. As soon as he finished his breakfast, Duny Gene started up East Mountain to take a few last runs on the sled, acting nonchalant because he didn't want his mother to know where he was going. She hardly noticed anyway, because this was the day for the Eastern Star white-bean supper, and she had more than enough to keep her mind occupied.

He took one run, sitting on the sled and guiding it with his feet, and with Wart gripped firmly between his knees. The dog held his mouth open, his nose up, as though trying to suck in all the air he could on the way down.

The slope was bumpy, with the snow melting down

around the rocks, but it was still fast. They started back up the hill, Duny Gene dragging the sled and Wart trotting along beside him, wagging his tail and wanting to talk about it. Halfway up the slope, his ears went forward and his tail stiffened, and Duny Gene knew someone was at the top. He supposed it was Hoadie.

Maudie Snowdon was standing in the snow, her hands in her coat pockets and a muffler wrapped around her head, giving her the look of some Arabian princess Duny Gene had seen in *National Geographic*. She was wearing a dress and heavy woolen stockings and laced boots that came almost to her knees. Her cheeks were cherry-colored and she was smiling. Duny Gene couldn't take his eyes off those wonderful teeth.

"Hi," she said, and when Wart went over to give her a good sniff, she bent and petted him, her eyes still on Duny Gene. Very blue eyes, bright and dangerously inquisitive.

"Hi," he said. "What're you doin' up here?"

"I had to take some turnips over to Mrs. Stayborn's place, from my mama. I thought somebody might be up here sledding."

"Nobody but me," Duny Gene said. "Snow's about all gone on this sunny slope anyway."

He finally managed to take his eyes off her face and get the sled aligned for another go at the hill. He sat down and waited for Wart to come jump on, but the dog was getting his ears scratched now, his tail whipping as he grinned up at the girl.

"Come on," Duny Gene said.

"All right," Maudie said, and as she came over to him, he had no intention of explaining that he'd been calling the dog. Somehow, she smelled like young willow shoots, the bark peeled off, fresh-scrubbed and clean.

"All right. I'll belly-down." He sprawled on the sled, holding it in place with his toes, and his chest was thumping a little. "Push off hard and then jump on."

Maudie had her hands on his shoulders, bent over the sled, and she pushed and the sled started and she was on him, taking the breath out of his lungs with the sudden weight of her body. She's heavy as hell, he thought, but only for a moment because they were flashing down the firebreak, him trying to steer the runners away from the rocks beginning to appear in the snow. The trees went past in a gray blur, and he heard her laughing and felt her body on his back and her hands gripping his shoulders.

Suddenly the sled struck the biggest rock on the run. It careened off the fenceline and into the trees, almost going over before it piled into the deeper snow alongside the firebreak, sending a cloud of white spray back into their faces. It flattened a gum-tree sapling, shaved a big oak, cut the bark from the side of a hickory, and overturned, throwing them off in a tangle of arms and legs, and Wart running to catch up, barking furiously.

Maudie was laughing still, lying there with her muffler pulled down off her head and snow making moist white patches in her hair. Duny Gene scrambled over her and took her shoulders clumsily in both hands and without even thinking, kissed her open mouth. He felt her teeth against his lips. It was quick and he pulled back almost at once. When he looked down at her he was surprised that she was still laughing. He was so close he could see the little gray flecks of light in her blue eyes.

"You'll knock my teeth out," she said. "That's no way to give a Yankee dime."

And she lifted her face to him and he knew she wanted to be kissed again and he did it, longer this time, and tasting strange things with his mouth and inside his chest, frightening and delicious all at once. She was just like she looked. Apple pie and cinnamon.

She finally pushed him away, and they stood up, laughing as they brushed the snow from their clothes. She turned for him to clean the powdery stuff off her back, and he could feel the line of her body and the firmness of it. He couldn't stop laughing, and it was the best laughter he could ever remember having, though there was nothing about it that had anything to do with funny. She turned and he looked at her teeth again and thought, I kissed her right there, on those teeth. I'd let her bite me if she wanted to.

Duny Gene was ready to wallow around in the snow until it melted, but Maudie was already retrieving the sled and starting back up the hill.

"Come on. This thing's heavy," she said.

He saw then that she wasn't wearing mittens, and he closed one hand over hers as she held the rope. They started up, not saying anything, just grinning and a little embarrassed. Off to one side, Wart tagged along, watching them warily. He was puzzled about all of this, and not too pleased with it, either.

At the top, Maudie slipped her hand from Duny Gene's and stood back from him and adjusted the muffler until she looked like that Arabian princess again, except that now a few strands of red hair were hanging out, damp with snow.

"I've gotta go," she said. "Mama's likely wondering where I am."

"We can take one more run," Duny Gene said expectantly. He thought his voice was shaking a little.

"I've gotta go." She started off abruptly, then stopped and looked back. "Are you gonna play next week, when West Fork comes?"

For a moment, he stood gaping, with no idea of

what she meant. Then he remembered the big ball game coming up. "Aw, I might," he said.

"I hope so. I'll be there." Then she moved back toward him, and he saw the light of some mischief in her eyes that left him completely unsettled. She's making fun of me now, he thought.

"Do you know where babies come from?" she asked, and Duny Gene was open-mouthed and stunned, and wondering what the hell this was all about. "Do you?"

"Aw, what kind of question is that? You think I'm some kind of kid or something?"

Maudie laughed. "I just wondered. Thanks for the ride. Bye-bye."

And Duny Gene stood there in the snow, dumbfounded, watching her go across the crest of East Mountain, her rear end swinging under her coat as if she was wearing nothing but step-ins. Then she was gone, looking back once to wave and grin at him, her strands of red hair shining in the sun.

"God Almighty," Duny Gene said, and sank down onto the sled to think about it.

He was still thinking about it that night, when he and Barton accompanied Lydia to the Eastern Star bean supper. But for a while, the music and marching and the beans and corn bread made him forget.

The Masonic Lodge Hall, where the Eastern Star met, was in a long room above Esta Stayborn's store. There was a single outside staircase that led up to it. Through the cracks between the steps, there was a cold breath blowing off the little stream that ran at the base of West Mountain behind the line of stores, one of the wellsprings of the West Fork of White River. Even with the clump and stamp of feet and the clatter of conversation, the water running over the rocks sounded like a moist whisper from the darkness.

Sometimes, outsiders who were not Masons or Eastern Stars were invited to attend the meetings—installations and social functions which had nothing to do with all the secrets involved in both orders. The annual March bean supper fell into that category. Whole families would arrive, and there would be a short meeting of welcome when the officers of the Star called each other brother and sister, and let it be known that everyone was in for one hell of a show.

After the greetings, the drill would begin. These were always planned and orchestrated by Lydia, who played the slightly out-of-tune piano, and Esta Stayborn's wife, Mona, who designed the drills and acted as a sort of sergeant major. The music would pound through the old hall, seeming to shake the building, and the ladies in their long dresses in various colors would troop back and forth, making patterns, crossing and circling and cutting square corners around the five stations that represented the star. Each station had a triangular table and a chair, painted in the color that delineated one of the sisters.

Duny Gene had heard about them so much that he knew them by heart. There was green for Martha, red for Electra, white for Esther, yellow for Ruth, and blue for Jephthah's daughter, who didn't have any other name in the King James Bible, but whom the Eastern Star called Ada.

Duny Gene liked Ada best. He wasn't sure why. Maybe because blue was his favorite color. Or maybe it was because she got such a bad deal. When her daddy came home after winning that big battle and sacrificed her to the Lord, all she got was a couple of months to go off into the hills ahead of time and worry about her virginity. She didn't even get a name out of it. She was just Jephthah's daughter.

When he asked Barton about it, Barton said he

guessed it was a lesson that a man shouldn't make any promises until he'd considered all the possibilities.

But how come we don't know her name? Duny Gene had asked, and Barton said he guessed whoever wrote the story had forgotten her name. It was a rotten deal all around.

Duny Gene sometimes turned to the Book of Judges and read the story for himself. In one place, it said Jephthah's mother was a strange woman. He thought that was funny. He'd never heard anyone call Violet Sims a strange woman. They called her a whore, like Jephthah's mother was.

Duny Gene never mentioned that part of the story to Barton.

After the drills were finished, there was some more sister and brother talk by the Eastern Stars, and then the Worthy Matron called on guests to speak. Barton Pay was always the first one asked.

"Once again, these fine ladies of the Weedy Rough Eastern Star have shown us their hospitality and talent. It is a great pleasure to sit here among friends and feel the fellowship that I have never failed to find in this hall. I speak for us all when I say we are deeply appreciative for having been invited. Thank you."

It was usually about the same, what Barton said. And Duny Gene couldn't help thinking that his father always fit his speech to the occasion. If he was among people who spoke as though they'd finished at least the fifth grade, his words were chosen accordingly. When he was in the tie yard or on the route with the sticks people, his speech became theirs.

After Barton, others were called on to add a few words. Olie Merton was always saved until last, because everyone knew what he would say.

"When do we eat?"

Halfway through his beans and corn bread, Duny

Gene started thinking about Maudie Snowdon again, about the bobsled ride and her teeth—the way they felt against his lips. Later, he tried to concentrate on the deep-dish peach pie, but the thing that had happened on East Mountain was hard stuff to forget.

Parkins Muller sat in the darkness of his living room, smelling the mustiness of the chair indented by his bony butt, and looked out into the snowy night, down across the tracks to the lodge hall where lights gleamed through the windows. The room was cold, because they seldom lit a fire here.

He knew the fire in the kitchen would be dead, too. From there, a coal-oil lamp burned, the only light in the house.

Parkins was in his nightgown and a frayed robe that he recalled buying the second year he had operated the bank. That had been a while ago, he thought. Maybe I ought to get me a new robe, and house slippers, too.

The Eastern Star meeting was finished soon, as he sat watching, and he could see people coming from the stairway door, all going their separate ways, calling to one another and laughing. Some of them carried lanterns and a few had flashlights. Parkins rubbed his hands together, hunched over and watching.

"Parkins, are you sick?" his sister called from her room.

"No, I'm not sick," he said.

"Why don't you get to bed and blow out that light?"

"In a minute."

But soon she appeared in the doorway, holding her own housecoat tight around her skinny frame.

"What's the matter with you?" she asked.

"I was just watchin' the people come out of the Star meeting," he said.

"You sit here in the cold, you'll catch the flu."

"Yeah," he muttered. The last of the people were disappearing now, going up the hills, their lanterns and flashlights making little wintry fireflies. "I found feathers all over the barn lot when I went to milk tonight."

"Was any of the guineas dead?" she asked, alarm in her voice.

"No. I almost caught that dog at it. He was just on the other side of the gate. When I came in the lot, he barked at me. That dog never barks at anybody, but he barked at me in my own barn lot."

"Well, why don't you say something to Barton Pay? It's his dog. Those are valuable hens. And that boy of his, teasing the goats. Every time it happens I can tell because they give down less milk."

"That's just your imagination," Parkins said. "But it's the idea of a boy like that not able to take a man's property seriously."

"Well, tell Barton Pay about it."

"No, I'm not going to tell Barton Pay about it," he said sharply.

"They're our goats and our guineas and—"

"I'm not going to get into it with Barton Pay," he said, cutting her off. "Now get to bed. Blow out the light if it bothers you."

And then he sat, hearing her go back through the kitchen to put out the lamp, hearing her bedroom door slam, hearing her bedsprings creak.

For a long time he stayed in the darkness, growing colder, thinking about his goats and his guinea hens. And about the little white dog, barking at him as though he were some railroad hobo.

Parkins Muller looked down into the town, deserted now and showing its white outlines in the snow. He thought he could still hear some of the people talking and laughing, somewhere up East Mountain along the road that ran below his house. He looked at the bank building, sitting on the snowy corner across from the tie yard, and he wondered why everything in life was not as simple and straightforward as loans and deposits and interest. Then he clenched his fist and beat it against the windowsill softly.

Nobody in Weedy Rough—except perhaps Parkins Muller—ever questioned the fact that the most important thing about the town was its basketball team. In some of the larger schools, football was the coming thing. In the smaller places, like the Rough, there weren't enough kids to field a football team. But any school, even the smaller ones, could find five boys to run up and down a dirt court in colored underwear, bouncing a round ball.

In Weedy Rough, the underwear was green and the team's name was the Chipmunks. Most people called them The Chips.

Before electricity, the games were played in the afternoon. Then came a gasoline-powered generator that could pump out about ten kilowatts, which shed a pale, malevolent glare throughout the old gym— enough light to play by, at least—and after that, all the games were at night. People called it the Delco, and it was the province of Tooth Snowdon.

In the year of the late March snow, Weedy Rough and West Fork were tied for the class B regional championship going into the last game of the season. Whoever won that contest was sure of an invitation to the county tournament in the National Guard armory in Fayetteville.

It was expected that West Fork would send a sizable contingent, arriving in town along the federal highway in their Fords and Chevys, prepared to be nasty. The two towns were generally on good terms, but during basketball season there was an animosity rivaling that of the Germans and the French.

In that year, with a championship in the offing, feeling ran so high that it spread into the sticks. A few of those folk came in for the final game, driving their mule teams and all the kids in the wagon bed along with the lingering litter of oak and hickory bark.

Tooth Snowdon ambled up toward the school about midafternoon. The snow was gone by now. The weather had turned balmy, but he figured he ought to stoke fires in the big fifty-five-gallon drums set along the walls of the gym for that purpose. Before that, he visited with Jacob Hubbs, who ran a small store just south of the Methodist church and within sight of the gym. Mr. Budd, the peg-leg man, was there, also Constable Sparks. They talked about the big game. There were a couple of fruit jars of clear corn whiskey involved.

"Say, Tooth, who'd you bet on tonight?" Mr. Hubbs asked. He was a gnomelike man with a glistening bald head and arms as tough and scaly as post-oak staves. But he was a good infielder on the town's ball team, and could run the base paths with such abandon that Weedy Roughers called him Cobb.

"Hell, Cobb, I ain't got no money to bet," Tooth said, passing along one of the fruit jars to the town constable. "But I'd bet a good milk cow on Weedy Rough. West Fork ain't got no chance at all."

"They got that big center," Leo Sparks said.

"Yeah, I wonder how much longer he's gonna be playing for West Fork?"

"He looks like he's twenty-nine years old," Cobb said.

They stopped talking and watched Mr. Budd ease off his chair and onto the floor, his back against the wall and his peg leg thrust straight out before him.

"Harmon," Tooth shouted. "You better lay off this corn. You'll be so goddamned drunk by game time you won't be able to see nothin'."

"I ain't goin' to no ball game," Mr. Budd said, his words gurgling out in a corn-scented spray.

"That's all right, Harmon," Cobb said. "You can look after the store."

Everyone but Mr. Budd laughed.

"Yeah, Harmon, you can beat off any robbers with that hickory leg," Tooth said, and they laughed again.

It was almost dark before Tooth got away. There were already a few automobiles and wagons parked in a scattered array near the gym, sitting under the scrub oak trees. People were waiting to get inside. Tooth got the Delco going after a few false starts, then unlocked the gym and went in before the others to set fires in the barrels. The cold had begun to creep in with the setting sun, and the people stood around the fires, butts to the flames.

Across town, Maudie Snowdon was hitching the team to the wagon. There was an older brother, called Little Tooth, but he was never around when she needed him. Old lady Snowdon had been a hard worker all her life, but she refused to hitch the horses, and none of the younger kids was strong enough to do it, especially since the mule colt came.

Maudie was good with horses. She'd been working with them since toddling age. But on this night, when she was in a hurry, the mule colt gave her more trouble than she wanted, kicking at the mare and biting Maudie on the butt at every chance and getting tangled in the traces.

"You stop talkin' like that, girl," old lady Snowdon yelled once from the back porch. "I never heerd such bad talk from a girl's mouth!"

With the hitching finished and all the kids and the

old lady in the wagon, Maudie thought her troubles were finished. But the mule colt picked the center of town to get so tangled in the harness that Maudie had to climb down and undo the whole thing and start from scratch, the colt prancing along the sidewalk in front of the post office and making occasional forays at his mother or at Maudie's butt, whichever offered the best target of the moment.

Finally, they made it up East Mountain, in time for the opening toss-up, the old lady complaining all the while about Maudie's cussing.

Later, Maudie guessed it was all worth the effort when two of the players from the year before who had graduated came and sat with her. She was glad they didn't smell of white whiskey, like her old man did. She knew the condition Tooth was in because she had made a point of seeking him out face-to-face and telling him what she thought of his goddamned mule colt.

It became a terrible night. Weedy Rough lost the ball game in overtime. All the players were crying, and their coach, and the parents. Maudie's face was wet. The players were in a bunch at the center of the court, consoling one another, and the West Fork boys were going past them, patting them on the shoulders and saying, "Nice game, fellows," but thinking, How you like that, you smart-aleck bastards!

Then Maudie was out there with the team, too, hugging and crying with them, and a few of them controlled their grief long enough to feel her where the mule colt had been biting. Watching it all, Tooth stood in one corner near a flaming barrel.

"If I'd knowed this, I never would have started the goddamned Delco," he kept saying.

Duny Gene moved around to Maudie, and she was wetter with tears than he was with sweat, he not having played any since the first half of the game. Of all the team, he alone was not crying. He put his arms around her and she hugged him and he almost kissed her right there in the middle of the gym with most of Weedy Rough watching. But then the coach hustled them all off to get dressed, and Maudie ran outside to the wagon, wiping her nose on her coat sleeve.

Duny Gene hurried out into the night after he was dressed, looking for Maudie. The grove around the gym was swept with dim headlights as the West Fork crowd pulled out in their cars, yelling and singing and generally rubbing it in.

Duny Gene found Tooth Snowdon leaning against a small hickory tree, dejected and wiping his nose with his fingers.

"She's done gone, boy," he said. "She was all tore up about the game."

Duny Gene looked through the trees toward the road to town, remembering how the rest of the team pawed at her when she ran on the court. She sure as hell hadn't offered much resistance, he thought bitterly. And before that, sitting up there in the corner while the game was going on with those two bastards from last year's team!

He moved through the trees, looking for Barton and the Ford. Behind him, he could hear Tooth grumbling to himself.

"That damned center must be twenty-nine years old."

But Weedy Rough got an invitation to the tournament anyway.

Soldier's Joy

ground the ...

the girl ...

ate th ...

thing, gi ...

oppor ...

coach ... and Maudie ran

· 5 ·

MANY THINGS IN WEEDY ROUGH ACTED AS
sounding boards about itself. One was the barbershop, another was the counter of Esta Stayborn's
store, and others included the Ladies' Aid Society
and the Eastern Star. Because of the efficiency of
such communications systems, it was virtually impossible to keep a secret. Everyone knew when some
poor girl got herself into trouble, and who the guilty
boy was; or when a good well went dry; or when Leo
Sparks developed gallstones; or when Cobb Hubbs
got tired of his wife throwing china at him and
locked her in the outdoor privy for the night.

Or that Duny Gene Pay had kissed Maudie Snowdon.

After that morning in the snow on East Mountain,
it happened again. Sometimes with regularity. Duny
Gene began hanging around choir practice every
Wednesday night at the Methodist church, where
Maudie sang soprano. There were opportunities that
presented themselves behind the parsonage.

When Maudie ate her lunch at school, Duny Gene
was always there, trying to spook the other girls
away with cutting remarks about how tacky their
clothes were or how drunk their papas got on Saturday nights. Once, a fight broke out on the basketball
court during practice for the tournament when one of
the other boys who had done some of that handling at

the West Fork game made a chance remark about Maudie, and Duny Gene started swinging.

The kids began calling her Duny Gene's girl, giggling about it but never saying it to his face, and when they were near her, moving away as soon as they saw Duny Gene coming.

When spring came on strong that year, Mona Stayborn began her Sunday-school get-togethers early, and between roasting marshmallows and wieners, Duny Gene and Maudie found time to slip back away from the fire's light now and again. But always for only a moment, because Mona had rigid ideas about what was supposed to take place at Sunday-school get-togethers.

There were times, too, in the school pump room at noon recess, and twice at the top side of Parkins Muller's goat pasture. And again on the night of the senior play at the schoolhouse, where Joe Sanford tipped over a tray of deviled ham sandwiches in the main hall during intermission, and some of the younger kids helping clean up the mess got into a bread-ball fight. During the confusion, Duny Gene and Maudie slipped into a dark classroom for a few seconds of fumbling at one another.

Each time, Duny Gene was amazed at the passion in Maudie, the way she came at him, threw herself against him and searched for his mouth with her lips, her eyes tightly closed. It always left his blood pounding, and he was sure nobody had ever experienced such emotions before. He started counting the times he had kissed her, hanging each occasion like a trophy on the wall of his thinking. Then he lost count, but it no longer mattered anyway.

And he was proud of his self-control. Because no matter what he and others like him had been taught, there was an almost overpowering urge to take this whole thing far beyond kissing on the mouth. He was uneasily aware that Maudie had the same kind of urgings, and with a little encouragement would have had no self-control whatsoever.

That spring, usual events took on unusual excitement. Wherever Duny Gene walked, the ground seemed to give each step a bounce, like the plank diving board that would soon be put up at the Slicker Creek swimming hole.

Lydia noticed an absentmindedness in her son. The old intensity was still there, but it sometimes became aimless. Frequently, he had to be shouted at before he seemed capable of hearing. She thought of taking him to Fort Smith to a doctor, to check his ears.

Wart was aware of neglect, and for the first time in his life he sulked, staying stubbornly away from Duny Gene, watching, waiting to be called for ear scratching or stick retrieving. But the calls were seldom made, and the dog sensed that some subtle change was taking place. He didn't particularly like it, and became irritable. Once, he almost bit one of Parkins Muller's goats.

When school was out, Duny Gene still managed to see Maudie almost every day—if not at some other time, then most certainly at the Frisco depot in the evening, when the townspeople and early arrivals among the Texas Trade gathered to watch Number Six come in. If anyone had doubts about what was going on, these doubts were dispelled on one such evening when Duny Gene gave Maudie a penny, squashed flat by the big locomotive drive-wheels.

The wagons and flivvers and a few expensive Texas cars were clogging the street in front of the post office. People were thronged along the depot platform, visiting, and the screen doors at the ice-cream parlor and drugstore slammed constantly. Mr. Harmon Budd was in his usual place, sitting immobile and a little drunk under the big maple tree beside the station house, his peg leg laying out before him like a peeled poleax handle.

For a while, they could hear the train pulling the long grade on the south side of Academy Heights. Then there was no sound of it, only the ground trembling as the locomotive entered the far end of the tunnel. The people grew quiet, waiting, and then with a bedlam of sound, drivers screaming, bell and whistle sending their warning, the train burst from the tunnel in a gunshot eruption of smoke, rounded the curve along the cut below the Pay house, and came into view, brakes shrieking. It roared past the platform, almost sucking the expectant people under the wheels, the kids squealing and holding their hands over their ears.

Finally, it was stopped and the baggage doors slid open, the engineer hanging from the cab of the locomotive, the front of his cap protruding from his head like a duck's bill.

Bending under the cars, Duny Gene retrieved his penny, placed on the rail before the train came from the tunnel. The coin was mashed paper-thin, with sharp edges, and was hot to the touch. He threw it back onto the platform and Hoadie Renkin caught it, laughing and tossing it from one hand to the other.

"Son of a bitch is hot, ain't it," Hoadie said. He spun the coin through the air, and Duny Gene took it like a hot line drive. Looking at it, Duny Gene could see all its features flattened beyond recognition, like hot butter pressed with a knife.

They moved through the crowd, looking into the car windows, watching baggage being unloaded and a few people coming down from the coaches onto the platform, treading carefully on the step the porter had provided.

"Bet there's good stuff on that Pullman," Hoadie said softly.

"Is that all you ever think about?"

Maudie was standing alongside the gray-painted depot, near the bay window where the telegraph key could be heard clicking inside. Their eyes met and she smiled quickly before turning her face elaborately away. Duny Gene moved to her, leaving Hoadie standing beside the Pullman car making faces at some well-dressed kid inside. Duny Gene held the penny out to her. She looked at it, and then into his face, and held out her own hand and let him place it there.

"Here's your fortune," he said. "It's cool now."

"I better get more fortune than that," she said. He looked at her lips and thought they were sweet as ripe cherries.

There was the press of people around them, and Duny Gene turned abruptly away and walked back to Hoadie. He tugged at the back of Hoadie's bib overalls.

"Come on. Let's go up to the engine."

Hoadie fell in beside him and they picked their way along the platform, shoving younger kids aside. Hoadie looked sideways at Duny Gene and grinned.

"You really after somethin' there, ain't ya?" he said. "You think that would be just keen, don't ya? Well, old Tooth may get ya, you don't watch out. He'll brain you with one of his gravediggin' shovels."

"Like hell," Duny Gene said. He looked back but could no longer see her standing near the depot telegraph window. "Nobody's gonna brain me with anything."

For an instant, he thought about his father's army pistol, lying cold and deadly in the nightstand drawer. That .45 was a defense mechanism in his brain that popped up unasked whenever he was threatened, whether the threat was real or imagined. He supposed that everyone else thought the same way.

* * *

"I reckon Duny Gene Pay's got the sweets on my girl," Tooth said. There was pride in his voice, because everyone in town figured that Duny Gene was growing into a good catch for anyone who could land him.

"She's a fine-lookin' young woman," Olie Merton said, picking at his teeth, leaning back in his barber chair, watching the pack of half-wild younguns playing in the street now that school was out. "So you need to be watchful. A young good-lookin' girl like that."

For a moment, Tooth had a twitch of apprehension about just how much was happening between his daughter and Barton Pay's son, but he brushed it aside, being always optimistic, even in the face of certain disaster.

"Hell, I can't do anything with her," he said. "It's like tryin' to control a good mare with spirit. She's growed way past the spankin' stage, by a long shot, and she can outtalk me and the old lady put together."

"Can't be too watchful."

"She's been taught right," Tooth said, a little huffy now with this prodding. "She knows how to act. She knows what's right. Now, she does have one hell of a temper and cusses a little when it goes off."

"Not much harm in that."

"She's a good girl."

"Yeah, and I'll bet Duny Gene ain't the only one got the sweets on her."

"I'll admit to that," Tooth said, once again a little proudly. "Leo Sparks's boy, down Fort Smith workin' in that furniture factory, he writes her letters all the time."

"He's a mite old, ain't he?"

"Hell, he ain't old," Tooth said. "Take me. I'm a good fifteen years older than my old lady. Say, Olie, I'd sure like to have a barber shave."

He scratched at the red stubble on his chin that always seemed to be there, never longer or shorter than the day or the week before.

"Costs a dime. Friend or foe," Olie said, sucking his toothpick.

"You're a damned hard man, you know that?"

"Shave costs a dime, haircut two bits, friend or foe."

"Shit, I'll go home and shave my ownself!"

If Tooth Snowdon knew Duny Gene Pay had the fidgets over his daughter, everyone else in town did, too. It was only a matter of time before some of the other boys tried to roast Duny Gene a little about having a sweetie, out of resentment or spite or just for the pure teasing hell of it. But it came unexpectedly, and from a strange quarter.

A few of the older boys were having their first baseball game of the season at the little diamond just north of town. There was a small patch of flat ground where the federal highway and the road out of Weedy Rough came together. This was where they played their games. It was a little lopsided, and left field disappeared into a tangle of persimmon and jack oak much too close to the infield, but it served its purpose.

This was a scrub game, with no sides being chosen. They were playing work-up, and Little Tooth Snowdon, the biggest player on the field, had been batting most of the afternoon. All the others were tired of his monopolizing the bat, but they said nothing because they were afraid of him. At least, most of them were afraid of him.

Little Tooth was on first, a base runner, when the batter swung at a pitch and missed. Little Tooth went down, and Hoadie Renkin, behind the plate, threw him out at second, with Duny Gene tagging Little Tooth at the bag.

"That gets your ass out," Duny Gene said.

Little Tooth was up from the cloud of dust his slide had created, his fists balled and his watery blue eyes bugging. He made a short charge at Duny Gene, who turned from walking away, the baseball still in his hand.

"I was safe," Little Tooth snarled.

"Like hell. You were out," Duny Gene snapped. "You may be too ignorant to know it, but you were out."

Little Tooth ran at Duny Gene and hit him in the chest with both fists, then leaped back and squared off like John L. Sullivan. The other players ran up, gathering in a circle to watch the maiming. Little Tooth was a foot taller than Duny Gene and outweighed him by at least forty pounds.

"You smart-aleck bastard," Little Tooth screamed, frothing at the mouth. "You think you're the big shit around here, don't you? You ain't nothin' but a smart-aleck bastard."

"You were out," Duny Gene said, and his eyes had suddenly gone rock-flat, lifeless as a snake's.

"You think you're the big shit," Little Tooth yelled again, edging closer, his fists up.

"You're so ignorant, you can't think of anything else to say, can you?"

"Oh yeah! You red Indian bastard. You sniffin' around my sister and puttin' on like you was layin' her anytime you want. I'm gonna break your damn arms. And you keep messin' around her anymore, I'm gonna break your damn legs, you smart-aleck bastard."

Duny Gene's face was pale now, the brown bleached out by his sudden realization that this thing had nothing to do with baseball. Everyone else knew it, too, maybe before Duny Gene had known, and they edged closer, waiting expectantly.

"You better shut your mouth," Duny Gene said.

"You little red Indian bastard," Little Tooth bellowed. "You come kissin' around on my sister like a white man. I'm gonna bust your ass. I'm gonna make you wish you was back in Oklahoma with all them others like you, all them black, greasy—"

Duny Gene threw the baseball with a hard, overhand whip of his arm. The pitch caught Little Tooth in the center of the forehead, just under the bill of his cap. Cap and ball flew out into center field and Little Tooth staggered back, arms flailing. But he didn't go down, and he started back toward Duny Gene, tears of rage in his eyes.

"You son of a bitch," Duny Gene said, almost too softly for anyone to hear. But Little Tooth heard him.

"What'd you call me?" Little Tooth sobbed.

"Son of a bitch. That's what I called you."

The other players leaned forward, eyes bright. Little Tooth took a deep breath, his fists up again, and weaved forward. Then he paused and stood there for a few seconds, tears running across his freckle-splotched cheeks and the red hair standing on his head like bunch grass. There was a growing purple welt across his forehead.

Suddenly, Little Tooth turned and walked out into center field, retrieved his cap, and slamming it on his head, passed across the outfield to the road and turned toward town.

Afterward, the boys told it around that Duny Gene Pay had faced off Little Tooth Snowdon with what appeared to have been a high, hard fast ball, and nary another blow. In their anticipation of a good fight, they had failed to see that as the squabble developed, Hoadie Renkin walked up close behind Duny Gene and stood there, grinning at Little Tooth, his long hands flexing into fists at his sides. But if the others had not noticed him, Little Tooth had. Like any town boy with a lick of sense, Little Tooth wanted no truck with a sticks kid, and besides, there had been those slate-colored eyes that turned suddenly deadly. Little Tooth may have been ignorant, like Duny Gene said, but he wasn't stupid.

The game fell apart after that.

PART TWO

·6·

THE FIRST SIGN OF HARD TIMES CAME IN the tie yard, where the price of timber dropped so low a man selling it could hardly buy flour on his earnings. Barton Pay fumed and complained each night to Lydia, and he wrote letters of protest to the Fort Smith office, though nothing ever came of them.

The wagons kept coming in, sometimes with packs of ragged kids riding on the ties, so they could have a look at Weedy Rough in this summer school's-out time. A few townspeople figured they were a plague set loose on decent folk, brought purposely by their daddies so they could steal a few items from any store at hand—whatever was loose and would fit inside the bib of their overalls.

Most days, Barton spent half his time squatting with some sticks man, whittling and trying to explain that crossties just weren't worth as much as they once had been, with no new track being laid anywhere and even some spur lines being shut down.

And out in the woods, good hickory and oak were beginning to get hard to find. Cuttings had decimated the virgin trees that had been growing close to the roads, growing since before the Osages had roamed these hills. Now, it was becoming more and more difficult to cut timber adequate for ties because most of it was off the beaten path and near impossible to haul out once cut—hidden down the narrow little sandstone outcrop hollows or along ridges that were as sharp and bristly as a wild hog's back.

The sticks men had more to complain about, too. There was the dry weather. It was a hard chore trying to coax beans and tomatoes from the rocky little fields. That year even the sorghum crop was bad, which could cause disaster in the winter, when most hill people survived largely on corn bread and molasses.

Sometimes, one of the timber cutters would tell of a postal card he'd had from a relative, writing about the fruit and vegetables to be picked in California, where a man could earn a hundred dollars a month just lying around under the orange trees. They usually brought these cards into the tie yard for Barton to read aloud for them. Then they would squat and ponder the possibility of selling their hill farms, buying a used tin lizzie, and heading west with their whole kit and caboodle.

Only there wasn't anyone around who wanted to buy a wild country farm that produced nothing much except rocks, and where mules sometimes had to walk spraddle-legged to keep from falling out of the hillside fields.

Nobody from the sticks was buying brogans or overalls from Esta Stayborn. It was a case of going one more year with patches and cardboard shoe soles and hoping next year would be better.

It was almost the dead of summer when old man Shayburg came. It was his annual visit, or maybe he'd call it a pilgrimage. He came on his old mule, in his old clothes, with his old hair and beard uncut, and all of it together with the old smell. He came from his shack or cave or den or whatever it was far back in the hills along the Oklahoma border, and the purpose of the trip was always the same—to buy a little sugar and a pint of cheap whiskey from Violet Sims, provided he could get anything for the ragged pelts he had trapped over the past twelve months.

Nobody knew much about him, though Tooth Snowdon was convinced he was some kind of red Indian. Nobody except Esta Stayborn or Violet ever talked to him. He was just a battered old man who never caused any trouble.

Duny Gene was in his mother's living room that afternoon, surveying the town below, when he saw the old man ride in and hitch his mule at Esta's sidewalk. And after a few moments, the old man went up the hill behind the bank to Violet's—he never went inside, just waited on the porch for the small brown bag she handed out—then came back down to the street, crossed to the tie yard, took a seat alongside the stacks of timber next to the tracks, and started drinking.

It was a hot, dusty day, with no breeze stirring. A real bum day, Duny Gene thought. He was restless and irritable. He hadn't seen Maudie for over a week, she having gone off to Benton County with her mother to visit some relative. Such separation was doubly irksome now that Duny Gene was growing tired of kissing games and was thinking about getting married when they'd finished school in a couple of years. Nothing had ever been said outright, but he assumed Maudie was thinking the same thing.

Dull as hell. Too hot to go sporting around in the woods, too hot to take the pistol out into the hills and pot-shoot cans.

Duny Gene looked at Barton's new Model A parked in the road below the house. It was black, a deluxe model, which meant two taillights. Duny Gene had mastered the clutch and steering wheel and brakes within a day after Barton brought it home from Fayetteville, attacking the problem with a fearless intensity that amazed but gratified his father.

He could see Barton in the tie yard, working with the grading hammer, stamping the marks on each timber that would eventually place it on some mainline track or spur, or as shoring along cuts and embankments. He could hear the hammer's soft thump each time Barton swung it into the butt of a tie.

He wished the black crews were in town, loading out the ties. They were always huge men, carrying the almost two-hundred-pound timbers into the boxcars, bouncing along a plank walkway, chanting some strange song he could never understand. But he enjoyed watching them, like great black panthers glistening wet in the hot sun.

Wart was on the front porch, watching Duny Gene through the screen door. Duny Gene went out to him and scratched his ears, and the dog followed him down to the road. The headlights on the Ford had a fine mist of red mud on the globes, and Duny Gene spat on them and wiped them clean with the heel of his hand. He was on the second headlight when the ruckus broke out in town.

Two cur dogs were suddenly going at one another in front of Esta Stayborn's store, almost directly beneath the belly of old man Shayburg's mule. They were making a terrible racket, and Wart's ears went up. Then the mule started raising hell, trying to pull free of the tether, and Esta Stayborn ran out of the store with a broom and started swinging at the dogs but hitting mostly mule.

Old man Shayburg heard his mule braying, too, and small wonder because the volume of noise now was enough to wake Mr. Harmon Budd lying under the depot maple. Old man Shayburg leaped up and secreted his bottle among the ties—Duny Gene watching it all from the road above—and ran along the tracks far enough to clear the tie yard, then into the street to save his mule. By then a third dog had joined the contest, and old man Shayburg disappeared into the roil of dust, his arms flailing.

Duny Gene moved without thinking about it. An impulse that didn't even register on his thinking. As he scaled down the steep bluff path to the tracks, Wart scrambled along after him. I know just where he hid that bottle, Duny Gene thought. I'll bet that crazy old bastard would raise hell if he came back and it was gone.

"Come on, you dog," Duny Gene called, jumping across the mainline tracks and the sidings, going directly to the stack of ties where the old man had hidden his whiskey. Then, with the bottle in his hand, Duny Gene turned back up the tracks and ran toward the tunnel, skipping across the flanged cowcatcher at the mouth of the cut and on between the steep walls, running on one rail like a fox along a snake-pole fence. Wart stayed close behind him.

Approaching the tunnel, he looked for a place to hide the bottle. The shale walls of the cut were always dropping loose rock into the ditches alongside the tracks, and he moved to one of these and scooped out a small depression. He started to lay the bottle in the hole, and then looked at it really for the first time. It was clear glass with a green label, and the liquid inside was oily-looking, amber-colored.

Duny Gene uncorked the bottle. He sniffed, and the heavy aroma made his nostrils flare. He looked at the bottle a long time, shaking it, making little foamy bubbles in the whiskey.

"What the hell," he said, and lifting the bottle quickly so he wouldn't have to smell the stuff again, took a drink. It scalded his throat, and the heat burned him down to his belt buckle. Wart watched apprehensively as Duny Gene gagged and choked.

"Damn!" Duny Gene said softly, wiping the tears from his eyes.

But now the burning was only a slow glow in his belly, not a bad sensation. He took a second drink. It wasn't nearly so raw as the first. He squatted there a long time, staring at the bottle, then drinking, then staring again. He began to feel light-headed and clean, too, as though all the pores in his hot skin were opening to the cool air in the cut.

Finally the noise of confused combat from the direction of town quieted. In a moment, old man Shayburg would be searching frantically for his bottle, thinking he'd forgotten where he hid it. Duny Gene giggled, then grew elaborately sober with the thought that maybe old man Shayburg might start up the line, looking for his whiskey.

Duny Gene moved back onto the tracks, wobbling a little. He threw the bottle—empty now—onto the crossties, and it shattered. Wart watched tensely, tail stiff and ears pitched forward.

"Come on, you dog," Duny Gene said, and went directly toward the tunnel, walking quickly along the deepening cut.

As he drew near, the great sandstone archway opened larger and larger, like a massive window into some dark cathedral beyond. He wasn't sure of the time, the realization coming with the momentary thought that the northbound freight was due. But he said to hell with that, too, and walked on into the tunnel, Wart following warily.

It was a straight tunnel, and from either end a person could see the tiny oval of light at the other, the rails shining all the way. But a few yards inside, all the shine disappeared from the track and it was black as night with only the far mouth opening to sunlight a half-mile away.

Water dripped from the arched roof, and it was

cold. There was a breeze coming through the great shaft, refrigerated by the falling water, and Duny Gene shivered but kept going. It was deadly quiet except for the falling water, even the sounds of summer birds outside completely shut off.

He'd walked through once before, with Hoadie Renkin, carrying squirrels they'd killed out of season and taking this route to avoid imaginary game wardens. But now he found it a great deal more unsettling. At any moment he expected to see a locomotive materialize at the far end. And behind him in the darkness, he could hear Wart, panting more loudly than was necessary just to let Duny Gene know he was still there.

"Come on, you dog," Duny Gene said, and his voice boomed against the walls and the high dome, as though he were shouting into a gigantic rain barrel. In the uneven footing where rock and brick had fallen from the roof he stumbled and fell, but there was no pain.

Walking into the sunlight at the far end, he felt a vast relief. Far down the slope, he could hear the freight train laboring upward, and he laughed in triumph.

"We beat you, you son of a bitch," he said.

He left the tracks and went into the woods alongside, climbing until he was directly above the tunnel entrance. He could see the smoke now, very near, and hear the sound of the engines. Wart watched suspiciously as Duny Gene selected a few large rocks and waited.

Everything was momentarily lost from sight as the engines passed beneath him, their smoke boiling up around him. Then the wind whipped the smoke away and he could see the long line of cars. He picked up the first rock.

It made a hell of a racket bouncing off the roof of

a boxcar. Duny Gene laughed and selected another boulder, and heaved it down onto the train. Then another, the report of the rocks striking the cars like small cannon fired off in the steep valley.

As the caboose came into sight, he could see a brakeman hanging out one window, waving a clenched first and screaming obscenities. Duny Gene—his hands empty of missiles now—stood quietly, smiling and waving, innocent as a first-grade kid at Sunday school.

When the last of the train had disappeared beneath him, he laughed again and threw a few more rocks at the empty tracks below. Wart watched him, intently.

"All right, you dog," Duny Gene said. "It ain't nothin' for you to worry about."

And he turned up the hill and walked home, still unsteady on his feet.

Duny Gene had passed beyond the dread of his father finding out about his escapades. Maybe it was because Barton never found out, as though he were insulated from what was really going on around him. Duny Gene was glad Wart couldn't talk.

It was a few days after the bombardment of the freight train when Barton suggested they go out in the late afternoon and do a little tin-can popping. They drove into the hills and found a spot they had used before and set up a row of cans on an old fallen log a few paces off the road. Duny Gene shot two magazines, missing only a couple of times.

It was a good day, not too hot and with a nice breeze coming in from Signal Rock. Duny Gene sat on the running board of the Model A, feeding .45 cartridges into the magazine, the still-hot pistol on his knees. Barton stood against the front fender, smoking a pipe and thinking as he often did that pistols were really not much good for anything except shooting people and popping tin cans. Sometimes now he wondered why he had ever brought the thing home from the war. But he had been a different man then, and besides, he enjoyed watching Duny Gene shoot.

"That old pistol brings back the memories," Barton said.

"About the war?"

"Not so much that. Later, back at home, in Fort Smith. I was mighty proud of that pistol then."

"You're not now?"

"Everything changes a little. Some things a lot. I was still a wild young man then like I'd been before the war."

Duny Gene slipped the loaded magazine into the butt and offered the pistol to his father.

"You wanna take a crack?"

"No, you go ahead."

Duny Gene opened fire on the cans, and when a slug struck home the can would bound crazily back off the log, a jagged hole showing. Sometimes a bullet would strike the slope behind the log and whine off through the trees.

"That's when you met Mother, I guess," Duny Gene said. "The wild times."

"I courted half the young ladies in Fort Smith before the war," Barton said and laughed shortly, with embarrassment or perhaps pride, or maybe, Duny Gene thought, with a little shame. "We hit it off, somehow, your mother and me. I never understood my good luck. But we hit it off."

"You were one of those young blades," Duny Gene laughed, a little embarrassed, too, because this was new ground, never plowed before.

"Yes. I'm glad you're a more settled boy than I was," Barton said. Duny Gene glanced at him and Barton was sucking on the pipe, looking off into the timber with an expression on his face that made

Duny Gene think of Brother Hammel about to deliver a funeral oration. It made him uncomfortable.

"Can't get in much trouble around here," Duny Gene mumbled.

"More's the blessing. I went for a spell without moorings, I suppose. But your mother helped change all that. Then there was the church. . . ."

Barton let it trail off, and Duny Gene was a little disappointed, even counting the discomfort, because it had almost turned into something that might have told him exactly how his father could ever have known—much less married—someone like Lydia. But there was no more.

"Well, better get on home," Barton said, knocking out his pipe against the front tire. "Get that gun cleaned. Your mother'll have supper ready before long."

· 7 ·

FEW PEOPLE IN WEEDY ROUGH KNEW WHAT it meant when they read or heard on the radio that there had been a stock-market crash on Wall Street. They made little effort to find out. It seemed to have no effect on their lives.

But the following summer, they began to see the signs. Little Tooth Snowdon had gone to Kansas City to attend one of those automotive schools that were springing up everywhere, and he wrote home that finding part-time work to support his education was becoming difficult. A few Weedy Roughers said Little Tooth would never return to town anyway, for fear of getting beaned with a baseball again. Even Tooth himself joked about it.

Leo Sparks's son, Jabo, had come home, laid off from what had been a good job in one of the Fort Smith furniture factories. At least, he had a new Model A to show for it. Some said it wasn't paid for and the town busy-bodies waited expectantly for some deputy sheriff to come and repossess it.

Mostly, they saw the change in the traffic of hoboes on freights that came through. Hardly a day passed without a few of these lank and ragged men stopping off in Weedy Rough, going from door to door, begging food in exchange for any work they might do. Lydia Pay began making more biscuits and frying more bacon each morning so she'd have something to feed them when they came. Wart watched them warily from a distance, but he never barked, seeming to sense that there was no wickedness in these men, only hunger and a desire to work for their dinner.

The barbershop gang watched with dismay and considerable awe as the parade of bums increased.

"They mark houses where they can get a handout," Tooth Snowdon observed. "I don't know how, but they do. Then the next one comes along, he knows the mark where he can get grub. You see all these fellas come through here, they always go to Barton Pay's or over to Violet Sims's or some such place, because they know somehow they'll get fed, even if there ain't no wood to stack or shit to shovel out of the barn. They know, somehow. You never see any go to Parkins Muller's house, do you? Because they know. The ones come before them has marked the good places."

Now, too, there were stories of a new kind of bandit, operating in powerful cars like LaSalles and Chryslers, and using sawed-off shotguns and tommies. One was a man named Charles A. Floyd out of Salisaw, Oklahoma. From what they'd read in the newspapers, most Roughers allowed he wasn't so bad, only robbing a rich man's bank now and again. He never hurt farmers or poor folks.

Leo Sparks said they'd sure as hell hurt a few peace officers, tapping the five-pointed star that was emblem of his office, sometimes apparent on his outer garments, sometimes not.

"You ain't a real peace officer, anyway, Leo," Tooth said. "You're just a constable. And if Pretty Boy ever comes around here, you'd better hide that badge and go fishin'."

And everyone in the barbershop laughed, except Leo.

Of all the Roughers, Barton Pay was most concerned about what was taking place. He read the *Kansas City Star* and the *Fayetteville Daily Democrat* each evening before the good radio shows came on, grumbling all the while, complaining about the country going to hell.

"More appeals from the chamber of commerce for businessmen to make odd jobs for people. More than four hundred men out of work in Fayetteville," he said one evening. "Says here farmers who can't make a living are coming into town, but no work there. Price of groceries so low. Some farmers even dump their milk, it says here."

"Why would anyone dump perfectly good milk?" Lydia asked, working on quilt pieces.

"Can't make enough on it to feed their cows."

"How will dumping milk feed their cows?"

"Run up prices. That's a lost hope. Sign of the times. No direction to it. But I guess our own hill farmers are no worse off than usual. They're broke now, but they always have been.''

''It's pitiful the way those people live.''

''Well, sometimes a man lives the only way he can. As long as the timber holds out and the railroad still buys it, and as long as there's squirrels in the woods, I guess they won't starve.''

''I saw that Renkin man in town today with his wagon. I never saw so many children.''

''Yeah, I never counted how many old Ike's got. He's no different than the rest. It says here another bank robbery over in Oklahoma. Hard times.'' Barton threw down the newspapers and bent to the radio dials. ''No help for it, I guess. But the foxes still run.''

When Barton Pay bought a foxhound bitch named Dixie, Lydia was so furious she went to Fort Smith for two weeks to visit her family. The dog had been brought into the hills by a man from Missouri for one of the hunts sponsored by the Washington County Fox Racing Association, and when Barton saw her and heard her run, he knew he had to own that dog. She cost him seventy-five dollars, and when he told Lydia, he shaved the price by about half, so actually she might have stayed in Fort Smith for four weeks if she'd known the real amount on that check from the Fayetteville bank where Barton kept his account.

''You won't have to put up with her around here,'' Barton said. ''I've arranged for Ike Renkin to board her. To keep her with his dogs.''

''And how much will that cost you?'' Lydia snapped, her mouth turned down and bitter.

''It won't cost much. Ike feeds his dogs table scraps . . .''

''What kind of table scraps would that Renkin

bunch have? They don't have enough to feed their children, much less any left over.''

''. . . and he kills squirrels for them, and now and again I can go up to Fayetteville to one of those packing plants and buy a couple of hundred-pound sacks of pig cracklings.''

''You take cracklings out there, and those Renkin kids will eat them. I know what you'll do. You'll haul a mess of food out there every time you carry the mail, or even have Alvie Haus take it out when you're not on the route.''

''Well, it won't cost much,'' Barton said weakly. And that's when Lydia marched off to the bedroom to pack her suitcase.

The summer vacation was still some distance away, but Lydia wanted to take Duny Gene with her. That would have meant missing a lot of classwork, so Barton prevailed in the name of education before Duny Gene himself had a chance to raise hell about having to go.

The two of them dutifully saw Lydia off on the south-bound passenger one morning, and she just as dutifully gave them each a peck on the cheek. Boarding the train, she turned the wrong way and came into the smoking car. Waving the cigar smoke away from her face with disgust, she wheeled about and went into the next coach, sitting in a seat on the far side of the car from the platform, where she knew Barton and Duny Gene were waiting to wave her good-bye.

It was too early in the morning for the barbershop gang to be assembled, but Olie Merton was there at his window. He watched Barton and Duny Gene standing on the platform together, looking a little forlorn. He observed that Duny Gene was as big as his father now, and mused for a while on the rapid passage of time.

Those two weeks were the first time that Duny Gene came to appreciate his mother. Most especially her cooking. Barton had little knowledge of the kitchen, and they survived mostly out of cans. Barton attempted a meatloaf the first Sunday, but forgot to season it or add eggs, and it tasted like greasy sawdust.

But at least there was fox hunting aplenty. Almost every night, Barton went to the woods, where the dogs were let loose, and now there was no one to complain when Duny Gene insisted on going, too.

Nobody around Weedy Rough had a large pack, usually just three or four dogs. In late afternoon, the hunters would amble into the drugstore or the barber-shop, and someone would allow that he would let his hounds loose out around Harragon Hollow or some such place that evening. Someone else would say that his dogs needed some running, too. By nightfall, a race would be arranged, although there was never any organization about it. The pieces just fell to-gether, somehow.

The object of these affairs was to hear the dogs run, not catch the fox. So they referred to them as races. Of course, sometimes when the ground was wet from recent rain, making the scent too strong for the fox to lose the pack, or sometimes when they jumped a young, inexperienced fox that had not yet learned how to toy with the dogs, the fox was caught and killed. Such a thing was considered only a little short of disastrous, because it meant one less fox to run the next night, or the next week, or the next month.

"Besides," Tooth said, "you let a hound catch a fox too many times, and he'll lose interest in chasing them one day. He'll finally figure out it ain't worth it, all that runnin' for a mouthful of hair and meat that tastes like soda acid."

"That ain't true," Olie said. "A foxhound is a

foxhound, and he'll run as long as he's alive, just for the fun of it.''

"What the hell do you know about fox dogs? You ain't ever owned one in your life," Tooth said testily, and stalked out of the barbershop.

During the time Lydia was in Fort Smith, Duny Gene was along on one of the better races anyone had heard in years. It was a Saturday night, the beginning of what Barton later called the dog weekend, because dogs figured into every part of it. The night was cool and clear, at least at first, and the new green was just coming onto the town maples. But the oak woods stood bare and crisp in the hills. It was always better when the leaves were off because the sounds of the pack came clearly across the ridges and through the valleys.

It was well past dark when they took the lantern down from the kitchen wall peg and Barton lifted the sack of groceries that had sat on the dining-room table since he'd brought it home after work. Wart moved along the porch with them, but only to the end, where the steps led down. He stopped there, knowing this was a trip he would not be invited to attend. He lay and watched them down through the steep yard to the road where the Ford was parked.

"You want to drive?" Barton asked.

Duny Gene slipped behind the wheel easily, having by now become accustomed to it. As Barton moved in beside him, he offered Duny Gene a cigarette, and they both lit up before Duny Gene jammed down the starter and switched on the headlights.

He had never been sure just when it was that his father knew he smoked. Nothing was ever said. But by now, when they were working timber in the tie yard, Barton always offered a Chesterfield when he rested and smoked himself. It never happened in Lydia's presence, of course.

They drove up the hill past Olie Merton's house, past the Methodist church, the lights making a pale yellow glare before them, then past Naulty's Ridge and onto the federal highway and south for about four miles.

"Turn off here," Barton finally said, and Duny Gene wheeled the car into a narrow, rutted road. They followed that another mile, and Duny Gene pulled off into an old field overgrown now with sassafras.

After the headlights were turned off, it seemed an extraordinarily dark night until their eyes became accustomed to it. There was a dense scatter of stars, the Milky Way making a sparkling pattern across the black dome of sky.

"Some Indians call it the Great White Road," Barton said.

"Our people?" Duny Gene said, and he was a little surprised at himself because he had never referred to his ancestry in just that way.

"No. Not the Cherokees. Some of the Plains tribes."

"The blanket-ass Indians?"

"Yes," Barton said, and laughed.

Far across the valley that sloped directly away under their feet, they could see the flare of a fire on the adjoining ridge.

"There they are," Barton said. "And the dogs are already at it."

To the east, Duny Gene could hear the pack, going away perhaps two miles off. Their voices came clear and trilling for a moment as they crossed high ground, and then the sounds faded and were gone in some far, deep hollow. But after a few moments they could hear the dogs again, coming back toward them, like the growing beat of music.

"Well, let's get across to the fire," Barton said, and scratched a match to the lantern.

They started down into the steep valley, Barton leading with the light, Duny Gene following with the sack of groceries. The lantern cast a pale glow, creating a tiny blurred world in the thickets of persimmon and jack oak, seeming to hold them captive. Beyond was only the darkness, the sense of deep woods. And from the blackness, always coming nearer, the frenzied voices of the dogs.

"Hear her?" Barton said over his shoulder. "Hear that high, clear voice? She's leading the pack. That's Dixie."

Duny Gene tried to distinguish a single voice, tried to imagine it ahead of the others, but he found it impossible. The whole of it was a wild, animal sound, pristine and brutal and somehow beautiful, too, and a little frightening.

On the next ridge they found a number of men grouped around the fire, squatting or warming their backsides, staring into the night and listening. All heads turned as Barton and Duny Gene walked into the circle of light. They nodded and spoke.

"Howdy, Mr. Pay. Howdy, Duny Gene."

Tooth Snowdon was there, although he owned no dogs, and Esta Stayborn and Reese Walls, the druggist and iceman, and Leo Sparks. Standing a little to the side was Ike Renkin, a tall gangling man wearing a tattered felt hat with sweat marks up the crown, and bib overalls. He was hard and knotty-looking, an older copy of his son. In the firelight, the stubble of a brassy beard showed. He nodded a welcome along with the rest, but said nothing.

"Got us a good one, tonight, Mr. Pay," Tooth said. "Got us an old gray, I allow, and he's teasin' them dogs."

"They're runnin' a wide circle," Esta said. "Right around us. They ought to come along the far side of that old wall in a minute."

"That's Mr. Pay's new dog out front, ain't it, Ike?" Leo Sparks asked.

For a moment, Ike turned his face to the others, but as quickly looked away. Duny Gene thought he acted a little embarrassed being here with all these town men, and him from the deep sticks.

"Yeah. That's Dixie," Ike said. "Mr. Reese's dog Cain was aleadin' a while ago. Now it's Dixie."

Duny Gene moved over beside Ike Renkin, and spoke to him and asked about his health. Ike never turned his head, staring still out into the night, where the dogs could be heard coming close now.

"Fair to middlin'," Ike said.

"Haven't see Hoadie for a while. He quit school?"

"He ain't said. You might ast him. He's out yonder."

Their fire was built alongside an old chimney, all that was left of what had once been a farmstead, burned years before. There was a rock wall about twenty paces to the north, barely visible in the firelight. Duny Gene could see a dark form, sitting on the wall.

"That boy of yourn gettin' bigger than you are, Mr. Pay," Tooth said.

"He drove out tonight," Barton said, blowing out the lantern and coming to take the sack from Duny Gene's hand. "Like to have run us into a canyon twice."

Everybody laughed.

The pack was coming onto the spur of ridge, and all talking ceased. The hounds came on with a rush, the yammering wail rising to a hysterical pitch. The sound broke from the edge of the clearing, where they expected at any moment to see the dogs. But they never did. Just as the pack was about to burst into the firelight, the racketing voices veered off along the far side of the old wall, and then as suddenly as they had come in violent crescendo, they were going away again, into the next hollow, the sounds of their voices more mournful, unlike the harsh chorus of their coming.

"Well, by Gawd, there they go," Esta Stayborn said.

"That ole fox is givin' us a show," Tooth said. "He's runnin' right under our noses, for the pure hell of it. He knows we're here, and he just wants us to know he can outrun them hounds."

"It sounds a lot better when they're a ways off," Leo Sparks said. "More like music then."

From the darkness, a long-ribbed black-and-white dog came to the fire, tail down and jaws gaped. He flopped down near the fire with a loud grunt and went to sleep, his sides still heaving.

"That's one of yourn, ain't it, Ike?" Leo asked.

"Yeah. That's Old Sam," Ike said, not looking at the dog, as though it was an embarrassment that one of his hounds would leave the race.

"How old is that dog, Ike?" Barton asked.

"Twelve."

"Gawd Almighty," Tooth laughed. "Surprised me he could get out of the yard at that age. What's that make him, Mr. Pay, human age?"

"About eighty," Barton said, reaching into the sack of groceries.

"What's that you got, Mr. Pay?" Tooth asked. "Tin Willy?"

They took the cans of corned beef from the sack, and the crackers and yellow rat cheese, and squatted around the fire, eating and listening as the dogs traced from the night the long circle through the hills around them. Ike Renkin had to be called before coming over and taking a small bite of meat and cheese, and then he stood back once more, chewing and listening, looking into the darkness.

"Where are they now, Ike?" Esta asked.

"Close to Signal Rock," he said.

Duny Gene moved over to Hoadie. The wall was like a barrier against the night, the fire making a dim flicker of light along its one side, but on the other, total blackness of the heavy timber. Duny Gene handed Hoadie a chunk of meat, and Hoadie bit off a large mouthful.

"It's a swell race," Duny Gene said.

"It's all right."

Hoadie called to Old Sam, and the dog lifted his head, rose with another grunt, and ambled over to them, ears hanging like empty burlap. Hoadie held out the meat and Sam sniffed it a second, and then with one quick gulp swallowed it whole.

"You been here long?" Duny Gene asked.

"No. Dogs kicked up the fox before we seen your lights over on the other ridge. What's the matter with you, Old Sam? You tared?"

The dog looked up at him with mournful eyes, and seeing there was no more meat, turned back to the fire, lay down, and went to sleep again.

"He ain't much for fox anymore," Hoadie said, and laughed softly. "He's a horny old bastard, though. He's still tryin' to make them puppies. He's sired more pups than any dog in these hills. He was a bull bitch for runnin' onct."

"He looks fagged out."

"Yeah. He's not much runner now. But he's a helluva singer."

"Singer?"

"Yeah. When the young-uns sing, he likes to join in. Sounds like holy hell."

"Maybe he ought to join the choir someplace," Duny Gene said, and they looked at each other a quick moment with the light of understanding and devilment in their eyes.

"Yeah. Maybe he ought."

The Weedy Rough Methodist church squatted on a bench of East Mountain above the town, like a white-washed shoe box dropped carelessly among the jack oaks and maples. Some folks called it Mr. Pay's church, Barton having become as closely associated with it as the minister, Leviticus Hammel. On the slope below it was the road that led down past the tunnel and the Pay house and into town. The tunnel was close enough so that any Sunday freight coming through from the south, exploding out of the ground with screaming drivers and rattling couplings, created a necessary interruption in the services. Even the high-pitched exhortations of Parson Hammel were swallowed in the racket.

Leviticus sent off letters to the Frisco railroad, complaining about the passage of trains just before noon on Sundays. Interruptions and distractions to his soul-saving sent him into a holy rage, but the Frisco railroad didn't give a damn about Leviticus Hammel's problems, because they had a few of their own. They suggested to him by return mail that he should offer five minutes of silent prayer for war dead at about the time he could feel the ground trembling and knew a train was about to emerge from the tunnel.

The correspondence became heated. Leviticus was not a hand-shaker and back-slapper, but a hard-line perdition preacher. Anger was a solid part of his ministry. Even in Sunday-school classes, teaching the sayings of Jesus, he was likely to remember that an unscheduled freight might arrive at some critical moment of his sermon later in the day, and he would belt into a raving oration about how all the startled kids listening were going to fry in hell if they didn't stop sticking their used chewing gum to the bottom of the church pews.

Leviticus was a small, mousy-looking man, with horn-rimmed glasses and intense blue eyes. He compensated for his diminutive stature with vocal bombast. But like most mortals, he lost his bout with the railroad.

The Sunday Old Sam came to church, few people paid it any mind. There were always dogs hanging about, and one more or less was not apt to arouse much interest.

But Sam was a sticks foxhound, a breed that during daylight stayed close to home, interested only in eating, breeding, and running foxes. Besides, Sam was so old, had anyone stopped to figure they would have known that he had not come into town from the Renkin farm on his own. Somebody must have brought him.

As he and Barton walked up to the front of the church, Duny Gene saw the dog at once, because he was looking for him. Sam was off to one side, doleful and sapped of all strength. And as soon as he saw the dog, Duny Gene knew how he came to be there.

Hoadie had not gone home the night before after the fox race. Instead, he'd brought Old Sam into town to enroll him in the Methodist church choir.

Now, Hoadie was nowhere to be seen, because he'd completed his part of the grand design. Besides, he had never come closer to a church than was humanly necessary.

Earlier, before he had grown to his almost six-foot height, the Ladies' Aid Society had tried to rescue him from his sins, tried to give him a solid religious foundation. Hoadie had never taken to it, and they finally gave up, reluctantly suspending their efforts to keep Hoadie out of hell as a result of his swearing and smoking and threatening the virginity of every girl within miles.

While Barton went inside to take his accustomed place in the front pew, Duny Gene paused at the door to smoke a last cigarette before the services. As he puffed, he watched the dog and nodded to the people who passed him on their way to their seats. And he thought for a moment about his increasing maturity. There had been a time when smoking had been done furtively, behind the parsonage, but now it was accepted, and the ladies all smiled at him as they walked past.

Before the Chesterfield was finished, all the people were in the church, and only Duny Gene and the hound remained. He flipped the cigarette away and snapped his fingers gently. Sam lifted his head soulfully. Perhaps in his dim old feebleness he recalled that this young man had been responsible for his having had a mouthful of corned beef only the night before. He rose and walked crookedly toward the church door as Duny Gene moved inside.

While the choir marched in singing the rising anthem, all in their white vestments, Duny Gene stood before his pew well back in the congregation, slightly turned so he could watch the door. It took only a moment. Before the second chorus of "Holy Holy Holy," Sam appeared and looked inside, some small light of appreciation for the singing showing in his faded eyes. Duny Gene turned toward the front of the church, his face stolid.

When the last chorus was finished, the congregation still standing, Leviticus Hammel drew himself up to his full five feet two inches beside the pulpit and pronounced a short invocation.

"And now, number three-seven-two," he shouted, and there was the shuffling of pages in hymnals as everyone turned to "Rescue the Perishing." Leviticus lifted his arms as though pinned to the cross, eyes closed, and Mona Stayborn played the opening bars on the piano. Leviticus's arms came down in a chopping motion and everyone burst violently into the opening stanza. By that time, Old Sam was halfway down the aisle, where he watched for a moment and then sat down, his long tail thumping softly against the floor.

Leviticus didn't see the dog at first, his eyes turned heavenward as he shouted out the verses. But then there was a long, low whine, like a sawmill blade biting into the first soft bark of a sycamore. Leviticus stopped singing and glared out into the congregation. From the center of the aisle, Old Sam looked back, his tongue hanging out like a piece of raw liver. As Leviticus watched, horrified, Old Sam launched into a long wail, louder this time, and seeming to catch the key, he lifted his head and howled.

Reese Walls was nearest the dog, and he aimed a kick, but Old Sam edged away without missing a note. Kids had begun to snicker. A few were hanging out into the aisle, watching the dog. Leviticus Hammel's face turned from purple to putty-color, his arms suspended in midcareer and his eyes bulging behind horn-rimmed glasses.

Slowly, the singing sputtered out, the choir itself finally muttering into silence. But the dog continued on for a few more bars, alone, with nothing but the laughter for accompaniment.

"Stop it," Leviticus screamed, his lips thin and spittle forming at the corners of his mouth like cotton froth. Reese kicked at the dog again, but missed and barked his shin on the pew in front of him.

"Stop it, stop it, stop it," Leviticus shouted. And now, even the kids' laughter was stilled, and then Old Sam, too. The dog sat there in the aisle, looking mournful and waiting for the singing to commence again. In the dead silence of the room, dog and minister staring into each other's eyes, Old Sam broke wind.

"Get him out," Leviticus screeched. "Get that son of a bitch out of my church, get him out, out, out!"

Mrs. Hubbs slapped her hands over her five-year-old's ears. Little Rex Snowdon began to cry. Reese Walls moved out into the aisle and delivered his first successful kick. Old Sam moaned and turned back toward the door, ambling along, Reese close beside him, kicking, his foot making a drumlike thump each time he connected with Old Sam's flanks.

And then, as Old Sam and Reese disappeared through the open doorway, the ground began to tremble and everyone knew that within a few moments a freight train would emerge from the tunnel in a fury of noise. Leviticus tried unsuccessfully to speak. His glasses had almost fallen off, and he jabbed them into place at the bridge of his long nose before he finally found his voice.

"Ushers, pass the collection plates," he gasped, and turning with a sweep of coattails he disappeared into the vestry. That was the end of the service.

"They tell me," Tooth said, "that ole Leviticus never called for 'Rescue the Perishing' again."

Walking home after the hound-dog service, as it came to be called, there was the light of merriment in Barton's eyes. Although nothing was said, Duny Gene knew that his father had enjoyed the Old Sam debacle as much as some of the kids.

Barton was serious about his religion, but Duny Gene had begun to realize that his father's God was different from Leviticus Hammel's. Barton's God was one that enjoyed a little fun now and again: the light in kids' faces when something silly happened, or when there was cherry cobbler on the table, or school was let out early. He was a God that could appreciate the innocent laughter of mortals, maybe because there was so little of it.

As for his own God, Duny Gene had almost decided that he had none, at least none recognizable in the church of Brother Hammel. There grew in him some sullen resistance to the patterns of people around him, their religion included. He often lay awake nights wondering if perhaps this was the spirit of his grandmother, Barton's mother, the wife of old Eben Pay. Of course, the one thing from his ancestry that his mother insisted he understand was that while Eben Pay's wife might have been a Cherokee, she was a Christian nonetheless.

But Duny Gene rejected that, too. He had begun to think that his bloodline ran back strongly beyond that acceptance of some white faith, back to deep and primordial beliefs, long since lost to conscious thought but always there in the stirrings of his dreams. Without being able to identify it, he sensed it when he was alone in the deep woods, or when he heard the dogs running in the night, or when he skinned a squirrel and felt the blood-warm meat coming out of the cocoon of fur between his fingers.

And he felt it sometimes when he looked at his father, and wondered if Barton had once experienced those same squirmings in the soul, and perhaps still did, but had managed to civilize such things within himself.

There was Hoadie, too. Duny Gene knew that one of the reasons he had been drawn to this sticks boy from the start was his wildness. As Lydia often pointed out, he was a thing of the timber, like a wolf. And Maudie. He tortured himself with the idea that she, too, was as wild as Hoadie, both of them with only a veneer of Leviticus Hammel's kind of refinement. And maybe, in both cases, a damned thin veneer.

Duny Gene wondered about his own motives in such things as the Old Sam business. He had found it mildly amusing, but his part in it was mostly for the pure hell of it. To disrupt pomposity or established routine. Like over-turning Tooth Snowdon's outdoor privy on Halloween. As much to see if he could get away with it as for any joy that came from the laughter.

Most of the congregation that day had preceded Barton and Duny Gene down the road into town as Barton had lagged behind, which he always did, to visit with a few of the men and their wives. Lydia would be back in a few days, he said to them, after a nice visit with her folks in Fort Smith. There had been time for Gertrude Merton to get ahead and stand waiting for them in the road before her house, holding a covered casserole.

"Made a nice chicken pie for you and your boy, Barton," she said, and Duny Gene took the dish and felt its heat. Barton tipped his hat and made a small bow.

"Why, that's mighty nice, Gertrude. Hear you make the best chicken pie of anyone around here."

"Well, it ain't much," she said. "But I made some up for my bunch and had enough left for this little one and thought with Lydia bein' away, you might like it."

"We surely will, we surely will."

"You tell Lydia when she gets back, come see me. I got a new quilt pattern started."

"I surely will."

They went along the sharp grade of the road, smelling the cinders and coal smoke from the freight that had passed only recently. Even though there were new leaves on the trees alongside, they could see through them to the dark mouth of the tunnel. Along the slopes of Academy Heights, there were milk cows, their bells making a discordant chorus, and above them on East Mountain, the sharp tones of a cock cardinal.

"Sounds like he's getting ready to nest," Barton said.

"It's a little early for that, isn't it?"

"Yes, but it sounds like his clock is fast."

It was a wonderful spring day, turning toward summer but with the prospect of many cool nights still ahead. It felt good to be walking.

"You want me to carry that awhile?"

"No. It's not heavy. A little warm is all."

As they mounted the steps to the house, Wart was nowhere in sight. Inside, Barton went to his bedroom to change, and Duny Gene took the chicken pie into the kitchen, took out plates and glasses and a quart of milk from the icebox. There was a little water on the floor, and he knew the drain pan under the box needed emptying. But he stopped and listened, uncertain of a sound he thought he had heard.

Then it came again, a low whining cough, and a scratching on the floorboards of the small back porch. He moved over to the door and saw the dog. Wart was lying on his side, eyes walled back, tongue out in a froth of slobber. His ribs were heaving and he was gasping, his hind legs jerking and stiffening convulsively.

"Daddy!" Duny Gene shouted. "Wart's down."

He ran out, but hesitated because he thought the dog might have gone mad or was having some horrible fit. Wart's eyes rolled up and looked at him, imploring, and Duny Gene went to him and lay his hands on the heaving flanks. When Barton came to the door, he took one look and turned back to find the lard can.

"What's the matter, boy, what is it?" Duny Gene could feel the muscle contractions under his fingers, and the choking for air sounded like a rasp file on sheet metal.

Then Barton was there with a fistful of hog lard. He knelt to the dog and tried to force the lard into the small stomach, his wrist deep down Wart's gullet. It had no effect. Wart tried to lift his head, his neck stretching pitifully. He coughed one last time, stiffened, and lay still, his eyes going dusty. There was a final convulsion, and he voided on the porch and went limp.

"Damn," Barton whispered. He felt Wart's neck for a long time, then rose above Duny Gene and shook his head. "I'm afraid he's gone, son."

Barton wheeled quickly back into the kitchen, swearing more than Duny Gene had ever heard him swear, and in the center of the room he bent over the table and started to cry.

Duny Gene stared down at the dog, his face flat and impassive, his eyes looking almost as lifeless as the dog's. He shuddered at the feeling of Wart's body beneath his hands, all the vibrant quality gone.

Duny Gene lifted the small white form in his arms, cradling it as he went up through the steep backyard and into the barn lot. Attached to the rear of the barn was an old chicken coop, long out of use. Duny Gene placed the dog's body there and went to the tool shed for a shovel. His mind was blank, his thinking at a dead stop, and he moved mechanically.

Inside the old coop, it was hot and there was the smell of chicken litter. But the earth was soft, and soon the hole was deep enough. Duny Gene spent a few moments getting Wart's eyes closed. He did not want to shovel dirt into those eyes, somehow. And he had brought the dog here, under cover, because Wart had always disliked rain intensely, running for the protection of the porch at the first spattering drop. Now, at least, he would lie dry.

Gently, Duny Gene laid Wart in the grave and covered him, then tapped down the earth with the blade of the shovel. He went back to the tool shed, replaced the shovel on its pegs, and latched the door. For a moment he stood against the wall, looking across the barn lot. There were billows of cloud forming over West Mountain, and Duny Gene figured that rain would be coming by nightfall. From high up the slope behind him, he could hear goats bleating.

Suddenly, hatred swelled in his throat like vomit, almost suffocating him. Barton had said nothing, but nothing needed saying. Duny Gene knew that Parkins Muller had poisoned his dog.

· 8 ·

AFTER WART DIED, IT SEEMED TO RAIN forever.

Lydia came home, and driving up the hill from the depot, Duny Gene had to operate the windshield wiper by hand because when the engine pulled hard, the blade came to a standstill. Barton escorted Lydia up the steep yard steps to the house, trying to hold an umbrella over her, while Duny Gene parked the Ford. On the long porch, she stopped and looked about for a moment.

"Where's Duny Gene's dog?" she asked, in her usual manner of not referring to Wart by name.

"He died," Barton said, and nothing more, not wanting to disturb her unnecessarily; besides, he didn't like to make any accusations he couldn't prove.

She made no comment, as though she didn't give a damn, but later, when Duny Gene was at the dining table struggling through the last few chapters of his world history book, she went in and hugged him from behind and kissed his cheek. And then hurried off to the kitchen to make a batch of black walnut fudge.

Duny Gene had told no one his own opinion about Wart's death. For most of his schoolmates, he figured it was none of their business. For Hoadie Renkin, he was sure if he told, Parkins Muller's barn might suddenly catch fire in the night, or else some evening when Parkins and Miss Veda went to milk the goats, they would find a prize nanny throat-cut and skinned and hanging in a tree on the edge of the pasture. If any such thing was going to happen, Duny Gene wanted to be the one who did it. For a few days, he had thought about revenge. But that passed, and now he had no intention of making any dramatic move.

Over the few days after Wart died, the weight of grief slowly decreased until he hardly felt anything at all, except when he heard one of Parkins Muller's goats bleating on the hill, and then the anger rose in his throat so hard and knotty he could not speak because of it. But that, too, slowly passed.

He was glad his mother had not come at him with her usual barrage of questions but had been content to give him the hug and the kiss and let it go at that. Duny Gene credited his father with making the point to her that it was a subject Duny Gene was not likely to enjoy talking about.

It was still raining the evening Gertrude and Olie

Merton came by in their Essex sedan and picked up Lydia for an Eastern Star meeting. Duny Gene was on the front porch, watching the gray light fade from the slopes of West Mountain, where the crest was shrouded with rain. Barton helped Lydia down the steps to the road, with the umbrella, and when he returned he sat in the chair next to Duny Gene and they smoked and put their feet up on the banister.

It was still light enough to see when Mr. Harmon Budd staggered up the road from town, his peg leg plunging deep into the mud with each step. He wore no coat and his cotton shirt and overalls were plastered tight against his fat body with the rain.

"I see Mr. Budd's been at it again," Barton said with a chuckle.

Almost even with the house, Mr. Budd fell, and Barton stood up suddenly, ready to go down and help. Mr. Budd floundered about in the mud and finally managed to get a hand up on the fence. They could hear him swearing thickly. He pulled himself erect and stalked on up the road, talking aloud, going crookedly around the Pay Ford parked alongside the road.

"Good way to catch the flu," Barton said, sinking back into his chair and lifting his feet to the banister.

"He's too oiled to catch anything," Duny Gene said.

"God looks out for drunks, I've heard it said."

"Where's he goin', up this way?"

"To church. To the revival meeting, I'd suspect. It's been raining ever since that tent meeting came to town, so I guess they'd welcome anybody they can get. Even Mr. Budd. I'd like to hear his testimony."

A traveling group of undetermined denomination was having a revival on Naulty's Ridge. Their tent had been erected only a few hundred feet down the slope from the schoolhouse, near the federal highway. It happened every spring, and on clear nights, when the wind was right, the townspeople could hear the shouting and singing. Many who were members of the more conservative churches characterized such taking on as blasphemous caterwauling. All such traveling revivalists, no matter their affiliation, were called Holy Rollers.

Barton and Duny Gene watched the darkness coming on, like a gray wall approaching from across the valley. There was the smell of damp earth and wet bark, and a chill was in the air. Water from the eaves of the porch made the sound of a sizable waterfall, taking the long drop into the yard below. Through the steady downpour, they could see the faint orange glimmer of houselights scattered across the slopes of Academy Heights above the tunnel.

"Your mother went to see Grandfather Pay when she was in Fort Smith," Barton said abruptly. "They had a long talk."

Duny Gene remained silent, puffing his cigarette, waiting for whatever was coming next. He knew that the purpose of any such visit could not have been social, and he knew before Barton spoke again that it was not a casual comment, either.

"Your grandfather's made a considerable amount of money in his time," Barton said. "He's always been a frugal man, too. After your Grandmother Bishop died, he took that little three-room house in south Fort Smith where he still lives. We had a colored lady named Cora, skinny little thing who kept coming in to clean and cook for him even after I was gone. She's dead now. Made the best chicken dumplings I ever tasted. About all I can recall him ever doing was going back and forth from that little house to the courthouse. Except the time he went off to the Spanish war."

For a moment, Duny Gene had to search his memory for the name Bishop, he had heard it so infrequently, and then he recalled that this had been the maiden name of old Eben Pay's wife, the Cherokee.

"It's been a long, lonely life for him, with a lot of thinking done, I suspect," Barton continued. "But now, he's well fixed. Matter of fact, I guess he always was, with his family in Saint Louis, his daddy a good lawyer there years ago, too. Anyway, your mother and him talked about your future, what you're going to be doing after you graduate."

Still, Duny Gene said nothing. The cigarette had burned down to his fingers, and he flipped it out into the yard, where it struck a white oak trunk and died with a shower of quick sparks in the rain.

"Your grandfather wants to send you to school. Pay for your education," Barton said softly, as though he were afraid of some violent reaction and wanted to make this as gentle as possible.

Well, there it is, Duny Gene thought. Grandfather Pay trying to make it up to me for being a red Indian, and me not giving a damn one way or the other.

"You mean college?" he asked.

"Yes. Up at the University at Fayetteville. He was always disappointed that I didn't take into the law or some such thing. But I had other things on my mind. I think he'd like to see another Pay get into law. It sort of runs in the family."

All of this came as a rather abrupt shock to Duny Gene, even as he saw it building. He had never thought beyond next year, when he would be finished with the Weedy Rough school. In fact, he had never thought beyond Weedy Rough. The idea of going into the outside world, away from the deep hills, unsettled him. His thinking went only so far as getting shed of school, marrying Maudie, and working in the tie yard with his father.

"I don't see anything wrong with buying ties for the Frisco," he said.

"Those kinds of jobs are hard to find."

"I mean working with you, here in Weedy Rough."

"But son, Frisco don't need but one agent here."

"Well, maybe I can take civil service and get on the mail route. Alvie Haus isn't gettin' any younger."

Barton sighed and leaned back deep into his chair.

"All right, there's no need to talk more about it now, I guess. You've got time to make up your mind."

"Yeah, we'll see," Duny Gene said, and was somehow disappointed that Barton was unwilling to push harder. But glad, too, because suddenly he knew he did not want to leave this town, had even an actual fear of doing it.

Duny Gene rose and walked to the end of the porch and stood leaning against the wall there, feeling a fine spray of rain coming under the roof and wetting his face. And behind him, Barton sighed again, knowing old Eben Pay's money would lie untouched in that Saint Louis bank. Well, he thought, let it just stay there, safe in a savings account, accumulating interest. Someday, maybe, the old man could brighten his life with a nice trip back to Cuba, to see the sights instead of getting shot at, or maybe even to Europe, to Wales, where his father's people had come from, or to Germany, where old Granny Ora Hasford's people had worked the fields of the beautiful Regnitz Valley.

Barton had no recollection of having seen any of his father's people, but he had heard their stories told by the old man before he was so old. When there had been the promise of traveling to Saint Louis and seeing the big city and all the relatives. A promise never fulfilled.

Well, Barton thought, we'll see. Meanwhile, that money can just sit there and accumulate interest.

"You want a game of dominoes or Chinese checkers?" Barton asked, rising and moving to the door.

"No, I don't feel much like it right now."

Duny Gene stood for a long time at the end of the porch, after Barton had gone inside. He could see only a few feet into the night, and no further into his own ambitions. His future seemed as dismal as the rain, and as impenetrable. Everything stopped short, just before him now, with graduation so near.

And he thought of Maudie Snowdon, taking Sunday rides with Jabo Sparks in his new roadster. Him a veteran and at least ten years older than she, maybe even older. Well, he thought, maybe it'll rain all year, and they won't have any good Sundays for joyriding, and maybe Jabo'll get his damned Ford stuck in the mud and it'll sink clean out of sight, and him in it.

He thought about Wart then. He was glad he'd had the foresight to bury the dog under cover, in the old chicken coop where it was dry. Wart would like that. Maybe even now he was chasing chickens. A ghost dog chasing ghost chickens.

The revival tent was a long canvas affair like all the revival tents of that time, and now with the rain stopped the sides were rolled up, revealing the wooden benches inside and the boxlike pulpit at one end alongside the piano battered and scarred from so many loadings and unloadings into and out of the old Mack bobtruck. The benches were full of worshipers, mostly sticks people, and scattered across the slope leading to the schoolhouse were wagons and buggies, a couple of rattletrap cars, and some saddle horses.

Although the service was young, there were already three people lying in the aisle, twitching and talking in tongues. A few people were standing, waving their arms and yelling in concert with the preacher, who paced back and forth before the congregation, shouting out his message. Now and again, he would charge into the crowd and grab one of the women and shake her, and she would wail with the holiness that seeped from his hands into her calico-clad shoulders.

Mr. Harmon Budd was there, as he had been every night since the first meeting, rain or fair weather. He sat in the rear, a little detached from the others. On this night, his religious fervor had become so overwhelming that he had unstrapped his peg leg and was waving it above his head like the blunt lance of some knight from the Middle Ages. He was only drunk enough to sharpen his sensitivity.

Up the slope, leaning against the fender of an old car, Duny Gene Pay and Hoadie Renkin smoked and watched. It was a good show.

"See that old woman wallowin' around in the dirt?" Hoadie asked. "That's my Aunt Cory. She's crazy as hell. What you reckon she's bellowin' about?"

"Damned if I know," Duny Gene said. "I can't understand what any of 'em are sayin'. Not even the preacher."

"Yeah, Pap used to take in all these tent-meetin' revivals," Hoadie said. "Take me and his old lady and the young-uns, and he'd get to talkin' tongues, crazy as hell. Worse than when he used to get drunk and beat hell outa everybody he could catch. Afterwards, I'd have to drive the team home, and him in the wagon bed still carryin' on like somebody'd died."

There was a renewed burst of frenzied shouting from the tent, as the preacher had someone at the front of the congregation on her knees. He was holding her head in his hands like a watermelon, screaming at the ridgepole.

"I see God!"

"I got that part of it," Duny Gene said, and

laughed. "I think I'd rather listen to a good fox race any day."

"Yeah, well there ain't any tonight. Still too wet. Jesus, look at 'em. Like some kind of red Injun scalp dance, ain't it?" Hoadie was grinning, but the remark irritated Duny Gene. He dropped his cigarette and mashed out the fire with his toe.

"Let's go down to Cobb Hubbs's for a soda pop," he said.

"Hell, we can't get no soda pop there. Cobb Hubbs catch us, he'd break our arms."

"I'm not talkin' about stealin' it," Duny Gene said, turning away. "I got some money workin' the tie yard today. Every son of a bitch and his dog came in to sell timber, with the rain finally stopped."

They moved to the store in silence, passing through the front screen door framed on either side by thin metal signs advertising Brown Mule tobacco, Lucky Strike cigarettes, and Arm and Hammer baking powder. Cobb Hubbs was bent over his single counter, reading by the light of a coal-oil lamp. It was a story entitled "The Primitive Lover" in a copy of *True Story* magazine.

Cobb eyed Hoadie suspiciously until Duny Gene produced his dime for the two grape sodas they took from the cooler, where there was no semblance of ice, the bottles submerged in a bath of only slightly cool water.

"You boys been to the service?" Cobb asked with a smirk.

"We watched awhile," Duny Gene said.

"Them ground stompers. They'd steal your eyeteeth when you ain't lookin'." Then Cobb glanced apprehensively at Hoadie, wondering if maybe old Ike Renkin was among the congregation.

They went outside with their pop, and around to the back, where Cobb had a horseshoe court. There was a full moon, making it almost as light as day except under the trees that marched up in straggling formation from the store to the gym. Duny Gene found a horseshoe in one of the pits and tossed it up and down in one hand.

"You ain't aimin' to pitch shoes in the dark, are you?"

"No, but I could beat your ass in the daylight," Duny Gene said.

"Uh-huh." Hoadie grinned, his teeth showing in the moonlight. "Next thing, you'll be tellin' me you're as good with shoes as Jabo Sparks."

The sound of that name gave Duny Gene a bitter taste in his mouth. He knew Hoadie enjoyed gouging him with it, so he gouged back.

"You ignorant sticks guys, you don't even have enough sense to stay in school. You don't show up for class but about once a week anymore."

"Yeah, well I been studyin' on quittin' altogether," Hoadie said. He took a long swig of the grape pop and made a face. "Warm as piss."

"You ought to go on and graduate, you're this close."

"Hell! Them teachers just pass me along to get rid of me. I ain't ever learned a damned thing in that school. They just pass me along."

Duny Gene threw the horseshoe toward the far pit and it rang as it struck the post there.

"See that? Even in the dark I could beat your ass." He felt for another shoe and held it up, aiming.

"Uh-huh. Well, speakin' of ass, you better get on your mule with that Maudie. The way ole Jabo is nosin' around."

Duny Gene slowly lowered the shoe and turned, the burn of slow anger rising under his throat.

"Let me worry about it, all right?"

"Yeah, well tell me somethin'. You ever popped

her? I bet you ain't. I bet you ain't ever popped anything.''

"Like hell I haven't,'' Duny Gene lied. He could feel the hot blood along his cheeks.

"Like hell you have,'' Hoadie laughed. "You ain't ever done nothin' but stroke your pole, and I had to show you how to do that.''

Hoadie's grinning face was like another moon hanging there in front of him, and Duny Gene swung the horseshoe and felt the impact along his arm as the shoe hit bone. Hoadie staggered back, dropping his grape pop, the grin still on his face.

"You're sure touchy, ain't you?'' he said. A dark stream was running down his cheek. In the moonlight, it looked like chocolate syrup. Duny Gene stepped in to deliver another blow, but it never landed.

Hoadie's first swing caught him in the short ribs, and all the air swished out of his lungs; the second fist hit him under the left eye and he was down, losing his pop and the horseshoe on the ground. He struggled up and charged in, his hands ready, and Hoadie caught him twice in the mouth and again in the belly and he was down again, thrashing around in the horseshoe pit.

"You better quit now,'' Hoadie said, watching Duny Gene rising. "Somebody's gonna get hurt here.''

Duny Gene came on hard, and Hoadie sidestepped him and hit him twice as he went past, and he was on his face, floundering about in the mud again.

"God dammit, Duny Gene, you better quit now.''

Silently, furiously, having by then forgotten why they were going at each other, Duny Gene swung a fist at Hoadie's face. He found nothing but the night air and took three more vicious punches in the ribs.

"You crazy bastard,'' Hoadie said, and by now his breathing was coming almost as hard as Duny Gene's. But Duny Gene never saw where the punches were coming from. They simply materialized like rocks against his face and sides. He had never known he could get hit so fast and in so many different places. Warm liquid was running across his lip. As he started to close in once more, he could hear the discordant jangle of the revival-meeting piano from beyond the store.

Neither of them saw Cobb Hubbs. He was suddenly between them with his fence-post arms, shoving them back from each other as easily as he might part bedsheets hanging on a clothesline.

"Hold up, here," Cobb said. "What's the matter with you boys? You all right, Duny Gene?"

Hoadie backed away, and they could hear yelling from the tent meeting. Duny Gene's chest ached as he tried to draw in air.

"Get away, Mr. Hubbs," he gasped. Cobb held him by the shirtfront, as though afraid he might fall.

"You're beat up, Duny Gene," Cobb said. He looked over his shoulder at Hoadie, glaring. "You've got yourself a peck of trouble, boy, fightin' with Mr. Pay's boy."

"I tried to tell him to quit," Hoadie said, and he was grinning once more, sardonically. "He like to have brained me with one of your damned horseshoes."

Cobb made no reference to the gash on Hoadie's face, and seemed unmindful of the blood running down and blackening his shirt collar and overalls.

"You get the hell out of here, boy. You get the hell out right now, and don't let me catch you around here no more." Cobb turned back to Duny Gene and peered closely into his swelling face. "You all right, Duny Gene?"

Duny Gene twisted free, tasting blood inside his mouth. His face and ribs felt as though someone had dropped a crosstie on them. Over Cobb Hubbs's shoulder, he watched Hoadie Renkin turn and walk back up through the trees, where the moonlight made patterns of black and silver, and then around the gym and gone.

"I'm all right," Duny Gene mumbled.

"You sure?" Cobb asked. But Duny Gene was already moving off, toward the road that led down into town. "I'll go along with you home, if you want."

Duny Gene said nothing, moving out into the muddy road, stumbling along the ruts. He felt inside his mouth, and two teeth were loose. But still in his head, at least. He swore and spat a mouthful of blood into the road. It looked like chocolate syrup, too, just like the blood on Hoadie's Renkin's face.

"I didn't hit him once," Duny Gene said aloud. "I didn't hit that son of a bitch one time, after the horseshoe."

He looked back, but saw nothing of Hoadie Renkin, only Cobb Hubbs, dark-shaped like a rain barrel in the moonlight. From beyond the store, he heard a long, high-pitched wail and the rattling notes of the piano.

"Go ahead, you ignorant bastards, bellow yourselves to salvation!"

There was a scheduled freight train that came through the Rough each night about 3:00 A.M., southbound. Although the grade leading to the tunnel from the north was not so great as the one on the other side of Academy Heights, it was enough to slow a loaded train to a crawl, and speed was not completely regained until well after the locomotive had snaked the cars through the tunnel and started down the long sloping valley toward the Arkansas River.

When Hoadie Renkin came out of the woods above the tunnel, the moon was lowering, but it was still light enough to see. He was carrying an extra pair of

Levi's pants and a cotton shirt in a bandanna knotted
to form a sack. He looked neither right nor left as he
trotted toward the railroad. In the deep woods, a
great horned owl was making his mournful hoots.

At the tracks, Hoadie squatted to one side, sitting
on his hams in the manner of his people. Gingerly he
felt the still-moist gash along his left cheek, and the
tips of his fingers found bone. He was sweating
because he had run most of the way through the
woods to the farm, and back again. He was glad that
he had wakened only Squib. That had been all right,
because it eliminated the necessity of writing a note
to his pap, explaining what he was about.

At first, he had told himself that he needed to get
away from this place, because after the beating he
had given Duny Gene Pay the constable would be
after him for battery, even though Duny Gene struck
the first blow. Everybody expected that when a town
man got into it with a sticks man, the one from the
deep woods was to blame. They might even set the
Washington County sheriff on him.

But he knew even before he had reached the farm
that such a thing was unlikely, that Duny Gene was
tight-lipped about such carryings-on. And if Duny
Gene said nothing, Cobb Hubbs wouldn't, either.

The law wasn't his reason for going, and he knew
it now, had possibly known it all along. He'd been
waiting for an excuse to take out. He'd wanted to go
for a long time. If Duny Gene had no notion of what
lay ahead, neither did Hoadie, but Hoadie at least
wanted it to happen someplace else, whatever it might
be.

Squatted beside the tracks, he could hear the train
faintly, on the far side of the tunnel, not yet even
whistling for its passage through Weedy Rough. He
looked at the tracks, and wondered where they led.

He had no conception of what was out there, no

idea of what might be waiting for him. But somewhere along those tracks there had to be something better than a lifetime of splitting fence rails and cutting ties, of scratching a living from rocky fields and never having much more to eat than hog jowl and molasses.

Hoadie had never been farther away from these hills than Fayetteville, and then only twice, going up in the Ford with Mr. Pay and Duny Gene when the Chipmunks played basketball in the National Guard armory. He'd liked it, especially once after a game, when Mr. Pay had treated the team to a bowl of chili and a bottle of Coca-Cola at a place called the Castle Luncheonette, and later escorted them all into a moving-picture show about cowboys, with some guy named Tom Mix, who had enough Vaseline in his hair to grease a large hog.

And there had been popcorn, from a vendor who stood in red-striped pants in the vestibule behind a miniature yellow panel truck with windows along the sides. In the truck, a toy clown turned the crank on the popper, and the white fluffy kernels bulged out and overflowed like a cotton cascade, to be scooped up in a sugar ladle and sacked, then drenched with melted butter, so much of it the sack turned greasy all the way to the bottom.

Thinking about it, Hoadie licked his lips and pulled a cold baked sweet potato from his pocket and ate it, hull and all.

Finally, he heard the whistle at the far end of the tunnel, and in a few moments saw the faint shine of the locomotive headlight in the mouth of the great arched hole a few yards up the track from where he squatted. He rose and stood back from the tracks, locating a level place on the right-of-way where he could make his run.

As the train came from the tunnel, he put his hand

over his eyes to keep from being blinded by the light, and as soon as the leading cars had swept past, gaining speed now, he looked for a place to connect with the passing train.

Just short of the caboose there was a boxcar with doors open, likely one the Frisco had started pulling on all its trains just to handle the hobo passengers, who otherwise would ride the rods at the risk of falling under the wheels when they went to sleep. He ran onto the gravel embankment and measured his jump and landed belly-down, halfway inside the boxcar. A pair of large hands grabbed his shoulders and hauled him inside, and he could smell hay and sweat and tobacco, and before him was a kneeling figure of a man, grinning through a stubble of black beard.

"Hey, it's a big-un, but a young-un, I'd bet," the man shouted. Behind the bearded man, Hoadie could see other dark figures lying asleep on the boxcar floor. "You takin' to the long road, are you?"

"I was aimin' to."

"You're welcome, boy," the man said, and indicated the sleeping figures. "You're right in amongst first-class passengers, travelin' in style on our own Pullman. Good as any Vanderbilt ever had. How far you goin'?"

"Far enough to get me a good job of work," Hoadie said.

The man laughed, his head back.

"By God. You are a new one, ain't you? Well, settle down for some sleep. We'll be halfway to Texas by sunup. Some damned fine jobs there. Only nobody's found any of 'em yet."

Duny Gene Pay said as little as possible about his bruised face. Just a friendly scuffle, he said, and was careful not to implicate Hoadie Renkin. Lydia raised hell over it, screaming about hillbilly roughnecks and pointing out once more the advantages of moving back to Fort Smith, where at least they could have a gas stove.

"I'll buy you a coal-oil stove, if you want," Barton said.

"That won't help having to live among these brutes who go around beating up on boys," she raged.

"Well now, I had a few scuffles in Fort Smith when I was a boy. There's some pretty tough ones there, too."

"His lip's split and his eye will be black for a month."

"Maybe it was just a last little fistfight before he grows out of it. I'll get some beefsteak for his eye if you want me to."

And as usual, after the first bombast, Lydia subdued her anger. But for two days, she watched carefully as Duny Gene ate and made no sign that it hurt his mouth. He didn't bother to mention the loose teeth.

It wasn't easy for Duny Gene to get a fix on how he felt about the whole business, once his own flashing anger had subsided. On the one hand, he hated Hoadie Renkin for saying things about Maudie. It was an especially sore spot now that she had begun making walleyes at Jabo Sparks. The thing that made it worse was that most of what Hoadie had teased about was true.

But on the other hand, there had been too much for too long between him and this sticks kid, too many quiet moments in the woods hunting for squirrels, where there was no conversation but a deep-felt fellowship nonetheless. There had been too many times that were not so quiet, standing alone and defiant against everyone, even though nobody else realized it but themselves. There had been too many secrets, some unspoken, things long-since forgot, but sealing their brotherhood like unseen padlocks and the keys lost forever.

It was three days after the fight. Barton and Lydia and Duny Gene were playing Chinese checkers at the dining table under a hanging light bulb, a part of the newly installed electric power system in the Rough. At first, they failed to hear the soft knock against a banister at the foot of the porch steps. When he did hear, Barton went out, a little irritated at this interruption of a game he had come to enjoy, but which he did not realize Duny Gene played only because he knew Barton liked it.

In a moment he was back, a puzzled expression on his face.

"Some kid wants to see you, Duny Gene," he said.

Duny Gene found a towheaded boy in overalls standing at the foot of the porch steps, and even in the growing twilight Duny Gene could see a familiar cast to the boy's eyes.

"You want me?"

"I'm Squib Renkin," the boy said. "I seen you a long time ago on the route, you and your pap, when you was handin' out them Christmas boxes."

"You're a Renkin?" For a moment he felt a small tug of apprehension, thinking that maybe this kid had come to lay down a challenge, to call Duny Gene out somewhere to meet Hoadie so Hoadie could finish the job he had started at Cobb Hubbs's horseshoe court.

"Yeah. I'm Squib. I seen you on the route."

"That was a long spell ago," Duny Gene said. "What was it you wanted?"

"Hoadie said tell you he's left," Squib said. He seemed a little embarrassed. "Hoadie said tell you. He taken out on a freight train, a couple nights ago. He said tell you he was gone. He wanted you to have this here."

The boy handed up a pocketknife and Duny Gene took it, feeling the familiar rough and cracked bone handles.

"Hoadie said you was supposed to have it and I ain't had no chance to get it in here till now, so I didn't want you thinkin' I wanted to keep it for my ownself. I just ain't had a chance to get in till now."

Squib, his message delivered, turned abruptly and started down across the yard, looking like Hoadie had years before, taking long strides and his straw-colored hair bouncing like wire.

Duny Gene looked at the knife, lying in the palm of his open hand, and he could remember all the squirrels he and Hoadie had skinned with it, and how they'd used it to cut their initials into the bobsled that year of the late snow, initials still showing now in the hard oak runners even as the sled stood in the barn rotting away with disuse. He remembered playing mumble peg with it, and how sometimes Hoadie would sit in school, with this same knife, slicing slivers of wood from a piece of short pine lumber until he had a pile of shavings under his seat and he would grin and whisper across the aisle that this here was kindling, just in case they needed to set the school on fire.

"Hey you, Squib," Duny Gene called. Squib was almost to the road, but he stopped and turned back. "Where'd he go?"

"He never said. He just took out." Squib turned again and leaped down into the road and was gone.

Duny Gene could feel the hard oily texture of the bone handles, and there was a tight knot in his chest.

"Who was that?" Barton called from the dining room, a little impatiently.

"Just a kid," Duny Gene said. "He brought me something I thought I'd lost."

· 9 ·

DUNY GENE'S LAST DAYS IN SCHOOL STARTED badly and got worse as they went along. There was something dismal about this first year of a new decade—as 1931 came on, everything seemed to fall on wicked times.

Apples of the fall were tough and tasteless, and the sweetness had disappeared from cherries. Ragweed and wild onion were so thick in most cow pastures that milk was bitter and harsh on the tongue. When the leaves turned, instead of the usual chorus of breathtaking color, everything went rust-brown, even the big maples that during most autumns were great balloons of red and yellow.

Chiggers and wood ticks were so bad that there were stories of hill dogs dying from their bites. It was dry, and everywhere a foot was placed a fine billow of white dust rose viciously, as though the earth despised the touch of feet. And there were more dogfights in the streets of Weedy Rough than anyone could remember.

One of Reese Walls's boys went a little crazy on the opening day of school and caught a tomcat and tried to skin him alive. Duny Gene and two of the other senior boys rescued the cat after only minor damage had been done to the belly fur.

Then the seventh and eighth grades had a riot.

They were playing hide-and-go-seek when Olie Merton's boy tried to kiss the wrong girl in the pump-room basement and a fistfight broke out—between Olie's boy and the offended girl. It spread across the schoolyard, boys against the girls and the girls getting the better of it until the faculty ran out and put a stop to it, lined the kids up in the auditorium, and gave them all a switching with willow sticks.

Even Halloween fell flat when some of the older boys were trying to hoist Joe Sanford's car onto the roof of a shed behind the ice-cream parlor and the thing slipped and fell on Donny Sparks and broke his leg. Duny Gene found himself wishing it had been Donny's older brother Jabo.

They held a Halloween party at the school, and it was the occasion of Duny Gene's only kiss with Maudie during the whole fall semester. It was little more than a peck, and Duny Gene wasn't sure she even knew who it was, the thing having happened in the dark and both of them with masks on their faces.

Christmas was no better. Boxing fruit and nuts for the kids along the route had lost its flavor somehow. And the present from Grandfather Pay—a brand-new Winchester Model 12 pump gun—failed to brighten the day for Duny Gene.

January and February. The Chipmunks lost all but two basketball games, and out-of-town fans began yelling that the West Fork girls' team could beat this bunch. Duny Gene fouled out of five games and was thrown out of one for starting a fight under the basket. It was the night he looked into the stands and saw Maudie sitting with Jabo Sparks. When they disappeared halfway through the first half and never came back, Duny Gene tried to take out his frustration on an opposing player.

Duny Gene pondered the possibility of joining the Methodist church choir. At least he'd have Sunday mornings with Maudie in the vestry, and better still, Wednesday evenings after choir practice. But it came to nothing because Duny Gene had never been much of a singer. Besides, by Easter Maudie had dropped out of the choir. Duny Gene began to suspect it had something to do with the Wednesday night dances held at Tip Top Tavern, a joint four miles south of town on the federal highway where they served near beer out front and homemade gin in back.

They were very strict at Tip Top Tavern about keeping out underage boys, what with the activities in back, so Duny Gene had never been inside the place. But he had heard that certain high school girls had been there, so long as they were escorted by men of age. It was also said that Jabo Sparks was a frequent visitor to the tavern.

Nobody was quite sure where Jabo got his money, but he always had plenty. In the barbershop, they figured he was running hill bootleg whiskey into Fort Smith in that new yellow Ford he'd bought when he worked at the furniture factory. He wore what were called snappy clothes. His patent leather shoes always had pointed toes.

Duny Gene studied for a while about slipping into the Sparkses' yard some night and blowing out the tires on Jabo's Ford with the Winchester Grandfather Pay had given him. But he finally decided it was a bad idea. Jabo's father was the constable, and by now most people in town knew Duny Gene hated Jabo's guts. Everyone else thought Jabo was a slick guy, so if his tires got vandalized with a twelve-gauge shotgun, just about anybody would be able to figure out who had done it.

That spring there was a torrential rain and the tie yard was ankle-deep in water for two days with the flow from the surrounding hills. Barton took a cold from working all day with his feet submerged. But the water ran off so fast it had little effect on the dry weather. When leaves came on, it was a halfhearted effort because of the drought. Redbud and dogwood blooms were sparse, coming to flower only along streams or near hill springs.

Cobb Hubbs caught the mumps from some sticks kid who came into his store with jowls swollen, not knowing what he had. Cobb very nearly died and his store was closed for almost two months. That left nowhere for the older boys to congregate at noon recess and lie about the girls they'd laid, and to smoke and chew licorice sticks.

When Mona Stayborn had her annual graduation party for the seniors, Duny Gene asked Maudie to go with him. She replied that Mona Stayborn didn't approve of boys and girls coming like regular dates to her parties.

"Well, you don't have to be so goddamned snotty about it," Duny Gene flared.

"Why don't you try acting your age once in a while," she said coldly. She whirled and walked away from him, switching her butt like a windshield wiper.

Duny Gene was so furious he played hooky that afternoon and took his shotgun into the woods to blast away at anything that moved—woodpeckers and crows and squirrels, even though squirrels were not in season. He was upset enough to miss most of what he shot at, but what he hit was left on the ground to rot.

God, he kept thinking, I sure miss that damned Hoadie Renkin.

Mona Stayborn had taken the idea of a spring party from the girls' school that had once stood on Academy Heights. She hung Chinese lanterns in her yard, the kind that used electric light bulbs instead of candles.

The Stayborn home was on the slope of Academy Heights, just above the north end of the tunnel and overlooking the valley of the Rough, with a big backyard that was ideal for parties. There was a barbecue pit, the first one in Weedy Rough, where a hickory fire could be kindled to roast marshmallows and wieners. Generally, it had the best lawn in town because Esta watered it and was using some of the new bone fertilizers on it. Only this year, Esta had left off the water because the well was going low, so the grass was nothing but a brown stubble, like everybody else's.

On the night of the party, Duny Gene wore a new white shirt with a clip-on bow tie, dark blue corduroy pants, and a pair of black-and-white oxfords Lydia had ordered from Montgomery Ward out of Kansas City. He walked down to the depot to watch the evening train come through, and the early arrivals of the Texas Trade were there, beginning to trickle into the Rough for their summer vacation. There was no sign of the Depression about these people. Duny Gene was more than a little envious of their sleek cars with white sidewall tires and twin taillights.

He had been driving for a long time, but Barton never allowed him to take the car on his own. Not until after you graduate, Barton always said. So wherever Duny Gene wanted to go, he walked, just as he had when there was a bean flip hanging from his rear pocket. He fumed about it to himself, but he held no grudge against his father, thinking it was Lydia who laid down such laws.

He thought, Boy, if I just had a car every night, like Jabo Sparks! Well, it won't be long now.

At the depot, Duny Gene watched some of the younger kids laying their pennies on the tracks, just as he had once done. Maudie was not there, nor had she been for a long time. From the platform, Duny

Gene could look up the slope of West Mountain and see the Sparks place, and it gave him a sour feeling in his stomach when he saw that Jabo's car was not there, in its usual place behind the house.

After the train came through, Duny Gene watched the Texas Trade get in their cars and roar out of town, kicking up dust on their way to the various resort hotels. He ambled down to Joe Sanford's for a fresh strawberry ice-cream cone. It was almost dark by the time he'd finished that and started along the tracks toward the tunnel, cutting back up Academy Heights before he got to the cowcatcher. As he came to the Stayborn home, he could see Esta and Mona, adjusting their Chinese lanterns. There were already a few kids gathered around the smoking barbecue pit.

"God," he said to himself. "I wish I had a good drink of whiskey!"

Arlene Kruppman was a tall, cheerful girl with little meat on her bones but a pleasant enough smile. She wore her blonde hair braided and coiled around her head in the fashion of a Bavarian barmaid. She was often seen in the company of other girls, including Maudie Snowdon, among whom she appeared to be lively and well liked. But no one had ever known her to have much truck with boys. Not because she was unwilling, but because she was never asked. It might have been because boys were afraid of her two older brothers.

Arlene's father ran the blacksmith and the machine shops, and the two boys, Pug and Archer, were the town criminals. They had both been in the pen, Pug twice, for such assorted activities as stealing live-stock and committing assault with intent to kill. When they were in town, people tried to stay clear of them. Archer had once borrowed twenty dollars from Barton, which he never paid back. Pug had been involved in a number of fistfights behind Esta Stayborn's store. Once, Leo Sparks tried to arrest him and Pug almost beat Leo to death with a singletree. That got him two to five at Cummins State Prison Farm.

Both the Kruppman boys were mean and sullen and quick-tempered, and people said it was a shame that such a sweet girl as Arlene had to be saddled with two such no-account brothers.

The night of Mona Stayborn's 1931 graduation party, Arlene was managing the hot dogs. There was a long folding table near the barbecue pit and she was arranging the wieners on a sheet of wax paper when Duny Gene came up the hill from the tracks. Maybe it was because sap was rising, but for whatever reason, Duny Gene looked at her and saw more than he ever had before.

They talked for a while about the horror of solid geometry and how the smell of the passing train seemed to hang in the air on these still spring evenings and about the rumors they had heard that the federal highway would soon be paved all the way to Fort Smith.

The yard began to fill with people, mostly seniors and a few juniors and even fewer parents, whom Mona had asked to come along to help maintain order and decorum. Like guards in a prison, Duny Gene said, and was immediately sorry, remembering Arlene's brothers. But she laughed and slapped his arm and said he was full of the old Nick.

Everyone gathered around the fire, which was shedding its orange glow in a wide circle through the new night. They sipped cherry-flavored punch with pineapple bits in it and held marshmallows and wieners over the blaze with long willow wands Esta had cut for the occasion. Then they sang some round songs, like "Row, Row, Row Your Boat" and "Old MacDonald," and finally they spread out in a loose circle under the Chinese lanterns to play Simon Says. There were prizes for winners: bottles of brilliantine hair oil for the boys, small blue vials of Evening in Paris perfume for the girls. Duny Gene found all of it dreary and childish. But at least Arlene kept close to him and touched his arm and smiled at him, as though she knew something he didn't.

Late in the evening a car came along the road toward the Stayborn house, and after the headlights went off Jabo Sparks strode into the firelight. Maudie Snowdon was hanging on to his arm.

Mona Stayborn was more than a little upset about Jabo being there, old as he was and not even invited, but she made the best of it. Soon he was playing Simon Says along with the high-school kids. When Maudie's eyes came to Duny Gene, her gaze went through him as though she were looking at smoke.

Soon the party went into its informal stage, with everyone standing around in groups under the Chinese lanterns, where early spring moths were fluttering in the faint light like bits of thistledown. Some of the kids roasted the last of the wieners, and Maudie was there at the barbecue pit, making a hot dog for Jabo, who seemed to strut even when he was standing still, his black leather bow tie shining and his snappy cap pushed back on his head rakishly.

That son of a bitch, Duny Gene thought, and went looking for Arlene Kruppman. She was among a group of girls at the well curbing, sipping punch from a paper cup. Duny Gene took her arm and pulled her off into the darkness, around the side of the house and across the front yard.

"Where we goin'?" she asked with a nervous laugh, but made no signs of protest. Duny Gene said nothing, but turned to her and threw his arms around her a little roughly and kissed her. Her mouth was flat, not like Maudie's in any way, but he kissed her

again before she could say anything. Then she pulled
back, but no farther than arm's length, and he could
see her eyes shining in the dark.

"Good Lord, Duny Gene, what's got into you?"
she asked.

"Don't talk. Just don't talk. If you wanna yell,
then say so now and you can go back to the party.
But if you don't wanna yell, just don't say anything."

"Good Lord! I'm not fixin' to yell. But I never
saw you act like this."

"Come on. Just keep still."

Along the front of the Stayborn yard there was a
patch of old rhododendron bushes, and Duny Gene
and Arlene found their way among them and went to
the ground, Duny Gene pawing and fumbling at her
and beginning to breathe hard. Arlene said nothing,
nor did she do anything, but only lay there passively.
They could hear the talk and laughter from the rear of
the house. The longer they were there, the brighter
the night seemed to become, until Duny Gene began
to feel that he could be seen from anywhere in the
valley. It was a frantic, terrifying few moments, and
Duny Gene had a hell of a time getting his belt
unbuckled.

Afterward, he helped her up and she was trying to
get her clothes back into order.

"You better go back to the party," he said.

"Aren't you comin'?"

"I've had all of it I want. Listen, I hope you don't
think—"

But he broke it off and, turning abruptly, walked
down the hill toward the railroad tracks. Behind him,
he could hear her saying something, softly, but he
couldn't make it out and didn't care.

So that's what it's like, he thought. He'd always
supposed that when it happened, everything would be
smooth and easy and fall into place without a lot of

ruckus. But there had been all that fiddling with fasteners he didn't know how to open and wallowing around on the ground like a hog, awkwardly, wildly, not knowing what the hell he was doing, and afraid she might think him a complete fool, and getting his shirt dirty at the elbows and his trousers at the knees, and her lying there like a limp sack, not doing anything to help, maybe laughing at him silently. And then over so quickly, and not all that damned much pleasure, either, with him afraid as he went through with it that somebody would walk up and discover what they were doing, and him with his pants down to his knees. And afraid afterward that she'd go right back to all her friends and tell them about it and what at mess he'd made of it, and what a poor dumb bastard he was.

He came to the tracks and walked along them into town, past the depot, seeing the lights in the drugstore, and up the slope of West Mountain, lights in Tooth Snowdon's house, too. He walked almost a mile north on the tracks, stumbling in the darkness when his feet failed to find the crossties. Then he turned and walked back into town again, and the drugstore lights were out now. He started up the hill toward home. He thought he could still hear laughter from Academy Heights.

God, I'd like to take a bath, he thought. He could never remember wanting a bath so badly. He felt somehow unclean and bruised and sticky, and he knew he'd best stop and brush the dirt off his knees and elbows or Lydia would start asking all kinds of questions.

No matter how much he tried to push it from his thinking, he kept seeing himself under those bushes. He couldn't imagine anything so damned undignified. Then, in a moment of panic, he wondered if he'd knocked her up. That would put a final end to it. That would bell the cat, he thought.

He saw lights from his living room and paused in the road to brush furiously at his clothes. Then he realized he'd lost his tie. Taken all together, it had been a complete disaster.

Graduation in Weedy Rough was like a wedding in some respects, a funeral in others. There was the happy sense of new things ready to happen, but at the same time sorrow at the loss of the boys who were leaving the basketball team and would no longer be available for the annual championship battle with West Fork.

The whole affair took on a churchy atmosphere, perhaps because Leviticus Hammel was always asked to say the invocation and the benediction, and this meant in effect that much of the ceremony would be concerned with hell's fire. And Leviticus always brought the Methodist church choir with their white vestments and hymnals.

The principal speaker was chosen after the citizens had had an opportunity to place their nominations with the president of the school board, Reese Walls. In the year that Duny Gene graduated, there seemed to be more than the usual number of recommendations. Someone suggested the deputy sheriff, who was well known by sight if not by name, being the one who made a trip to the Rough once every two weeks to deliver Violet Sims her supply of labeled whiskey. But Reese figured such a speaker might not be appreciated by all, what with his connection with Violet.

Duny Gene Pay suggested Mr. Harmon Budd one afternoon while he was sitting at the marble-top soda-fountain counter and sipping a lemon Coke. Reese was behind the counter, scooping ice cream, and the suggestion tickled him so much he dropped a scoop on the floor.

"Yeah, he could tell us how he fell under that freight train and lost his leg," Reese said, laughing so hard he had to stop with the ice cream and wipe his eyes on a paper napkin.

The school board finally settled on the mayor of West Fork, who was a section boss on the Frisco and had two sons playing for the West Fork basketball team. It was a gesture to show that Roughers held no grudges for the past season of play, when West Fork had beaten the Chipmunks in three games by a total cumulative score of 123 points.

The night of graduation was one of those wonderful spring evenings in the hills. There had been a little rain the day before, not enough to fill many wells, but enough to give a fresh smell to things. The little pin oaks that stood around the school were popping out bravely with their luscious green, and in the hollow on the far side of Cobb Hubbs's store and across the federal highway a mockingbird provided a background symphony for the whole proceedings.

People drove up in cars or wagons, and a few riding horseback. They stood around outside at first, reluctant to march back into the school where most of them had matriculated. The seniors were hustled inside as soon as they appeared, so they could be arranged in proper order on the stage. The boys were mostly red-faced, tugging at collars and neckties. The girls were all pretty in cotton dresses and bows, their faces shining as though they alone realized that this was the moment of their coming to womanhood.

There was no opportunity for Duny Gene to speak with Maudie. She and the other girls were on one side of the stage, the boys on the other. Arlene Kruppman was there, looking well scrubbed. Like a peeled willow pole, Duny Gene thought. Maudie was wearing a trace of lipstick, and looked more beautiful than ever.

The ceremony seemed to go on endlessly. The seniors fidgeted, anxious to be away. Some of them had plans for that first trip to Tip Top Tavern, and Duny Gene was one of these. After many protests, Lydia had finally given in to Barton's appeal that graduation was a special night, meant for special concessions. So after the diplomas were awarded, Duny Gene would drive them home and then take the car for the rest of the evening. Lydia had agreed only after Duny Gene promised to be home in bed before midnight.

Duny Gene had it all mapped out in his mind. As soon as Leviticus Hammel pronounced the benediction, he would go over and take Maudie's hand and lead her to the Ford and have her sit with him in the front seat while he took Barton and Lydia home. Then on the way out to the tavern, he would stop a few times in the dark for some hugging and kissing. They would dance, holding each other close, and he might go into the back room for a few sips of gin. Then they'd drive back, with a few more stops for the spooning. Duny Gene even had places picked out along the federal highway where he could pull over without going into a ditch.

But none of it worked out that way. As soon as Leviticus had blessed the assembled citizens and sent everyone away with a reminder of sin's destructiveness, Maudie dashed off the stage. Duny Gene watched her disappear from the hall with Jabo Sparks. All right, he thought, I'll go out there where he's taking her and I'll kick that slick-ear in the balls, and maybe tear hell out of his new blue serge suit. Driving Barton and Lydia home, he said nothing, gripping the wheel viciously and thinking about what he would say to Maudie after he'd peeled some hide off Jabo's head.

As she got out of the car, Lydia gave him a little peck on the cheek.

"Congratulations, Duny Gene," she said. "I know you're glad to be finished with school. Now be careful with the car and get in early."

All of his fantasies about what he would do to Jabo Sparks didn't work out, either. Maudie and Jabo were not at the tavern, nor had Duny Gene seen the little yellow roadster parked anywhere along the way. He had watched for it at every bend in the road, driving at a breakneck thirty-five miles per hour. He stood around, he danced, and he went to the rear room for drinks. He was sullen and soreheaded, and even Arlene Kruppman finally got tired of his silence— and of his stepping on her feet when they danced— and started avoiding him. By eleven, he was a little drunk and the owner asked him to leave.

After he drove home and parked the car, he fell once on the yard steps and barked his shin and cursed a little too loudly. He went into the dark house, banging into furniture, and Lydia called from her bedroom.

"Is that you, Duny Gene?"

"Yeah. It's me," he said. Who'd she think it was?

"Did you have a good time?"

"Yeah. It was all keen. Just keen."

The Crown Coach Company ran two buses between Fayetteville and Fort Smith. They were big and uncomfortable, powered by White truck engines. Each had four spare tires strapped on the rear. The southbound came through Weedy Rough in late afternoon, about an hour before the northbound Frisco passenger arrived. Most generally, there were a few Roughers who rode the Fayetteville bus each day. It was slower than a train, taking about two hours to make the twenty-mile trip, what with all the stops to let people off or pick them up, and with the flat tires. But it was cheaper. A round-trip ticket to the county seat cost four bits.

When Tooth Snowdon alighted from the bus that day at the ice-cream parlor, which served as bus terminal as well, he had not paid a round-trip fare. He had gone to Fayetteville earlier in the day with Maudie and Jabo Sparks in the yellow roadster. Now he stood beside the big cumbersome-looking vehicle, wiping dust off his face. He looked along the street toward the depot, and there were some of the Texas Trade already gathered, waiting for the train. He saw Barton Pay's car parked near the platform, too. He heaved a deep sigh and adjusted the straps on his bib overalls. Then he turned and walked around the long front bumper of the bus and across the street to the barbershop. Olie Merton, sitting in his chair, watched Tooth coming.

Tooth banged through the screen door and glared around with red eyes. Olie thought maybe he'd been crying. Tooth sighed again.

"Olie, I need a drink real bad," he said. "I got a chore I hate worse than sin, and I need a drink."

Olie said nothing, but slipped from the chair and went to his glass-fronted cabinet and drew out a bottle with a hair-tonic label on it. He handed the bottle to Tooth and watched as Tooth unscrewed the cap. Tooth took a long swallow, then another, his head back and his big Adam's apple bobbing. Olie counted seven bobs.

"That ain't bad lightnin'," Tooth said, smacking his lips. But even the good whiskey failed to put any spark back in his eyes. He pulled out a soiled hand-kerchief and wiped his nose.

"Yeah, I got it from Ike Renkin," Olie said.

"Gawd, Olie, I got a chore that's about to kill me."

"Best way to go about things like that is to get 'er done quick and have it over with. Like pullin' teeth."

"I seen Mr. Pay's car over at the depot. He in town?"

"Not that I know of," Olie said, taking the bottle from Tooth's hand before he could lift it again. "Duny Gene drove down a while ago, to see the train come, I reckon."

"Gawd! I gotta go up and talk with Mr. Pay. Hardest thing I ever done."

With that, he turned and left. Olie figured that after a time he'd learn the particulars. In Tooth's good time, he'd learn.

Tooth spoke to a number of people sitting in front of the post office as he passed. They could see that he was preoccupied. He walked on slowly but steadily, beyond the buildings and up the East Mountain road. Along the way, he paused and looked down into the tie yard and saw that the little shack there was locked. He sighed once more and swore under his breath and went on up toward the Pay house.

Just ahead were Parkins and Veda Muller, hurrying home from the bank to milk their goats. Tooth slowed his pace, not wanting to be seen by them. Parkins had been pestering him for years about that loan he'd taken on his wagon, before those three men rode in on horses and robbed the bank.

"Pesky little bastard," Tooth said to himself.

Barton Pay was sitting on his front porch, smoking, Lydia beside him working on some quilt pieces. Tooth took a long time mounting the yard steps and then the porch steps. His feet seemed to drag as he approached the two, his face red and his eyes watery. He took off his hat.

"Howdy, Miz Lydia. Howdy, Mr. Pay," he said.

"Hello, Tooth. What brings you up this way?" There was a note of apprehension in Barton's voice, uneasy about what this might mean. Lydia smiled and nodded but said nothing.

"Mr. Pay, I need to talk to you a minute," Tooth said.

"You can talk out here," Lydia said, rising. "I've got to get supper started. How's your family, Tooth?"

"Tol'able, tol'able," he said. After the screen door slammed behind Lydia, Tooth moved in a little closer and took a deep breath. But he seemed unable to speak.

"Well, what can I do for you, Tooth?" Barton asked. "I have to warn you ahead of time, I'm stretched for cash right now."

"No. No, it ain't anything like that," Tooth said. He took out the handkerchief and wiped his face. "It's about . . . well, Mr. Pay, it's about my girl Maudie. I wanted to tell you because I know your boy was always kind of taken with her. You know."

"Yes, I know," Barton said. He flipped his cigarette out into the yard and Tooth watched it arch all the way to the ground.

"This mornin', I went to Fayetteville. I went with my girl in Jabo Sparks's car. Well, sir, Mr. Pay, they got married up there. They're headed out to California."

Barton looked at him a long time without saying anything, and then he leaned back in his chair and closed his eyes.

"I guess it's been comin' for a long time, now," Tooth went on. "I was hopin' it wouldn't, me and my ole lady both. We was hopin' it wouldn't. I hate it like sin, knowin' how Duny Gene felt and what a fine boy he is, but there was nothin' I could do about it."

The expression on Barton's face was calm, as though he were perhaps thinking that even with this hurt for Duny Gene, at least there was no longer the rather horrifying prospect of becoming one of Tooth Snowdon's in-laws.

"No. There was nothing you could do about it," he said, eyes still closed. Tooth turned his hat in his hand, looking down across the yard again, and past the bluff to the tie yard. He wondered if he'd told it right.

"I appreciate your telling me," Barton said.

"Well, hell, Mr. Pay, I wanted you to know from me, at least. And how I feel about it. I don't think they tole anybody what they was aimin' to do. Didn't tell us till the night of graduation, and my ole lady like to have raised Cain. Jabo and Maudie come to us and tole us. She ain't but eighteen."

"Lots of girls marry younger than that."

"Yeah, I reckon. But anyway, I wanted to tell you right off, Mr. Pay, so you could tell the boy. Better than hearin' from some of the other kids. Me and Leo talked about it, and he was tore up, too, because he sets a store in Duny Gene, just like I do. Always thought the world of that boy of yours."

"I appreciate it," Barton said. There was something final in the tone of it, and Tooth, not usually sensitive to such things, caught it this time and pulled his hat on roughly.

"Well, I'm sorry, Mr. Pay. Wasn't nothin' I could do."

Barton rose and they shook hands. "I hope your girl will be happy with Jabo."

"They say California's a nice place. I hope she writes sometime. She's a fine girl, Mr. Pay, but I told her she taken the wrong man."

Before Tooth was down the porch steps, Barton moved back into the house. He found Lydia standing just inside the door, looking at him with her eyes almost full but held back from overflowing. Barton knew she had heard everything.

"Do you want me to tell him?" she asked.

"No. No, I'll tell him when he gets home after train time."

Barton put his arms around her and she lifted her hands to his shoulders and they stood like that for a

moment. It was the first time in many years that
Barton could recall an embrace between them.

There was a congregation of flies on the barbershop
window. The afternoon sun slanted in through the
dirty glass and flooded the room with blinding light.
Olie Merton was cutting Reese Walls's hair, and
Tooth Snowdon was sitting near the door, staring out
into the street. Farther back in the shop, Mr. Harmon
Budd was sleeping in a chair, his wooden leg detached and lying on the floor beside him. There was
the smell of hair oil and talcum powder about the
place. The flies buzzed and the scissors in Olie's
hands made their little *snip, snip, snip* as he trimmed
around Reese's ears.

"You heard from that girl of yours, Tooth?" Reese
asked.

"No. It's only been a couple weeks and they was
plannin' on goin' through Yellowstone Park, maybe
spendin' a little time there."

"I guess it's nice to have enough money to spend
a little time in Yellowstone Park," Olie said, and
Tooth made a sour face.

Mr. Harmon Budd woke for a moment, gurgled
and spat and glared around the room with bloodshot
eyes.

"Is it train time yet?" he asked.

"No, Harmon, it ain't," Olie said. "It's a while
yet."

Mr. Budd slumped down in the chair and was
immediately asleep again.

"I guess Mr. Pay's boy took it kindly hard," Tooth
said, staring out into the street still. There was some
note of pride in his voice, thinking that his own girl
Maudie could have such an effect on anyone as fine
as Duny Gene Pay.

"I hear he left town for a spell," Reese said.

"Yeah, he taken that shotgun of his and went down on Lee Creek and camped for a week," Tooth said.

"Where'd you hear that?" Olie said, snipping. Unlike some barbers, Olie liked to check the credibility of his sources before he passed along stories.

"Mr. Pay told me," Tooth said. "Duny Gene taken off all by his self. Me and Mr. Pay was jawin' one day in the tie yard about it. He said Duny Gene went off to camp on the creek by his self, gig a few frogs and shoot some. Mr. Pay drove him down and let him off, and went back for him. He taken his gun and some fishline and a few cans of beans and a blanket roll. Wanted to be in the woods by his self awhile, I reckon. Like a red Injun."

"He comes by that natural," Reese said.

"I ain't seen him at the depot for a long spell," Olie said.

"No," Tooth said. He thought about it for a moment. "I reckon Duny Gene's all frazzled out by it all. Wasn't nothin' I could do." He rose and walked to the door and stretched, his hands in his hip pockets.

"Ike Renkin was in town today," Reese said. "Says he's gonna let the dogs loose tonight, out around Clovis Springs. Think I'll take a couple of my hounds out, too."

"They tell me Mr. Pay's dog Dixie gets better every race," Olie said. "Mr. Pay must sure be proud of that dog. You ought to go tell him there's gonna be a race tonight, Tooth."

Tooth thought about it for a minute and stretched again.

"Naw, I have an idea Ike already told him. But I don't think Mr. Pay wants to hear no race right now. I think he's a little frazzled out his ownself."

PART THREE

· 10 ·

Cobb Hubbs had served in the infantry during the war and he knew what a Browning automatic rifle looked like, but after he left France in 1919 he never expected to see another one. But he did. It was lying in the backseat of a blue Model B Ford sedan. Beside it were two twelve-gauge pump guns, both with viciously short nineteen-inch barrels and enough ammunition to bribe a Mexican bandit.

When they paved the federal highway, which ran in front of Cobb's store, he put in a gasoline pump. It had a high glass cylinder at the top that showed the level of gas, and the glass vial was filled by yanking a pump on the side of the apparatus. It held ten gallons, and if anyone wanted twelve Cobb would run the cylinder dry and then pump more of the amber-colored liquid up from the tank buried just beneath. Five gallons was usually the most he sold at any one time.

There was a new, brightly painted sign hanging near his door now, proclaiming this as a Magnolia service station. Below that was a hand-lettered placard that indicated gasoline was twenty cents a gallon, oil two bits a quart. The oil was in clear glass bottles in a rack against one wall.

It was spring. Warm weather had come early in that year of 1933. Cobb was enjoying the shade, leaning back against the front of the store with Mr. Harmon Budd. Mr. Budd was considerably more sober than usual because his pension check from the railroad was late getting in that month and he had no money for anything more than a thick elderberry wine. This commodity Cobb manufactured and marketed himself when he had the opportunity. It was sweet and gritty, a concoction even Mr. Harmon Budd refused to drink until it became a matter of absolute necessity.

"You make the worst wine I ever saw," Mr. Budd complained, eyeing the level of evil-looking purple liquid in the vinegar bottle he held in his hand.

"I ain't tryin' to compete with Virginia Dare," Cobb said, undisturbed. "But I sure'n hell sell cheaper."

They watched the occasional automobile that came up the hill from the direction of the baseball diamond, laboring to the crest immediately in front of them, then gaining speed as it passed. Being an expert on automobiles now that he ran a service station, Cobb identified each one. Mr. Budd had no way of knowing whether all the designations were correct, and he really didn't care much.

The Model B, a dark blue one, came in from the south. It had a great deal of mud and dust on it, testifying that it had been run on something other than paved roads recently. It pulled into the service station, stopping before the pump and throwing gravel about. A slight bareheaded man in a three-piece dark suit was driving. He slipped out of the driver's seat, the door opening toward the front of the car, and stood blinking with eyes that seemed somewhat beady to Cobb.

"Fill the tank," he said. "And wipe off the windshield."

There was something prissy about the way the man

talked, Cobb thought, maybe a little hidden lisp. Cobb had the vague feeling he'd seen him somewhere before. He opened the tank cap and took down the hose and inserted the nozzle. The odor of gasoline came up as he pressed the lever. The woman in the car, he could see through the back window, was smoking a cigarette. She looked familiar, too.

When he went around to wipe the windshield, Cobb got a better look at her. She was frail and had a pointed chin, and her hair was parted in the middle, pulled back tight along her head. She was wearing a dark brown French beret. She watched Cobb with cold, unblinking eyes, and suddenly Cobb knew who they were. Then he saw the guns lying on the back seat, and that confirmed it.

"Get some smokes," the woman called to the man still standing by the door. Cobb saw then a large bulge in the man's coat and took it for the butt of a pistol.

"This place got a name?" the man asked, in that strange voice.

"Uh . . . it's . . . uh, Weedy Rough," Cobb stammered.

"That's a helluva name, ain't it?" the little voice said. "Hurry it up, will ya? I need some cigarettes."

"Yes sir," Cobb said. He went ahead of the man into the store, feeling the flesh along his neck crawling. Mr. Harmon Budd sat listlessly, fondling his wine beneath the bib of his overalls.

By the time Cobb reached the back of his counter, his hands were shaking. The man seemed to smile a little. Cobb started throwing cartons of cigarettes out onto the counter, all he had. Chesterfields and Camels.

"That's all the cigarettes I got, mister," Cobb said. The man laughed.

"We don't sell many here, you see, so that's all my stock."

"How much are they?"

"That's all right, you take what you want, don't worry about it."

The man laughed again, a soft little laugh that came from the top of his throat. With his fingernails he slit open a carton of Camels and took out three packs. He threw a handful of coins on the counter along with some wadded bills.

"That ought to take care of the gas and the smokes," he said.

"That'll be fine, mister," Cobb said.

"Ain't you gonna count it?"

"It's plenty, I can tell. More than enough. Much obliged to you."

The man lifted his slight shoulders in a shrug, turned back to the door, and sauntered out to the car. He tossed the cigarettes into the front seat beside the woman and got in and drove out onto the highway. Cobb crept over to the screen door and watched them go.

But they only went about a hundred yards down the road and pulled onto the shoulder. Cobb watched as they both got out and moved into the backseat, leaving all four doors open. Then he realized they were cleaning their guns, sitting right along the federal highway in broad daylight, cleaning that Browning automatic rifle and the shotguns.

Cobb hissed at Mr. Budd, but Mr. Budd sat on his stool by the oil rack, fingering his wine bottle. Cobb whispered again, louder now, and Mr. Budd turned his head.

"Come in here," Cobb said softly. Mr. Budd did not move. "God dammit, Harmon, come on in here."

Mr. Budd rose and stalked toward the door, his peg leg making a jarring sound each time it cut into the gravel of Cobb's driveway. Cobb held the screen door open and grabbed Mr. Budd and pulled him inside.

"What the hell—"

"You know who that was?" Cobb asked, looking down the road where the Model B was still parked, doors hanging open. "That was Bonnie Parker and Clyde Barrow. I seen their pictures lots of times in the *Kansas City Star*."

"Who the hell is Bonnie Parker and Clyde Barrow?"

"Jesus H. Christ, Harmon, don't you know nothin'? Bonnie Parker and Clyde Barrow. The bank robbers and killers. Did you see his eyes? He had a pistol on him and guns in the car. You shoulda seen the way she looked at me."

"Hell, then," Mr. Budd sputtered, pulling out of Cobb's grip. "Go over there to your telephone and call Leo Sparks and get him up here to arrest 'em."

"You crazy! I ain't gonna set no law on them two people. Jesus H. Christ, Harmon. Lookee there. They've finished with the guns. One of 'em is a Browning automatic rifle, like I seen lots of in the war."

The man and woman moved from the back into the front of the car, slamming all the doors shut, and a small cloud of blue smoke issued from the exhaust pipe as the engine started. Cobb and Mr. Budd watched as the Ford inched out onto the concrete slab and gained speed, then went out of sight toward the baseball diamond.

"Jesus H. Christ," Cobb breathed.

It was one of the high moments in Cobb Hubbs's life, or so he thought at first. He told the story around town, but in his exuberance he told too much— about shoving the cigarettes over the counter, about not asking for pay, about not counting the money on the counter for fear of getting shot. Much as they sympathized with him—or maybe because they got tired of hearing the story—they began to make fun of him, joking about Cobb's bravery and sense of public welfare. They started calling him Hoot Gibson, the man who scared the criminal element out of town.

So the whole thing went sour on him. He raised the price of gasoline by two pennies a gallon, and he refused to sell Mr. Harmon Budd any more cheap elderberry wine because he suspected Mr. Budd was going around behind his back elaborating on the story. He was mistaken about that. The only contribution Mr. Budd made was to ask the recurring question: "Who the hell is Bonnie Parker and Clyde Barrow?"

For Cobb and a lot of others during that time, bad luck seemed to come in bunches. That spring, Cobb's wife, Eliza, dropped her dentures into the privy. It wasn't unusual for people to lose things now and again down the holes of those old outdoor toilets, but a set of false teeth was a new kind of record. The boys in the barbershop heard about the teeth, but they said very little about it. They always felt a little underhanded making dirty talk about one of the town's ladies. Tooth wondered how Eliza had gotten into a position that would allow her teeth to fall through the hole, but he finally put it out of his mind because of the strange possibilities that occurred to him.

It was a great embarrassment to Eliza, knowing all the Eastern Star ladies knew what had happened, but they said nothing to her face out of consideration for her feelings. She would have stayed away from the Star meetings, but now she was an officer in the order: Ada, one of the five sisters of the star.

When Duny Gene heard about it, he laughed. But there was a little bitterness in it. There was good old Jephthah's daughter again—Ada—he thought, having all the bad luck an ungrateful Providence could heap on her.

Burma Shave signs appeared along the highway north and south of Weedy Rough, a sure indication of encroaching civilization. The number of cars passing along the road came to be a nuisance, and a few fox dogs were killed crossing the concrete slab late at night. It was disgraceful.

"And what the hell are people doin' out in the middle of the night in a car goin' up the highway?" Tooth Snowdon wanted to know. "Decent folks ought to be in bed by midnight. Unless they're listenin' to a race."

"A lot of drunks, too," Olie Merton said, slouched in his barber chair and chewing a toothpick. "Homer Gage, down at North End Garage, went out the other night in the rain to fix a car stalled somewhere on the highway. You hear about that?"

"I heard there was four of 'em. All drunk."

"Yeah, and when Homer fixed their car and asked for seventy-five cents, they told him to go to hell and beat him up and drove off and left him in the mud."

"If I was Homer, I wouldn't go nowhere on that highway at night to fix nobody's car without carryin' a gun."

"Not much tellin' what kind of people you might run into on that highway."

There were good things happening, too. A telephone call could be made all the way to Little Rock and beyond, with some expectation of getting through and even of hearing what the person on the other end was saying. But nobody in Weedy Rough made too many long-distance calls, except for Parkins Muller. He found that riding the Frisco to Fayetteville twice a month for his groceries gave him backache, so he placed all his orders by phone. He used Reese Walls's instrument in the drugstore because he and Miss Veda had not installed one yet in their home or at the bank. It cost a dollar a month, sometimes more.

Everybody was listening to "Amos 'n' Andy" on the radio. On Tuesday mornings, after the show the night before, the barbershop gang would congregate to laugh about the antics.

"You ever heerd anybody talk as ignorant?" Tooth asked. "And some of them people is crazy. That Kingfish."

"There's only two people do all the voices," Olie said.

"The hell you say!"

"I read it in *Collier's*."

As the spring came on, there were fierce arguments about the upcoming baseball season in the big leagues. Tooth was a Cardinal fan, claiming he'd known the Dean family that produced Dizzy and Daffy. Olie and Reese insisted that the Dean boys came from Oklahoma, saying since Tooth had never been out of Arkansas, how the hell would he know their family? It always made Tooth mad, and he'd stalk out of the barbershop fuming. Then the others could get in a word edgewise about their own favorites.

"In the American, I say Philadelphia," Reese said.

"I say the Yankees," Olie said.

"How about that guy Jimmy Foxx, though, with Philadelphia."

"Well, what about the Nationals?"

"I say Saint Louis."

"Me, too. But don't tell Tooth I said so."

Sometimes they talked prizefighting. Olie had a photograph of Jack Sharkey clipped from a *Police Gazette* pasted to his wall. But they all agreed Jack Dempsey could have whipped any of the present herd of heavyweights with only his left hand.

They were learning a lot, for a small hill town. Like the fact that Listerine prevented halitosis and that Palmolive soap gave the schoolgirl complexion. Every week, there were a few new magazines on Reese Walls's racks at the drugstore. They were laced with ads about how to learn to be a radio mechanic at night, and how to develop enough muscles to beat hell out of that son of a bitch who kicked sand on you. The favorites among the pulps were Street and Smith's *Wild West Weekly*, for the he-man types, and *Rangeland Romances* for those who thought a cowboy ought to spend some time kissing girls.

There were undercover publications, too. Reese kept them hidden in his storeroom. Although it had happened years before, there were now pictures of famous murderers, and the snapshot of Ruth Snyder at the moment of her death in the electric chair in New York or some such place. There were reprints of love-nest slayings, with faked photographs. And there was a book entitled *Hell on the Border*, which explained in some detail the executions in Fort Smith during the tenure of old Judge Isaac Parker when he was on the federal bench there. Barton Pay bought a copy, and when Lydia saw it she threw a fit and hid the thing in one of her hatboxes. Duny Gene found it anyway, and read it between unloadings at the tie yard.

"Your Grandfather Pay was involved in a lot of that, but he's not mentioned," Barton said one afternoon, Duny Gene sitting beside him on a stack of posts, reading the book.

"Yeah, I guess he was a pretty good lawyer."

"Still is. It's a pity he lost all his savings in that bank that went busted in Saint Louis. He should have had more faith in some of our own banks."

Duny Gene looked along the tie yard and across the street to the Bank of Weedy Rough. He thought about Parkins Muller standing there in his wire cage, where all the money was locked up.

"Yeah. I guess so."

"Too bad you took so long to make up your mind about going to the university on that money."

"Yeah. I guess so."

"You could still go, if you wanted to."

"I'm all right where I am for now."

'Well, maybe with Mr. Roosevelt in there, we

won't have to worry so much anymore," Barton said.

"Sure," Duny Gene said, and laughed. "Maybe we won't be feeding so many hoboes now."

"It's hard times," Barton said. "People over in Oklahoma leaving their land, going west. Some of our own hill folks, too. The old rattletraps they leave in, surprised if they get to Tulsa, much less California."

"Another kind of hobo," Duny Gene said. "Tinlizzie hoboes. Esta says he's sellin' a lot of pork and beans to the train bunch. And they throw their cans all along the tracks. South of the tunnel looks like a garbage dump."

"Hard times," Barton said again. "And violent. All these poor people taking law into their hands. All these banks being robbed. Your grandfather was involved in that kind of thing years ago. And I think he enjoyed it."

"Maybe some people like fast cars and holdups," Duny Gene said, and Barton looked at him sharply. But Duny Gene was reading, not really listening anymore.

The Frisco tie buyer in Chester, a small town south of the Rough, had been laid off. Barton went there twice each week to do the buying. On those days, Duny Gene ran the Weedy Rough yard. It worked out all right, but the only money Duny Gene got was what Barton paid him from his own salary.

It didn't seem to matter much. Duny Gene had settled into a routine. He worked and hunted and fished, and about once a week he took the Ford out to Tip Top Tavern and got drunk and chewed a whole package of Sen-Sen before coming back home. Lydia never suspected that he was drinking so much, or if she did she said nothing.

When he could afford it, Duny Gene would take one of the local girls to Fayetteville to watch a moving-picture show. He watched *Little Caesar* three times, but none of the girls thought it was so hot. On the way home, he would usually pull over to the side of the road, and sometimes he and the girl would wallow around in the backseat. Each such occasion was just as disappointing as the first time had been with Arlene Kruppman. Duny Gene began to worry about himself, but he passed it off in his mind by saying it was just because he was afraid someone might walk up on them with a flashlight.

Lydia was proud of his appearance as he grew, well aware that he caught the eye of every woman in town when he passed by. He was a handsome, stalwart young man, and he always looked well groomed even in his work clothes. Like his father, he wore a dark suit coat over his striped railroader's overalls in the tie yard. He also wore a woolen bill cap. He shaved with a straight razor, again like his father, and he used a little brilliantine every morning. It made his black hair shine like a crow's wing.

Often, without saying anything to anyone, he took the old Army .45 out of Barton's nightstand and went to the woods to shoot at cans. He liked the feel of the gun in his hand. He even enjoyed all the racket and his ears ringing afterward. He had by now come to realize that all men did not hold such strong attachments to firearms as he did, and he began to wonder about that, too.

Repeal came, but Violet Sims was in no danger of losing her label-whiskey business for a while yet. Kruppman, the blacksmith, converted his machine shop into a beer hall. Parkins Muller tried to raise hell about it, since the building sat on the back side of the bank, but old Kruppman was one of the few businessmen in the Rough who were not somehow obligated to Parkins and his bank, so he ignored the fuss.

After that, Parkins's friend the deputy sheriff appeared regularly to check out the premises. He was likely looking to catch Pug Kruppman swilling brew. Pug was out on parole at the time and he spent many hours at the tap, but the deputy never caught him drinking.

The beer hall was viewed by most of the townspeople as a plague worse than a Holy Roller revival. They enjoyed old man Kruppman successfully going against Parkins Muller's grain, but the business with Mr. Barton Pay was shameful. Everyone in town knew about it.

It started when Kruppman discovered it took a lot of interior carpentry work to turn a machine shop into a beer joint. Kruppman was short on tools of that nature, so he went to Barton Pay to borrow his. Long since, Barton had bought a number of fine saws and hammers and levels and planers for modifications in his own house. He did not particularly enjoy working with tools, but he became tired of having to depend on Tooth Snowdon every time he needed something repaired or a new pan shelf put in Lydia's kitchen.

Kruppman carried the toolbox down the hill from the Pay house and past the bank and into his new beer establishment. For a few days there was the sound of hammering and sawing from within. Then the hammering and sawing stopped and Parkins Muller and a few others saw Kruppman carry the toolbox up the slope of West Mountain to his house, only a few hundred feet from Violet Sims's. That's where it stayed.

At first, Barton thought little of it. Then he began to worry that one of the Kruppman boys would take his tools to West Fork or Chester and sell them. One morning in front of the drugstore, he stopped Kruppman and asked about it.

"Listen, don't egg me on," Kruppman said, in

that mean way of talking he had passed on to his two
sons. "I ain't through yet. You loaned 'em, and I'm
still usin' 'em. Don't egg me on."

A number of men, including Reese Walls, heard
the exchange. Some thought that son of a bitch
Kruppman had no intention of ever returning those
tools.

It was no surprise that Barton Pay took it calmly
and walked away, being such a passive and religious
man. But everyone thought it was a crime, talking to
the leading citizen of the town like that, a churchgoer
every Sunday and supporter of the basketball team,
and whose wife was now Worthy Matron of the
Eastern Star. But nobody said anything to Barton
about it.

From the very first, it seemed, Roughers tried to
protect Barton Pay from the truth. They had said
nothing of their suspicions about Duny Gene and that
last school fire, nor about his drinking in more recent
years, nor the fact that most girls in town had begun
to consider him a fast boy in a rear seat. At this time,
too, they tried to protect Barton by pretending that he
had not been insulted by old man Kruppman.

But if the town tried to keep Barton in the dark
about things he might think unpleasant, they had no
such code with Duny Gene. When Reese described
the confrontation between his father and Kruppman,
Duny Gene sat at the marble counter of the soda
fountain sipping his chocolate Coke. And he said
nothing. But later, Reese told Olie Merton that Duny
Gene's eyes had suddenly taken on a flat, lusterless
look like old dry charcoal.

Lydia was in Fort Smith again. She was spending a
lot of time there with her ailing father. The day after
she left that spring, it was time for Barton to go to
Chester to run the yard there. He took the morning

freight south as he always did, leaving Duny Gene in charge.

The town was busy that morning, but by noon most of the wagons and cars had disappeared from the streets. Duny Gene sat on a tie pile, looking past the bank to the beer joint. It was padlocked this day, Kruppman having run out of his first shipment of 3.2 beer, and no new load yet arrived. Duny Gene looked up the slope of West Mountain, where the Kruppman house sat. He could see Archer Kruppman in the backyard working on an old Ford. Duny Gene thought about what Reese Walls had told him.

About two o'clock, Duny Gene locked up the shack, crossed the tracks, and went up the bluff. He knew his father always kept a good bottle of whiskey hidden in a back closet for those cold days after being on the route or when he was tired from working timber all day. Duny Gene had never touched it before, but he had no trouble finding it.

He held the bottle up, measuring the level of the liquor. It was about half full. He uncorked it and took a snort, looked at the level once more, and drank again. Then he went into the kitchen and poured a little water in, shook the bottle, and checked the level one last time. It looked about right. He went back to the closet and hid the whiskey where he'd found it.

For a moment, he thought about the .45 in his father's nightstand, but finally he shook his head and went for his own shotgun. He loaded it with three shells, number-four shot.

Bee Schirvy was on the sidewalk in front of the post office talking with Tooth Snowdon when Duny Gene came down the East Mountain road carrying the shotgun. He crossed the tracks and went around Esta Stayborn's store.

"Wonder where Duny Gene's goin' with that scattergun," Bee said.

They watched as he disappeared behind the line of buildings on the far side of the tracks, then reappeared again above and behind them on the slope of West Mountain.

"Looks like he's headin' for either Violet Sims or Kruppman's," Tooth said.

Watching, they saw Archer Kruppman in the backyard look up from beneath the hood of the car he was working on, but Duny Gene paid him no mind, walking right past him. He went to the front steps of the Kruppman house, up onto the porch, and banged on the door, the shotgun cradled carelessly in the crook of an elbow.

It took a long time for anyone to answer the knock. Duny Gene slammed his hand against the side of the house. In the yard, Archer Kruppman was stock-still, leaning under the car hood but peering out with his mouth open. After a third knock, the door opened. Tooth thought he saw Duny Gene saying something. He wished he was close enough to hear.

"Who was it?" Bee asked. "Who come to the door?"

"Can't see. Maybe Pug. Maybe the old man."

The door closed and Duny Gene stood on the porch, but he did not knock again. Then the door opened once more and a foot shoved a toolbox out onto the porch, then disappeared back inside and the door closed.

"Well, I'll be damned," Tooth said.

Duny Gene lifted the toolbox and turned and went down into the yard. Archer Kruppman was still staring at him. Duny Gene came even with the car and stopped and looked at Archer for a long time, and Archer ducked his head back under the hood and did not look up again. Duny Gene came down the hill, going out of sight behind the stores, then coming around them and onto the tracks and across them to the East Mountain road.

"Yes siree," Bee said. "That boy's gonna amount to somethin' yet."

The day Duny Gene recaptured the carpenter tools, Barton came back from Chester on Number Six, looking fagged. He spoke only briefly to Duny Gene as he passed through the living room. Duny Gene was there trying to find a station without static on the new Philco radio Barton had found in Fort Smith for almost nothing in a store that was going bankrupt.

Barton walked into the back room and on to the closet and took out the bourbon. He took only a small sip, all he ever allowed himself, and even then feeling a little guilty about it now that he had religion. Somehow, the whiskey seemed not to taste so strong today. After replacing the bottle and starting back to the kitchen to prepare one of those dismal bachelor meals he fixed when Lydia was away, he saw the tool kit sitting beside the icebox.

"Where'd this toolbox come from?" he called.

"Kruppman gave it to me this afternoon," Duny Gene said.

"Well, I guess he decided he didn't need it anymore."

"Yeah. I guess that's what he decided all right."

· 11 ·

PUG WAS THE TOUGHEST OF THE KRUPPMAN breed. If any of them was ever to try revenge on Duny Gene Pay for retrieving his father's tools, everyone figured it would be Pug. But then the railroad detective came to town and started asking questions about some Frisco boxcars that had been broken into one night while they sat in a Fort Smith freight yard. A great quantity of automotive parts had been taken, along with some cases of glass mason jars.

The detective inquired into the whereabouts of Pug and Archer Kruppman on the night in question. He spent some time with Homer Gage at North End Garage, and he asked if Homer had ever seen either of the Kruppmans driving a Dodge panel truck. Homer said as a matter of fact he had seen Pug in such a vehicle once, in the company of another man he didn't know.

Archer had taken to helping his father run the beer joint, passing out the tall amber bottles of brew, acting as bouncer when required, and swamping out the place each morning. His nights had obviously been spent on endeavors other than stealing salable property from boxcars. So everyone figured Pug was the target of the detective's questions. Apparently Pug thought so, too. The day after the detective arrived in the Rough, Pug disappeared.

The barbershop gang heaved a sigh of relief. Not that they wouldn't have enjoyed seeing Pug go back to Cummins Prison Farm, even though they didn't really give a damn about a few car parts and some empty fruit jars. But it was good that Duny Gene could at least temporarily feel safe from Pug's retaliation. After the affair of the shotgun on the Kruppman front porch, Duny Gene had become even more of a barbershop favorite than before.

"Ain't that the limit!" Tooth Snowdon said. "It takes a Frisco policeman to run the likes of Pug off."

"Archer may take it on his mind to light into Duny Gene," Homer Gage said.

"Hell," Tooth snorted. "Duny Gene'd knock Archer flat as Lottie's sock."

"I'm not too sure about that," Olie Merton said from his throne. "But I don't think Archer's got the guts to try."

"I'll tell you," Reese Walls said. "I wouldn't want to tangle with that little Indian. He may look slick, but he's tough as old hide."

"Them Injun people are that way," Tooth said authoritatively. "You start givin' 'em shit, they rare up on you."

"I'm glad Pug's gone," Olie said. "He was a blight on the town."

"He belongs in the pen," Homer said, nodding.

"Archer ain't too bad. A little mean and backhanded, but he ain't wild and wicked like Pug," Olie said.

"Maybe Pug'll come back," Homer said. "That'd make one helluva fight, him and Duny Gene."

"Gawd damn, Homer, Pug must outweigh Duny Gene fifty pound," Tooth said. "And he's a lot older."

"It'd make a good fight," Homer insisted.

"I dunno," Olie said. "I feel like Reese. I'd not

want to tangle with that boy if he had a stick, or a gun. I think he'd lay you out any way he could. But with his fists, I don't know. He had to use a baseball on Tooth's boy. And Cobb Hubbs told me Hoadie Renkin beat hell out of him one night.''

''Well, for Christ's sweet sake, who's in the same class with Hoadie Renkin? I don't know anybody much around here is,'' Tooth said.

''I understand Hoadie was nobody to fool with up at the school when he left, and him only a junior. Wasn't he a junior when he left?'' Reese asked.

''Who knows what he was?'' Tooth said.

''If he was still here, I'd bet he'd be in the same notch behind the beer hall with the big boys,'' Homer said.

''Yeah,'' Olie said. ''I wonder what ever happened to Hoadie?''

They all thought about that for a while, silently. Then they began arguing about the merits of various catchers in the National League. But before it became anything approaching a good argument, Homer went back to the original subject.

''Hoadie was best dog, for his grade,'' he said.

''He never had to prove it much,'' Reese said.

''Hell, Reese, best dog don't have to prove nothin','' Tooth said knowingly. ''It's all them other boys has to tie into one another, see who's got the moxie to sidle up to best dog.''

''Yeah, well, Duny Gene Pay never had to prove nothin', either,'' Homer said.

''He never lowered his self much to fistfights,'' Tooth said. ''He looked down his nose at it. But he wasn't afeared, 'cause he tied into Hoadie Renkin, like Olie said.''

''With a horseshoe,'' Olie said.

''The boy's got good sense. And now, after he seen how the Kruppmans acted when he showed a shotgun, you ain't gonna see him use bare fists any more than before.''

"He seems like a young man who likes some iron in his hand," Reese said.

"Well, if Pug comes back, it'd be a helluva fight," Homer insisted.

Reese was right. After the affair with the tools, Duny Gene thought a lot about the look on old Kruppman's face when he'd seen the twelve-gauge. Duny Gene thought about Archer, too, rooted to his spot under the hood of that old car. He began to think more surely than ever that the sight of a cold steel muzzle could immobilize anyone. But in thinking that, he slowly began to forget what the consequences could be if victim turned attacker, no matter the cost. Or even worse, if the victim had a gun, too.

Lydia Pay watched her son entering manhood and concluded that it was disastrous. She had always known it would come, of course, but she had forced herself not to think about it. When Duny Gene had first weighed a hundred pounds, she was horrified because she still thought of him as a little boy. Now he weighed considerably more than a hundred pounds, solid as an ax handle.

From the time he had been able to walk, Lydia had seen some kind of quietness in him, some detachment that cut her off, and it seemed to grow more pronounced as the years passed. He looked so much like his father once had that it shocked her. But the resemblance stopped there.

Barton had always been vivacious, joking, full of good spirit and laughter, even after he got religion. Even then, he was a man who enjoyed life and its people and could find a chuckle in most of what he saw, and most of what he did. He was still able to laugh at himself. Lydia had come to think that it was a physical impossibility for Duny Gene to laugh at himself, or, for that matter, at anything else.

Duny Gene was withdrawn, speaking only when spoken to, even with Barton. He had become almost sullen. Lydia saw it, even if Barton failed to, what with his church business and tie buying and fox hunting and mail carrying.

Reflecting on it, Lydia thought that perhaps it was not a thing happening now, that it had been going on all along, too slowly developed for Barton to notice. At first, she thought that Duny Gene's behavior had gone sour after Wart died, or perhaps when Maudie Snowdon ran off to California with that Sparks man. But the more she pondered it, the more she was certain it had always been there. Even as a child, he had been largely unsmiling. When she scolded him then, he would look at her with that expressionless stare, without recognition, without passion of any kind—certainly never any hurt—regarding her as though she were a fence post or a cloud of dust.

It was difficult to pinpoint. Duny Gene was not disrespectful. He was not given to violent fits of temper, or at least when he was, he controlled them so well they went unnoticed. He would engage in conversation when someone else initiated it, but more and more shortly, as though impatient to be off alone with his own thinking. There was something stand-offish and queer about him.

When they had moved from Fort Smith, one of her prized possessions had been the upright grand piano her father had bought her when she entered high school. It sat now in the place of honor in one corner of the living room. Wherever she placed it, that was the place of honor. She had become an accomplished player. When she was alone, she sat at the instrument for hours, chording the hymns she sometimes played at the Methodist church choir practices while Mona

Stayborn instructed the singers, or the sharp, staccato marches she played for the Eastern Star drills. Or sometimes the Gilbert and Sullivan tunes from sheet music that she still regularly bought at a music store on Garrison Avenue in Fort Smith.

She could play by ear, too. She could hear a song on the radio, one that particularly suited her mood, and the next day would find the right key, pick out the melody, and after only a few tries have the tune sounding through the house as though she had been playing ragtime and jazz all her life. She could improvise, too, sometimes in a rather stilted and restrained way, but improvise just the same. The simple chord progressions of most popular music of that time made such things easy for anyone as familiar with the keyboard as she.

Neither Barton nor Duny Gene was aware of much of this because all of what she played when they were around was straight from a sheet of music or a Methodist hymnal. And had they known, there would have been little recognition of her talent because both of them had what was called by musicians a tin ear. Even in church, with the congregation standing and singing one of the old hymns, Barton's lips were always seen to move, but no one had ever heard a true note issue from them. Duny Gene didn't even bother to move his lips.

Her playing became a part of her agony, a cherished thing unshared with these two strange men with whom she lived, and neither of whom she understood or was sure she even loved, yet who were by now so much a part of her that she had begun to find her trips to Fort Smith more and more unsatisfying, because she was then away from them.

By the spring of 1933, Lydia began to try sharing in their lives when she could. It was a change, one of which she was sure they were acutely aware and a little uncomfortable with, but she was determined to establish herself in their world. They had no idea why, nor for that matter did she. But she felt compelled.

It was a warm June evening that year when all of the Pays went to the depot to watch the train come in, and there were more than a few surprised glances from other Weedy Roughers who could not remember ever having seen Lydia here to greet Number Six. Ladies wondered what she was doing in town, and this not even meeting night at Eastern Star. The fox hunters wondered if Barton would get away for the race planned that night.

Tooth Snowdon walked over and took off his hat and discussed early turnips. Homer Gage stopped a moment to remind Barton that he should get his Ford into the garage for an oil change. Joe Sanford and his wife visited for a while, and Joe invited them to the ice-cream parlor after train time. He said he had some nice fresh bananas for splits.

Lydia was amazed as she watched kids putting pennies on the track. She allowed that such a thing could derail the engine. Barton said it never had, that they'd been putting pennies on the track since Frisco first appeared in the Rough. Duny Gene placed a penny on the near track, too, a thing he had not done in many years.

When the train arrived, the engine and cars hurtling past with brakes screaming, Lydia drew back and held her hat on her head to keep it from being blown off. That evening, nobody arrived, nor did anyone get on, so they had to be content with watching mail and baggage being unloaded. When the train pulled away, Duny Gene got his flattened penny, allowed it to cool in his hand for a moment, and handed it to his mother.

"You could get a hole punched in it and wear it on a chain around your neck," Barton said.

"Yeah, and turn your skin green," Duny Gene said.

"It's a nice token anyway," Lydia said. "It doesn't look much like a penny anymore, does it?"

Duny Gene said nothing, thinking of the time he had given such a penny to Maudie Snowdon on this very platform.

They went to the ice-cream parlor, Barton holding Lydia's arm and Duny Gene walking on the other side. Joe Sanford was pushing his splits because his bananas were beginning to go black on him, but Lydia ordered a strawberry sundae and the other two followed suit. Neither Barton nor Duny Gene liked bananas.

There were a number of people in the place, sitting on the wire-leg chairs around the little marble-topped tables. In the center of each table was a napkin dispenser. Lydia used a number of napkins, daubing at her lips daintily. Duny Gene bent over his ice cream and finished it in a few gulps. Lydia's eyes turned to the old piano in one corner, the key cover down and dust-coated. No one could recall ever hearing anyone play the thing, but Joe Sanford kept it because he said it added some class to his place.

The fox race had been mentioned earlier, and now Barton was reluctant to bring it up again. He looked a little stunned when Lydia asked him when the hunt was supposed to begin. In a moment of panic, he thought she was going to ask if she might go along.

"They'll be taking the dogs out soon," he said.

"I suppose your dog is going to run?"

He tried to detect the usual rancor in her voice when she mentioned the dog, but failed.

"Dixie? Yes. She'll be there, right at the head of the pack again."

"I'm going to the car," Duny Gene said, rising. "I'll drop by the post office, see if the mail's made up yet."

"Had you planned using the car tonight?" Barton asked. Lydia had to swallow her rage. Who does he think owns that car, him or the boy? she thought.

"No, I didn't have any plans."

"Well, you want to come with me? Ike said he'll set the dogs loose out around Devil's Mountain. Says there's a couple grays out there, good ones, haven't been run much this year."

He starts thinking fox and he talks just like some sticks man, Lydia thought, dropping his words and running it all together.

"I thought I might," Duny Gene said. "I'll be at the car."

They watched him go and then turned back to their sundaes. Barton's spoon scraping against the dish irritated her, but she said nothing.

"Shouldn't you be going, too?" she asked, startling him again.

"Well, I need to buy a few groceries, I guess. Some cheese maybe, and some corned beef."

"I suppose those others would starve if you didn't carry along a sack of food for them." She was sorry she'd said it.

"It don't amount to much. But there's plenty of time."

"You go ahead. I'll walk home. I'd like a little walk, it's so nice this evening."

"Well, if you think that's all right," Barton said, on very uncertain ground.

"Go ahead. I may have another sundae."

"I thought you weren't hungry."

"I might try one with the pecans," she said.

Barton rose, still unsure of what was happening, and with a mumbled word turned and walked out. He was so trained to respond to her whims that he could make no argument, even had he wanted to, which he didn't.

Lydia watched him through the screen door, and then her eyes turned to the piano again. She had a sudden urge to walk over there and play the dusty old thing. But she quickly controlled any such foolishness.

Joe Sanford walked from behind the counter, acting a little startled, too, because Lydia Pay had never sat alone in his ice-cream parlor.

"Would you like anything else, Miz Lydia?" he asked.

"No, thank you," she said, dabbing her mouth with her third paper napkin. "It was very good. Are you going to the fox hunt tonight?"

"Well, I reckoned I might slip out after a while, yes ma'am," Joe said, more flustered than ever.

"How nice," Lydia said, and rose and walked to the door, leaving him standing there gaping.

It was growing darker on the street. Barton's car was nowhere in sight. They didn't lose any time about getting away, she thought, with a touch of bitterness.

She walked along the street to the now deserted depot platform, crossed the tracks where the street did, and went to the outside stairs at Esta Stayborn's store. She mounted the steps slowly, opening her purse and taking out the lodge-hall key.

The meeting room was in gloomy shadow, and she started to switch on a light, but changed her mind. She walked slowly around the familiar room, touching the tables that stood at each point of the star. At last, she found herself at the Worthy Matron's lectern. She reached up and touched her gavel lying there. She looked at the piano in one corner and moved to it, lifting the cover and fingering the keys, but not with enough pressure to make any sound.

She slipped off her hat and pulled back the stool and sat down. At first she played softly, remembered marches and snatches of an old hymn or two. She paused and looked from one of the windows, out into the street, seeing the gray depot with the lettered sign WEEDY ROUGH.

Her fingers strayed over the keys, and she chorded randomly for a moment and then played "Among My Souvenirs." She played it a second time, much louder, the notes coming boldly now and shaking through the empty and darkened hall.

Abruptly, she stopped, lowered the cover, replaced her hat, retrieved her purse from the floor, and rose from the stool. She did not bother to push it back under the keyboard but turned and walked through the room and down the stairs. On the street, there was still a little light, and she saw Esta Stayborn, locking his store for the night. He glanced at her and touched his cap.

"Evenin' Miz Lydia," he said. "I thought that might be you up there playin'."

"Yes," she said, but nothing more, and walked quickly across the street and the tracks. As she went up the East Mountain road, she was aware of the spring night sounds starting around her—the cicadas and tree frogs and the inevitable dog barking on some far ridge. The evening star was a pinpoint of diamond light in the western sky. She could hear behind her the slamming of the screen door at the beer hall.

She moved up the familiar yard steps, onto the porch, and into her living room. She sat on the sofa, her hat still on, her purse still in her hand. She sat there a long time, in the dark, fingering the Eastern Star pin on her blouse.

·12·

ARLENE KRUPPMAN HEARD ABOUT THE AF-
fair with the shotgun and her old man, but only
indirectly. She no longer lived with her father and
Archer in the West Mountain house, and since she'd
left, it had begun to go to seed. Weeds grew up
around the building and screens were falling off windows and empty beer bottles were scattered in the
backyard around the old wrecked cars that Archer
spent most of his time tinkering with—when he wasn't
drunk at the beer hall.

There had been no tears at her leaving. From the
moment her mother died, when Arlene was ten years
old, she had thought of little else but getting away,
out of reach and hearing of that crew. The old man
treated her like dirt, and after Mrs. Kruppman died—
some said she was tired of putting up with her
menfolk—there was no one to defend her. Sometimes there were beatings, and the boys harassed her
constantly without fear of discipline from the old
man. They were a trio of sons of bitches, as Arlene
had known most of her life.

So when the job at Sycamore Lodge opened up,
Arlene took it gladly, almost frantically. And now
she spent her summers working in the dining room
along with other town girls. In winter, she stayed on
with the woman who cooked and owned a part inter-

est in the place—Parkins Muller owned the other part—acting as caretaker without pay, only for her food and lodging, keeping up the place, painting and waxing and checking all the cottages to see that possums or squirrels had not burrowed in to chew up the bedding.

Sycamore Lodge was the last of the summer resort hotels for the Texas Trade. All the others had gone bust. It wasn't the Depression, because most of the summer vacationers were little affected by hard times. It was lack of interest. The young people who were well enough fixed to take summer vacations wanted things more modern than Weedy Rough could offer. So they were going to places like Florida or Canada, posh places with heated swimming pools, big bands, and snails on the menu.

As a result, most of the Texas Trade now was old people. There were few of the hell raisers who had once roamed the hills in their Stutz Torpedos and Pierce-Arrow Runabouts, swilling fake gin and yelling "twenty-three skidoo" as they swept past local girls on the road, leaving them in a cloud of dust. Now it was more the quiet set, who drove big Chryslers and Caddies, some of the men wearing golf shoes and plaid socks, and the ladies with half-length, dark coats with fox fur collars, even in summer.

Some brought along drivers for their cars, and they wore caps like policemen, and some brought housemaids to cater to their whims and eccentricities. But most of them depended on Arlene for the little things, for which they could well afford to tip, and handsomely.

Sycamore stood on a long ridge east of the federal highway. A single road led up to it, branching off the highway at the baseball diamond. The lodge itself was a large rock structure with a reception room and lounge, a ballroom, a dining room, kitchen, and rooms in the basement for the hired help, who lived in during the summer. The road wound past the lodge and on along the ridge, where the cottages were scattered among the oak and wild cherry. These were mostly owned by Texas people, who came back to the same one every year. Now, about half of them stood empty during the tourist season.

At the end of the line of cottages was a golf course. Here, the Texans played the game that a few Roughers found fascinating, but most thought foolish. Once, in 1928, a barnstorming pilot had landed his biplane there and the whole town gathered to look at it, touch it, marvel at how the flimsy thing held together. But none of them paid the dollar for a ride. Tooth Snowdon said the thing didn't weigh any more than his mule colt and wasn't half as tough.

But most generally, Weedy Roughers stayed away from Sycamore. It was a little hilltop world, self-contained and aloof. That suited Arlene. She liked the people who came, and they liked her.

Sometimes they took Arlene with them when they went slumming at Tip Top Tavern, to see how the unruly hill-folk set lived. Or sometimes she went with them into town to watch Number Six arrive in the evening. She made little picnic lunches for them when they wanted to roam the wooded perimeter of the links.

They gave her presents, like a red silk ribbon for her golden hair that she wore now in a pageboy bob, or a pair of kid gloves. Some of the ladies gave her articles of intimate clothing with a Dallas marking. Nobody tried to pat her fanny when she was waiting tables and she was never asked to one of the cottages by any of the male guests when their wives had driven to Fayetteville for a matinee moving-picture show.

There had initially been a little problem with the caddies. These were local boys, much younger than

Arlene, who often came to the lodge after a day of chasing balls into the timber off the narrow fairways, hoping for a sandwich of strawberry preserves on the good homemade bread served at Sycamore. They tried to feel her legs as she passed, but she usually managed to avoid their clumsy attempts. But once, one of Olie Merton's boys had made contact, and she slapped him so hard he carried the mark of her hand on his face for two days.

The guests held dances in the ballroom, and Arlene served them finger-sized deviled ham sandwiches. They played bridge there, too, and she would bring them coffee and pineapple upside-down cake about nine o'clock, just a short time before the games broke up.

Everyone thought she was a wonderful girl. She smiled all the time, and she was pretty. A bit skinny, but pretty just the same. They called her by her first name, and each of them hugged her when it was time for the summer vacation to end.

Arlene didn't date Weedy Rough boys now—partly because her only free time was usually in the afternoons, when she would go along the slopes below the lodge hunting huckleberries or wild flowers for the dining-room tables, and partly because nothing much had changed since her high school days. Nobody ever asked her. She was lonely for her own kind—exclusive of her old man and the brothers—but it was a satisfied kind of loneliness.

She had worked at Sycamore for two years when Duny Gene Pay bearded her father with the twelve-gauge. Too bad he didn't pull the trigger, Arlene thought.

Duny Gene was in her mind a great deal. She'd seen him a few times at the Frisco depot, where he had acted cool toward her, speaking only enough to be civil, and she had seen him twice at Tip Top

Tavern during the past summer, when he'd been drinking too much. They had danced, she struggling around the floor trying to avoid being stepped on and not sure he was sober enough to realize who she was, because he never called her name. When she thought about it, she could not recall Duny Gene ever calling her name.

Arlene thought a lot about that night under Mona Stayborn's rhododendrons. Duny Gene had never once suggested since that such a thing happen again, by word or glance or gesture. She had known from the first it had been a disappointment to him, without his ever saying anything. And she was convinced that it was her fault.

She hadn't wanted it to be that way. She had wanted it to be fine and glorious and even better than was hinted at in *True Romance* magazine. But it hadn't been. Maybe because she had been as new to such a thing as Duny Gene.

But for Arlene, there had been at least one time before, when she was fourteen, and maybe part of the failure was because her first time had been a horrible experience with her brother Archer.

And so she knew what Archer represented, and she thought she knew what Duny Gene represented, too. The old man and Pug and Archer, all of them sons of bitches, she thought, and not fit to live in the same world with Duny Gene Pay.

If business in the summer resort lodges had all but disappeared, trade at the many tourist cabins that had sprung up along the highway after it was paved never got started at all.

These were simple, often tacky little places meant to house passing folk who found themselves in the hills at nightfall. Unlike the former Texas Trade resorts—and unlike Sycamore Lodge still—these were for transient, night-by-night guests. But the kinds of people who normally billeted in such spots were not on the road much now, and if they were, they could not afford the six bits for a night's lodging. They simply pulled off onto the roadside shoulder and slept in their cars or on the ground.

The Depression killed most of the roadside tourist courts in the hills, leaving them falling into decay before they had a chance. But a few were tough enough to survive.

The Ridge View Tourist Camp sprawled among the jack oaks and gum trees alongside the federal highway about six miles south of Weedy Rough. It was a place where the Ozarks made their last wild scramble of canyons and ridges before dropping off into the valley of the Arkansas River.

There was a main building, as always, with signs claiming SCREENED WINDOWS, CABINS, GROCERIES, AND ICE-COLD POP, RUNNING WATER. A tank on somewhat crooked stilts reared up behind the place to add credence to the last. The pipe leading to the ground was wrapped in burlap to avoid freezing in cold weather.

Running back into the trees, away from the highway, was a twisting gravel road or driveway. Here, there were log cabins, designed to look rustic. Each had its own name. Oak Ridge Haven . . . Bide-A-Spell . . . Traveler's Rest. The last and most pretentious of these was called Mountain Manor. It was nothing more than two of the smaller cabins stuck together with a connecting door between. Behind it, the ground dropped off into a wooded and tangled hollow, and beyond that the hills stretched away to the horizon in the east, blue and gray and translucent.

Some of the far mountains had rimrocks and flat-tops, like buttes in the West. But here, unlike those arid plateaus, the rimrock was crowded close at the base and crowned across the top with hardwood jungle green.

Two cars were parked beside Mountain Manor that August afternoon: one was a 1928 tan Packard touring car with top down, the double strips of chrome bumper and the shiny radiator cap—with a thermometer glassed inside—patterned with sunlight filtered through the overhanging leaves; the other car stood like a square packing crate with windows, a blue Studebaker, the spare-tire cover with a red Texaco star decal. Both cars bore Texas plates.

It was hot, almost ninety-five. A breath of breeze from the south did little more than stir the heat. From inside Mountain Manor an electric fan droned, and in one of the rooms a radio was playing soft music, an afternoon dance concert from some hotel lobby in New Orleans.

There were three people in this room. Lounging on the bed in a litter of motion-picture magazines was a young woman. She was about thirty, but it would have been difficult to guess her age. Her face had a hardness that very nearly negated the soft, full curve of her rouged lips and her large, heavily penciled eyes.

Her hair was shoulder-length and bleached so constantly it looked lifeless as a drugstore mop, snow-white and metallic. She was wearing spike-heel pumps, a short silk slip, and orange step-ins. Her hose were rolled halfway up her thighs. Her legs were very shapely and her knees were dimpled.

As she leafed through *Photoplay* magazine, she chewed gum rapidly, her lips parted. It made a moist little popping sound.

A man was sitting at the only table, wearing an undershirt and nothing more. The skin of his face looked like faded leather, as though he had once worked all day in the sun but now was washing out the color in the shade of poolrooms and cabins like this one. His hair was dark, cut close around the ears but long on top, and long across his shoulders and along the backs of his hands. He flipped out cards one at a time, playing solitaire, the aces at the top of the table lying near a .45 Colt automatic.

A tall, younger man was at the dresser, peering into the round mirror, combing his straw-colored hair. He could not control a cowlick at the back and finally gave it up and pulled on a woolen cap with a snap-down bill. He arranged it jauntily over his left eye. Below the eye, a long brutal scar ran across his cheek. He wore a loosely fitting seersucker suit and black-and-white shoes, wing-tipped. On the dresser before him lay a second army automatic, a large revolver, and a Thompson submachine gun.

"I reckon I'll take a run in, Lester," the man with the scar said.

"You gonna see that friend of yours?" Lester asked.

"Yeah, I'm gonna see him, and take another look at that ole bank."

"Don't fuck anything up."

"Bring your friend out to visit us. We can have a picnic," the woman said from the bed, still looking at her movie-star pictures.

"Yeah, if you want to, kid. Bring him on out," Lester said. "Maybe Ruby'll find herself a hillbilly stud."

"Kiss my ass," Ruby said, but without any heat.

"I hear these hillbillies are real studs," Lester said. "Are they all like you, kid?"

"This one ain't," the tall man said. "He's a real keen guy."

"What's keen got to do with it?" Ruby asked, and laughed a harsh little cackle.

"You better leave that thing here," Lester said, waving a hand.

"Sure," the tall man said, and pulled a .38 Savage automatic from beneath his seersucker coat and dropped it on the table beside Lester's Colt. "But ain't nobody in that little ole town gonna say anythin' about a man with a pistol."

"Leave it anyway. I don't want you fuckin' it up."

"Yeah, well, see ya."

The tall man went out and the screen door slammed behind him. They heard the Studebaker starter grind and the engine take hold and then go into gear. They heard the car back into the driveway, then a clatter of gears as it went into low. When the car passed before the cabin on the way to the highway, a fine powder of dust drifted through the screen door.

"I wanna go to one of them creeks around here he's been tellin' about," Ruby said. "Have a little picnic and go swimmin'."

"If that's what you want."

"I can go up front and get some baloney and a few bottles of pop."

"If that's what you want. See if that old geezer's got some sardines, too. I like them."

"And some canned beans. We can have a picnic and a little swim." Ruby's gum popped furiously.

"Yeah, well you better get some clothes on."

She snorted. "Hell, I thought I'd just traipse up there like this. Get that old man randy as a goat. I wonder they got any goose liver."

"These hicks ain't ever heard of goose liver," Lester said.

Ruby slid off the bed, her hips slithering. Her spike heels snapped across the floor. As she passed Lester, she bent and slid a hand down his belly below the undershirt.

"Speakin' of makin' somebody randy," he said, but he sat motionless, unaffected, flipping out the cards, a few of them sliding across the table to lodge against one or the other of the two pistols.

When he first saw Hoadie Renkin, Duny Gene Pay did not recognize him. The face was much the same, except for the scar down the left cheek. But the seersucker suit and the winter cap with the blond hair splayed out all around was a getup seldom seen there, and certainly not to be associated with Hoadie Renkin. Worst of all were the wing-tip shoes. Everything about him was out of place and awkward in the Frisco tie yard of Weedy Rough among the mules and the overalled timber sellers and a Rhode Island Red rooster that had wandered down from some coop on Academy Heights to strut for a while in town.

Hoadie came into the yard leaving the blue Studebaker parked across the street at the bank, grinning and strutting a little himself. Duny Gene stood with the grading hammer hanging from his hand, mouth gaped open, staring until Hoadie was within a few feet of him.

"Well, I'll be damned," Duny Gene said.

Duny Gene took an uncertain step toward Hoadie, and then Hoadie's hand was out and Duny Gene took it. There was a strangeness in the feel of it, and then Duny Gene knew what it was—the flesh of Hoadie's hands was soft and mushy, and Duny Gene could feel the bones in Hoadie's fingers like lead pencils with a covering of putty.

"You ole mulehead you," Hoadie laughed. "What the hell you doin'?"

"Where'd you come from? What's it been, two years?"

"More like three. You runnin' this shebang now?"

Hoadie looked around the tie yard and at the tim-

ber cutters standing a little distance off, staring. A
few of them knew Ike Renkin and they were trying to
associate in their minds that old hill farmer and this
dude, wearing two-colored shoes and a store suit.

"I am while my folks are gone," Duny Gene said.
"They're visitin' down Fort Smith for a few days."

"Don't have to worry about your ma runnin' my
ass off then, do we?"

They both laughed, shaking their heads and remembering. It was hard to find anything else to say,
and they laughed again, nervously, shuffling their
feet like boxers. Hoadie took off his cap, swept a
hand back through his hair, and repositioned the cap,
slanted over his left eye.

"Damn!" Duny Gene said. "Where'd you get that
suit of clothes and those shoes? You a scissor
salesman?"

"Hell, kid, I'm in the investment business. Other
people's. See that blue Studebaker? Paid for in cash.
Ain't but four thousand miles on it, either."

"You found a way to feed on hard times, then?"

"Like a hog at the trough."

"Where you been all this time?"

"Out in the world, kid. A cake eater, that's me.
Good stuff all around, and me wallowin' in it."

"You're crazy as ever," Duny Gene said.

"I been in Texas and Baton Rouge and Oklahoma.
Doin' a lot of whoopee."

"Yeah, I'll bet."

There was another painful lull, then Hoadie looked
at the timber cutters and waved a hand casually. A
few of them nodded slightly, but their faces remained
stolid.

"You just get in?"

"Naw," Hoadie said. "I been out at a tourist
cabin on the mountain couple days."

"You seen your pap?"

"Not yet. I might run out there in a day or so. I thought maybe he'd be in here, sellin' timber."

"He don't come much anymore," Duny Gene said. "He gets to a fox race sometimes, but that's about all he gets out."

Hoadie's face clouded, the grin fading. He looked up East Mountain toward the goat pasture.

"Yeah. Pap's pretty old now, and all banged up, I reckon. But I guess he'd fox-race if he had to crawl."

"Squib and Audie bring in a load of posts now and then."

"Yeah." Hoadie continued to stare up East Mountain. "Parkins Muller still got them goats?"

"Yeah. He's got a bigger herd than ever."

"You ever get another yard dog?"

"No." Duny Gene wondered why Hoadie would think of Wart in the same breath with Parkins Muller, wondered if maybe all this time Hoadie had known what had happened to the dog. But then he knew that wasn't it when Hoadie spoke again.

"You oughta get another dog to chase them goats," and Hoadie was grinning once more. "God, this town is a dismal little place, ain't it? I don't see how you put up with it. How long you gonna be workin'?"

"Couple more wagons to unload is all. I don't expect any more this late in the day."

"All right. Look, you finish up here, I'll go to Violet Sims, get some whiskey. You still drink whiskey?"

"Or anything else I can get."

"Violet still in business?"

"Sure. There's a beer hall now, but I guess that don't bother her trade."

"She's gettin' a little old for a whore, though, ain't she?"

"Beats me."

"Yeah, I know," Hoadie laughed. "That still ain't

your department, is it? Well, it's mine. Listen, I'll go up, see old Violet, get some hootch. She'll get a big thrill, seein' me back. Then I'll come by, pick you up. Wanna take you out to the cabin, meet some folks I got with me.''

As he watched Hoadie walk away, past the parked Studebaker and around the bank and up the hill behind to Violet Sims's house, Duny Gene thought, Hell! He's never been in Violet Sims's place before. She probably won't even know who he is, she'll likely take him for some scissor salesman, too.

"All right," he shouted. "Let's get 'em off the wagons. Don't bother to stack 'em, I'll grade 'em and make out your drafts for you. I'm in a hurry."

Duny Gene worked in a kind of feverish excitement, grading the ties as they were thrown off the wagons. Hoadie back! But different, even in those few moments talking with him. Another light in his eyes, another twist to his smile, another hardness to his talk.

As he slammed the hammer into the butt of each tie, Duny Gene's mind worked back over some of the old times.

The night he had slipped from the house and met Hoadie and they had sat in one of Parkins Muller's goat sheds, drinking a pint of home brew Hoadie had hijacked from his old man's supply, and the next morning almost throwing up trying to get down a batch of Lydia's biscuits and sausage.

And the Halloween he and Hoadie had overturned Homer Gage's outside toilet, and Homer inside, screaming and bellowing as they ran back into the woods along the slopes of West Mountain.

The bean-flip fight with one of Olie Merton's boys, when they used the drainage ditches on either side of the cut into the tunnel as trenches.

And the squirrels they'd killed, and some of these

skinned on the spot and roasted over hickory twigs. Then eating the dark red meat, and the smell of smoke and hot fur and fallen leaves all around them.

And the day in school when Hoadie goosed one of the Reed girls and she'd thought it was Donny Sparks and knocked hell out of him with her fist.

But now it was all changed, not kids anymore but men, and Hoadie looking like a rumpled Chesterfield cigarette advertisement hung up beside the road, in his seersucker suit and wing-tip shoes. Nothing the same, Duny Gene thought, slamming home the hammer. Not Hoadie's hands, gone soft from lack of manual labor while his own had hardened here in the tie yard. Even the grin different somehow, looking pasted on, misplaced in a long bony face hard and stony as Parkins Muller's.

Well, he thought, maybe that's just the scar.

Barton and Lydia had taken the train to Fort Smith, leaving the car for Duny Gene. They wouldn't be home until the middle of the next week, and it was only Friday now. So there was time for one hell of a party, Duny Gene figured, and he wasn't sure he'd get back to the tie yard by Monday once he and Hoadie and Hoadie's friends started on the whiskey. So he left a note tacked to the door of the yard shack.

> *If you bring in timber and nobody here, put your mark on it and you'll get your draft sometime next week when you're back in town again. Gone to Lee's Creek fishing.*
>
> *—Duny Gene Pay*

He gave no thought to the certainty that a few timber cutters bringing in ties and posts while he was gone would be mad as hell, having to make an extra trip to town for their money.

Hoadie dropped Duny Gene off at the Pay house, and he followed the Studebaker out the highway to the cabin in his father's Ford. He wasn't sure why he wanted to take his own car, but part of it was that he needed to show Hoadie he had an automobile now, too, whenever he wanted it, although it wasn't anything like as good as a Studebaker. In fact, parked under the trees at Mountain Manor, the Model A looked a little battered, rusty and forlorn beside the other two cars, like a destitute relative at a family reunion.

Duny Gene liked Lester right off, and he was fascinated with the Thompson submachine gun, of course. When he saw it, he began to understand how these people made their living. It wasn't something that bothered him particularly. Lester showed him how the gun worked and he dry-fired it a few times, pressing the wide trigger and feeling the impact of the heavy bolt slamming forward. Lester said they'd take it on the picnic and shoot it, along with the handguns.

"You got an arsenal here," Duny Gene said, with some overtone of admiration in his voice.

"Yeah, but the chopper ain't for work," Hoadie said. "Lester got it from a guy in Mexico. He just keeps it for a play-pretty. I think he sleeps with it."

"It ain't that pretty," Lester said, and they laughed.

But if Lester was all right, Duny Gene wasn't so sure about Ruby. When they arrived at the cabin, she had returned from the store-office out front with the picnic grub and was back in her bedroom uniform—the slip and rolled hose and orange step-ins. It made Duny Gene wildly uncomfortable looking at her. And she kept coming up and feeling him, breathing on his neck and walling her eyes while he was fiddling with the machine gun. She touched his hair once.

"God, kid, you got nice black hair," she said,

sounding like she was panting. "Why you put all that grease on it?"

"Leave him alone, Ruby, for Christ sake," Lester said.

"Piss on you, Lester. I ain't hurtin' him. Hey kid, how you like this?" She fluffed out the ends of her dead-looking silver hair.

"It's okay," Duny Gene said.

"Remind you of somebody?"

"Aw, for Christ sake, Ruby," Lester said. She ignored him.

"Don't it look a little like Jean Harlow?"

"I guess so."

"It sure ought to. I work my butt off keepin' it this way."

She talks like a Frisco section hand, Duny Gene thought. Between Ruby and Lester, he'd never heard such swearing and obscenities. They seemed to pass off such words as easily as breathing, automatically. That made him uncomfortable, too. Especially to hear such things from a woman's mouth, and a pretty mouth at that. A few "God damns" were all right, but some of that other stuff was pure filth.

Hoadie had laid in a good supply of whiskey, enough to last the weekend, although it didn't matter because Violet Sims sold label whiskey on Sundays as well as any other day. They had a few drinks before loading up in the Packard for the picnic. Ruby brought a dress from the other room and slipped into it with Duny Gene watching. He'd never seen a woman putting on her dress. When Ruby lifted her arms, he could see patches of black hair and figured that was her natural color. Then Ruby smoothed her hose, running both hands up her thighs and smiling at Duny Gene as he stared at the dimples in her knees.

"I got dimples in other places, too," she said, and laughed.

Lester observed all of this, but remained unperturbed, even though Duny Gene supposed Ruby was his woman.

When they went out to the Packard, Duny Gene was surprised that Ruby got behind the wheel. He didn't know many women who drove cars. Mona Stayborn was about the extent of it, hauling her Sunday-school kids to the swimming hole in summer. But Ruby had been at it awhile, he figured. She moved the shift lever easily and without any racket from the gearbox, and generally she held only one hand on the wheel.

Duny Gene sat in back with Hoadie, the picnic sack and the guns at their feet on the floorboards. Once, after Ruby had skidded the Packard around one of the hairpin turns, he leaned forward and looked at the speedometer. They were going better than fifty miles an hour, faster than Duny Gene had ever traveled before.

They drove down into one of the deep hollows to a big hole on a stream called Frog Creek. There was a long gravel bar where the road forded the creek, and Ruby pulled the Packard under some sycamore trees.

The car was hardly stopped before she jumped out and ran down to the stream, kicking off her spike heels and peeling down her stockings. She waded in, holding up her dress high enough so they could see the orange step-ins.

The men took out the pistols and ammunition and were soon blasting away at spots on the trunks of trees nearby. Finally, Lester took out the submachine gun and snapped the drum magazine into place.

"She'll rise on you, if you don't get a good grip," he said. "Rises and kicks a little to the right, so she'll climb right up on you. Don't lay too much pressure on the trigger, so you can turn it loose when you want to. Some guys get on one of these and hang on for dear life and shoot the magazine dry, most of it goin' right straight up. You gotta show her who's boss. Get a good hold on that front pistol grip and lean into her a little.''

It all came as natural as walking to Duny Gene. The hard bounce of the heavy gun in his hands was as intoxicating as the whiskey. He let off a few bursts, blowing bark from trees.

"You got it, kid,'' Hoadie said, laughing. "I told you, Lester, this little son of a bitch can shoot anything that shoots.''

Duny Gene emptied the drum and Lester took the gun. It smelled of burning oil, and the barrel was smoking.

"Don't touch that bitch now, along the barrel,'' Lester said. "Burn right into you. I think we better let it go at that.''

"Yeah, some farmer around here's likely to think the Mexicans has come,'' Hoadie said.

They fired the pistols again, and two of them felt familiar in Duny Gene's hand. Just like the one his father had brought from the war, he told them.

"Bring it along next time we shoot,'' Lester said. "We can try all of 'em out.''

"One of them big automatics is like all the rest,'' Hoadie said.

"No they ain't. Each one's a little different. Each one's a little sweetie you got to get acquainted with before she'll come across for you.''

Duny Gene liked the way Lester talked. And he had this direct way of looking at people, like he was interested in them.

"Duny Gene, you handle a chopper good,'' Lester said. "You sure you never shot one before?''

"That's the first one I ever saw.''

"I told you,'' Hoadie said. "Son of a bitch can shoot anything.''

Lester called Ruby up from the creek then, and they spread a blanket on the gravel bar and made sandwiches. They ate the baloney and fingered sardines from a can, drinking lukewarm soda pop and chasing it with large belts of whiskey. Duny Gene thought it tasted as good as anything he'd ever eaten.

"This is nice, ain't it," Ruby said. "Come on somebody, let's go for a real swim."

She dashed off to the water again, and Duny Gene, drunk enough by now so that things were beginning to look a little crooked, watched with his mouth full of baloney and bread, staring as Ruby stood on the edge of the water and this time stripped down to the skin. She waded out into the middle of the creek and turned, the water coming just below her bare breasts. They flopped and bounced as she waved.

"Come on, you guys, let's all have a swim."

"Oh for Christ sake," Lester muttered, but he rose and went down the gravel bar and slipped off his clothes, too. Duny Gene watched Lester's naked ass disappear into the water as he waded out to the woman, and then the two of them splashed and hugged and ducked one another, like two Sunday-school kids. Ruby was squealing with laughter.

"Damn," Duny Gene said. "This kind of thing happen all the time?"

Hoadie was lying back against the trunk of a sycamore, his cap pulled over his eyes.

"Hell, it gets better'n this sometimes," he said. "Hand me one of them bottles."

Duny Gene didn't remember much of the rest of that day. It was dark when they drove back up the mountain to the highway and turned onto it toward the tourist cabins. When he got out of the car, Duny Gene threw up beside the running board, and he was vaguely aware of Ruby holding his head and stroking his belly.

"You're the best-lookin' boy I seen in a long time," he heard her say, and he threw up again.

She led him into the cabin, and his feet were not working too well. Lester was in the other room and Hoadie was on the bed in this room, face to the wall, already asleep. Duny Gene sagged onto the bed and Ruby started undressing him. Then he knew the lights were out and he lay back and could still feel her fingers groping around, fumbling with him. But he was to sick to give a damn.

Sometimes Duny Gene dreamed after he'd been drinking. Usually they were strange and confused dreams, with images he couldn't identify that were often large and formless, and even terrifying.

But on this night, his dream was concise and clear and almost touchable, recalling a time he knew so well in his memory that none of it woke him, and when it was done he slept on, without stirring in the bed beside Hoadie Renkin.

From his subconsciousness came the vision of a day long past, when he and Hoadie and one of the Walls boys had played hooky from school and were wandering in the wild hollows east of Naulty's Ridge, shooting at squirrels with their bean flips. They were in the deep woods, so far from any house or highway that the only noises were those made by their own feet moving through the dry husks of fallen leaves. Even the birds were still, as though observing some law of silence so powerful it took precedence over all others.

There were sharp outcrops of limestone bluff along either wall of this narrow valley. Sweet gum and shagbark hickory contested with the oaks up each slope, and beside the twisting, shallow stream in the hollow floor the sumac and honey locust grew thick and lush, somehow thriving in the shade of taller trees.

And as they moved beside the stream, they saw the wild dogs.

There were four of them, looking unlike any hound or yard dog they had ever seen. The dogs stood on a ledge of limestone above them, with cold yellow eyes, unmoving and making no sound.

It was devastating to wonder how long the dogs had been watching them as they came through the thick timber. Now, the boys stood rooted for a moment, returning the silent stare, holding their bean flips ready but each knowing that these were puny weapons against such targets.

Without a word, they moved cautiously away, though keeping their faces turned back so that, until they were lost in the timber, their eyes were locked with the dogs' eyes.

They had heard of wild dog packs in the hills, domestic breeds that had somehow wandered off into the woods and stayed there, feeding on rabbits or ground squirrels and sometimes preying on chicken coops of isolated farms. But they had never seen such dogs before, and until that moment none had really believed the stories they had heard.

And ever afterward, when Duny Gene stood on some high ridge and looked across the hazy blue distance of hills and timber, he wondered what might be hidden there. The far hollows and ridges and woods became the reflection of his own mind, because he often wondered what was hidden there, too. But he never spoke of it to anyone. Even mention of having seen the wild dogs came hard for him, because it was somehow sacred and personal and a part of his own inner self that was painful to reveal.

· 13 ·

"YOU GOTTA TAKE WHAT YOU WANT OUTA this life, that's all," Hoadie Renkin said.

He was driving the Studebaker along the federal highway, going toward Fayetteville. They had risen before the others for a ride in Hoadie's coupe. Getting Duny Gene out of bed and dressed had been no easy effort. Now they had traveled almost twenty miles, Hoadie talking all the way, and Duny Gene feeling as though he might throw up again. His face was gray-green and his eyes were bloodshot. His tongue tasted like a strip of horse blanket that had been on the horse a long time.

"I almost starved to death," Hoadie said. "Livin' in them hobo jungles and them Hoovervilles. You ought to see 'em. Shantytowns, made outa cardboard boxes and tin cans, and God, they stink! Men from all over, lookin' for work, tryin' to stay alive. I seen men from all them Yankee states, too. You can't understand a damned word some of 'em say."

Duny Gene held his face close to the open window, feeling the rush of wind, opening his mouth to catch some of it. A heavy gray cloud cover had rolled in from the west overnight. He thought he could smell rain.

"I hijacked many a garbage can," Hoadie continued. "In alleys behind cafés or sometimes at one of them swanky houses you find in big towns. But you had to get there early. You got to know when they'd throw out their scraps, because good garbage cans didn't last long. Mostly what you got was rotten turnips and moldy carrot tops, and stuff like that.''

Duny Gene retched and pushed his face farther out into the slipstream of air. Oh God, he thought, let him spill it all out, he's got it coming, after living all his life on that rocky hill farm and then going out to find a world of rotten turnips and moldy carrot tops. Let him spill it all out fast, before I puke again. Let him show off a little now, with this Studebaker and the Savage automatic and his wing-tip shoes. He ought to have at least that much coming to him.

''It was in Shreveport, in one of them shantytowns beside the railroad tracks. This spiffy-dressed guy comes along one day and parks his big Packard and starts jawin' with all the men, and we thought he was lookin' for men to work someplace. In a way, I guess he was,'' and Hoadie laughed.

''Lester?'' Duny Gene asked.

''Yeah. That's who it was. Ole Lester. He comes over to me after a while and we jaw. Then he says, 'You look like you might be a good man,' and I says, 'I guess I am, good as any other.' Hand me that bottle.''

Duny Gene passed across the quart bottle of rye and Hoadie pulled the cork with his teeth and held it between his fingers like a cigarette. With his head turned to one side so he could watch the road as he drank, he lifted the bottle to his mouth. The smell of the liquor made Duny Gene's stomach tighten dangerously.

''So anyway, he says, 'Come for a little ride.' And we got in the Packard and we drove along and he ast me if I was in trouble with the law anywheres? And I says, 'No.' And he says, 'Have you ever had your fingerprints made anywheres?' And I says, 'No.' And he says, 'Well, you're about to make yourself some money.' "

A dog ran across the road and Hoadie swore and yanked the steering wheel and the Studebaker swerved violently.

"Son of a bitch get his self killed," Hoadie said. "So we drove over into Texas and stopped at this fillin' station that was sort of out in the country. Lester handed me a pistol and we went in and that's all there was to it. Only made eleven dollars on that one, and a few cigarettes. But Lester wanted to see how I acted. I says, 'How you know I wouldn't shoot somebody?' And he says, 'I knew you wouldn't because there ain't no bullets in the gun.' But Lester had bullets in his," and Hoadie laughed again.

Hoadie took another drink and passed the bottle back to Duny Gene and lit a cigarette.

"Better take some of the hair of the dog," Hoadie said, but Duny Gene shook his head. "Makes you feel better.

"Well, anyway, after that it was a good thing all around. We went to Midland and picked up Ruby. We went all over, and I bought me this suit of clothes after we'd visited a few more places. Didn't stay long in one place. But that Texas is a big son of a bitch. We went all over 'er. I ain't gonna say too much, though, 'cause then if the law was to ast you somethin' you wouldn't know nothin'. Lester has taught me a lot about how the law works."

"Yeah, I guess he would," Duny Gene said. He thought about Hoadie being involved in some of those stick-ups he'd read about in the newspapers, even some where there had been shooting. It didn't affect him one way or the other. He thought, What the hell. He deserves all he can get.

"Lester says a man got to be careful in this business or he might get his head blowed off. But Lester, he's careful. And smart. But he drives too fast. He drives so fast it even scares Ruby, and it takes one helluva lot to scare her."

"Listen, can't we stop and get some breakfast and something cold to drink?" Duny Gene said. "My gut's on fire."

"Sure, we'll stop. In Fayetteville. It ain't far. You remember onct when your pap brought us to a ball game and we ate at that place close to the armory? You remember?"

"Castle Luncheonette. I been in there lots of times after a picture show."

"That's it. I wanna get me some chili. They got the best chili I ever ate."

"Chili?" Duny Gene asked incredulously. "For breakfast?"

"Hell, it ain't all that early in the day. Besides, I like chili any ole time."

The concrete ribbon of the highway twisted and turned gently here, the terrain becoming less rugged the farther north they drove. Fayetteville sat on the lift of a number of rounded hills, and they could see the high clock tower of the courthouse as they came up the valley. They drove into the town's streets and there were many other cars there, this being Saturday and people in from the country to do their shopping and visiting. They circled the square, around the red brick post office, and drove down a street called Smoky Row, the courthouse looming up directly in front of them.

Standing on the sidewalk before the yellow-brick-and-sandstone building was a man with a large hat and an equally large pistol showing at his belt.

"Look at that goddamned deputy sheriff," Hoadie said. "Lester's told me plenty about them bastards.

Standin' around protectin' the rich people and the banks.''

"Yeah, but from what I've heard nowadays, banks don't have all that much to protect.''

"Hell! There's still money in plenty banks. Take ole Parkins Muller. You ain't seen him go bust yet.''

Duny Gene couldn't argue with that.

Hoadie turned left and passed the courthouse, and then a narrow alley and a movie theater. A number of black men lounged there, eyes turning slowly to watch the Studebaker pass, the gears grinding as Hoadie shifted into second.

"You drive like hell, you know it?" Duny Gene said.

"I get 'er there.''

The Castle Luncheonette was on the far side of the theater, and Hoadie pulled over and parked and yanked on the emergency brake. They left the bottle under the seat. It was a long, narrow room inside, with no tables, only stools along a counter that ran the length of the place. They slipped onto the rotating stools and a fat man with a stained waist apron and chef's cap sauntered up and leaned on the counter from the far side.

"What'll it be, pardners?"

"Bowl a chili and a Coke," Hoadie said.

"Beans or no beans?"

"Beans.''

"How about you, pardner?"

"You got scrambled eggs?"

"I can do that. What to drink?"

"I guess I'll take a Coke, too. A cold one.''

Bottles of catsup and Tabasco sauce were lined up like soldiers on a shelf behind the back bar and griddle. The cook swirled his spatula in two eggs, breaking the yolks. He threw a thick chunk of light bread down beside the eggs, doused it with melted butter from a tin pitcher, and let it toast. The beans and chili came from a steam table under the counter. It all smelled greasy and hot and like a hamburger booth at a county fair.

They ate, and Duny Gene tried to avoid looking at Hoadie's chili. He managed to get down a few mouthfuls of egg and drink three bottles of Coke. When Hoadie finished, he wiped his mouth with the back of his hand, leaving a smear of red grease.

"Gimme some hamburgers to take," Hoadie said. "Put some fried onions on 'em."

"How many, pardner?"

" 'Bout four ought to do 'er." Hoadie grinned at Duny Gene. "I like hamburgers, even if they're a little cold."

While the hamburgers cooked, Duny Gene went to the glass door and watched the rain start.

"How much?" Hoadie asked.

"Chili a dime, eggs a dime, Cokes a nickel, burgers fifteen."

Hoadie dropped a silver dollar on the counter and it made a metallic ring. Going out to the sidewalk, they could see the large drops of rain making flower-shaped patterns on the concrete. The black men had moved under the theater marquee.

"Burrheads don't like gettin' wet, do they?" Hoadie said.

"Who the hell does," Duny Gene said. "I'm drivin' from here on."

"Sure, climb in."

Duny Gene drove back to the square, the rain falling harder now. The vacuum wiper made a little gulp each time it moved back and forth across the windshield. A few people were moving quickly along the sidewalks, and under a metal awning a line of men in overalls stood against the wall, splattering tobacco juice in the general direction of the gutter. A sign over them read POOL. Duny Gene pulled in to the curb.

The poolhall was in the basement of the building that housed an insurance company, a realtor, and the city administration offices. There were a half-dozen tables, only one in use. Duny Gene and Hoadie took cues from a wall rack and played a game of eight ball, Hoadie winning after only three shots.

"You had some practice at this," Duny Gene said.

The other men in the place watched them closely, because they were strangers here. They played another game and Hoadie bought two bottles of beer. It was icy cold and it felt good going down, and Duny Gene drank a second one. Hoadie won the next game, and the next. Altogether, Duny Gene drank four beers.

Back in the car, Duny Gene drove into the west end of town and they looked at all the houses with the big maple trees in front and cars parked beside the curbs. The streets glistened with the rain, and everything smelled fresh, like wet lettuce. Duny Gene was feeling a good deal better, and he took a drink from the rye bottle.

Soon, the houses came farther and farther apart, and then there was a marker indicating that Siloam Springs was twenty-two miles away, the Oklahoma border just beyond.

"Let's see what they got in Siloam Springs," Hoadie said.

The pavement ran out before they were outside the city limits, and the dirt road was already going a little mushy. They drove in silence, past groves of hickory and a few small apple orchards. I guess he's talked it all out, Duny Gene thought.

Ahead in the rain, they could see a Conoco station,

rimmed beside the road in a stockade of white oak trees. Hoadie leaned over and looked at the gas level on the dash gauge.

"Better pull in, get some gas," he said.

The attendant appeared, a teen-age boy in oily coveralls and a railroader's cap. Hoadie got out and moved to the back of the car.

"Howdy," the boy said.

"Fill it up," Hoadie said. Duny Gene sat in the car, slumped behind the wheel. He took another sip from the bottle.

"Texas plates, huh?"

"Yeah, that's it. You had a good business today?"

"Hell no. Ever'body gets their gas in town, 'cause it's a penny a gallon cheaper," the boy said. "What part a Texas?"

"Down around Midland," Hoadie said. "You know who that is in the car?"

The kid gawked through the rear window and shook his head.

"I don't reckon so."

"That's Pretty Boy Floyd," Hoadie said. "I'm takin' him to see his ma, over Salisaw."

The kid gulped.

"It is?" the kid said.

"Pretty Boy Floyd, that's who it is," Hoadie said. "You've heerd of him, I guess."

The kid sloshed gas onto the ground, running the tank over, and he had trouble getting the nozzle of the hose back into its slot in the pump. Hoadie handed him two dollar bills.

"That enough?"

"Yes sir."

Hoadie walked around the car and got in, grinning. He winked at Duny Gene.

"You crazy bastard, why'd you tell him that?"

"Just for the hell of it," Hoadie said, and they both laughed.

Duny Gene pulled out into the road, headed for Siloam Springs, leaving the kid in the railroader's hat standing in the rain gawking. Hoadie looked back once and laughed again, and then he took the automatic from his belt and wiped it with the tail of his coat.

"Let's have a drink," Duny Gene said.

The road was getting sticky. Duny Gene tried to stay out of the old ruts, but without much success. The Studebaker began to fishtail.

"Son of a bitch is gettin' gummy. I reckon we'd best turn around."

"That suits me," Duny Gene said. "I wanna go by the post office at home, see if there's mail. We can stop and pick up Daddy's pistol. It might clear off after while and we could go down to Frog and shoot some more."

"Yeah, well, get this damned thing turned around."

But it was too late. The Studebaker hit a quagmire and the rear wheels spun as Duny Gene gunned it.

"Shit!" he said.

"Lemme have a look," Hoadie said. This time, before he stepped out into the rain, he took the automatic from his belt and slid it under the seat. He splashed around in the mud, bending down to look at the rear wheels. When he got back in the car, the seersucker coat was plastered to his shoulders.

"To hell with it," he said. "We'll just set here and wait 'er out, and when it's finished we'll find some farmer with a mule."

They opened the sack of cold hamburgers and began eating, and the car was filled with the smell of fried onions. They passed the bottle back and forth. The rain beat steadily on the roof of the car, and they were beginning to get a little drunk.

That's when the carload of deputy sheriffs found them.

In the Washington County courthouse, His Honor Judge Orvil Pitt was arraigning various citizens who had offended the dignity and decency of the state of Arkansas. The crestfallen hog stealers and knife fighters sat about the pit of the courtroom with their lawyers—if they had any—awaiting their turn before the bench.

It was a large room, built in the style popular for such functions at about the turn of the century. There was a downstairs gallery and a balcony for the curious, separated by a wooden railing at the lower level from the official arena, much like fences at cattle-auction barns. In the pit were the standard number of tables and chairs for the contestants and court personnel. The jury box sat to one side under high arched windows of many panes, each of which was in need of a dose of soap and elbow grease. Extending across the front of the room was the bench itself, its top lifting above all else in the room. The decor was massive Arkansas white oak. Over it all were the hanging chandeliers with bare light bulbs, not a few of which were burned out.

Judge Pitt glared down from his perch like a defeathered eagle, his bald head gleaming in the light. Leaning forward in his black robe, elbows on the bench before him, he gave the appearance of great stature when actually he was a rather frail and bony man. The robe sagged a little at the neck, revealing a collarless shirt fastened with a large mother-of-pearl button.

Beside him on the floor, and hidden from the view of those in the courtroom, was a large cuspidor, of which he availed himself frequently. He was clean-shaven, but occasionally when he waited too long to spit, a fine dribble of juice ran from the corners of his mouth down his chin, making it look as though he had begun to cultivate a Fu Manchu beard.

It was Judge Pitt's fourth term on the circuit-court bench, and he knew what he was about, confident and strident and taking no nonsense from anyone in his courtroom, except from time to time the prosecuting attorney, whom he called by first name even during the course of a trial.

As each supplicant stood before him this day, he did his work quickly and decisively. This was a chore he despised and would have done with as soon as possible. After each consultation and decision on bail, the men who had stood for only a brief moment before him were hustled off to the county jail by a deputy. It was Monday, and some of the weekend offenders were in serious trouble; few of them made any bail, looking forward to a couple more days where they would be fed at county expense and kept out of the wet.

In the midst of setting bail for a young man accused of stealing the spare tire off an automobile parked on the square, Judge Pitt glanced at the door and stopped talking. He lowered his head and glared over the tops of his steel-rimmed glasses. A deputy sheriff had just brought in Duny Gene Pay and Hoadie Renkin.

"Are those the boys you caught on the Siloam Springs road Saturday?"

"Yes, Your Honor."

"Well, don't bring 'em in here. I don't want 'em in here. Take 'em to chambers and stay with 'em until I get there. I'll be along in a minute. I don't want 'em in here."

The judge's chambers overlooked Smoky Row, from a kind of bay-window arrangement. The room was crowded with bookshelves and legal volumes, many of which had collected considerable dust. There was a large desk and some chairs, and the deputy motioned the boys to take a seat near a window. He stood back near the door, one foot propped against the wall behind him, his nickel-plated revolver angled out at the hip like a moving-picture cowboy's.

Duny Gene and Hoadie stared from the window, streaked by the rain that was still coming down. But in the west, the sky was brightening, a sure sign that the rain was about to pass. They looked rumpled and dirty, having slept in the jail's drunk tank for two nights. Duny Gene took a black rubber comb from his pocket and, throwing his cap on the windowsill, got his hair into shape. Most of the brilliantine had washed out, but it was still blue-black.

"You wanna use this?" he asked, holding out the comb.

"Naw. It don't do much good with this hair I got," Hoadie said.

"Well, at least take off your cap before that judge gets in here."

It didn't take long. Judge Pitt appeared at the door, yelling instructions over his shoulder to the clerk. All of it was unintelligible to Duny Gene. As he crossed the room, glaring at the two boys, the old man pulled off the black robe. His shirt was damp with sweat.

"Which one is Pay?" he asked abruptly, throwing himself into the chair behind the desk. But before they could answer, he turned to the deputy. "Carl, is their car still down at the jail?"

"Yes, your honor. Parked in the jail lot."

"All right. They'll be down to pick it up in a few minutes. You run on along now, I wanna talk to these boys."

Turning back to Duny Gene and Hoadie, his eyes darted from one to the other. He yanked open a drawer and took out a celluloid collar and began the struggle to fasten it about his neck with a silver stud.

"Goddamned things are a pain in the ass, boys," he said. "Don't ever let anybody talk you into wearin' one."

He got it secured, then pulled a red tie from the same drawer and whipped it around his neck and tied a lumpy knot.

"All right, which one is Pay?"

"I am, sir," Duny Gene said. It surprised him that he'd tacked on the "sir." He wasn't in the habit of using that word, even with his father. But somehow, this was solid authority sitting before him, and he felt that if he didn't respect it in some obvious way he might be in peril.

"I knew your granddaddy," Judge Pitt said. He leaned sideways and opened his mouth, and a soggy cud of black tobacco fell precisely into the cuspidor behind his desk. "Practiced with him in Fort Smith. He was prosecuting attorney down there for a while, wasn't he? You don't look a helluva lot like him."

"No, sir."

Judge Pitt rummaged through a stack of papers, came up with a yellow sheet, and stared at it, adjusting his steel-rimmed glasses on his nose with the heel of his thumb.

"I guess that means you're Hoadie Renkin," he said, looking over the glasses at Hoadie, and Hoadie nodded. "Well, how you boys like our jail?"

"It's all right," Duny Gene said. "I'd as soon not go in it again."

Judge Pitt laughed.

"Son, I hope you don't ever have to find out that it's as good as most. Jails ain't meant to be resort hotels. You boys from Weedy Rough, then?"

"Yes sir," Duny Gene said. "My daddy's a timber buyer for Frisco, and his is a farmer."

"I guess I heard that's what your daddy did, buy timber for the railroad. How is he?"

"He's all right."

"Never knew him. Knew your granddaddy, though. Well, boys, you might near got yourselves in a peck of trouble. Sheriff says when his deputies found you, you was stuck in the mud, and drinkin' pretty heavy."

"We was stuck. We didn't have much else to do," Duny Gene said.

"Yeah, and you made them deputies pretty mad. They said they spent most of the afternoon gettin' your car out, and then got their own stuck, too. Things like that make deputies mad as hell."

Judge Pitt produced a cigar from the desk drawer, bit off the end, and spat the wad of tobacco toward a volume of *The Civil Statutes of Arkansas*. It took a while for him to get the cigar going, and then he blew smoke rings that floated out across the desk for a few feet before they fell apart. He was obviously proud of the feat, and he blew a number more, one after the other. Duny Gene and Hoadie sat unimpressed, their caps in their hands.

"Now, drinkin' is bad enough, boys. You get into all kinds of trouble with it. I'm a little surprised at you . . ." He bent and stared at the yellow paper once more. ". . . Duny Gene, that it?"

"Yes sir."

"Drinkin' is bad."

"I just drink now and then, sir."

"Some people do, not much doubt about that. But what bothers me most is what you boys did at that gas station. You told that kid workin' there that one of you was Pretty Boy Floyd. Now why would you do a thing like that?"

"Just for the hell of it," Hoadie said, speaking for the first time.

"Well, it's dangerous. That kid called on his telephone to the sheriff and the sheriff called Siloam Springs. Did you know they had a bunch of police officers waitin' for you there?"

Duny Gene and Hoadie said nothing, turning their caps in their hands. But when the judge looked at them, their eyes did not waver.

"If you'd drove into Siloam Springs and they'd waved you down and you'd hesitated just a second, you know what they'd've done? They'd've shot your ass off."

He waited for a response, but there was none.

"You hear what I'm sayin'," Judge Pitt yelled.

"Yes sir, we hear," Duny Gene said.

"They might have killed both of you. Police officers around here don't mess with people like Floyd and all the rest of that bunch. They shoot and then start identifyin'. You know that?"

"Yes sir." Duny Gene's eyes had taken on a flat, lusterless look.

"You'd better bet it's so. Now don't either one of you ever let me hear about you doin' such a fool thing again. Go on, now, pick up your car and get back home where you belong. I gotta get to a Rotary Club luncheon."

As they moved out of his chambers, Judge Pitt thought, I don't think I impressed those two at all.

"Next time you see your granddaddy, tell him I said howdy," he called after them, thinking, Damned young men nowadays going to hell, a good family like that, and he don't act like he gives a good God damn for anything.

Duny Gene and Hoadie walked silently through the courthouse halls, past the men's toilet, which smelled like acid, disinfectant, and old urine. Outside, the rain had stopped, and they walked on to the jail in silence.

In the sheriff's office a deputy looked up and said, "Well, if it ain't Baby Face Nelson and John Dillinger."

Well out of town in the Studebaker, driving on the still-wet pavement, Hoadie reached under the seat and came up with the automatic. He grinned.

"Dumb bastards, didn't even find this," he said, and shoved the pistol into his belt.

"You better be damned glad they didn't," Duny Gene said.

· 14 ·

IT WAS ONE OF THOSE TYPICAL AUGUST days after a good rain, when the sun and wind had dried out the surface dust so thoroughly that it billowed and swirled and made a mess of everything, as though there had never been any rain at all. Weedy Rough subsided into its accustomed afternoon lethargy that day, waiting for evening, when it might cool a little and everybody could go to the depot and watch Number Six come through.

Parkins Muller stood at his post, staring out into the street. Nothing moved except the flies on the bank's plateglass window. There was an unloaded wagon in the tie yard, the mule team halfheartedly switching their tails. A timberman had come in earlier, read the note on the shack door, walked back alongside the bank—cursing softly—and disappeared into the beer hall.

In the bank, there was an L-shaped counter, with metal screening that ran up about two feet toward the ceiling. Two openings in this cage, marked "Teller" and "Cashier," were sally ports for money passing back and forth, the windows to the bank's business. Parkins was at the long side of the L, at the teller's position. He was more than teller, of course, and when required would trot back and forth between there and the cashier's post. He operated both windows himself because he trusted no one else to do it, not even his own sister.

His hat sat tightly pulled down on his head, as always, but on this day he had taken off his coat. He wore sleeve garters that bloused his shirt above the elbows. Under the counter hung a Remington shotgun. It was loaded with double-ought buckshot.

At the far end of the room, behind the shorter leg of the L counter, Miss Veda sat at a draftsman's table working over sheets of ledger paper with a number-two lead pencil. Near her was the potbellied safe, the round door standing open, and beside that a desk with stacks of paper neatly arranged across the top.

They said nothing to each other, which was also usual. Their conversation during banking hours concerned business and sounded to anyone listening like the vocalization of addition and subtraction. They had worked together a long time, and each knew what was expected, and therefore talk was considered by both to be a waste of time and energy. It was even less desirable because it didn't draw any interest.

Parkins was thinking about FDR. Someone had brought in a cardboard picture of the new president, but Parkins had refused to put it in his window.

It was torn in half and lying near the stove, to be used to kindle a fire when winter came.

Damn Roosevelt, Parkins Muller thought bitterly. He had never enjoyed the prospect of politicians meddling in private business, and this new man—former governor of New York or some such Yankee state—was not only meddling, he had jumped in with all four feet. Bank holidays, for God's sake, Parkins thought.

Then he thought about the doles pushed through Congress. They were not called doles, of course. They were called WPA and CCC and PWA and God only knew what other letters, each one designed to put people to work on wages paid from the money of honest taxpayers. Worse than Russia, Parkins thought, although in fact he knew nothing of Russia except that he'd heard they ate fish eggs and drank clear whiskey.

But, at least, perhaps a few more people would have money. Or with the prospect of it, a few might want to ask for loans. That's what he liked, loans.

He thought of the $1,400 resting in his safe, all in neat bundles of greenbacks. Railroad section payroll. He liked that, too. Some of these section hands owed him money. It was good to be the local depository for their payroll, because then Parkins knew exactly when they got paid. It wasn't so much as it had been, what with layoffs and cutbacks. But then, it didn't take much to run the Bank of Weedy Rough, so long as one watched each transaction carefully and made no bonehead mistakes. Parkins Muller was proud of the fact that he seldom made bonehead mistakes. In fact, he could not remember ever having made one.

Parkins Muller kept his bank open all day, five days a week. He did not approve of city banks that worked their people until only a couple of hours after noontime. If there was any chance for business after two o'clock, Parkins wanted to be available to transact it.

Therefore, it was almost three on that day when he watched as a large Packard touring car rounded the corner from the West Mountain road and slid to a halt in front of the bank. He was cursing the dust boiling through the open door, and perhaps that was why his usual alertness deserted him for an instant. Suddenly through the cloud of dust, leaping into the bank, three men appeared wearing brown fedora hats and red bandannas pulled over their faces up to their eyes. He heard Miss Veda gasp and he knew she had seen their entrance, too, and the pistols they carried in their hands.

On the lift of West Mountain behind the bank, Violet Sims also saw the Packard. But she had not looked closely and failed to notice the strange apparel of the passengers. She was hanging clothes, moving along a cotton rope line behind her house, her mouth full of clothespins. She was worrying again about the effect repeal of Prohibition would eventually have on her bootleg business. She was beginning to get a little old for the other enterprise that had sustained her for so long and was afraid that her only recourse soon would be to take that job old man Kruppman had offered, serving up beer in his joint.

She was vaguely aware that the Packard had not reappeared after making the turn at the bank. She knew without thinking that the car had stopped there, but there was nothing unusual about that, so she continued to push the wicker basket of clothes along the ground with her foot, the pins jutting from her mouth like the tusks of a walrus bull.

Then she heard the first shot, a deep roaring bellow enclosed within the steep valley walls. It was followed almost instantly by a second report, this one different, sounding like the whack of a hoe handle against an empty rain barrel. She stood still, looking down into the town, taking the clothespins from her mouth.

Suddenly, the Packard burst into view again, going toward the railroad crossing at the depot, across the tracks and along the line of buildings at the foot of East Mountain, past the post office and barbershop, and out of sight again behind the ice-cream parlor. With the roar of the car fading, Violet heard a high wailing moan, and it took a few seconds to realize that someone was screaming.

"Dear Jesus," she whispered, and started running down the slope.

She came to the street at a dead run, holding her skirt up above her ample knees, going along the sidewalk in front of the beer hall as Archer Kruppman and his father appeared on the high porch of their establishment, looking along the street toward the bank.

"What the hell's goin' on?" Archer yelled.

Violet ran on to the bank, turned the corner, and almost stepped on Parkins Muller. He was on his back in the doorway, the shotgun beside him and still smoking. He was moving, his arms and feet jerking with little spastic motions, and there was a blue hole in his face, and behind his head across the doorsill a deep red pool, thick and growing rapidly larger.

Violet stepped over him and into the bank. Miss Veda was still at the drafting table, her mouth open and the noise coming from it like bubbles of metal, exploding at her lips in a harsh shriek. Violet ran behind the counter and to the rear, where Miss Veda sat on her stool shaking and screaming, her hands flapping at her sides. Her eyes were glassy and she did not know that Violet was there, even after Violet touched her.

"Holy God, look what they done," Archer Kruppman shouted from the street, he and his old man staring down at Parkins Muller, who was lying still now, his eyes half open. Esta Stayborn was running from his store, carrying a Winchester lever-action rifle, and from beyond the depot others were coming, too. Olie Merton and Tooth Snowdon and Reese Walls.

"Oh my God, look at that," Archer wailed.

Somebody had already called Leo Sparks—afterward, no one could recall who it was—waking him from his afternoon nap. He was running down the hill into town, pulling on a belt and a holstered pistol. He kept thinking as he ran, Oh shit, I forgot my badge.

They began to swarm like bees in the street before the bank, eyes large as they stared at Parkins and his bloody head. Inside, Miss Veda was still wailing, Violet trying to quiet her. They saw blood splattered across the street, and from the tie yard a voice called out once, words they could not understand.

A dog came nosing along the street, tail stiff, avoiding the people and trying to move in close enough for a sniff of Parkins Muller. Olie Merton kicked him away, and the dog whimpered and ran into the middle of the street and there found the bloodstains in the dust and paused to inspect them.

Tooth Snowdon leaped over Parkins Muller, straddling him, arms up and face flushed with excitement.

"Give him air," Tooth shouted.

"Air? What the hell's the matter with you, Tooth," old man Kruppman said. "Can't you see he's dead?"

There was another low shout from the tie yard, and they seemed to realize for the first time that someone was there, likely well armed and dangerous. They scrambled through the door, Leo Sparks leading them, drawing his pistol. In the scuffle of feet, someone kicked Parkins Muller, and he rolled to his side, exposing the harsh wound behind his right ear.

The timber cutter, whose wagon was still in the tie yard, was yelling almost incoherently, once safe inside the bank.

"Them's my mules out yonder, I don't want my mules shot."

"For God's sake, man, nobody gonna shoot your damned mules," Tooth said.

They crouched along the edges of the door and the plate-glass window, Leo holding his pistol ready, Esta Stayborn standing well back with the rifle, uncertain and confused. In rear of the room, Miss Veda had subsided into broken sobs. Violet Sims made her blow her nose. She had somehow managed to get Miss Veda into the chair at the desk, and she knelt there making a soothing croon, stroking Miss Veda's hair.

"We gotta go get him," Leo Sparks said.

"Yeah, and get our butts shot off?" Archer Kruppman said. "I ain't goin' out there."

"They've killed my brother," Miss Veda screamed, and all the men jumped and looked embarrassed.

"We gotta get him out of that tie yard and call the doc and have him give Miss Veda somethin'," Leo said. "We need to get her home to bed, or somethin'."

"You wanna walk out this front door with her?" old man Kruppman asked. He was peering through the open door, watching the tie yard. Now and again his gaze turned down to Parkins Muller's body. "Damn. He don't look as big now, does he? Like he's started shrinkin' already."

"Why don't you shut up," Reese Walls said.

Then they saw a stooped figure, beyond the tie yard, stumbling toward the tunnel.

"There he goes," Leo shouted. "He's goin' to the tunnel."

"Get some flashlights, Esta, we gotta go after that son of a bitch," Tooth yelled, and he was the first to leap back over Parkins's body and start running across the street to the tie yard. But he stopped short, and turned, waiting for the others, who were boiling out of the bank door now.

Leo Sparks took command, badge or no badge. He sent Esta back to his store for more weapons and some flashlights. He ordered Olie Merton to get his car and drive up Academy Heights and get down to the far end of the tunnel to cut off their fugitive.

"Gotta get to the far end of the tunnel with some men before he does," Leo said. "Else, he'll be gone in the woods."

"Hell, Leo, my car's up at the house," Olie said. "Time I get up there, he'll be halfway to Chester."

"I'll drive some of you boys up the Heights," Archer Kruppman said. "But I ain't goin' down to that tunnel."

"Well, get at it, a couple you men go with him. Get some rifles from Esta. Here he comes now. Damn, I hope he got ammunition."

Esta ran to them awkwardly, carrying rifles in the crooks of both arms, and flashlights. One flashlight fell, bouncing in the street, but Esta came on, running crookedly, his pockets bulging with boxes of ammunition and batteries.

Esta passed out the rifles, and then they were shoving shells into the magazines, working the levers.

"Watch where you're pointin' that damned thing," Tooth yelled at old man Kruppman. "It's cocked, you know."

"I was workin' one of these when you still pissed your pants," Kruppman snorted.

Now the timber cutter broke from the group, going to his wagon. He scrambled up and unwound the lines from the brake handle, whipped the startled mules around in a half-circle, and drove into the street heading for West Mountain, whipping all the way.

They dispersed into two parties, one going with Archer Kruppman to get his car. The rest started through the tie yard to the tracks and turned along them toward the tunnel. They could see splatters of blood on the crossties and glistening on the rails.

"Son of a bitch is bleedin' like a hog," Tooth panted. "Maybe ole Parkins got one of 'em anyway."

Leo Sparks and Esta Stayborn led them across the cowcatcher, and as they approached the high arch of the tunnel entrance they all paused.

"Better hold up a mite," Leo said. "He may just be waitin' to shoot."

They tiptoed closer, hearts pounding, holding their borrowed rifles ready, waiting for a blast of gunfire. But nothing came. Soon, they were close enough to see the tunnel's far entrance, the tiny oval of light a half-mile away.

"I don't see nothin'," Tooth said.

"He's sure as hell in there. Look at that blood on the tracks."

"Bleedin' like a hog."

They moved warily, some of them peering closely along the steep banks of the cut to ensure that their quarry had not climbed up and gone away over Academy Heights. But there were no such signs, only the trail of red that led directly into the gaping maw of the tunnel. They inched forward, feeling the cool draft of air from the great hole through the mountain. Soon, they could hear water dripping from the tunnel roof, and then they were inside, the light fading as they advanced, feeling the icy drops on their backs.

"Think we oughta turn on a flashlight?" someone whispered.

"No. We'll go in the dark. Flashlights make too good a target," Leo said.

"For Christ's sake, Leo, he can see us against the light that's at our backs, from the entrance," Olie said.

"Can't help that. Come on."

Their feet scraped through the gravel and chunks of fallen brick. They moved bent over, cursing the noise their feet made. They were well into it when Reese Walls made a hissing sound.

Everyone stopped. The water falling from the roof made a loud splatter in the ditches that ran along either side of the tracks, next to the walls.

"I found something," Reese whispered. He was bent over, searching with his hands. "Here. I got it. It's a gun."

"Lemme see," Leo said. They fumbled in the dark, passing the gun back and forth. "It's a pistol, all right."

"Turn on a light."

"No. He may have another one."

They moved again, deeper into the tunnel, in total darkness now, and a few of them shivered as the water fell on their backs. Leo led them, his pistol pointed and ready.

"What's that over there?"

They stopped again, bunching as before.

"You got cat's eyes, Reese," Tooth said.

"Eyes gettin' used to the dark," Reese whispered. "Over there. In the ditch."

"I don't see nothin'."

"Turn on a light."

"Wait a minute."

"No, turn on one of them flashlights."

The bright beam suddenly cut through the darkness, a circle of light playing along the wall of the tunnel. The beam wavered and moved down so that the spot was on the ditch.

"By God," Leo said.

There was a figure lying in the ditch, facedown. They moved slowly, more lights snapping on. The water running in the ditch was like scarlet dye.

"Jesus," Tooth said. "Turn him over."

Leo bent and touched the figure, running his hand under the hair behind one ear, feeling for a pulse.

"I think he's dead," Leo said.

"Turn him over," Tooth repeated.

Leo holstered his pistol and rolled the body over, and the front of the lightweight suit and shirt was a spongy mass of blood just below the rib cage. They turned the beams of their lights to the face, and then stood back quickly, like a hand being retracted from a hot stove, involuntarily.

"Jesus Christ," Tooth whispered. "Oh Jesus Christ. It's Hoadie Renkin."

It took a long time to get Miss Veda out of the bank and up to her house, where all the ladies who had gathered made her a pot of hot tea, which Violet Sims laced with a snort of gin. It was all right. In this time of disaster, the other ladies felt that the blush of sin on Violet would not likely rub off, and it was obvious to all of them that she knew more about soothing battered emotions than any of them did. A few even guessed that such techniques were part and parcel of her trade—and not the liquor trade, either.

But even that part of it was all right, too, thinking about Violet's bedroom business. This was a crisis, when the ladies of the town realized their role was to comfort one another, as they always did when the menfolk got themselves into serious and sometimes lethal situations. At such times, they flocked together, clucking, past transgressions forgotten. They were all sisters, if only for a little while, and even Miss Veda was included, though she had never been a member of the Eastern Star, the Ladies' Aid Society, or a supporter of the basketball team. And even Violet Sims. Tomorrow, she would be the town whore again, but today she was one of them. A few ladies went so far as to smile at her.

There was almost a party atmosphere about it. Not around Miss Veda, of course, who had taken to her bed. But none of these ladies—excepting Violet Sims— had ever been inside the Muller home, and this provided a good opportunity to nose around. As some of them passed the front window, they looked down into the town, where they could see the front of the bank. There, the men had laid out the two bodies, like crossties, on the sidewalk, waiting to be stacked.

Leo Sparks himself made the call to the county seat. When he got Sheriff Geehyle Ramey on the telephone, he said, "Sheriff, there's been a little shootin' down here in Weedy Rough."

It took some time for the law to arrive. The men stood in a semicircle around the bodies on the sidewalk, staring at the two upturned faces. One man, who had voted against Geehyle in the last general election, said that likely the sheriff had to finish a pitch game before he started to Weedy Rough.

Then they could hear the siren, coming along the valley from the north, just a faint whine at first, but growing louder, and accompanied by billowing dust once the sheriff's car left the federal highway and started into the cup of valley where the town stood. The same discontented voter explained that Geehyle blew his "sireen" wherever he went, just to show what a large dog he was.

It was true that Geehyle Ramey was large. Flesh was distributed about face and body in such a way that it resembled muscle, and some of it was, because there were always stories of his lifting a grown man in his hands and throwing him into the rear of a police car, like a sack of meal. He habitually wore

brown pants and a short jacket, high-heeled boots
and a western belt. But no weapon was ever visible
on his person. Some said he carried a nine-millimeter
Luger in a boot top. There were stories, too, that he
had taken the pistol from a German officer during the
war at the moment the Hun was trying to shoot him
with it. Geehyle never confirmed either story. He
never denied them, either.

If the sheriff was a good man—and most agreed
that he was—his deputies were issued from a different lot. They were mostly seedy and rough and sometimes crooked as hell, but people said what can you
expect, no more than the county is willing to pay for
such service.

When the sheriff and his three men arrived, they
went about their business quickly, asking a lot of
questions and looking at the bloodstains and examining the Savage automatic Reese Walls had found in
the tunnel. They learned very little about what actually took place at the bank. Most of the Weedy
Rough men were a little reluctant to talk about any of
it, because they knew Hoadie Renkin, lying dead
now and a part of the robbery, had always been close
as skin with Duny Gene Pay. But the sheriff remembered the incident on the Siloam Springs road only
that weekend.

"You see that Indian-lookin' kid around anywhere?"
he asked.

"What Indian-lookin' kid?" Tooth asked innocently.

"This boy here," and Geehyle indicated Hoadie
Renkin, lying there on the sidewalk, "he was runnin'
around the county a few days ago with some Indian-
lookin' kid. Dark-headed kid. We arrested 'em last
Saturday afternoon for bein' drunk. Name was Pay, I
think."

"Oh," Tooth said. "That kid."

Most of the other men had drawn back now, all of

them looking as though this was the first time they'd thought of Duny Gene Pay, but each of them having thought of little else since they'd turned Hoadie Renkin over in the tunnel.

"Why, he's down at Lee's Creek. Fishin'," Tooth said. "He put a note on the tie-yard shack. That's where he's at."

"When did he do that? Put up the note?"

"Let's see. Friday, I reckon."

"He sure as hell wasn't at no Lee's Creek fishin' Saturday."

"Well, that's where he's at now."

"When'd you see him last?"

Tooth looked up at the sky and scratched his chin. He frowned and wiped his nose on his sleeve.

"I don't recall, sheriff."

"He lives around here, don't he?"

"Oh yeah. But nobody home now. His folks is down at Fort Smith, visitin' family. Duny Gene, he's fishin'," Tooth said stubbornly.

"Yeah. We'll see," Geehyle said coldly. "All right. Get these bodies covered. But leave 'em here. I got the coroner comin' down, and I want him to see 'em before they're moved." He turned to his deputies, who were standing around with their hands on their pistols. "Boys, I'm goin' up to the Muller house, talk to that lady. Stay here till I get back. Shut this bank up and lock it. One of you town men wanna take me up there?"

"I'll do it," Tooth said. "I know the way."

When Number Six came through that evening, so one was on the depot platform to meet it. The crowd had disappeared from the streets and there was just Mr. Harmon Budd, lying drunk under the big maple tree, the one person in town not aware of what had happened at the bank that afternoon.

There were more lights burning in the Muller house than anyone could remember having seen there before. Violet Sims was still in attendance as the sheriff slowly tried to question Miss Veda. The other ladies had all gone to their homes.

Astonishingly, only Violet Sims had seen Hoadie that day when he came back, at least to recognize him. Those who saw the man in the seersucker suit, driving the blue Studebaker, likely had taken it as someone from Sycamore Lodge and paid little attention. But Hoadie had come to her house for whiskey, and he had told her he and Duny Gene Pay were going on a drunk. Violet failed to mention any of this to the sheriff.

When the train came through, shaking the hills as it always did, there were only the deputies standing about the still forms on the sidewalk before the bank. The bodies had been covered with a canvas tarp, and now only the feet of the two dead men showed. The coroner had not yet arrived, and the deputies smoked and swore impatiently, and stood about with their hands on their pistols.

They watched Number Six roar to a stop at the depot, and then after a few moments pull away again, the whistle sounding and steam coming from the coupling hoses. They continued to hear the whistle, each time fainter, as the train rolled north out of the valley. On the slopes of Academy Heights, a mockingbird began his evening song, and across the tie yard there were lightning bugs, and beyond that the dark form of the Pay house, and nearby the lighted windows of the Muller place.

And then the wagon came.

Nobody ever understood how news traveled through the back country, nor why it always seemed to move so fast. Maybe one rider on a mule, passing word-of-mouth to a wagon driver, and he to a squirrel hunter.

However, things got around quickly in the sticks. So there was nothing surprising about it when Ike Renkin drove his wagon into town, only a few short hours since his son had died.

Old Ike sat in the seat alone, his face stony. All the rest of the family was in back. There was Audie, the oldest now, standing behind his pap and looking stony, too, amazingly like his half brother Hoadie in younger years, except that Audie seldom grinned as Hoadie had. Then there was the old lady with a shawl over her head, and all the girls clustered around her, some so small their little faces barely came above the sideboards. And at the rear, Squib, standing too, looking like a smaller copy of his older brother, with straw-colored hair hanging over his eyes and his lips grim.

Ike pulled the mules into the edge of the tie yard, and sat for a long time, looking across the street at the canvas tarp. Then he spoke quietly, and Audie stepped up into the seat and took the reins, and the old man climbed down over the wheel.

All eyes in the wagon watched the old man cross the street, except for Audie, who sat holding the lines and staring at the mules' rumps because he'd seen all he needed to see. As Ike approached the bank, a deputy stepped before him and lifted a hand.

"Hold it, old man," he said.

Ike looked down at the deputy with his cold eyes, hard bones showing under the leathery skin, and the deputy shrugged and dropped his hand to his side. Ike went on to the sidewalk, to the edge of the tarp, and squatted there in the manner of his people. After a long time, he reached down and drew back one corner of the canvas to reveal Hoadie's face. Watching from the wagon, the family was as silent and immobile as plaster statues.

After a long time, his expression never changing,

old Ike put his hand across his son's face. He gently closed the eyes with his fingertips, feeling the coldness.

Then he replaced the canvas over Hoadie's face, rose, and walked into the street. He paused before passing the deputy who had tried to stop him, but he said nothing and went on to the wagon. As he climbed up, Audie handed him the lines. He clucked the team around, never looking back at the still forms under the canvas. Only the old woman and all the kids in back of the wagon looked, until they had passed beyond the corner of the bank.

The deputies listened to the rattle of trace chains and the clop of mules' hoofbeats for a long time after the Renkin family was out of sight. In the growing darkness, they looked again at the canvas tarp, the two forms under it, only the feet showing, the small brogans looking somehow grotesque beside the wing-tip shoes.

· 15 ·

THE BARBERSHOP BUNCH WATCHED THE events of the next few days unfold with bewildering speed. Later, Tooth Snowdon would say things were happening in so many places, a man didn't know which way to look. Nobody could have kept up with it all without the newspapers and Geehyle Ramey.

Fort Smith and Fayetteville newspapers were as

sensitive to sensational news as the rest of the country's press at that time. They were no longer as strident and messy as they had been in the twenties, but when there was a robbery and men left lying about with gunshot holes in them, the coverage was bound to be impressive. And so it was with the Weedy Rough bank job.

There was even a little pride written into the stories, as though some social station were at stake. Maybe there was, with banks being knocked over in various parts of the Midwest, and now northwest Arkansas had one to brag about, too.

As for Sheriff Ramey, he was looking to the next election. He wanted to leave the impression of speed and skill in solving the county's crimes, whether anything was actually accomplished or not. Had the Weedy Rough thing been a simple robbery, nobody would have given much of a damn one way or the other. But with the killing of a banker, it became a different-flavored hog, a case that required action.

Usually close-mouthed about official business, Geehyle on this occasion was not reluctant to explain the status of his investigation to any interested citizen. Especially Democrats, and almost everyone in Weedy Rough was a Democrat except the Mullers. Geehyle had recognized the significance of the last general election. When Roosevelt ran, there was the largest turnout for the party since Wilson's time, an encouraging thing to contemplate.

Like all good politicians, Geehyle Ramey had a sense of where the talking was done. He knew that anything said in the Weedy Rough barbershop was like a speech made into a ten-thousand-watt radio microphone, because within minutes of his departure his words would be spreading around town and through the back country. So he made sure Roughers were aware of his efforts. He spiced his facts with some fiction, of course, having by this time in his career learned that office seekers who didn't sling a little bullshit seldom got the opportunity to run the county.

Besides the newspapers and the official line expounded by the sheriff, Roughers were able to see some of the case developing. They were as good as anybody and better than most at watching one another.

There was no lack of action in Weedy Rough. Parkins Muller's remains were shipped to an undertaker in Fayetteville and the funeral was planned for the coming Sunday at the Methodist church, services to be said by Leviticus Hammel. Parkins had never been a Methodist, nor anything else that people could remember, and Leviticus was reluctant about preaching over him just in case Parkins at some time in his past had been a Baptist.

Reese Walls and Olie Merton made a special call on Leviticus. They explained that no matter what people thought about Parkins in this world, he at least deserved a proper introduction to the next, having been for so many years the town's only bank owner. What he deserved, they said, was the best funeral in town. Leviticus had to agree that he would himself have to be involved in any service thus described. And besides, they had to consider poor Miss Veda's feelings.

Hoadie Renkin's body lay all night in front of the bank after the coroner had gone. Nobody was quite sure what to do about it. Esta Stayborn got a stool from his store and sat the night through alongside the canvas tarp, because someone always stayed awake beside the dead until they were buried, and just as importantly, the dogs had to be kept away.

"We can't just leave that boy out there in the street under a tarp," Esta said the next morning. So with Tooth Snowdon's help, he wrapped Hoadie tightly in the canvas and they stored him in Esta's back room.

It wasn't until just before noon that Audie Renkin came back into town, driving his pap's log wagon, to take his brother home. Esta got a lump in his throat and couldn't talk, so Tooth had to tell Audie where they'd put the body.

"I figured maybe the county had taken him off to cut him up, and look at his insides," Audie said. "I heerd they do that sometimes."

The three of them loaded the long bundle into the wagon. Audie stood looking at the tie yard, where no wagons had appeared that day and where the shack was still padlocked.

"I'd like to leave him here a minute," Audie said. "Pap wanted me to see Mr. Pay. See if he'd come out and say words over his grave."

"Well, son, I'm afraid Mr. Pay ain't here," Tooth said. "He's down Fort Smith with his missus, visitin' her relatives."

"Well, I guess Pap'll have to say words his ownself," Audie said. He climbed up to the seat and took the lines and whipped the mules along the street and around the corner at the bank.

After Audie was gone, Tooth said he'd best get over to the barbershop. He was a lonely figure walking across the tracks. No one else was on the street. Everybody seemed to be staying close to home on this day after the robbery. Esta watched Tooth go and then looked back in the direction Audie had gone. He thought about the times he'd let Hoadie come into the store and steal little things, Duny Gene Pay usually with him. He was having trouble swallowing the hard knot in his throat.

That same night, Barton and Lydia came back on Number Six. The moment he saw Barton, Tooth knew they'd heard about what had happened. Barton looked drawn and sick, and he seemed to have trouble walking. Tooth helped Lydia get him up the hill to the house, and before Tooth was gone Barton had taken to his bed.

Later, in the barbershop, Tooth made his report.

"He didn't seem right," Tooth said. "He was all drawed out and weak-lookin'. He never asked a thing. After we had him abed, Miz Lydia asked where at was Duny Gene, and I said he'd gone off fishin' on Lee's Creek Friday night.

"Then when I started back to town, I heard the car. I stopped and looked back and Duny Gene was pullin' in. He parked Mr. Pay's Ford and walked up the steps to the house, and it was still light enough to see he was carryin' what looked like a string of fish."

"I have an idea hearin' about Hoadie tore Duny Gene up some," Homer Gage said. "Them boys was thick as thieves."

They all glared at Homer, and Homer realized what he'd said and his face got red.

"Well, what the hell," Homer muttered. "I didn't mean nothin'."

Then, there was the car wreck. A good car wreck was pretty sensational in itself because safety glass was a long way from perfection and generally unknown in many models. When an automobile began coming apart under the impact of one thing or another, flying crystal shards made for horrible injuries. But there was more than flying glass in this particular crash.

The night of the robbery, Crawford County police reported that a tan 1928 Packard touring car—heading for the Arkansas River bridge into Fort Smith—had gone out of control on the main street of Van Buren. The Packard leaped the curb and ran along the sidewalk, sheared off a telephone pole, and smashed into the solid brick wall of a hardware store.

The woman passenger apparently had seen what was coming and thrown herself on the floorboards. She came out with a few minor cuts and bruises and a broken arm. The man driving hadn't been so lucky. Flying glass had very nearly taken off his head, and he died from loss of blood before they could get him to a hospital.

Searching through the bloody wreckage, officers found a small canvas bag. Stenciled across it were the words *Bank of Weedy Rough*, and inside was a little over $1,400, most of it still neatly bundled. And in the car, too, were enough weapons to start a war, the officers said. Included was a Thompson submachine gun.

The Crawford County sheriff made a long-distance telephone call to Geehyle Ramey. He had known about the Weedy Rough robbery only a few hours after it happened because the information had been passed along the Frisco telegraph lines. He figured Geehyle might have some interest in that tan Packard.

The dead man was identified as Lester Bains, out of Midland, Texas. When officers asked the woman who she was, she made a number of obscene suggestions about what they might do with their badges. But they found letters and other items in her purse indicating she was one Ruby Denton. A telegram from the Midland County sheriff in Texas confirmed her identity—the platinum hair was hard to mistake— and informed that she was wanted for shoplifting and automobile theft and God only knew what else in Ector and Upton counties, among other places. There was a hint of prostitution, too, but nothing had ever been proven.

Within two days, Geehyle Ramey had Ruby in the women's section of the Washington County jail—

stitches, arm cast, black eyes, and all. She arrived the same day Judge Pitt called the grand jury. Everybody knew that Ruby would be indicted for armed robbery and murder. They didn't need a grand jury to tell them that, because she'd been caught with the goods. So the line of reasoning was that somebody else must be suspect.

Audie Renkin was in the lower field when he heard the car. He knew it wasn't the mailman, because it was coming from the wrong direction. He dropped his hoe between the corn rows and started for the road, his younger brother Squib following close behind.

"You better stay on your hoe," Audie said, but Squib came on anyway, the two of them finally stopping at the mailbox, watching as the Pay Ford came into view.

Duny Gene Pay braked the car to a stop and got out, and the two Renkins stared at him with little or no expression on their faces. Duny Gene took out a package of Chesterfields and lit one and offered the pack to Audie.

"I'd sure like to have one of them tailor-mades," Squib said.

"You ain't old enough to smoke," Audie said. He took a second cigarette and handed it to his brother. They bent their heads over Duny Gene's cupped hands to light up. Silently, they stood in the sun and smoked. There was a hot breath of air blowing across the ridgelines from the south. It moved the Renkin boys' hair like corn silks.

"Esta Stayborn said you came in and got Hoadie yesterday," Duny Gene said.

"I got him," Audie said. "You wanna see the grave?"

"Yeah. I'd like to."

They started up the rocky path toward the house.

Duny Gene could see the faces of other kids at the windows. Audie led them around the house and went past it and down through the backyard alongside the pigsty and the pen where old Ike kept the dogs. Hounds came from their shade at the rear of the pen, where some persimmon trees struggled in the stony soil. The dogs watched silently as the three walked past, and Duny Gene tried to find Dixie among them, but he didn't recognize her.

Behind the privy was a scattering of debris long past use—a rusty washtub, the handle from a meat grinder, a few tin cans. Beyond that was a line of oaks, and a few stumps where Old Ike had cut trees for making crossties. At the edge of the woods was a new grave, mounded with large rocks, and beside that an older one with a pumpkin-sized sandstone at its head. The marker was overgrown with a gray-white moss.

"We put him in the ground as soon as I got home," Audie said.

"Yeah," Squib said. "He was stiff as a board."

"Pap wanted your pap to say words, but they told me in town he was gone visitin' someplace."

"Pap looked at Hoadie's face. But he wouldn't let none of us."

Duny Gene pulled off his cap, looking at the grave. They could hear jays somewhere in the timber to the west, down a deep hollow there. The trees dropped off quickly into the sharp valley, and above them the blue hills stretched off toward Oklahoma.

"We put him beside of his ma," Audie said. "Pap buried her here when she died, years back."

"They say he was robbin' the bank in Weedy Rough," Squib said, and his eyes were bright thinking about it.

"Yeah," Duny Gene said after a while. "That's what they say."

"We never got to look at him," Squib said.

It was uncomfortable, standing there. Not just the heat and wood gnats, but all of it. The Renkin boys kept staring at him, waiting for him to say something.

"The one that did it to him got his ass shot off, too," Squib said. "Old Parkins Muller."

"Why don't you shut up," Audie snapped.

Duny Gene pulled his cap onto his head and turned back up the slope. He could hear them behind him, following closely. As they came near the house old Ike Renkin came out onto the porch, stooped and hard-faced. Duny Gene paused a moment, then walked up to the porch and he and old Ike shook hands.

"I'm sorry Daddy wasn't able to get here," Duny Gene said.

"It don't make no difference," old Ike said.

Going down to the car, only Squib followed Duny Gene. At the mailbox, Duny Gene stopped and fished the old bone-handled knife from his pocket and handed it to the boy.

"You might like to have this," he said. Squib looked at the knife and shook his head.

"He said you was supposed to have it."

"All right. I'll keep it, then," Duny Gene said. Squib looked at him with those pale Renkin eyes.

"You was there at the bank, too, wasn't you?"

Duny Gene turned and got into the car, started it, and turned around in the road. His face was set in hard surfaces and his eyes had a flat look. He'd thought the old man was going to ask the same thing. There had been the question in his eyes, the same question Duny Gene had seen when his father looked at him over these past few hours. But they only looked, with the question left unasked.

He was strangely unaffected by it all. He had thought it would be different when he saw the grave. He tried thinking of old times, as he had after their fistfight and Hoadie had gone away. He tried hard to bring on some sorrow or remorse, anything that he could count as emotion. But none of the images came, and he felt cold even in this August heat. It was as though all of it had been from another time, from somebody else's life, and now the curtain was drawn down. Over and finished, and none of it holding any interest for him.

Olie Merton watched it all with a growing sense of frustration. That damned grand jury was meeting in Fayetteville and Miss Veda had gone up to testify. Lyle Proctor, the prosecutor, had come to Weedy Rough to take her there. With the proceedings secret, and Judge Pitt threatening legal action against anyone who talked about it, there was nothing to do but wait. At least it was a short wait.

Olie had counted the times the sheriff had been to town since the robbery. Four times, and on each trip, he had stopped at the barbershop to jaw a while. Now, he came again, with Lyle Proctor, riding in the Model A sedan with the white five-pointed star painted on each front door.

Geehyle didn't stop at the barbershop this time. He drove directly up East Mountain to the Pay house. It was Saturday and the tie yard was closed. Which meant Duny Gene Pay would likely be at home, as Geehyle must have known. After only a few minutes, the sheriff and Lyle Proctor came down from the house with Duny Gene between them.

When they drove past the barbershop, headed north toward Fayetteville, Olie saw that Proctor was driving and the sheriff and Duny Gene were in the backseat. He thought he saw handcuffs on Duny Gene's wrists. He ran to the telephone.

Olie twisted the handle viciously, hearing the bell

ring on the switchboard at the central office. After a long time, the operator came on.

"Miz Tillie, give me Barton Pay's house."

"It won't do any good, Olie," Tillie said. "I already called about them people bein' there and takin' Duny Gene. Lydia won't talk about it and Barton's still sick in bed."

But as he hung up, Olie knew what had happened as surely as if he'd been there. Everybody in town had been expecting it, without saying so. The damned grand jury had returned a true bill charging Duny Gene Pay, and now he was on his way to the county seat to answer charges.

Olie yanked the toothpick from his mouth and flung it hard against the picture of Jack Sharkey hanging on the wall. Then he turned to the glass-fronted cabinet where he kept the whiskey in a bottle labeled "Hair Tonic."

· 16 ·

LYDIA PAY WASTED NO TIME PONDERING the irony of circumstance, once she made up her mind that Eben Pay was the best man to defend her son. She had always disliked the old man—she was the only one in the family who thought of him as the "old man"—and she had never made any bones about letting people know how she felt. But once the notion came that Eben Pay was a good lawyer, as good as any in the state perhaps, she put all past feelings aside.

Some might have thought she made the decision in the full knowledge that Pay would charge very little, if anything, for his services to a grandson. That had no part in it. Lydia was fully prepared to pay whatever was right, even though she would have to borrow the money. She wanted Eben Pay because he had a large reputation in criminal law, albeit primarily from the standpoint of a prosecutor. But what she expected to be the natural scheme of things became an infuriating experience for her.

The first frustration was Barton. Listlessly and looking a little forlorn, he had gone back to work in the tie yard a few days after Duny Gene's arrest. Not because he wanted to, but because if he didn't, he knew he would likely be canned. By then Judge Orvil Pitt had appointed an attorney to Duny Gene's defense. Lydia found it astonishing that Barton was ready to accept this man, who was no man at all but a boy hardly any older than Duny Gene himself. Lydia raged at Barton for playing the game of comewhat-may and letting it go at that.

They had gone to visit Duny Gene in his cell at the county jail. Barton sat there on the bunk beside his son, crying the whole time, unable to control himself. It had been embarrassing and humiliating, and it set her resolve even harder to get rid of this youngsquirt lawyer and hire old Eben Pay for the job.

Driving home afterward, Lydia had stated the point flatly, and to her continuing amazement Barton refused to consider it. Lydia realized then that Barton was ashamed for his father to know such a thing could happen in the family—a Pay arrested and charged and being held without bail on first-degree murder.

"Don't you think your father ever reads a newspaper?" she shouted. "Don't you think he's known about this all along?"

But Barton just sat there with his hands gripping the steering wheel, shaking his head stubbornly. As though it would all disappear if he could just ignore it long enough.

Lydia felt no pity for him. She was furious. As soon as they arrived in Weedy Rough, she packed her suitcase—the same one she had packed after Barton bought that damned foxhound.

"If you want to sit here like a lump, go ahead and be damned," she shouted. "But I will not allow this thing to happen without a fight."

And she walked down the hill into town to the ice-cream parlor and bought a ticket on the southbound bus for that evening.

Eben Pay was sixty-five in 1933. He was concerned about being old, noticing little things in his behavior that seemed to be associated with advancing age. He left items lying about carelessly, like books on chairs and dirty brandy glasses on end tables and wet towels on the bathroom floor. He thought too much about the past, too, the time he had served with old Judge Isaac Parker and the Federal Court for the Western District of Arkansas, when just across the Arkansas River was the Cherokee Nation and not Oklahoma.

Always when he thought of The Nations, he remembered his wife, Missy Bishop, a Cherokee who had been bred and born in a place called Going Snake. She had been gone almost forty years, but he still thought of her every day, especially the way she smiled at him. His memory of her face sometimes faded, and he would take out the tiny hand-tinted photograph of her that he carried in the back of his pocket watch.

It was good to see her likeness, never changing. Yet it bothered him, too, because while she appeared to remain the same, he had changed a great deal. If there was a hereafter, and he made it there, she would greet him as a young woman and wonder who this old man was, with his gray hair and lined face, old enough to be her grandfather. It was one of the disconcerting aspects of a hereafter that made him think about it as little as possible.

All of this was a part of belittling himself, which he had made a habit of doing all his life. For his years, he in fact looked quite young, even with the white hair. At least there was plenty of it. He had a long Welsh face, with a straight, prominent nose and well-shaped mouth, and his sagging jowls were not too noticeable because he carried his head high, as though sniffing.

He held his six-foot frame—which showed little evidence of fat—perpendicular to the floor when he stood. Some said he must have served a long time in the army, always standing before a jury in the posture of a sergeant major on parade. Actually, he had served only a short while during the trouble in Cuba, and had come away without having spent enough time in uniform to develop any habits from the experience, good or bad.

Now there was no time to dwell on old age and the fact that since retirement he had not worked as often as he would have liked. His daughter-in-law, Lydia, was in Fort Smith and was about to arrive, having made an appointment from her father's telephone, and any meeting with Lydia was bound to require special resources. Besides, he fairly well knew why she wanted to see him.

So he was prepared for her brisk arrival, his demeanor more gentlemanly than she had ever known it to be, at first. He was solicitous and gentle and showed great concern about the whole matter.

"I'd been waiting for you to call," he said. "I hope I can be of help."

"I came alone because Barton seems to be broken in spirit over it. I don't think he believes it's happening," she said.

"Such a thing is a shock," Eben Pay said. "But I've been in this business long enough to know that one's worst enemy can be hopelessness."

Soon the subject of a fee came up, branching out into other things, and that's when the shouting began, carrying their conversation all along the halls of the third floor of the City National Bank building, where Eben Pay had his practice, overlooking Garrison Avenue.

Eben said he knew that Barton had no money, and Lydia said she would not take a lawyer or anybody else on charity and would get whatever was necessary. Eben Pay rejoined that he knew where she'd get it, and he had no intention of taking her family's money, what with the way they felt about the Pays in general and himself in particular.

They wrangled on about what everyone thought of everyone else, and not much of it was complimentary. Lydia said her father's money was as good as anybody's and Eben Pay said he would not take a cent from such a bigoted old bastard as her father, and that launched them into a loud discussion of interracial marriage.

Eben defended it for anybody who felt so inclined. Lydia took the generally accepted view. She commented on red heathens, and Eben Pay said if his wife had been a heathen while she lived, then there ought to be more of them around. And besides, whatever Lydia called the late Missy Bishop she had to apply equally to her own son, Missy Bishop having been Duny Gene's grandmother.

Then they got back to the money. Eben Pay said he could see no reason why he might not be expected to defend his own blood without fee, whether the boy was guilty or not. Maybe even more so if he was guilty. With that, Lydia flew into one of her rages, explaining at the top of her voice that Duny Gene was not guilty of anything except maybe a little laziness that one had to expect from a boy his age, and Eben Pay said nobody had been convicted yet, but it was always a possibility.

"He's innocent," Lydia said. "He'd never do such a thing as they claim he did, and you can prove it."

"My dear, the defense doesn't have to prove anything," Eben Pay snapped. "The purpose of a criminal trial is for the state to prove guilt."

"I don't care about your legal jargon," she said. "It all sounds like the same thing to me."

"It is not the same thing. Our job is to show a jury that the state failed to prove guilt beyond a reasonable doubt. We are not looking for 'innocent.' We are looking for 'not guilty.' There is a difference."

She started to respond and then realized the sense of his pronouns.

"Then you'll take the case?"

"Yes," Eben Pay said. "In fact, I had already packed when you called, and purchased a ticket on tonight's train to Fayetteville."

That infuriated her, too, even though she felt that, with his acceptance of the case, her duty had been fulfilled.

"You were going up there, then, whether we asked you to come or not?"

"If by 'we' you mean yourself and Barton, yes. It is not you who will determine Duny Gene's counsel, but himself. He just turned twenty-one."

"I know that! I'm his mother."

"I am capable of keeping track of time on a calendar, too," Eben Pay said. "And in his majority, he will decide if he wants me."

"Then why did you let me sit here going through this, knowing all along that you were going to defend him?"

Eben Pay suddenly laughed. "Lydia, it is the best conversation we have had in a long time."

He remained alone in his office until dark, his mind on the future of his grandson, and whether he could preserve it. Conviction for murder committed in the act of robbing a bank could mean a rapid trip to the electric chair, in this time and place. Eben Pay had himself sent a few on that last trip.

It was disturbing as hell, all the newspapers making it appear that there was a tight case against Duny Gene. But he would know more about that once he'd gone to Fayetteville and found a place to stay and started prying and pumping and cursing to get all the information he could from the prosecuting attorney, Lyle Proctor. Eben Pay had met the young man once at some sort of bar association meeting in Little Rock, but he could not recall the man's face.

He didn't have time to consider his own son's dismal part in all of this. Lydia had come alone to ask for help, a chore which he knew she detested and for which he admired her a great deal. And leaving Barton brooding in his tie yard up there in the damned sticks, wounded either because he thought his son had done a terrible crime or else was sure that he had not but would be convicted for it anyway. Eben Pay had found that fear of punishment and fear of injustice were often indistinguishable among those involved.

Well, he didn't have time to think about his son's withdrawal, or whatever it was. It didn't bother him too much, either. Barton had always wanted to go his own way, make a life for himself without any kind of education, tomcat around Fort Smith when he was young, drinking and raising hell and whoring and finally knocking up the daughter of one of the town's best families. Although bigots, all of them.

Barton had always owned a stubborn streak wide as Garrison Avenue. He'd never sit still for help from his daddy, once he'd found a few ways to make money on his own. He'd always been apart from Eben Pay. He'd never once sat down and talked about his conversion to the Methodist church, nor had he ever hinted that he'd like help in getting a position that paid well and that would make the Pay name proud. Stubborn as hell, and maybe that was part of it. Not just lack of backbone, but stubbornness. Even now, with his son facing the electric chair at Tucker Prison Farm, he wouldn't come forward and ask for help.

Well, no time to think about all that. Now came the work, a hell of a lot of it, he suspected, to avoid that electrical contraption at the pen. None of it looked too promising. He knew Orvil Pitt, a feisty little bastard with all the polish and dignity of a hill-country hog, and he knew that Pitt would not sit still for dillydallying on bringing this one to trial. So pretrial discovery of the prosecution's case could be a major problem. But at least there would be the grand jury's true bill, and that should provide the major portion of prosecution witnesses. Maybe that alone would tell him something.

He'd have to see Duny Gene right away. That bothered him a little. The boy wasn't easy to talk to, with that pair of gray eyes like his father's that never hinted at what might be working in the mind behind. He'd just have to make the best of it.

At least the boy had always seemed to like him.

But even that was hard to tell, what with Lydia hovering about scolding and watching like a hawk. Eben Pay had no idea whether or not Duny Gene would tell him the truth. He would simply have to listen, and go on from there.

The September flies worked in and out of the open door of the tie-yard shack, making their constant drone. Barton Pay sat there on his stool beside the drafting table he used as a desk. He stared out into the bright yard where the oak and hickory crossties gleamed white and hot in the sun. Beyond the stacks of timber, he could see the lift of the bluff to the road, and then his own house above that, framed in the dark green foliage of the trees that ran on up the slope to the edge of Parkins Muller's goat pasture.

Three times now he and Lydia had been to Fay-etteville to visit Duny Gene in his jail cell. Barton despised it. The old limestone building looked like a medieval fortress, cold and forbidding, and each time he entered the steel door to the line of cages where they kept the people waiting their turn in circuit court, he was violently depressed.

For the first time, he was entering the world his own father had known throughout his professional career, a world of jails and lawyers and bail bonds-men and courts and iron bars, faced on one side by armed officers and on the other by men with no laces in their shoes.

Lydia had each time taken a deep-dish cherry pie for Duny Gene, but he never ate it while they were there. He said little, answering his mother's ques-tions in a monotone, with as few words as possible. He hardly spoke to Barton at all. Barton wanted to hold his son's hands and ask, "Did you do this terrible thing?" But the thought of an answer terri-fied him, and so he never came close to asking.

Each time when they left the jail, Barton handed Duny Gene a few packs of Chesterfields and some cash, to buy little things from the jailer, like candy bars or hamburgers. Duny Gene always took this offering without a word, only a short nod of his head, as though he were taking change from some store clerk.

Barton thought of Eben Pay, his own father. He had never been at the jail when Barton and Lydia visited, and although Barton knew he had taken lodging at the Washington Hotel in Fayetteville while preparing Duny Gene's case, at no time had Barton seen him. He wasn't sure about Lydia. She had gone to the county seat twice while Barton stayed behind, working the tie yard. But if she had seen Eben Pay, she never mentioned it.

Barton thought about the times his father had taken him to the circus when it came to Fort Smith, and Barton still a child. The performance wasn't the important thing. It was the setting up and breaking down that had fascinated Eben, a fascination he passed along to Barton as he held the boy's hand and pointed out the things that were exciting.

They would eat hot dogs with kraut, the juice running through their fingers, and then popcorn and soda pop, and Barton always ended with pink cotton candy. Then, with the performance near, they would take their tickets through the menagerie tent that led to the big top, seeing the tigers and lions behind the bars of their wagon cages, snarling and pacing, glaring yellow-eyed at the passing people.

The noise and smell and glittering costumes were still strong in Barton's memory.

Always the best part was afterward, when the circus started breaking down, loading out for the next town. The big tents gently lowered, air still trapped beneath until men walked across the canvas, making canyons with billowing walls, until finally the tarp was flat enough to roll and lift onto the wagons.

The tent stakes were pulled by elephants, going down the line where the big top had stood, pausing only a moment to lift each four-foot oaken shaft from the hard ground like a toothpick from an angel food cake.

Eben Pay would take his son home at last, and Barton would lie awake in his bed until almost dawn, thinking about all he had seen. The cats growling and the elephants stamping and the working men sweating in their undershirts, all of it smelling as only a circus can smell. For all his life, when Barton thought of Barnum and Bailey, or Sells Floto, or Ringling Brothers, the odor of elephant droppings came to him.

As he sat in the fly-buzzing shack that afternoon, Barton recalled the times his father had taken him to the circus. And he was painfully aware that he had never taken Duny Gene to see such things. Of course, they had been in other places together. There had been the fox hunts and the meetings at the Eastern Star and a few moving-picture shows in Fayetteville. And there had been those times along hill roads when they sat on the running board of the car and shot at tin cans with the pistol. When Barton thought of that, he shuddered.

But he had never taken his son to a circus, and remembering how it had been when he was a boy, he suddenly felt a sense of admiration for his own father, and of ignored obligations in himself.

But again, he told himself, how could such a thing make any difference? If that strange, emotionless hard streak in his son had been there all along, how could elephants and tigers and a big-top tent have made any difference?

PART
FOUR

· 17 ·

JUDGE ORVIL PITT, HIS BLACK ROBE BIL-
lowing, moved to his place at the high bench, seated
himself, and glared around the courtroom. In the jury
box were the twelve men, selected in an amazingly
short time, the judge thought, for a trial on such a
serious matter. At the prosecution table sat Lyle Proctor, reared back in his chair, thumbs in the armholes
of his vest, looking confident but grim. On the table
before him was an impressive stack of legal-looking
papers, and beside him sat a deputy prosecutor.

Opposite Proctor in the courtroom pit was Eben
Pay, his gray hair brushed back from a high forehead, relaxed, with his elbows on the defense table.
Across his flat belly, he wore a gold watch chain
from which was suspended a polished wolf's tooth.

Beside Eben Pay was his grandson, Duny Gene, in
a new dark suit, white shirt and necktie, all purchased from Montgomery Ward only two days before, according to Judge Pitt's sources, which in this
town were numerous.

You'd never know they were kin, Judge Pitt thought,
glancing from Eben Pay's blue eyes to the slate-
colored ones of Duny Gene, set off strikingly and a
little defiantly by the crow's-wing hair, black as a tar
barrel. The gray eyes were focused on Judge Pitt's
face, but it didn't bother him. He'd had plenty of

hardcase defendants stare at him over the years in this courtroom.

Beyond the railing that separated the pit from the spectators, every seat was filled. The balcony was jammed, too, people standing along the back walls. Judge Pitt could see a few black faces there. None were in the lower section, of course, because in the courthouse hallway was a large arrow sign that pointed upward and had a single word printed thereon: COLORED.

And in the balcony, he saw a large, rather stooped man, dark-faced with close-cropped hair and broad, high cheekbones. Down one side of his flat face was a line of black tattoo dots. It was all over town that Eben Pay had brought this man from Fort Smith, to be a companion or an assistant in preparing the case, or something else no one could imagine. But he was a very old Indian, not one to cause any disruption to the peace and tranquility of Fayetteville, and something of a curiosity that added to the fascination of the business at hand.

Judge Pitt finished his survey of the courtroom and turned to the sheaf of papers before him that he had carried from chambers. This thing is getting off like a scalded cat, he thought. Two days for jury selection and opening arguments yesterday afternoon, short and to the point. That was good and bad all at the same time. Good because it might indicate a short trial, which meant less burden on the taxpayers—a concern constant on his mind—but bad because he was looking forward to this one and hoped it wouldn't all be over before he could savor some of it.

Judge Pitt once again peered over the tops of his glasses. The room was still, all eyes on him. For the first time, he noted that there were a number of unfamiliar faces at the press table beside the jury box. He looked across the room at the double doors opening into the main hall. There were two deputy sheriffs there, on either side of the doors, nickel-plated revolvers hanging from their cartridge belts. Through the small window in each door, he could see faces gawking into the courtroom from the hallway.

"Now, I want to say this one more time," Judge Pitt said, his eyes running back and forth across the spectators' section. "I said it yesterday and I'll say it again. I want quiet in this courtroom. I won't put up with any noise or foot scuffling and coughing. If you got to cough, go outside to do it, and go without making any noise. I want no talking or laughing.

"Now, when I excuse the jury from the box, I want everyone here, including counsels and defendant, to sit where they're at until the jury is out and in their room. I don't want to catch anyone talking to a juror or winking or waving at him or anything else. I want this jury left alone, and you let 'em come and go while you sit still."

He paused a long time, letting it sink in, and then he turned to the prosecuting attorney.

"Are you ready, Lyle?"

"The state's ready, Your Honor."

Judge Pitt looked at Eben Pay.

"Are you ready, Mr. Pay?"

"The defense is ready, Your Honor."

"Call your first witness," Judge Pitt said, and Lyle Proctor rose from his chair.

In the front row of spectators, Tooth Snowdon jabbed an elbow into Olie Merton's ribs. They had claimed these choice seats before six o'clock that same morning.

"Now, by Gawd," Tooth whispered. "We'll get at it."

Lyle Proctor ran out his stable of early witnesses, designed to set the stage for the ones to follow. During this process, Eben Pay and his grandson exchanged a number of short, written notes, but they did not whisper together.

The coroner testified that Parkins Muller and one Hoadie Renkin had both died as the result of gunshot wounds. They were identified by citizens who had known them for a long time. He said Parkins Muller had been a registered Republican in the county for years, but that so far as anybody knew, Hoadie Renkin had never registered for anything.

"Mr. Muller died when a large-caliber bullet passed through his head from the left eyebrow, exiting behind the right ear," the coroner stated. "The Renkin boy was the victim of shock and loss of blood and the disruption of vital organ functions due to a shotgun blast in the lower chest cavity."

"Your witness," Proctor said, turning and smiling at Eben Pay. But Eben Pay waved his hand and the coroner was excused.

Then came Violet Sims, dressed like a country school-teacher with a blouse buttoned high around her neck. She was not wearing lipstick, but her nails were painted bright red, like horny-backed bugs sitting on the ends of her chubby fingers.

Violet told what she'd seen before the robbery, which wasn't much, and what she'd found in the bank when she arrived there. When Proctor was finished with her, Eben Pay rose and moved over to stand near her, straight and formal-looking, fingering the wolf's tooth on his watch chain. Like Proctor, he did not carry notes to the examination of witnesses, and old court hangers-on took this to mean that both men had prepared well.

"Miss Sims, when you found Miss Veda Muller in the bank, what was her condition?"

"I object," Lyle Proctor said, on his feet. "It's irrelevant."

"Your Honor, it is not irrelevant at all," Eben Pay

said calmly. "It is my privilege and duty to determine the condition of witnesses at the time they claim to have observed various things pertinent to this case."

"He's trying to impeach a witness I haven't even called yet," Proctor said.

"All right, Lyle," Judge Pitt said. "But he knows you're likely to call her, because her name's on the true bill the grand jury returned, and he's seen that. I'm gonna overrule you, Lyle. Go ahead, Mr. Pay."

"What was Miss Veda Muller's condition when you saw her in the bank immediately after the robbery?"

"She was all upset. She was screamin' and cryin' and it was a while before we could get her quieted down."

"What was the expression on her face?"

"Objection! Calls for an opinion."

"Your Honor," Eben Pay said patiently, "I am simply asking what this witness observed. I'm not asking for a clinical evaluation."

"Overruled."

"What was her expression, Miss Sims?"

"She was all glassy-eyed. She was sayin' things nobody could understand. Her hands were floppin' around like a bird's wing."

"Thank you, Miss Sims. I have no further questions."

The Weedy Rough constable was called. Tooth jabbed Olie Merton again.

"He don't look too comfortable, does he?" Tooth whispered.

"Shut up before you get us both thrown out of here," Olie hissed.

Leo testified that he and other citizens had come to the bank after they'd heard shooting. They found bloodstains leading across the street and into the tie yard. He and the other men went into the tie yard, he said, and saw a brown hat and a discarded red bandanna handkerchief, and later, following the stains, had gone into the railroad tunnel and found a dead man there. All the citizens recognized him as Hoadie Renkin, a boy who had lived in the hills outside Weedy Rough until only recently.

"Constable Sparks," Lyle Proctor said, "who was Hoadie Renkin's best friend?"

"I object, Your Honor," Eben Pay said quietly, without rising.

"Sustained," Judge Pitt said. He was leaning on his elbow, chin cupped in hand, watching the witness.

"Constable," Proctor continued, "how long have you known the defendant in this case?"

"Since he was a mite." Not once did Leo Sparks look toward the defense table.

"How often did you see him in the company of this Hoadie Renkin?"

"I don't know, Mr. Proctor. Pert' near ever' time Hoadie was around town, you seen Duny Gene with him, since they was little boys, huntin' with bean flips."

Proctor returned to his place and some of the spectators thought they saw a smile play on Duny Gene's face for a moment, but it wasn't there long.

Once more, Eben Pay took his stance for cross-examination.

"Constable Sparks, you mentioned a brown hat and a red handkerchief. Why would you mention those things?"

"Why, that's what the robbers wore."

"Ah. Then you saw the robbers?"

"I seen Hoadie Renkin in the tunnel."

"But before that, did you see any robbers either going into or coming out of the bank? Did you see them fleeing in their car?"

"No, they was all gone when I got down to town."

"Where were you during the robbery?"

"I was takin' a nap," Leo said, and as the spectators laughed his face puffed up and grew red. Judge Pitt tapped with his gavel.

"Well, then, if you were taking a nap through all of this and did not see the robbers at any time before or after they took money from the bank, how did you know they were wearing brown hats and red handkerchiefs?"

"Sheriff Ramey told me."

"How long after the robbery did he make this revelation?"

"I don't know. A few days, I guess. Maybe the next day."

"Did the prosecuting attorney tell you there were brown hats and red handkerchiefs involved in all of this?"

"I don't remember if he did or not."

"How much more were you told about this robbery by officers of the court?"

"I object to that, Your Honor," Lyle Proctor shouted.

"I withdraw it," Eben Pay said, and turned back to the defense table.

"Your Honor, I ask that you instruct the jury," Proctor said.

"About what?"

"Defense counsel did not allow this witness to answer his question."

"Your Honor, I asked a legitimate question," Eben Pay said. "I asked how much more some official of this court told the witness about the facts in this case. But I changed my mind. It is of little consequence, perhaps. At any rate, if prosecution wants an answer, he can ask the question again on redirect."

"Mr. Pay, are you trying to run your own case and mine as well?" Proctor snapped, bristling.

"You might need a little help."

"Now look here," Judge Pitt said. "I won't have this wrangling between you two."

"I apologize, Your Honor," Eben Pay said. "I accede to prosecution's request and add my own that the jury disregard the question, and that it be stricken from the record. For the sake of clarity, I suggest the question be read as stated."

"No," Judge Pitt said, trying to hide a smile. "I'll instruct that it be disregarded and stricken from the record, but I won't run it past the jury a third time."

This is one sneaky son of a bitch, Judge Pitt thought, watching Eben Pay take his seat. Then when Lyle Proctor released the witness without asking the question himself, Judge Pitt could hardly hide his astonishment. Not only a sneaky son of a bitch, he thought, but a damned good bluffer. I'd enjoy playing a little poker with that man.

It didn't seem to bother Lyle Proctor much. He was about to bring in some of his big guns. Everyone sensed it as he leafed through his stack of papers. Finally, Judge Pitt's patience wore brittle and he leaned forward, peering over his glasses.

"Well, Lyle, have you rested your case, or do you intend to call another witness?"

"I call Sheriff Geehyle Ramey," Proctor said, and the bailiff went to the main hallway doors, opened them, and called out.

"Geehyle, it's your turn."

Sheriff Ramey told the jury about being called to Weedy Rough, and what he'd found there. Nobody at the defense table showed any interest until Ramey testified that he and his deputies had dug a spent .45 slug from a counter just inside the bank doorway. Then Eben Pay looked up, his eyes alert.

Lyle Proctor went to one side of the bench, where the bailiff sat. They whispered a moment, the bailiff rummaging in a brown grocery sack beside his chair. Finally, he produced a small sealed envelope. Lyle Proctor moved quickly to the stand and handed the envelope to Geehyle Ramey.

"Do you recognize this, sheriff?"

"Yes sir, it's a sealed envelope I picked up from Professor Themore Bates at the university. It has his signature on it and the date he sealed it."

"Open it, please."

The sheriff ripped open the package and poured into his palm a single copper-jacketed bullet, flattened on the nose. He peered at the base and nodded.

"This is the bullet I found at the robbery scene," he said. "I put my mark on it there with a pocketknife, right after we found it."

"Did you have the bullet in your possession from the time you recovered it until you placed it in Professor Bates' hand?"

"I did. And after he called me to say the examination was finished, I picked up this package along with two others and I've had them all in my safe until this morning when I gave them to the bailiff of this court."

"Your Honor," Proctor said, "I will ask that this and other items be admitted to evidence at a later time, when I have completed the chain of custody."

Eben Pay rose. "Your Honor, allow me to compliment the officials of this court for the obviously well disciplined way in which they establish the chain of custody with physical evidence," he said. "And the defense has no objections to entering it at this time, if the prosecution so desires."

Lyle Proctor was taken aback only momentarily. He stared for a moment at Eben Pay, suspicion plainly written on his face. "Prosecution is grateful for small favors," he said.

"It's of no consequence," Eben Pay said. "You'd get it in anyway."

"Your Honor, I ask it be entered."

"Mark it prosecution number one, Ed," Judge Pitt said to the court reporter. And the fatal bullet was placed gingerly on the broad railing at the front of the jury box.

"Now sheriff," Lyle Proctor said, "you served a warrant on the defendant on Saturday, August 26, or thereabouts?"

"I did."

"Were other documents served that day?"

"Yes sir. A search warrant for the home of Barton Pay of Weedy Rough, the home of the defendant."

"And did you find any items specified in the warrant?"

"We did."

Once more, Proctor went to the bailiff, and again they carried out the brown-sack routine until the bailiff came up with yet another envelope, this one larger than the first. The sheriff opened it and identified it as a box of Peters .45-caliber army service ammunition. He inspected the box and lifted a few of the cartridges and looked at the nose of each bullet. The box was about half full.

"That's what we found. I marked the box and each bullet. There were twenty-two cartridges in the box. There are twenty-one now."

"I'll come back to that missing round in a moment, Your Honor," Proctor said. He glanced at Eben Pay, and after receiving a short wave asked that the box be entered in evidence, along with the remaining cartridges in it. This was done, and the box, open, was placed beside the single spent slug on the jury railing.

"Was anything else found in Barton Pay's house specified in the warrant?"

"Yes sir. A service automatic, Colt .45."

The bailiff handed up another sack, largest of all, and from it Geehyle Ramey pulled an automatic pistol. He identified it by serial number, and once more without objection it was entered in evidence. The jurors stared at it lying on the rail, a deadly chunk of cold metal, while the spectators in the rear rows half stood, craning their necks to get a look at the weapon.

"Now, sheriff, from the time you took these items until now, did they ever leave your custody?"

"Only when I took them to Professor Bates. He took all these items under lock and key in his laboratory. In three days I returned to his place and picked them up again. As I said before, all have been in my safe until I turned them over to the court."

"When you gave these items to Professor Bates, did you tell him the nature of the case?"

"I did not."

"Did you tell him where you had obtained these items?"

"No sir. All I told him was the nature of tests required. This meant firing a round in the pistol, and he asked if he could use the ammunition in the box, and I told him he could."

"All right. Now going back from that time, sheriff, had you ever seen the defendant before the Weedy Rough bank robbery?"

"The Saturday before the robbery, my deputies arrested him on the Siloam Springs road. That would have been August 12. He was driving a blue Studebaker coupe."

"And was anyone with him?"

"Yes sir, that boy Hoadie Renkin was with him."

"Is that the same Hoadie Renkin whose body you observed at the bank immediately after the robbery?"

"The same. I recognized him right away. He was a tall, skinny kid with light-colored hair."

"Why was that arrest made on the Siloam Springs road, sheriff?"

"We got a call from a service station on the Siloam Springs road. Kid there says these two had drove in and the tall one got out and said the guy at the wheel was Pretty Boy Floyd."

"Hearsay, Your Honor," Eben Pay said.

"Overruled," Judge Pitt said. "It states the reason for the sheriff responding to the call."

Lyle Proctor asked a few more questions, establishing how the boys were caught that rainy day, stuck in the mud. Then Geehyle testified that the blue Studebaker had turned up abandoned in Van Buren, Arkansas, on the day after the robbery.

Eben Pay glanced up sharply, then looked at Duny Gene and nodded, before rising to cross-examine.

"You saw Hoadie Renkin with Duny Gene on the Saturday before the robbery?" he began.

"That's right."

"Did you see them together after that?"

"When we released them from the county jail on the following Monday."

"And after that, did you see them together?"

"No, I didn't."

"You said your deputies apprehended these boys on the Siloam Springs road, is that right?"

"That's right."

"Why weren't you there?"

"I had other business at the jail."

"Are you trying to tell this jury that there was something more important than the apprehension of Pretty Boy Floyd? Or were you afraid to go, thinking it might be Floyd?"

"Now looka here . . ." Sheriff Ramey started, but Eben Pay waved his hand and was already turned back toward his seat.

"Your Honor?" Lyle Proctor asked, clearly angry at this prodding of his witness.

"All right, Lyle, all right," Judge Pitt said. "Jury disregard the last comment by defense counsel. It has no bearing on this case anyway."

"I must protest this business of the defense counsel making unseemly remarks reflecting on elected officials of this county," Lyle said.

"All right, Lyle, all right."

And in the front row of the spectators' gallery, Tooth Snowdon jabbed Olie Merton in the ribs again.

"That'll make 'em forget half of what ole Geehyle said."

At noon recess, Eben Pay walked back to the jail with Duny Gene and the pair of escorting deputies. They walked side by side, Duny Gene in handcuffs, the deputies behind them. No one said anything until they were back in the jail and the cuffs were taken off Duny Gene and his cell door was locked. Eben Pay waited for the deputies to go back to the outer office, standing with his hands locked on the bars.

"You feel all right?" he asked.

"Sure. It's not so bad. It's better than the waiting."

"We're lucky. Old Pitt wanted this thing tried. Sometimes you've got to wait months for your date to come up."

"Have they hurt us yet, Grandfather?" Duny Gene looked through the bars at Eben Pay, but little concern showed in his eyes.

"Not yet they haven't. But they'll try this afternoon. Is there anything else you want to tell me about this Veda Muller?"

"No. I think I covered it all. But don't forget about the goats."

Eben Pay smiled. "No. I won't forget about the goats. Well, I'll see you back in court. Joe Mountain's waiting for me, so I guess we'll catch a bite. You need anything?''

"No," Duny Gene said, and suddenly thrust his hand through the bars. Eben Pay took it for a moment and then pulled away. "I like the way you do it, Grandfather."

"If I'm not good at it by now, you've got an idiot for counsel."

Eben Pay started toward the exit door, meeting the jailer coming with a tray of food—white beans and corn bread and buttermilk. Duny Gene called to his grandfather, and he turned back.

"I didn't see Daddy or Mother today."

"No," Eben Pay said. "I asked them to stay away until I call them. They'll be here, when the time's right. You can believe that."

"If you say so."

"I say so. You got plenty of cigarettes?"

"Yeah, but you might get me a pack of Spearmint."

Down in the street, Eben Pay took a deep breath of the sharp fall air. Along College Avenue to the south, where it dropped into a wide valley, he could look to the hills in the distance, starting to turn brown. Toward the north, large elms and maples overhanging the street were already going bright red and yellow in this dry October.

Not far along the walk Joe Mountain waited, grinning, his large teeth showing in the dark face and the line of tattooed dots looking like ink spots. Eben Pay moved along the sidewalk and the Osage fell in beside him, standing a head taller than Eben Pay even with his old-man stoop. Under his narrow brim hat, Joe Mountain's hair was white but still stiff and thick.

"You laced a few folks this mornin', Eben Pay."

"It didn't amount to much. They'll start throwing it at us this afternoon, I suspect."

"Well, I'll tell you, this here is a good one. I like these murder trials. They're the best kind."

"Yes, I know. Come on, let's get a hamburger and a Coke."

A stripped-down roadster flew along the avenue, loaded with kids wearing porkpie hats. There was a buggy whip attached to the windshield frame, and from that a white flag with a red hog painted on it whipped back in the slipstream. Across the sides of the car was the printed message *Get 'em, Razorbacks*.

"These damn college kids." Joe Mountain laughed. "Crazy as hell, ain't they?"

Miss Veda Muller sat on the stand, having some difficulty keeping her dark blue straw hat in place. She wore an old-fashioned dress that came almost to her ankles, and at the ruffled collar was an ivory brooch. She was also having difficulty focusing her left eye on the prosecutor standing before her.

In the front row of spectators, Tooth Snowdon whispered, "That bad eye keeps wanderin', don't it?"

"Miss Muller, let me recall for you the date of August 16, this year. Could you tell the jury what happened to you on that day?"

"From the first?"

"Yes ma'am, from the first."

She straightened her hat, and the eyes of the jury on her obviously made her nervous and uncomfortable.

"We went to the bank like we always do, me and my brother Parkins," she said. Her voice was high-pitched. It seemed to go up a note now and again, into one of those high keys that hurt the ears. Then she would pause a moment and start again.

"It was a bad business day. There were a few customers in the bank that morning. We had our lunch. Do you want to know what that was?"

"It won't be necessary, Miss Muller. Just go on with what happened."

"It was about three o'clock, or thereabouts. I was working the ledger at the back counter. My brother Parkins was at the front, in the teller's cage. This big car came in front of the bank and stopped. It was the kind that had the top down, and there were two seats in it and it was tan."

She made another stab at her hat, pushing it back from her casting eye.

"Three men ran into the bank, and they yelled at us to throw up our hands. They had on brown hats and red handkerchiefs. They all had guns."

"What kind of guns, Miss Muller? Were they long guns, or handguns?"

"They were pistols," Miss Veda said. "They told us to stand still and one of them ran behind the counter and back to where I was, and to where the safe was. The safe was open like it always is when we're doing business. Two stayed by the door, pointing their guns at us. The one who had run back found a bank money-sack and he went to the safe and took all the money out and put it in the sack."

"How much money was that, Miss Muller?"

"Well, we had a railroad payroll of fourteen hundred dollars, and then there was some loose money. About two hundred dollars. The railroad payroll was still bundled."

"What happened then, Miss Muller?"

"Then the man ran out from behind the counter and all three of them backed out the door. There was still one of them sitting in the car."

"You mean there was a fourth man in the car?"

"Yes. There's a small plate-glass window in the bank and the car had parked far enough along so that I could see the front end of it. There was a man there behind the steering wheel. He was wearing a hat and red handkerchief, too, like the others.''

Miss Veda gulped and clutched her throat and Eben Pay came over from the defense table with a glass of water. Lyle Proctor took the glass from Eben Pay and handed it to his witness.

"Now, please go on, Miss Muller, I know it's hard, but you need to go on.''

"Well, as soon as the last man had left, my brother Parkins reached under the counter where he had always kept his shotgun since we were robbed back in 1925. He ran to the door and I heard the gun go off, and then another gun went off and my brother Parkins fell down in the doorway.''

She coughed, lowering her head and covering her mouth with both hands. But she did not cry, and after she had her hat in place again she looked at Lyle Proctor with one eye, the other still casting toward the jury.

"Now please recall for us, Miss Muller, did you recognize any of those four persons who robbed your bank and killed your brother Parkins?''

"Yes sir'' Miss Veda blurted. She turned to face the defense table for the first time and pointed. "I recognized him. Duny Gene Pay.''

The spectators made little rustling noises, and Judge Pitt glared over his steel-rimmed glasses and pecked at the bench with his gavel.

"Let's be still, now,'' he said. "Go ahead, Lyle.''

"And Miss Muller, did you recognize the person who shot and killed your brother Parkins as he stood in the doorway protecting his property?''

"He did,'' she said, pointing again.

"Let the record show that the witness pointed out the defendant, Duny Gene Pay,'' Lyle Proctor said, whirling around in the pit like a dancer, his number finished without missing a step. "Your witness, Mr. Pay.''

Eben Pay approached the witness with a second glass of water, and this one he handed to her himself. After she had sipped from the glass, she passed it back to him and dabbed at her lips with a lacy linen handkerchief that looked like it might have come out of the eighteenth century. Eben Pay took the glass back to the defense table deliberately. Duny Gene sat with vacant eyes, looking toward the jury but not really seeing them, and his jaw worked slowly on a cud of Spearmint chewing gum.

"Miss Veda," Eben Pay began, speaking gently. "I have only a few questions. You stated that you were at the rear of the bank, and you say you recognized Duny Gene in all of this. Where was he?"

"He was at the door. He was one of those two at the door."

"When the robbers left the bank, I assume they went toward the car?"

"I guess so."

"There is between the door and the small plate-glass window an intervening wall, is that correct?"

"Yes."

"Now you have testified that you saw the man shoot your brother."

"Yes, I did."

"How could this happen, Miss Veda? Did he remain in the doorway while his companions ran for the car?"

"I don't know what you mean."

"If he had gone toward the car, he would have been hidden from your view by that portion of wall between door and window."

"I saw him do it," she said defiantly, tugging at her hat.

"The man who shot your brother simply remained conveniently in your view, until your brother pursued him?"

"Object, Your Honor, he's badgering the witness," Proctor said.

"No, he isn't, there's nothing wrong with the question. Go on, Mr. Pay," Judge Pitt said.

"Perhaps I can clarify the question for you, Miss Veda, and for the jury," Eben Pay said. He moved across the pit and took three empty chairs from the defense table, and arranged them in a row, gaps between the chairs.

"Now, this first gap represents the door. This second one, the window. Where I am standing represents the position of the car, only partly seen through this second gap, or the window of the bank. Is this an approximation of the scene, Miss Veda?"

"I suppose it is," she said.

"Well, then," Eben Pay said, pointing to the first gap, "if I ran from this door and started for the car"—he placed his hand on his chest—"as you can see, I would be hidden from anyone observing me from inside the bank by this wall," and he placed a hand on the center chair. "Are you telling this jury that the man who shot your brother simply stood fairly in the doorway, waiting, thus allowing you to observe him?"

"I saw him," Miss Veda said, her jaw set.

Eben Pay slowly returned each chair to its place, then stood in the center of the pit, one hand to his chin. After a long pause, he turned back to the witness.

"Quite naturally, Miss Veda, you were upset when this occurred."

"Yes, I was."

"You were so upset that your friends and neighbors found it necessary to put you in bed, is that correct?"

"I lay down at home, a little later."

"You were so upset that a certain Doctor Barr, of

Weedy Rough, was called and gave you a sedative, is that correct?''

"I don't recall."

"Miss Veda, I can call Doctor Barr, if you like, but I had supposed it would not be necessary."

"He gave me something to make me sleep, I guess."

"On that day, did you speak with Sheriff Ramey?"

"A little bit. I was too upset to talk much. They'd just killed my brother Parkins." She dabbed at her nose again with the lace handkerchief.

"How long after the robbery was it, Miss Veda, when you identified Duny Gene Pay as one of the persons involved?"

"Well, I don't recall. The sheriff and a lot of people talked to me."

"Isn't it true, Miss Veda, that you identified him only *after* someone had told you that Hoadie Renkin was one of the robbers, and you assumed they were together?"

"Object," Lyle Proctor shouted.

"Overruled," Judge Pitt snapped. He was bent forward, almost lying on the bench, listening to the testimony. "You may answer, Miss Muller."

"I don't recall exactly when it was I told anybody," she said. "But it was him, all right."

"Isn't it true, Miss Veda," Eben Pay continued, moving closer to her, "that you identified Duny Gene Pay as one of the robbers after you had talked for some time with officials of this county, and that you made no positive statement in that regard until you knew Hoadie Renkin was involved and you were called to the grand jury?"

"I don't recall when it was," she said stubbornly. "It was a very hectic time and my memory isn't what it used to be."

Eben Pay turned back to the center of the pit to

stroke his chin once more. At the defense table, Duny Gene sat unmoved, but in his mind he had finally begun to realize that these little stances and posturings by his grandfather were not to give him time to think of the next question. They were for dramatic effect.

"Miss Veda, do you keep a herd of goats?" Eben Pay asked, and for the first time Duny Gene smiled and looked out into the crowd, his gaze going boldly along each row. Tooth Snowdon winked at him.

"Yes, my brother Parkins and me kept a herd of goats for many years."

"Did it ever come to your attention that Duny Gene Pay threw rocks at those goats?"

"Yes, he rocked them all the time, and sicced his dog on them, too. People who lived on West Mountain and could see across the valley to our pasture would call on the telephone and tell us about seeing him and Hoadie Renkin rocking our goats."

After the pressure of the previous questioning, she seemed eager to talk about something else, and Duny Gene chewed on his gum faster.

"How long did this go on, Miss Veda?"

"For as long as I can remember."

"It made you angry that someone would rock those goats, didn't it?"

"Of course it did, they were good milking goats."

"So for as long as you can remember, you have hated Duny Gene Pay for abusing your herd of goats."

"I object," Lyle shouted.

"I think she ought to answer it," Judge Pitt said.

Miss Veda adjusted her hat.

"I've never liked the boy," she said.

"Yes, and in fact, you hated him, didn't you Miss Veda," Eben Pay said, moving in close to her again, his words coming like popcorn from a hot skillet. "And you told this jury that he was one of the robbers, that he killed your brother when actually you didn't recognize anyone at all during the robbery, and identified him only after someone else *told* you that Hoadie Renkin was there. Isn't that true?''

''Objection!'' Proctor was around his table and charging the bench. ''He's testifying. He's badgering. He's asking her to answer a basket of questions all at once, and she's already answered all of them.''

''All right, I'll sustain that,'' Judge Pitt said.

''I think it's a good question, Your Honor,'' Eben Pay said, his own voice showing the rough edges of anger.

''This court will be the judge of what's a good question, Mr. Pay,'' Judge Pitt said, a little tightness showing around the corners of his mouth. ''The objection is sustained and the last statement by defense counsel will be disregarded and stricken. You'll have to do some rephrasing, Mr. Pay.''

''Your Honor, I ask an exception,'' Eben Pay said.

''Get it on the record, Ed,'' Judge Pitt said. ''Now go on with your cross.''

''I'm finished with this witness,'' Eben Pay said, and sat down.

Duny Gene leaned toward him and whispered, ''Grandfather, what's an exception?''

''It means I don't agree with the judge's decision on the objection. It'll come in handy if we lose this thing and have to appeal. It's called saving for a rainy day.''

Lyle Proctor tried a lot of patching on his witness's testimony, but not much came of it. The jury sat impassively. As he watched them, Eben Pay could see very little. They were a typical group of men from this hill country, some from towns, some from the sticks. A few wore bib overalls, and equally as many were wearing neckties. The only thing Eben

Pay knew about them was that over half were Masons. He'd seen to that on *voir dire*. He figured that might also come in handy later.

On the east side of the square next to the Palace Theater was the Smoke Shop. A man named Brad was the proprietor, selling fine cigars and canned tobacco from the best line of that type merchandise in town. He also made the best cherry malts and chicken salad sandwiches in the county. Eben Pay had taken most of his evening meals there since arriving in Fayetteville, but on this night he wanted something more private.

He went to the Piggly-Wiggly grocery store at one corner of the square and bought a can of salmon, a small box of crackers, a hunk of yellow rat cheese, and a quart of milk. The total tab was fifty-eight cents.

It was just dark as he walked across the square to his hotel. There were a few guests sitting on the long porch that faced the street, in wicker rocking chairs, and he nodded to them as he went past and into the lobby. The clerk watched him suspiciously, which was not unusual. The entire hotel staff had watched him suspiciously since he had first registered for two rooms, one for himself, the other for Joe Mountain. The Washington Hotel was not accustomed to hosting large Osage Indians with dots tattooed along their cheeks.

On the second floor, he tapped on Joe Mountain's door, then went on to his own and keyed it open. Joe Mountain came from his room and followed Eben Pay into the corner suite that overlooked the square with windows looking out in two directions. The lights from the street below illuminated the room dimly, but they did not turn on any lamps.

"Let's eat," Eben Pay said, and Joe Mountain started taking things from the brown grocery bag.

Eben Pay sat down beside a window with a sigh, slipped off his shoes, and lifted his feet to the sill. Looking past the post office at the center of the square, he could see the Palace Theater marquee, in electric lights. They were playing a Tarzan movie with Johnny What's-His-Name, and that trained ape.

"Where you been at, Eben Pay?"

"Law library at the university," he said. "A hunch I had today when they introduced that bullet. More than a hunch, I suppose. I thought I'd stock up on a few recent citations."

"I been over at the pool hall," Joe Mountain said. "Them fellas don't act too friendly."

"Hell, Joe, you're out of your home country. They never saw anything like you up here. You should've whipped out that old French trade hatchet. That'd give 'em something to talk about."

"Hell, I don't carry that thing no more, you know that."

The room was suddenly filled with the smell of salmon as Joe Mountain cut open the can with a large pocketknife. They ate the salmon from the can, with their fingers, breaking off chunks of the cheese to go with the crackers. Joe Mountain shook the milk bottle to mix the cream, holding his thumb over the cap. They drank from the bottle, passing it back and forth.

"I like them bones," Joe Mountain said, his teeth crunching the mealy backbone of the canned fish. "How they get 'em so soft?"

"They cook it, very hot," Eben Pay said.

After they'd finished, they sat in the darkness, watching the cars cruising the square. Some walkers were on the sidewalks, window-shopping.

"I hate to think of that boy down there in jail," said Eben Pay, almost to himself. Joe Mountain said nothing.

They had been together for a long time—from the

first week Eben Pay had arrived in Fort Smith, back
in 1890, he a young law clerk and Joe Mountain a
scout and tracker for some of Judge Parker's deputies. They had seen a great deal together, in Fort
Smith courtrooms and in the old Indian Territory—
some of it good, some bad—and they knew each
other so thoroughly that often they went for hours
without speaking. But with a great deal of communi-
cation going on just the same.

"Tomorrow, they'll bring out the real stuff," Eben
Pay said.

"We'll be ready," Joe Mountain said. "Won't
we?"

"I sure as hell hope so."

The breeze was from the north, and at his open
window, looking through the bars, Duny Gene Pay
thought he could smell the chili at the Castle Luncheonette. He could see the dim outline of the courthouse in the streetlight glow, and the grassy plot of
ground between the courthouse and the jail. One of
the deputy sheriffs had said that in the old days that's
where they'd erected the gallows when somebody
was hanged.

That particular deputy was a son of a bitch. He
enjoyed talking about such things, standing out in the
jail hallway, leaning against the wall well back from
the bars, toying with his nickel-plated revolver. He
said Duny Gene would like the old electric chair at
Tucker Prison Farm. It was handmade, built by the
cons themselves years ago and still in use.

"It ain't too comfortable, I reckon," the deputy
said, grinning. "But you don't have to sit in it very
long."

Duny Gene kept his mouth shut. When any of
them spoke to him, he looked at them with his flat
stare, and usually they would not meet his eyes with

their own. At least Geehyle Ramey was decent to him, and the jailer, who lived in the rear of the building with his wife and prepared the meals and swamped out the cells and hallways and such like.

They all called Duny Gene "Chief," and some kidded him about his black hair, straight as strung wire, and asked him to do a scalp dance. He said nothing, watching them, waiting for the blows he'd heard always came when one was in jail. But no one ever abused him, even though he expected it every night.

We're putting on a nice show for all the folks, he thought, watching the last of the lights go off in the courthouse windows. He had seen all the Weedy Rough gang in the courtroom that day. Tooth and Homer and Reese and Olie. Once, when he looked into the balcony, among all the black people he'd seen old Ike Renkin and Audie, faces long and showing no emotion. He thought he saw Arlene Kruppman there, too, but he wasn't sure.

Just a goddamned show, he thought, showing all these bastards how the state goes about sending a man to the chair at Tucker.

"Hey, Chief, you want some coffee?"

Duny Gene turned. The jailer was passing a tin cup, steaming with coffee, through the bars.

"I'd rather have a long shot of good whiskey," Duny Gene said, taking the cup. "Thanks."

The jailer stood back against the hallway wall as Duny Gene sipped the coffee.

"I gotta watch till you're finished, then take the cup. They're afraid you might make a knife out of it and cut yourself."

"Yeah, that sounds real likely," Duny Gene said. "Your wife make this?"

"Sure. She makes all the grub here."

"How long you and your wife been doing this?"

"Three years."

"Why'd anybody want to live in a jail?"

"It's a job. That's more'n lots of folks got nowa-days. I'm a car mechanic by trade."

They were silent then until Duny Gene finished the coffee and handed the empty cup back through the bars.

"Tell your wife thanks," he said.

"You're welcome," the jailer said. Before turning away, he looked at Duny Gene's face for a long time. "From what I hear, Chief," he said, "they're gonna fry your ass."

"It looks like they're sure as hell gonna try."

·18·

WHEN RUBY DENTON FIRST CAME INTO THE courtroom and took her place on the witness stand, the spectators gawked and gasped at the stunning effect of the sunlight from the east windows across her platinum hair. But from the jury box, where a closer look was possible, the light only served to illuminate the hard circles under her eyes and the fact that the roots of her hair had gone dirty brown during her stay in the county jail. Her left arm was in a blue cloth sling.

She was the second witness Lyle Proctor called that day. The first had been the man who operated the Ridge View Tourist Camp. He had testified that a man and woman in a Packard touring car arrived at his place about six or seven days before the robbery. The woman came into his store, paid a week's lodging in advance, and said their name was Mr. and Mrs. Smith.

"There was another man, too," he testified. "In a blue coupe. I didn't see what he looked like."

The Ridge View Tourist Camp man said he had seen a car he thought was Barton Pay's Model A parked at the Smiths' cabin a number of times, but on cross-examination admitted that he'd never actually seen Duny Gene or anyone else driving it. On the day of the robbery, which he hadn't heard about until later, he said all three cars pulled out at one time or another, and had not returned. He couldn't recall the sequence in which they had left, or who was driving them at the time. "Mrs. Smith seemed like a real nice lady," he said.

Now, it was Ruby's turn, and she sat on the stand as though she were born to it, relaxed and smiling and showing her ankles below the hem of her dress. Duny Gene noted it was the same dress he had watched her strip off at Frog Creek swimming hole, and he wondered if she was still wearing those orange step-ins.

"My boyfriend was named Lester Bains," Ruby was saying. "He'd found this kid named Renkin on some garbage dump in Louisiana. We were pals and spent some time in Texas. Then we came to Arkansas when this kid Renkin said he knew about a bank here that was a crackerbox. We got this cabin, close to the town, you see. Close to Weedy Rough. Then this kid named Renkin brought out one of his old friends to meet us and to help us make this bank."

"Is that man in the courtroom?" Lyle Proctor asked.

"That's him over there," Ruby said, pointing. "The kid with the black hair. Duny Gene Pay."

"Did you spend some time with the defendant?"

"Sure, we all four of us went down to some creek a couple times and had a swim and ate picnic stuff and the boys shot the guns. The second time, I guess it was, Duny Gene brought out his daddy's gun, and they shot that, too."

Lyle Proctor lifted prosecution exhibit number three from the jury railing and held it before Ruby's face.

"Miss Denton, would this be the pistol you say defendant brought along for this target practice?"

"I never took no numbers off it," she said, and laughed. "But that looks like it. It was that kind of gun, a Colt .45 automatic."

"Very well, now," Lyle said, and gently placed the gun back before the jury. "Tell us about the day of the robbery."

"We all got in the Packard and drove down the federal highway towards the south. Then we took out on a dirt road and wound around through these mountains so we could come into Weedy Rough from the west side. Lester said he didn't want to come and go the same road. This Renkin kid and Duny Gene both knew the way.

"We stopped on a hill west of town and Lester gave us all a hat and a red bandanna. We had a few drinks of whiskey. Then we put on the hats and fastened the bandannas around our faces, and drove in to the bank. I was at the wheel."

"You were driving?"

"Yeah, Lester and me always argued about it, but I'm a better driver than him."

"Go on, Miss Denton."

"At the bank, the others went inside, and I stayed in the car with the motor runnin'. It didn't take long. About two minutes. I was lookin' back to the bank door and Lester run out first. He was carryin' a canvas sack. Then the other two came out, this Renkin kid and Duny Gene. Duny Gene, he jumped in the car, in the backseat, and this Renkin kid was still makin' it towards the car when an old man run to the door of the bank with a shotgun. Lester was lookin' back, too, and seen this old man and he yelled out, and this Renkin kid turned around.''

"You mean Hoadie Renkin stopped and faced the bank again?''

"That's right. Still in the street behind the car. Then this old man let go with the shotgun and I seen this Renkin kid go down and Lester started yellin' for me to get the hell out of there. Then Duny Gene shot from the backseat, and I stepped on the gas.''

"From what you've said before, I assume you did not go out of town the same way you came in.''

"Naw, we tore right through the middle of it, what there is of it, and came to the federal highway and turned south toward the cabins. When we got there, we pulled in, and Lester wanted me to drive this Renkin kid's car out of there. Lester run into the cabin for a minute seein' that we hadn't left anything, and Duny Gene jumped out and got in his Ford. Then we all pulled out, me in the coupe and Lester drivin' the Packard now. One after the other, we turned down south towards Fort Smith. Duny Gene was trailin' us, but in a minute he turned his car off into some dirt road and that's the last I seen of him until now.''

Then she told about stopping to have another drink of whiskey and Lester counting the money. Most of it was in bundles, she said, and Lester leafed through the bills without taking the bands off because he thought that made it look so clean and neat. They had a laugh about Duny Gene going rabbit on them and leaving before he got his share. They drank some more whiskey and waited until it was dark.

"We drove to some place called Van Buren, and I ditched the coupe."

"You drove it into a ditch?"

"Naw, I just left it parked beside the road. Then I got in the car with Lester and we went on. He was a little drunk by then and driving too fast, and we had a wreck right in the middle of this town."

In the spectators' section, Tooth Snowdon whispered, "That may wean the calf."

On cross-examination, Eben Pay proceeded slowly at first, picking up speed as he went. None of it seemed to bother Ruby Denton one way or the other. Tooth Snowdon observed later, as he related all the details in the barbershop, that she was cold as a woodyard wedge in winter and tougher than a boiled owl.

"Miss Denton," Eben Pay began, "you observed that this pistol, prosecution exhibit number three, is a Colt .45 automatic. This indicates to me that you have some knowledge of firearms."

"You couldn't be around Lester long and not pick up a lot about guns."

"Lester had a number of guns, didn't he?"

"Yeah, he sure did," she said.

"Did Lester have a Colt .45 automatic?"

"He had two of 'em."

"I believe that when you and Lester were picked up in Van Buren by the police there, a submachine gun was found in your car?"

"That's right. It was Lester's."

"But in the robbery, the machine gun was not used?"

"Naw, it was just sort of a toy for Lester. He had a pistol."

"Just like this one?" Eben Pay asked, pointing to prosecution exhibit number three.

"That's right. Like that one."

Eben Pay paused and looked at the jury, each one in turn.

"Miss Denton, at the time Parkins Muller appeared in the doorway of the bank with a shotgun, you testified that you were turned in the seat so you could see him."

"I saw him."

"And when Mr. Muller fired, Lester began shouting to get the hell out of there, I believe those were your words."

"That's right."

"And did you get the hell out of there?"

"I sure did."

"As you drove off, were you still looking toward the rear?"

"I watch where I'm drivin', not like Lester a lot of times. He was an awful driver."

"Then how could you have seen anyone in the backseat fire a second shot?"

"Well, then, I heard it. The kid was the only one in the backseat."

"Couldn't it have been Lester who fired?"

"I heard the shot from the rear seat. Lester was in front beside me."

"But you were excited and concentrating on your driving. How could you be so sure it was not Lester who fired?"

"It came from the backseat."

"You mean it sounded as though it might have come from there."

"It came from there."

"But you did not see who fired that shot."

"No, but I heard it."

"You did not see it."

"No, I didn't."

"But Miss Denton, that's what you implied in your previous testimony. You left the impression that you *saw* the shot fired, and now you contradict yourself, admitting that you were not even looking in that direction."

Proctor came out of his chair. "Objection. He's not asking a question, he's making a statement. He's always making statements."

"Sustained. Mr Pay, you'll have to rephrase so the witness will know what question you want a response to," Judge Pitt said.

"Miss Denton, at the bank, did you see any shot fired other than the one that felled Hoadie Renkin?"

"How many times does he have to ask it?" Proctor said, looking disgusted.

"No, I never," Ruby said.

There was another long pause, and Judge Pitt waited patiently along with everyone else. Finally, after taking a turn around the pit, scratching his chin and fingering his wolf's tooth, Eben Pay stopped before the witness.

"You had the opportunity to observe Duny Gene Pay and Hoadie Renkin over some period of time, is that right?"

"Little less than a week in all."

"Would you say they were close friends?"

"Objection. Opinion."

"Sustained."

"Miss Denton, you said that after you arrived in the vicinity of Weedy Rough, Hoadie Renkin brought Duny Gene to you. Now, you were planning the robbery at this time, is that correct?"

"Yeah, that's right."

"Why would you and Lester have allowed some person who was a complete stranger to become a part of this operation?"

"Because the Renkin kid said Duny Gene was all right and a friend of his for a long time. I said that before."

"That's hearsay, Your Honor," Lyle Proctor said.

"Overruled. It's stated as a cause for her action."

"Miss Denton," Eben Pay said, "did either of these boys indicate any affection for one another?"

"Objection, Your Honor. Opinion again."

"I don't think so, Lyle. Overruled. Answer the question, Miss Denton."

"They seemed real close. They were always horsin' around together and talkin' about the good times they'd had when they was kids."

Eben Pay smiled and made a small bow. "Thank you, that's very helpful. Now please explain to me why Duny Gene Pay would have stayed in a car, driven away in it, when his close and dear friend for many years was lying wounded in the street."

"Now Your Honor," Lyle Proctor said, standing red-faced at his table. "That's asking her for an opinion."

"Sustained."

"I withdraw it," Eben Pay said, but he looked at the jurors again and was still smiling. Duny Gene saw one juror smile back, and he figured that was a nice sign. But by his stance, Eben Pay indicated his jokes were finished and very serious business was at hand. He crossed his arms on his chest and stared hard at Ruby.

"Miss Denton, how long have you known a man named Kid Tabor?"

For the first time since she'd appeared, Ruby allowed the trace of a frown to crease her penciled eyebrows. But it was only for a moment.

"I never heard of him."

"When you said you stopped on the road before going into Weedy Rough—to drink whiskey and put on those hats and bandannas—didn't you meet a man at that time, whose name was Kid Tabor?''

"We didn't meet anybody."

"Didn't you meet him and take him on the robbery with you, and wasn't it this man in the backseat with Hoadie Renkin and who later drove Hoadie Renkin's car away from the tourist camp after Hoadie was shot?''

"Your Honor, he's testifying there," Lyle Proctor shouted, "and I object to this repeated reference to someone the witness has already said she doesn't know."

"Your Honor, I am in the process of impeaching this witness."

"With some imaginary person?"

"Your Honor, we know that Ruby Denton, Lester Bains, and Hoadie Renkin were in that robbery car." Eben Pay paused for a full ten-count before he continued. "I am concerned here with the *fourth* person."

Judge Pitt looked agitated and yanked off his glasses. "Approach the bench," he snapped.

Eben Pay and the prosecutor moved to the bench, with the reporter standing close to them, an ear cocked to hear what was being said and scribbling his notes. They whispered for a long time, and when they turned back to their places Lyle Proctor was smiling.

"The objection is sustained," Judge Pitt said, replacing his glasses. "And the jury will disregard any reference made by defense counsel to this fourth person."

"Exception, Your Honor," Eben Pay said, and Ed recorded it.

In the front row, Tooth Snowdon whispered to Olie, "By Gawd, maybe the calf ain't weaned yet."

Eben Pay turned back to Ruby and smiled, and she smiled back.

"Miss Denton, in those days before the robbery—at

the cabin, when you first saw Duny Gene Pay—did you find him handsome?''

Ruby looked across the room at Duny Gene and shrugged. "He's a pretty-good-lookin' kid."

"Miss Denton, isn't it true that during this time, before the robbery, you tried to seduce him?"

Ruby looked back into Eben Pay's eyes, her own unwavering. A little smile tugged at each corner of her mouth, and she glanced at Lyle Proctor, who shrugged.

"We played around a little bit."

The jurors sat immobile and stoic, but the spectators seemed to lean forward and make a sound like wind passing through oak leaves. Judge Pitt gently rapped with his gavel.

"Isn't it true he refused your advances?"

"I object to this whole line of questioning," Proctor said.

"Overruled. You can answer that, Miss Denton."

"I wouldn't say he refused all of it," Ruby said.

"Isn't it true that he would not in the end have sexual intercourse with you and that this enraged you against him?"

"Objection, it's irrelevant."

"No, Lyle," Judge Pitt said. At some point on this morning he had slipped a cud of tobacco into his cheek, and he shifted it now, one side to the other. "But Mr. Pay, you've got to ask your questions one at a time. And Miss Denton, none of this one way or the other business. Just answer the questions directly with the truth."

"Thank you, Your Honor," Eben Pay said. "Miss Denton, did you succeed in having Duny Gene commit adultery with you?"

"No, not all the way. But I ain't married," she said. The spectators laughed, and it was some time before Judge Pitt could restore order.

"Then you lied, didn't you Miss Denton, when you told that tourist-camp attendant that you and Lester were man and wife, and you lied about your name with him, too."

"You never give your right name unless you have to," she said.

"In other words, Miss Denton, you are an habitual liar!"

"Objection!" Lyle Proctor was up waving a yellow pencil like a baton.

"I withdraw it, Your Honor," Eben Pay said. "I suppose the facts speak for themselves."

"There he is again, making statements," Lyle yelled.

"Mr. Pay, you've got to stop throwing out these comments," Judge Pitt said. "The jury will disregard that last one."

"I apologize, Your Honor."

Eben Pay marched back toward the defense table as though he were finished. Lyle Proctor was halfway to the witness stand before Eben Pay turned back.

"I have more questions," he said. Proctor went back to his place, muttering to himself and frowning.

"Miss Denton," Eben Pay continued, "you have confessed under oath that you were a part of this robbery and murder."

"Well, the robbery, anyway. We didn't want anyone to get shot."

"And you are wanted in the state of Texas on various felonies, are you not?"

"Objection!"

"Sustained," Judge Pitt said. "Now, Mr. Pay, you know that charges against a witness cannot be cited to impeach, only convictions. You know that. The jury will disregard your question."

"I ask it be stricken," Lyle Proctor said.

"Yes, Lyle, I've just done it. Ed, strike Mr. Pay's comment."

"Which comment, Your Honor?" Eben Pay asked, straightfaced.

"They know which comment," Judge Pitt said, growing a little pink around the ears. "I'm getting sick and tired of all this folderol. Can't we just get on with the case?"

"Your Honor, I cannot believe you are calling my efforts to defend my client folderol," Eben Pay said. "It appears to be a comment from the bench on the evidence."

"No, no, it is no such thing," Judge Pitt said. "I'm talking about counsels' bickering. Once more, prosecution's objection is sustained. And the jury will disregard your comment regarding comments from the bench."

"I ask an exception on both counts."

"All right, all right, get it in there, Ed."

For the first time, Eben Pay went to his table and took a sheaf of papers, leafing through them and frowning. He stood so that the jury could clearly see certain and various seals and ribbons and other official-looking markings. After a few moments, he advanced on the witness and read from his papers.

"Miss Denton, did you on or about January 17, 1932, steal a black, four-door Hupmobile from one Albert Craneburg, of Odessa, Texas?"

"I object, Your Honor," Lyle Proctor shouted.

"Overruled. Answer it, Miss Denton."

"I never done that," she said calmly.

Eben Pay pulled forth another paper with a gold seal at the top. He made sure the jury saw the seal.

"Miss Denton, on or about March 3, 1927, did you not take a blue felt coat with an imitation-fox collar from the Winston department store in Monahans, Texas, without paying for same?"

"Objection."

"Overruled."

"I never done that, either."

Once more, another paper, legal-sized and with print running all the way to the bottom, held so the jury could see it.

"Isn't it true, Miss Denton, that on or about April 5, 1933, you were soliciting for prostitution on the streets of Lubbock?"

"I never done that."

Eben Pay looked at her a long time, shrugged, and dropped the bundle of papers on the jury railing. Lyle Proctor was enraged, running forward, his tie stringing out behind.

"What's he doing, what's he doing?" he shouted. "That's not evidence, it's not evidence."

He snatched up the papers and ran across the pit and threw them onto the defense table.

"Mr. Pay," Judge Pitt said, his voice raised for the first time during this trial, "unless you intend to introduce evidence, you keep your papers in your own place."

The audience sighed, and Tooth glanced at Olie, who was scratching his neck. In the balcony, Joe Mountain was leaning on the railing, grinning.

"Now Miss Denton," Eben Pay said at once, "have you been arraigned in this very court for armed robbery and murder?"

"That's right."

"And isn't it true that the prosecuting attorney offered you a deal if you would testify against the defendant here, a deal that would ensure a light sentence for yourself?"

"I object," Lyle Proctor said, and he came toward the bench. "May I approach the bench?"

Judge Pitt waved them forward once more, and the

two lawyers and the reporter leaned against the bar. They spoke in tones too low for the jury to hear.

"What're they doin'?" Tooth whispered.

"How the hell do I know?" Olie said.

Then the little huddle broke up and everyone returned to his station, and Lyle Proctor's face was working furiously.

"Ed, repeat the question," Judge Pitt said, and Ed read it from the notes. "All right, Miss Denton, answer it."

"Mr. Proctor said if I cooperated with him, he'd cooperate with me."

"In other words, if you helped convict Duny Gene Pay, the prosecutor would repay you with recommendation for a light sentence?"

"Objection."

"Overruled."

"I don't recall exactly what we said. Just that if I cooperated with him, he'd cooperate with me."

After Lyle Proctor finished his redirect, which was not much except a rehash of what he'd gotten on direct, Eben Pay rose to request a recess for the remainder of the day.

"Mr. Pay, I see no reason to waste a whole half-day," Judge Pitt said.

"Your Honor, this case came to trial very quickly for charges so serious, and I had inadequate time to prepare. With certain turns of events now, I request these few hours, and will ask for nothing more."

Judge Pitt fumed about it for a while and finally recessed court until the next morning at eight o'clock.

For most of the afternoon, Eben Pay stayed in his hotel room, going over his notes and watching the people on the square below. On the bed, Joe Mountain lay with his feet hanging over the end, reading a recent issue of *Wild West Weekly*. Since Eben Pay had been in town, one of the things Duny Gene had asked for was western magazines. Once he'd finished them, Eben Pay picked them up for Joe Mountain to read.

There was no conversation between them that afternoon, except once when Joe Mountain laughed.

"Eben Pay, these here stories are crazy as hell. I never saw anything like this happen in Fort Smith in the old days. Maybe it happened out in Arizona or somewheres."

"I doubt it," Eben Pay said.

That evening, toward time for the *Daily Democrat* to come out, Eben Pay walked across the square to the Smoke Shop and had a cherry malted. He smoked a cigar, sitting at the counter and talking with Brad, the proprietor, until the boy arrived with the bundle of newspapers. Eben Pay bought the first one and folded out the front page. He started to smile. He hoped the jurors were thinking like the newspapermen who'd been in the courtroom. The banner head proclaimed: NEW 4TH PERSON HINTED.

He knew the jurors would never see this newspaper, at least not until after the trial. Judge Pitt had them sequestered at the Mountain Inn Hotel. But if only Mr. Kid Tabor was in their minds, it would be good. And the recess would give them plenty of time to think about it before the next prosecution witness tomorrow, and without their thoughts being cluttered overnight with a lot of other evidence that Eben Pay knew was coming.

·19·

"MY NAME IS THEMORE BATES. I AM A LIEU-
tenant colonel in the ordnance corps of the United
States Army Reserve and am presently a member of
the university faculty in the physics department. In
the past, I have been assigned at the army's ordnance
arsenal at Springfield, Massachusetts, where .45 service automatic pistols were then manufactured, and
have for the past fifteen years been involved in the
identification of firearms through examination of bullets fired therefrom."

He was a large, ruddy man with a sandy mustache
and a tweed coat, and he held an unlighted pipe in
his hand as he gave his qualifications as an expert
witness.

Before him, Lyle Proctor was the image of confi-
dence, well combed but still grim, still businesslike.
And now, as he questioned, he held notes in his
hand.

"Would you explain the nature of this procedure?"

"All gun barrels, except shotguns, have a spiral
cutting in the surface of the bore called lands and
grooves. This is also sometimes called rifling," Professor Bates said. "When a bullet passes through the
bore, these tooled lands and grooves give a rotation
to the bullet that stabilizes it in flight. Passing through
the bore, the bullet will be engraved along those

surfaces touching the lands and grooves, giving each bullet a distinctive marking which is called a signature.''

"Professor," Lyle Proctor said, "by examination, can you determine if a bullet has been fired from a particular weapon?"

"Almost without fail—by firing a second test bullet in that same weapon and making a study of the signature under a comparison microscope."

"What is that?"

"It's a microscope that displays two images in the eyepiece, and in the case of bullets they can be rotated under the lens to line up the appropriate markings."

"So it is a science, this identification of firearms by such a method?"

"Yes, over the past few years, I would say it has become a science."

Lyle Proctor said, "And the .45 automatic is your particular province?"

"I have worked with that weapon more than any other, and have been personally acquainted with its manufacture for some years."

Then Proctor showed him the fatal bullet and the .45 pistol, and Bates identified them as those having been brought to him by the sheriff. Proctor produced another sealed envelope from the bailiff's grocery bag, and inside was a slug that the professor identified as one he had fired through Barton Pay's gun.

"Where did you obtain this cartridge that you fired?"

"From a box of ammunition the sheriff brought along with this other material," he said.

Lyle Proctor handed him the half-empty box of ammunition, and Bates examined it and said this was the box, according to his own markings. Lyle Proctor continued to glance back toward the defense table, as though expecting an objection, but none came.

"Please tell the jury of any examination you made with these items."

"I inspected the evidence bullet—"

Proctor interrupted him and held up the flattened slug.

"You mean this bullet that you have just now identified?"

"Yes sir. I inspected it and determined that it was a Peters Cartridge Company make, and that it was a two-hundred-and-thirty-grain bullet—"

"What is that, professor? These grains?"

"It's a measure of weight in the United States customary system, an avoirdupois unit equal to a little over point zero, zero, two ounces."

"Go ahead, professor."

"I then took a bullet from the same manufacturer, and of the same weight, and fired it in the evidence pistol."

"This pistol, which you have identified?" Lyle Proctor pointed to Barton Pay's pistol on the jury rail.

"Yes sir. I took a bullet from the box brought to me by the sheriff, because these were of Peters manufacture and of the correct weight."

"And what was the result?"

"I found that the test bullet which I fired through this pistol had the same signature as the evidence bullet."

"Which means?"

"It means that both my test bullet and the evidence bullet were fired through that same pistol."

The spectators murmured until Judge Pitt rapped them to silence. After they had quieted, Eben Pay rose to object.

"On what grounds?" Judge Pitt asked.

"On the grounds that the witness is usurping the prerogative of the jury," Eben Pay said. "In a most recent case concerning the testimony of an expert witness, *State of Iowa* versus *Steffen*, the Iowa Supreme Court held that an expert witness may not act as a juror. An expert witness can only state his *opinion*. The fact of the matter is the province of the jury alone.''

"I'd like to see that citation," Lyle Proctor said.

"I will be glad to provide the volume, page, section, and paragraph, as well as the stack where the volume may be found in the law library at the same university that employs this witness," Eben Pay said.

"All right," Judge Pitt said. "I'll sustain the objection, with instruction to the jury to disregard that portion of the testimony where the witness stated as fact that both bullets came from the same gun. You'll have to rephrase, Lyle."

"Professor," Proctor said, "may I ask if your test revealed information upon which to base an opinion?"

"Yes sir, it did. My opinion is that both bullets came from the same weapon."

"That is your expert opinion?"

"That is my opinion."

Lyle Proctor went to the bailiff and returned with a large sheet of cardboard on which were mounted, side by side, two enlarged photographs of bullets. The marks of the lands and grooves were visible on them. The professor identified the photographs, stating that he had made them. He said the bullet on the left was the evidence bullet, the other his own test bullet. He then proceeded to show similar markings on each, using his pipe as a pointer. Lyle Proctor proposed to have the photographs entered in evidence, and this was done without objection.

"Your witness," Lyle Proctor said, and marched off to his seat.

"Professor," Eben Pay began, "I have just now

seen these photographs, so I may ask some foolish questions about them."

Eben Pay retrieved the large cardboard matt from the jury railing where Lyle Proctor had placed it, and turned so that jury and witness could both see the pictures.

"I can see some similarities in these bullets," Eben Pay said. "But they show on only one side, is that true?"

"Yes sir."

"Why is that?"

"This view of the bullets provides the best comparison of signature."

"So we don't know what might be on the other side of these slugs, do we?"

"Well, you see—"

"Just a yes or no answer will be adequate, Professor Bates."

"No, not from these photographs."

"So we don't know how they compare on that far side, do we?"

"No, but—"

"Thank you, professor," Eben Pay cut in. He bent to the photographs and peered at them closely, frowning. He tapped one of the photographs with his finger, being sure the jury could see where he was pointing.

"Now this little spot here. It appears on one bullet, but I fail to see it on the other. Why is that?"

"There will sometimes be distinctive markings on a single bullet fired through a particular weapon."

"That is to say, bullets fired through the same weapon will sometimes have dissimilar signatures?"

"It can happen, to some degree."

"And isn't it true as well that often bullets fired from different weapons can have similar signatures?"

"Well, that's true, but—"

"Thank you, professor. Now another question." Eben Pay placed the photographic enlargements on the jury railing, then drew back his hand and wiped it along his trousers, as though he might have just touched a snake. "Why did you fire a bullet from this box of ammunition the sheriff brought you?"

"Because he said I could, and it was the right make and weight. The same as the evidence bullet."

"But *any* Peters Cartridge Company ammunition in this caliber and of this weight would have done as well?"

"Yes. This was simply convenient."

"I see. Then in examining a fired bullet, you can't tell if it came from a specific box?"

"No, you can't even tell the lot number. Only weight and manufacturer."

"Then firing a test bullet from the box that came from the defendant's home has no significance?"

"I don't understand the question."

"Let me put it this way, professor," Eben Pay said. "You could have gone to Lewis Brothers' Hardware up here on the square and bought a box of Peters .45's, with a bullet weight of two-hundred-thirty grains, and used one of those as easily?"

"Yes."

"And with the same result?"

"I suppose so."

"So the fact that the bullet came from this particular box doesn't mean anything, does it?"

"No."

"Good," Eben Pay said, and looked significantly at the jury. "In firearms identification, are there any means available to you other than the bullet?"

"Yes sir. Examination of the spent cartridge case."

"Does examination of a spent case as well as the bullet make a stronger case for identification?"

"Yes, it does."

"But no spent cartridge case was examined here?"

"No sir."

"Why not?"

"I asked the sheriff if he had a spent case, and he said he'd never found one."

"So in effect your identification of this weapon was based only on a partial examination, wasn't it?"

"Well, no—"

"Thank you, professor." Eben Pay turned to the bench. "Your Honor, I have no further questions of this witness at the time, but I would request that he be held under subpoena."

"For what purpose, Mr. Pay?" Judge Pitt asked.

"I shall want to call him for my case in chief, as a defense witness."

Lyle Proctor's mouth dropped open, but he recovered enough to rest the state's case after Eben Pay was back at his place beside Duny Gene.

"Now, it's our time," Eben Pay whispered, and he reached over and squeezed Duny Gene's arm.

When Olie Merton was called as the first defense witness, Lyle Proctor made a small fuss about his having been in the courtroom all along, but Judge Pitt pointed out that neither attorney had asked for an exclusion of witnesses. Olie took the stand nervously, but Tooth Snowdon tried to reassure him from the audience with elaborate winks and smirks. It took no effect because Olie never looked in Tooth's direction.

After Eben Pay had established that Olie Merton had known the defendant for many years—since Duny Gene had been a tyke—he asked, "Mr. Merton, did you ever see him up close?"

"All the time. He'd come into the barbershop for a haircut at least once a week."

"How well did you come to know his general

appearance? Not just his features, but his bearing and his build.''

"Nearly as well as I know any of my own kids'.''

"On the day of the robbery, would you tell the jury what you saw?''

"First, I heard these shots from the far side of town. I run outside of my shop onto the sidewalk and this big Packard went past, goin' fast. There were three people in it, all with hats and red bandannas around their faces.''

"How close were you to them?''

"Close as we are now.''

"Did you recognize anyone in that car?''

"No, I didn't.''

On cross, Lyle Proctor gave Olie a hard enough time to make him angry, and Eben Pay was happy to see it didn't sit too well with the jury. Proctor finally got Olie to admit that with those hats and bandannas it would have been difficult to recognize anyone in the car.

"Mr. Merton,'' Eben Pay said on redirect, "you have just told the prosecutor that it would have been difficult to recognize anyone with those hats and masks,'' and everyone in the room was thinking about the prosecutor's own witness, Veda Muller. "As well as you knew the defendant, and supposing he had been in the car—just supposing—I assume from your answer that it would have been difficult for *anyone* to positively identify a person in that car.''

"That's right.'' Olie got it out before Proctor could make his objection, but it didn't matter. The harm had been done with the question, and after Judge Pitt released the witness Eben Pay smiled.

Back in his seat, Olie leaned against Tooth and whispered, "That son of a bitch made me a little mad.''

"You done all right," Tooth said.

When Lydia Pay walked into the courtroom, Duny Gene half rose. She looked at him and smiled before she turned to the clerk and raised her right hand. Duny Gene looked back toward the hall doorway, expecting to see his father, but Barton was not there.

Not until she took the stand did Duny Gene notice the Eastern Star pin on Lydia's left breast—the side nearest the jury. It was the largest such ornament he had ever seen. Behind the spectators' railing, Tooth nudged Olie Merton.

"Look at that," he whispered. "It's bigger'n a deputy sheriff's badge."

Eben Pay took his time, allowing all the Masons on the jury to absorb the idea of the pin. Lydia testified that she was the defendant's mother, and that she and her husband had been in Fort Smith visiting relatives on the day of the robbery. They returned to Weedy Rough the following day, she said, and found Duny Gene gone.

"He got home that night. He'd tacked a note on the tie-yard office door saying that he was going to Lee's Creek, fishing. He went there a lot, sometimes alone, sometimes with his father."

"How did he appear when he came home?"

"He was tired and his clothes were dirty, like they always are after a fishing trip. He had three sun perch and two blue catfish. I had to clean them."

"What else did he have?"

"All the usual stuff. His bedroll and his fishing gear and some canned food he had left over and his father's pistol."

Eben Pay lifted the automatic from the jury railing.

"Would this be the pistol?"

"It looks like my husband's pistol, yes. All I

know is, the sheriff took my husband's pistol when he arrested my son, and that looks like the pistol.''

"How frequently did your husband and Duny Gene take the pistol on fishing trips?"

"Anytime they went. They always took it. They took it out sometimes just to shoot at tin cans, too."

"After these times, when they'd fired the pistol, what did they do on returning home?"

"They cleaned the thing. They were always sitting in the kitchen, cleaning it, taking it apart on a newspaper and smelling up the house with gun oil. Sometimes they cleaned it even when they hadn't shot it.''

"How often after they had fired it did they fail to clean it?"

"Never in my memory! They pampered that pistol because my husband had brought it home from the war. They'd clean it just for the fun of it, I suppose. I never understood it.''

"She's stating her opinion," Lyle Proctor said, but he did not rise, and Judge Pitt waved it aside.

Eben Pay moved about the pit, silently rubbing his chin. He seemed in no hurry, and Judge Pitt made no move to hurry him. Later, Tooth Snowdon said Lydia sent off heat waves of class from that stand just sitting there with her head up, and that Eastern Star pin shining, and it made everyone a little afraid of her somehow, or perhaps respectful, because she was showing herself to be such a fine lady. You couldn't help thinking about the difference in Lydia Pay and Ruby Denton, Tooth said. In that light, she made one hell of a good impression.

When Eben Pay came back to the stand, his questions were so softly spoken that spectators in the rear of the room had to bend forward, trying to catch the words. From the balcony, they were hanging over the rail.

"Lydia, I see that you are a member of the Order of the Eastern Star. What is your position in that order?"

"I am the Worthy Matron of the Weedy Rough chapter."

"Tell us, on what is your order founded?"

"I object, Your Honor," Lyle Proctor said, and now he was up. "This is all irrelevant."

"Your Honor," Eben Pay said, "I am trying to show this jury the atmosphere in which the defendant has lived all his life."

"But Your Honor," Lyle Proctor said, "this goes to credibility only if the defendant . . ."

He stopped, and Eben Pay watched him, waiting for him to say more. Their eyes met, and each knew that if the prosecutor mentioned in any way the defendant taking the stand—or failing to take it—it would make a strong argument for reversible error on appeal.

"I withdraw my objection," Lyle Proctor said, and sat down.

"Very well then, Lydia, you may answer my question," Eben Pay said.

"The Order of the Eastern Star is founded on brotherly love and kindness and charity. It is founded on the teachings of the Bible."

"Were these teachings a part of your family life?"

"Your Honor, I must object to all of this—"

"No, now Lyle, I'm going to allow him some latitude here," Judge Pitt said.

"Lydia, were these teachings a part of your family life?"

"Yes. We are members of the church, and we have always tried to teach our son in the Christian Way of Life. We go to church together each Sunday, my husband and my son and I. We often attended social gatherings at the Star. From the time he was a little boy, Duny Gene has asked questions about the Bible, and he read it often, and he knew the women from the Bible that the stations of the star represent.''

"Lydia, how many Bibles are in your home?"

"Three."

"Is there an American flag there?"

"Oh, for heaven's sake," Lyle Proctor yelled. "Now he's leading her, too."

"I'll take that as an objection and sustain it," Judge Pitt said.

"Lydia, how often has your son been in trouble with the law?"

"Only that once, when he was picked up for something another boy said."

"I object!"

"Your own witness has so testified," Eben Pay said.

"Overruled. Go on, Mr. Pay."

"How many times has your son been accused of crimes such as car theft or shoplifting or pandering?"

"Never!" she said emphatically.

"He's beating it to death," Lyle Proctor said.

"All right, Lyle. Mr. Pay, I think that's enough on that subject."

"Very well, Your Honor. Lydia, explain to the jury how Duny Gene has occupied himself in recent years."

"After he graduated from high school, we were planning to send him to college. But he said he wanted to stay in Weedy Rough among his own people and help his father in the Frisco tie yard."

"What kind of work is that?"

"They buy and ship timber," Lydia said. "Sometimes, it's very hard work. They handle heavy crossties all day long."

"I have no more questions for this witness," Eben Pay said. Proctor hesitated, then indicated he would not cross-examine, and Eben Pay helped Lydia down from the stand. As she passed from the courtroom, she looked at Duny Gene and smiled once more.

When Judge Pitt recessed for lunch, Duny Gene asked his grandfather where he had found such an outlandishly large Eastern Star pin. Eben Pay looked at Duny Gene and grinned.

"You're beginning to catch on to this business, aren't you?"

Eben Pay went to his hotel room with Joe Mountain, and they ate sardines and drank beer from two dark amber bottles Joe Mountain had brought from the pool hall. It was one of those unseasonably hot days that sometimes come on in the fall, and Eben Pay was changing his shirt and underwear, making himself fresh for the afternoon session with clouds of talcum powder.

"Eben Pay, if you had a jury of them people from Tin Cup, you could rest your case right now," Joe Mountain said.

"Tin Cup?"

"Yeah, that's the place all them colored people live," Joe Mountain said. "Them colored people I sit with up in the balcony."

Eben Pay smiled to himself. Joe Mountain was as darkly colored as most of the blacks Eben Pay had seen in this town.

"You think they might acquit him?"

"I think they would have acquitted him as soon as he walked into the courtroom and they seen his black hair." Joe Mountain chuckled. "Besides, they ain't much love lost between them colored folks and most white bankers."

The sardines were gone then and most of the beer. Joe Mountain pulled a small box of vanilla wafers from his coat and offered them to Eben Pay.

"Want a cookie?"

"No. The damned sugar hurts my teeth."

Joe Mountain shoved a cookie into his mouth.

"You know, Eben Pay, there's more to this case than a man can read on the label," Joe Mountain said.

"There usually is."

"Yeah, but this here one's got your own grandson in it, facin' the hangman."

"It's not the hangman now, Joe, it's the chair."

"Same thing."

Joe Mountain pushed another cookie into his mouth and crushed it with his massive teeth. He started to say more, but there was something about the set of Eben Pay's backbone that made him stop this conversation short.

Eben Pay had buttoned his shirt and was pulling the suspenders up over his shoulders when there was a gentle knock at the door. Eben Pay went to open it. Standing in the hallway clutching a beaded purse with a fringe was a tall girl. She was not unattractive, in a bony sort of way. Her blonde hair was cut short and mostly hidden under a hat pulled close down around her ears.

"Mr. Pay?"

"Yes, young lady, what can I do for you?"

"Sir, my name's Arlene Kruppman. I need to talk to you for a minute."

·20·

"PROFESSOR BATES, I REMIND YOU THAT you're still under oath," Judge Pitt said.

Eben Pay took the .45 from the jury railing and held it in one hand.

"Professor, you have established your credentials as an expert on this weapon, I believe. Now, I am going to perform a little experiment here and I would ask that you observe closely."

"Just a minute," Lyle Proctor said, coming toward the bench.

"You don't intend to shoot that thing do you?" Judge Pitt asked.

"Of course not, Your Honor. I only intend to disassemble it. I have a purpose in this for the defense of my client."

"All right, go on with it."

Standing at the jury railing, Eben Pay depressed the recoil-spring retaining plug, turned the barrel bushing, slipped back the slide and pushed out the barrel retaining pin, pulled the slide from the frame, and lay the disassembled parts on the rail. Then carefully lifting the slide once more, he pulled the barrel from the front of the slide and held it up.

"Would you identify this part, professor?"

"That's the barrel."

"In the identification of firearms from lands and grooves markings on *bullets*, how critical is this part?"

"It is the only critical part of the piece. The bore of that barrel is what makes the markings on the bullet, the signature."

Eben Pay passed the barrel to the witness, and Bates clamped his unlit pipe between his teeth and took the barrel in both hands, like an ear of corn.

"Inspect the interior of that barrel, the bore, and tell the jury what you see."

Professor Bates held the barrel up toward the light coming from the east windows.

"I see lands and grooves, rotating in a counter-clockwise direction, about a quarter-turn for the complete length of the bore."

"Is there anything else at all that you can see on the surface of the bore?"

"There are some rust marks and pits."

"What causes that?"

"Rust will accumulate after the weapon is fired. The burning powder creates all sorts of particulate matter that is highly corrosive. This causes rust and pitting."

"What is pitting?"

"Small depressions on the surface of the bore. It's caused by rust."

"After the rust is cleaned from the barrel, will the pits remain?"

"If the bore has been pitted—as I say, by rust— cleaning cannot remove the pits. They are depressions in the metal itself."

"How does one avoid this?"

"By proper cleaning. By working the bore with solvent and oil after firing."

"Would you explain why you did not mention this rust and pitting before?"

"In my opinion, there isn't enough of it to affect the signature."

"Only enough to indicate what, then?"

"Lack of cleaning."

"Now, this weapon was in your possession for some time after you fired it, and in possession of the sheriff. Was the weapon cleaned during that time?"

"Not to my knowledge."

"Would you explain how this might have affected the bore?"

"It would account for the rust, but not the pits."

Professor Bates was then asked to inspect the frame and the slide, and indicated that in his opinion they showed no signs of rust and appeared to have been well maintained.

"Thank you, professor. Now, let me recall for you that I disassembled this weapon before your eyes. I am not any sort of expert with a weapon such as this, but how long would you estimate it took me to do that job?"

"I'd say less than a minute. Perhaps less than thirty seconds."

"How long would you say it would take a person experienced with this weapon to disassemble it?"

"To the extent that you disassembled it, I'd say about twenty seconds. You have only field-stripped the weapon, broken it down into major component parts."

"How long would it take to disassemble *two* of these .45's, supposing I had another one here?"

"I would say less than a minute. One of the favorable features of this pistol is the ease with which it is disassembled."

"Good," Eben Pay said, and he lifted the barrel once more. "Now, explain to the jury how this barrel differs from a revolver barrel."

"A revolver barrel is factory-threaded into the frame. This barrel is not. It is held in place by the pin and the bushing. A revolver barrel cannot be removed as simply as you removed this one."

"What happens when a revolver barrel has to be replaced?"

"It has to be sent to the factory, or to a very good gunsmith."

"And with an automatic, like this one?"

"Anyone who can disassemble the weapon can replace the barrel."

Eben Pay now lifted the frame and grip from the railing and passed it to the witness.

"On the right side of that frame, above the trigger guard, what do you observe?"

"Your Honor," Lyle Proctor said. "I object to this lesson in pistol nomenclature."

"Overruled."

Bates looked at the slide, still chewing on his pipe-stem. "There are various standard markings in the metal. The ordnance stamp, the model number—this one is M1911 U.S. Army—the fact that when manufactured, this pistol was United States property, and the serial number."

"United States property?"

"Yes sir. After the war, the market was flooded with these pistols, many of them sold by the War Department."

Eben Pay took the frame from Professor Bates's hand and replaced it with the slide.

"Are there markings here as well?"

"On the left side of the slide, the dates of patent, Colt Firearms stamp, and a place of manufacture—Hartford, in this case."

"A serial number?"

"No sir."

Eben Pay replaced the slide with the barrel.

"Would you tell the jury where to find the serial number on this barrel?"

"There is no serial number on the barrel."

"Then can you explain how one goes about establishing that a particular barrel goes with a certain serial-numbered weapon?''

''You can't determine that. Like all internal parts, the barrel is not numbered. They are interchangeable.''

''Now I want to be sure the jury understands what you are saying, professor. You are saying that *any* barrel, purchased from a gun shop or hardware store, or *any* barrel from another weapon of this type, would fit this pistol, and you wouldn't be able to tell the difference?''

''That's correct.''

''He's leading the witness,'' Lyle Proctor said.

''Your Honor, I am simply rephrasing what the witness has already said.''

''Overruled.''

''Thank you, Your Honor.'' Quickly, with the jury and witness watching, Eben Pay reassembled the .45, pulled the slide to the rear, pointed the pistol toward the ceiling, and snapped the hammer down.

''How long would it take a person familiar with this weapon to disassemble and reassemble it?''

''Less than a minute.''

''And how long would it take for such a person to disassemble *two* of these things, *exchange the barrels*, and reassemble them?''

''I object, Your Honor. Now he's got the witness usurping the prerogative of the jury.''

''I commend your memory, Mr. Proctor,'' Eben Pay said. ''But I am asking nothing except his opinion as an expert. And besides, you yourself did see me take this pistol down and put it back together.''

''All right,'' said Judge Pitt. ''I rule that the questions are properly put but admonish the jury to take the witness's testimony as his opinion.''

''Your Honor, the jury saw me disassemble and reassemble this pistol.''

''Mr. Pay, I know that. Now, if you want something more in testimony, ask your questions.''

"I think I have none other to ask."

Lyle Proctor made no cross-examination, and Eben Pay leaned toward Duny Gene and whispered as the professor left the courtroom, "You see, if he crossed, about all he could have done was let the jury hear again what I'd already gotten from the witness. So he's smart enough to let this one wiggle off the hook and be forgotten."

"I doubt if they'll forget it," Duny Gene whispered. He took the wad of chewing gum from his mouth and stuck it to the underside of the table. "This is pretty good. Maybe I should have gone to law school after all."

"It's not always this much fun," Eben Pay said.

As he walked to the stand, Duny Gene remembered what his grandfather had said to him, over and over again, when they visited in the jail cell.

"Don't lose your temper. Don't get that vacant look. Act like you're interested in telling that jury your story. Look at them as though every man there is your old and dear friend."

Duny Gene told about meeting Ruby and Lester and how they had gone to Frog Creek to shoot and swim; how he'd brought his daddy's car and pistol to the cabin; how they'd killed off a lot of whiskey.

"On the morning of the robbery, I knew they were up to something. They didn't say much to me, but I heard them talking. They said they were going to pick up a guy named Tabor. Kid Tabor, Lester called him," Duny Gene testified. "I was drinking a lot of whiskey. By noon, when we ate some hard-boiled eggs and some pork and beans out of a can. I was pretty far along."

"You mean you were drunk?"

"Yes sir," Duny Gene said, remembering, too, that one of the things his grandfather had told him was to say "sir" to anyone asking him anything, or even acting like they might. "Right after we ate, I lay down. I went to sleep. I guess I passed out. They were all sitting around the cabin, talking and drinking whiskey. Ruby would come over to me and try to wake me up, and ask me how I liked Jean Harlow. Daddy's pistol was on a little table beside the bed."

"Let's interrupt your story a moment here, Duny Gene, and let me ask you: how many guns were in that room?"

"I don't know. Lester had a bunch of guns, and a Thompson—"

"A submachine gun?"

"Yes sir. He had a .45 like Daddy's, or maybe two. They had a lot of .45 ammunition, for the Thompson and Lester's pistols. They had a half-dozen boxes of Peters and some Remingtons and a few Winchesters."

"Were all the guns loaded?"

"Lester kept his guns loaded all the time. He had the magazines full for his pistols and he had a drum magazine for the machine gun. All loaded. Earlier that morning, we'd done some shooting down the mountain behind the cabin. Afterwards, I cleaned Daddy's gun, drinking whiskey and cleaning it. Lester said he'd clean his later. The magazine for Daddy's pistol was on the table with the pistol, Daddy's pistol. I hadn't reloaded it."

"All right, son, let's go on now. You've testified that you went to sleep. What then?"

"I woke up in the afternoon," Duny Gene said. "Nobody was around anywhere. It was hot and I got up and had a drink of water. I saw all their stuff was gone. They'd had clothes and stuff scattered all over the cabin. It was all gone. I went in the other room, and there was none of their stuff there, either.

"Daddy's pistol was still on the table by the bed,

and the empty magazine. I took it and was going to load it and go to Lee's Creek. I'd had enough drinking and laying around, so I wanted to go dry out at the creek and do some fishing. But I couldn't find any ammunition. It was gone, too. So I got in Daddy's car and drove on down to Lee's Creek. I found me a campsite about dark.''

It was over very quickly. On cross-examination, Lyle Proctor leaped at Duny Gene like a bass taking the bait, Tooth Snowdon said later. He started by reminding Duny Gene that he was under oath, and that the whole system of justice rested on the sanctity of telling the truth, to which Eben Pay objected. Lyle Proctor charged again and again, asking if it wasn't true that he had helped plan the robbery, that he had been in the Packard, that he had shot Parkins Muller.

"You killed that man, didn't you?" Lyle Proctor said coldly. "You went to rob his bank and then you killed him when he resisted, you shot him dead!''

"I told you what happened," Duny Gene said, his voice flat.

Eben Pay rose and moved over to stand close beside Proctor, so Duny Gene could see him, because that glaze had come to the gray eyes. After seeing his grandfather's face, Duny Gene got control of it.

"What's defense counsel doing standing out here?'' Proctor said. "Your Honor, please instruct defense counsel to take his seat.''

"Your Honor, the prosecutor is badgering my client," Eben Pay said. "I am simply placing myself in the best position to defend him. I'm not in anybody's way, and I am not aware of any procedural rule that requires that I remain in some far corner.''

"Would you like to go up and hold his hand while I'm questioning him?''

"Your Honor, I must make it a point of record that

I deplore prosecution's attempt to belittle the relationship between myself and this boy. I've made no effort to hide the fact that he is my grandson, and I am in fact proud of the fact, and proud that he is a fine young man.''

"Nobody's making an issue of your kinship," Proctor fumed. "But when I'm making a cross-examination, I don't expect to have to pull the defense counsel out of my hip pocket at every turn.''

"All right," Judge Pitt broke in, "none of this little exchange has anything to do with the cause in hearing and I admonish the jury to disregard it. Now, Mr. Pay, please stand back a little and allow the prosecution to make his examination.''

But by then Lyle Proctor was finished, too, and Duny Gene came back to the defense table, Eben Pay ushering him there with an arm about his shoulders, as though he were protecting this poor boy from an angry dog.

Duny Gene felt good about it. It hadn't been so bad. He'd managed to hold his temper, and except for that one small lapse he had looked directly at the jury when he spoke. He had seen no sign of hostility in their faces.

He thought it was over then, except for arguments. But Eben Pay called Arlene Kruppman, and Duny Gene watched her coming into the courtroom looking skinny and plain and very frightened. He wondered what in hell was going on. He could barely hear her voice when she answered to the oath.

"Now just speak up so these gentlemen can hear you, Arlene," Eben Pay said. "Tell them exactly what happened on the afternoon of the Weedy Rough robbery.''

"Yes sir. I work at Sycamore Lodge. That's a summer place for folks from Texas, mostly. It's on a hill east of the federal highway and sort of above the place where the Weedy Rough road comes out and runs into it—''

"Runs into the federal highway?''

"Yes sir. That afternoon, after we'd cleaned up the dining room and kitchen after lunch, I had a little time off before supper. We were fixin' roast chicken and dressing, and there wasn't much to do in the kitchen until close to suppertime.

"I got my basket from my room and went along the hill, looking for wood violets. I do that sometimes in the afternoon, so we'll have flowers for the tables at suppertime.''

"Please speak right up, Miss Kruppman,'' Judge Pitt said.

"Yes sir.'' Arlene said it loudly and her voice broke a little. She cleared her throat, trying to avoid looking toward the jury. "I was just above the federal highway where the ball diamond is at. That's where the Weedy Rough road comes in. I saw this big car coming and it was going fast and I watched it.''

"Describe the car, Arlene,'' Eben Pay said.

"I don't know about cars. I don't know what kind it was. But it was long and had the top down and it was tan. There were three people in it.''

"Was there anything unusual about these people?''

"No sir, not that I could see. They were just driving fast.''

"Could you describe them?''

"There was a woman driving. She had this white hair. There was one man in front and one in back, and there wasn't anything peculiar about them.''

"What kinds of hats were they wearing?''

"They didn't have on any hats.''

"How far were you from the road when they passed?''

"Not very far. I saw the car come around the bend

in the Weedy Rough road and onto the federal highway and turn south, and it was just below me on the hillside.''

''How many of the people in that car were you able to recognize?''

''I didn't know any of 'em.''

''All right, Arlene, do you know the defendant in this case?''

''Yes. Duny Gene Pay. We went through school together in Weedy Rough.''

''Your witness,'' Eben Pay said.

Lyle Proctor tried to make a great deal out of the distance Arlene stood from the car when she saw it pass. He asked her why she wasn't wearing her glasses now, and she said she'd never worn glasses. ''At such a distance, and that car going fast,'' Proctor asked, ''how could you have known anyone in the car?''

''I'd know Duny Gene Pay anywhere,'' Arlene said softly.

When Proctor released the witness, Eben Pay rose and rested the case for the defense. Judge Pitt pulled a large gold watch from beneath his robe and popped it open and shifted his cud and recessed until the next day, when he would charge the jury and arguments would be presented.

Duny Gene slipped another stick of Spearmint from his pocket, unwrapped it, and stuffed it in his mouth, then rose to be cuffed and taken back to the jail. He was glad this much was over.

Eben Pay and Joe Mountain sat in the hotel room as the evening came on, watching the college kids screaming around the square in their jalopies. There was a pep rally that night, over on the campus, in anticipation of a football game the next day with some Texas team. Now and then, a group of the brightly painted and ribboned cars would collect in a bunch at one corner of the square, like water bugs congregating, and the kids would give a long, wailing yell. Eben Pay knew it was a glamorized hog call, intended to exhort the Razorbacks to victory.

"You ever see a football game, Joe?"

"Never did," the big Osage said. He was cleaning his fingernails with his oversized snap-blade pocket-knife. "Never much wanted to."

"Some of your people were pretty good at it," Eben Pay said. "At a place called Carlisle."

"Osages play football?"

"Well, I'm not sure about that. But some pretty good ones with Indian blood of one kind or another do."

"What's this Carlisle, a reservation?" Joe Mountain asked, and grinned.

"Don't try to haze me, Joe. You know what Carlisle was as well as I do."

After dark, Joe Mountain went to the pool hall for some beer and to the Smoke Shop for chicken salad sandwiches, and Eben Pay sat waiting, his feet up on the windowsill. Scattered on the bed behind him were a number of issues of *Wild West Weekly* that he had brought from Duny Gene's jail cell for Joe Mountain to read. He took one and idly leafed through it, looking at the line drawings of men with a pistol in each hand, shooting down evil-looking characters in clouds of powder smoke.

One story title caught his eye. "The Kid and the Murder Steer." He glanced down along the double columns of type, and suddenly sat up straight. The hero of this particular epic was named Kid Tabor.

· 21 ·

AFTER JUDGE PITT INFORMED THE JURY ON
points of law, and emphasized at Eben Pay's insis-
tence that a defendant is innocent until proven guilty
beyond a reasonable doubt, Lyle Proctor stood to his
opening argument and ran over his witnesses' testimony. It took a long time, and the sun climbed high
enough so that by the time Lyle was finished its light
was no longer shining into the courtroom from the
east windows. Tooth Snowdon went to sleep twice.

Eben Pay, when he had his turn, started off with
the "fourth person" business, and before he was
finished he had used the term at least twenty times.
He reminded the jury about the fine home from which
Duny Gene had come, and about his choosing a life
of hard work instead of college, to help his father in
the tie yard. Among the jurors, as Eben Pay knew
quite well, there was not a single college graduate.

He spoke of credibility, and Tooth Snowdon was
bruising Olie Merton's ribs with his elbow until Olie
leaned against him and whispered, "God dammit,
stop pokin' me ever' time he says somethin'."

"Who would you believe?" Eben Pay asked. "An
hysterical woman, who saw four *masked* people, three
of them with pistols, and who somehow failed to
identify Duny Gene until *after* she'd heard that Hoadie
Renkin was involved?

"Who would you believe, a Texas woman come to these hills to make her own manner of mischief, fighting to stay clear of the pen, willing to say anything to do it, willing to lie to do it? After all the other things she's done, do you really think she would hesitate to lie to save her own neck?

"Or would you believe a woman, pillar of her community, a good Christian woman you saw on that stand, she and her husband, a hardworking veteran of the war, raising a son on the teachings of the Bible?"

Lyle Proctor groaned loud enough to be heard, and Judge Pitt was about to admonish him, but Eben Pay was going on like a runaway Frisco train, pounding home his points, striking the jury railing with a clenched fist to punctuate his words.

"Or instead of an hysterical spinster or a Texas outlaw, would you believe the son of that household, hardworking and never in trouble, caught in a wicked circumstance because like so many of us he enjoyed the taste of a little whiskey now and then, tangled at every turn in the web of deceit spun by these spiders that came to prey on your communities, your institutions, your citizens?"

Eben Pay paused, breathing hard, standing straight and fingering his wolf's tooth. After only a few seconds, he launched into it again, going to that fourth person once more.

"There *was* a man named Tabor. The fourth person. When those three—Lester and Ruby and Hoadie—left the cabin that afternoon, they picked him up somewhere. We don't know where. We don't know if he had his own car or not. I suspect he did, but we don't know because Ruby refused to tell us. The fourth man, dropped off somewhere afterwards. We don't know where. Because Ruby refused to tell us. But he's out there somewhere. We don't know where because Ruby won't tell us. She was here for one purpose: to cooperate with the prosecutor in sending that boy to the chair,'' and he pointed at Duny Gene.

"Oh yes, gentlemen. Ruby had been caught with the goods in that Packard, and she had to cooperate to save herself. She had to put Duny Gene in that car. But where was he? Sleeping in the cabin!

"They went into Weedy Rough—Lester, Ruby, Hoadie, and that fourth person—and they robbed the bank. But something went badly wrong. They had to shoot a man. Lester had to shoot him with one of his .45's, and Lester knew the pistol he'd used could send him to the electric chair. And back at the cabin— Ruby told us this much, anyway—they stopped to pick up their things, and there that fourth person went his own way, we don't know where because Ruby refused to tell us.

"But they stopped there. And in those few minutes, maybe two or less, Lester saw the opportunity to rid himself of that incriminating bit of evidence. Of course, they had found the spent cartridge case in the car, from where the shot had been fired, and Lester had thrown it away. So Lester knew that the only thing that could mark him as the killer was the bullet that had passed through Parkins Muller's head!

"And in those few moments at the cabin, he saw the pistol on the bedstand, the pistol that belonged to Duny Gene's daddy. And gentlemen, he *switched barrels*. He knew that as much as Duny Gene cherished that gun his daddy had brought back from the war, the boy almost surely knew the serial number by heart, and because of that, Lester could not switch the *whole* pistol intact. So he *switched barrels!*

"And they drove away, gentlemen. They ditched more than the blue coupe. They ditched Mr. Tabor, that fourth person as well. Oh yes, Ruby said, they laughed about not having to split the money. But they weren't laughing about not splitting it with Duny

Gene. They laughed about not having to split it with Hoadie Renkin, dead in the street, and with Mr. Tabor, whose whereabouts we don't know, but we do know he isn't likely to come forward. Oh yes, I can hear Ruby and Lester laughing about it. And Duny Gene sleeping in the cabin.

"And when he woke and went fishing and then home, he replaced his daddy's pistol in its place without cleaning it, as he *always* did. Why? Because, gentlemen, Duny Gene *didn't know the pistol had been fired!*

"Recall, please, gentlemen. Lydia Pay testified that her son and husband have always, *always* been avid in their care of that pistol. Cleaning it when it was fired, cleaning it when it was not. Doesn't that seem terribly contradictory to you, those pits in that barrel, pits that had to develop over a long period of time due to *lack of cleaning!*"

He stopped again and the courtroom was so still some people thought they could hear Judge Pitt's gold pocket watch ticking.

"As His Honor has told you, the law requires that you convict only if the state has proven guilt *beyond a reasonable doubt*. An abiding conviction to moral certainty. And I tell you, gentlemen, there is much more here than a reasonable doubt. I tell you my grandson is not guilty! I thank you for your attention, gentlemen!"

Proctor rose for his rebuttal, and he made a good deal of the fact that the rust in the evidence gun barrel could have formed during the long period it was in the hands of court officials. He didn't try to explain away the rust pits, because he couldn't. And at the defense table, Duny Gene knew he couldn't, and he also knew that those pits had been in the barrel the day his daddy brought the .45 home from the war. Barton had told him so.

It went to the jury a few minutes past noon, and as they filed out past the spectators, the only sound was the thump of their shoes against the polished hardwood floors. Eben Pay touched Duny Gene's arm, then quickly went into the hall before the people could clog it with traffic. He hurried to the clerk's office and asked to make a long-distance telephone call, to number thirty-two at Weedy Rough.

"Lydia?" Eben Pay said into the mouthpiece. "It's over. The jury's out, just a minute ago. You and Barton better get on up here if you want to see the finish. I don't think it's going to take long."

"We're starting now," she said, and hung up.

They didn't take Duny Gene back to jail. Sheriff Geehyle Ramey came and sat in Eben Pay's vacated chair at the defense table. They didn't put handcuffs on him, either, and after a while, as the afternoon wore on, Duny Gene walked aimlessly around the pit of the courtroom, going to the jury rail a number of times and rubbing its smooth oak surface with his fingertips. The bailiff had removed all the physical evidence to the jury room.

Some of the spectators had gone out, but others remained in their seats and waited, whispering among themselves. Tooth had another little nap, but Olie Merton was wide awake. Once Duny Gene walked near the front row of the gallery and nodded to Olie.

"Hi, Olie. How you?"

"Tolerable, Duny Gene, just tolerable."

There were three deputies in the courtroom, and once one of them came into the pit close to Duny Gene, but Geehyle Ramey waved him back again.

Eben Pay was on the street, walking up and down College Avenue in front of the courthouse. Joe Mountain and some of his black friends were on the sidewalk in front of the Ozark theater, and Eben Pay walked over to them and talked for a while.

"These are some of the folks from down in the Cup," Joe Mountain said. "They gonna cook up a bait of pork ribs tonight and asked me to come down and eat with 'em."

"You welcome, too, Mr. Pay," one of the men said. He had red hair, the color of copper shavings.

"I appreciate it," Eben Pay said. "But I may be detained elsewhere. But Joe can eat enough for two of us anyway."

"You done good in the court," the red-haired one said. "I seen it all."

"Yeah, you don' get on back to wuk 'fore long, they gonna lay you off," a woman in back of the group said, and they all laughed.

"Yeah, they lay me off, I go to Detroit."

"They's more comin' back from Detroit than goin'," the woman said, and they all nodded and laughed again.

Eben Pay turned back toward the jail and walked with his head down, his hands behind his back. There was little traffic on the streets this Saturday afternoon, and it was very quiet. Once he heard a strange, faraway sound, like brittle thunder, and he paused and listened for a long time until it came again. He knew then it was the crowd yelling at the football game across town. The wind was blowing from that direction, and it was cold. He wished he'd brought his overcoat.

He saw Barton Pay's Ford coming down Smoky Row, with Barton driving and Lydia beside him, sitting straight as a bed slat. He hurried to meet them as Barton parked the car along the Row.

"I'm glad you're here," he said, and they both shook hands with him. Barton's grip was weak and wet, and he looked haggard and drawn. "How you feeling?"

"I'm not too bad," Barton said. "I can't seem to get any strength up since this thing happened."

"Well, it's almost over," Eben Pay said. "Let's go to the Castle Luncheonette and get some coffee. It's turned coffee weather."

"Shouldn't we be in the courthouse?" Lydia asked.

"They'll get me before anything happens. I told them where I'd be."

"How's Duny Gene?"

"He's fine. He did a good job on the stand."

"I don't know why you insisted that we stay away," she said.

"I wanted the jury to see you once on the stand, and nothing more. Sometimes you can make too much of a good thing."

She started to reply but stopped, and he took her arm and guided her along the sidewalk, Barton walking close behind with his head down.

It took longer than Eben Pay had thought it would. They were on their fifth cup of coffee when the messenger came from the clerk's office to say that the jury was coming in. As he held her arm on the way to the courtroom, Eben Pay could feel Lydia trembling.

Duny Gene was slouched in his chair, his back to the door, and he didn't see them arrive. The spectators' section was packed again, and Tooth and Olie got up so the Pays would have a place to sit. They stood along the wall near the door, and a deputy sheriff started to usher them out into the hall, but Geehyle Ramey said leave 'em be.

Joe Mountain had been watching Eben Pay in the street, and had followed into the courthouse with his entourage of black friends. Now they were tumbling into the balcony seats, creating a terrible racket.

Judge Pitt mounted the bench, and the bailiff called the court to order and everything was suddenly still.

His Honor glared around and adjusted his glasses. He had disposed of his cud.

"Bring in the jury."

The twelve men filed in, looking somber. After they'd taken their seats in the box, Judge Pitt asked if they'd reached a verdict. A man in bib overalls stood up and said they had.

"Hand it to the clerk," Judge Pitt said. The slip of paper passed from foreman to clerk to judge. Judge Pitt read it at a glance and passed it down to the clerk once more.

"Defendant rise," he said. Duny Gene pushed back his chair and stood facing the jury, Eben Pay beside him.

"Read the verdict," Judge Pitt said.

The clerk read, "We the jury find the defendant, Duny Gene Pay, not guilty!"

Duny Gene watched it all dissolve into a heaving, flowing mass, like a school of minnows when the bass comes near. The judge was releasing him, adjourning the court and moving out of the courtroom. The jury was standing, a few moving tentatively toward the gate from the box. He watched the crowd going from a well-ordered formation, like soldiers, to a milling, chattering mob, reminding him of a gaggle of geese. Then he felt a tug at his sleeve and turned to find his grandfather, hand extended, but Eben Pay was not smiling.

"I hope you've learned something from this," Eben Pay said, and they clasped hands.

"Thank you, Grandfather. I never saw anything like it."

"Good-bye, Duny Gene," Eben Pay said. "Your folks are here to take you home." And he turned abruptly and walked away.

Barton and Lydia were moving across the pit toward him, and Lydia was crying. Barton was not, and Duny Gene thought, Daddy always picks the wrong times to cry. She fought for me, while he sat in my cell and cried and acted like it was the end of the world, or else he didn't bother to come at all. He gave up on me. But she never did.

Later, Tooth Snowdon would say in the barbershop, "I never figured to see Lydia Pay hug anybody in public. She never made no sign or show of that kind of thing. But she hugged Duny Gene and he hugged her and it looked like they'd never turn loose of one another. Then after a long spell of huggin', Duny Gene shook his daddy's hand, and his daddy kissed him on the cheek. I never figured to see anything like that happen with Miz Lydia."

"What the hell you expect?" Olie Merton said, and his ribs were still aching.

"Duny Gene went over and shook hands with all the jury," Homer Gage said.

Back in one corner, Mr. Harmon Budd roused himself.

"Is it train time yet?" he mumbled.

"No, ain't time, yet, Harmon," Olie said.

"Then Mr. Pay and Miz Lydia and Duny Gene left, and she was still huggin' at him and he had his arm around her, and Mr. Pay walkin' along behind with his head down like an old dog. I never figured to see Miz Lydia carry on like that in public. She was even cryin'."

"What the hell you expect?" Olie repeated. "He's her own son, ain't he?"

The Sunday train carried few passengers. Eben Pay and Joe Mountain had the whole smoking car to themselves. They sat facing each other, Joe Mountain eating peanuts and Eben Pay puffing on a cigar. He watched the rolling landscape flow past the window, growing rougher as they rode south. They were silent, each with his own thoughts, or more correctly Eben Pay with his, and Joe Mountain not wanting to intrude.

The train made the final long bend into Weedy Rough, stopped long enough to unload mail, and then labored on into the tunnel, where the only light came from the oily yellow glow of bulbs hung along the ridgeline of the car. Then they were out into the blinding sunlight once more, and the rugged hills and hollows peeled back from the tracks in all directions as they moved closer to Fort Smith.

"Well, I'm glad it's finished," Eben Pay said softly.

"That was one fine case, Eben Pay," Joe Mountain said, happy the silence was broken.

"It had a few good moments. I hated to hand Lyle Proctor's head to him, he's a good lawyer. I like Judge Pitt, too. He asked me to come back up sometime for a little poker and sour mash."

"That part about the pistol barrel, that was good," Joe Mountain said. "You couldn't do that back in the old days, when about all they ever brang into court was a Winchester or an old Colt six-shooter."

Eben Pay sat silent again, watching the landscape beyond the window. The ridges were covered with hardwood, their leaves still hanging on, colored yellow and orange and red and shining in the sun. They crossed High Bridge, and far below Eben Pay could see the sparkle of the small creek that meandered through the deep hollow like a silver garden snake. He puffed the cigar and let out a dense cloud of blue smoke.

"You know, a man never gets too old to learn something new about himself," he said. "All my life, I've worked for justice. It's been the one thing that has consumed my thinking, after Missy died. I've always thought that justice was the strongest urge inside me. But I just found out. Blood is stronger."

"I coulda told you that," Joe Mountain said, and he was grinning, but there was no mirth in it. Grinning was Joe Mountain's set expression, even in the old days when he was on posse duty for Judge Parker and had to shoot somebody.

"It's disturbing."

"How long did you know he done it?"

"I'm not sure. It came to me slowly. I think the thing I hate worse about it is that little girl committing perjury."

"Maybe some of it was true," Joe Mountain said. "Maybe it could count as just a little lie. Anyway, that pistol-barrel thing would have won it."

"Maybe," Eben Pay said, looking out the window. "But it amazes me. My mother always talked about it. That family meant more than anything else in life. She'd learned that from her mother. Stronger than the land, stronger than any other faith, she said. I never completely believed that."

They were coming down into the last deep valleys of the Ozarks, and ahead the land opened and flattened along the Arkansas River. Beyond that broad plain rose the blue outline of other mountains, far to the south.

"It's a funny thing, Joe. You look down the years instead of backwards. Your mother and father, they fade into the history of things, they become the past, and you always have a reverence for them. But you view it from arm's length. Your own children and their children, that's what family really means to a man my age. Maybe a man not my age, too, but I never fully realized it before."

"You and your boy was never very close," Joe Mountain said, dropping peanut hulls on the floor, popping meats into his wide mouth.

"No, that's true. It all amazes me. I guess somewhere in me, some hidden place I'd never found before, was my mother still speaking to me about family. This was the first time it got the test. But I know now, for me anyway. It finally came to the surface. When push comes to shove, blood is stronger than anything."

"I coulda told you that," Joe Mountain said again. "Blood is stronger than lye soap. You feel better now, don't you?"

"I suppose I do. But it all amazes me."

· 22 ·

THE BANK OF WEEDY ROUGH WAS NEVER opened again. Miss Veda retired to her goats and guinea hens, and the only time people ever saw her was late each afternoon when she went to her milking. Her only contact with the town came through Tooth Snowdon, who went up every month to clean out her privy. Each time, when he was finished, he knocked at her door to collect his four bits for the job, but more importantly to see that she hadn't died since his last visit.

It was almost a year later when she left town, coming down to the depot to catch the morning train, carrying two canvas bags that might have come into the state with reconstruction Yankees after the Civil War. One of Reese Walls's boys, by now a man, was the new ticket agent and telegrapher for Frisco, and he said she bought a one-way fare to Paris, Texas.

It didn't surprise anyone. Miss Veda had been trying to sell all her property for a long time, but with the Depression it was hard to find much money around for buying empty bank buildings, musty old houses that needed roofing, and a herd of French Alpine goats. She finally made a deal with somebody from Oklahoma, but it was still a long time before the old bank building was opened again, this time as a grocery store.

When she left, Tooth Snowdon took the goats to board until she finally sent him the money to ship them to Texas.

"You gotta give Frisco credit," Tooth said. "If you got the price, they're willing to put anything on their freight cars. Even them gawddamned goats."

Later, a lot of people figured the town's decline began when the bank closed forever. A town without a bank, they said, wasn't much of a town. But there were other factors, too.

Each year, the Texas Trade grew smaller until, finally, only a few of the big cars came to the streets in summer, and almost all of the cottages on Sycamore Lodge hill began to rot and fall into ruin.

And there weren't as many babies born in Weedy Rough as there once had been. Baby-bearing-age women were going to Fayetteville or Fort Smith to find jobs and husbands, or else they married a man in Weedy Rough who went off someplace for work and adventure, some even to California.

Alvie Haus had retired, and the mail was being carried back through the sticks by Joe Sparks's youngest son. Alvie and his wife picked up and went to Missouri to live with a daughter and her family.

On Christmas, Barton Pay helped with the mail as he always had, and he carried the little animal-cracker boxes of goodies to the hill kids, as he always had. Only now there were not so many of them. The old folks along the mail route were still dying as usual, from hard work and bad diet, and Barton spoke over a lot of graves, as he always had.

Lydia was still active in the Star and the Methodist church, but other things had changed. Barton never went fox racing anymore, and it seemed that all the running packs were dwindling. One reason was the traffic on the federal highway. Unlike yard dogs and city mongrels, fox dogs never made a satisfactory adjustment to automobiles. Dixie was run over and killed just north of the ball diamond one night when she was coming in from a race. That took all the remaining starch out of Barton's desire to race dogs.

The biggest change at the Pay household was Duny Gene's absence. Three days after the trial, he did not appear for breakfast. When Lydia went to his room, she found a short note, informing that he was hitch-hiking to Tennessee to join the Civilian Conservation Corps.

It didn't surprise her. It didn't surprise anyone in town. It was just another of those changes taking place after the robbery. They began to measure everything by that. A thing happened before the robbery, or after.

That same day, when Duny Gene slipped away, Lydia posted a letter to Eben Pay in Fort Smith, and this became a matter of public knowledge as soon as Bee Schirvy could get to the barbershop from the post office. Everybody figured Lydia was letting the old counselor know that his grandson had moved on, and they were right.

To Barton's surprise, his wife and father began to correspond on a regular basis. It seemed a little absurd to him, that they would communicate by mail living so close together, and Lydia often being in

Fort Smith once more, almost as much as she had when they'd first come to the Rough. Before the robbery, it would have pleased Barton. But now, he could work up little enthusiasm for it. The barbershop bunch noted that since the robbery Barton had worked up very little enthusiasm for anything.

Lydia got her first letter from Duny Gene almost five months after he'd gone. It was from Tennessee, where as near as she could make out, he was part of a work force building dams. It was a short letter, but at least it had a return address. She sent him more than a dozen letters before she got a second one back from him, all of which Bee Schirvy reported.

It didn't seem to matter to her that her son was far away and seldom heard from. She had come to think of it all as part of the bad bargain she had struck in the back of that buggy in Fort Smith more than twenty years ago.

And she never lost faith in the jury verdict. It was a thing that Barton should have rejoiced in, but instead it weighed heavily on his soul, knowing that Lydia was unaware of their son's capacity to commit a felony. And the worst part of it was his knowing the truth in his heart, but unable ever to bring himself to tell her.

Barton still ran the tie yard, but the work seemed to give him physical pain. He no longer squatted and talked with the timbermen, but as soon as the load was marked and credited, he went into the office shack and shut the door. The Frisco had to send another man up to do the work finally. That was in 1934, when Barton had his first stroke.

"God," Tooth Snowdon said, wiping his nose on his sleeve. "It's goin' to hell in a poke. My younguns growed and gone off. No more little ones to wool around and hug. Maudie writes she's had her second baby, and I ain't even seen the first one yet."

"We're just gettin' old, Tooth," Olie Merton said. "Things are bound to change."

And they were changing, fast. Esta and Mona Stayborn had left for Alabama, where Esta was going into business with some of Mona's people. A stranger came to operate the store where Esta had been a fixture in the town for as long as anybody could remember. He still called it the Muller Mercantile—in memory of one of Weedy Rough's finest citizens, he said. Leviticus Hammel had received the call to a higher ministry and gone to a West Memphis church. Now a stranger was in the pulpit each Sunday at the Methodist church. There were strangers everywhere.

Cobb Hubbs was getting too old and stiff to play shortstop, and Leo Sparks had hung up his badge, and his pistol was rusting away on some closet shelf. He was the last constable Weedy Rough ever had. After Leo, they left law enforcement to the county sheriff. Joe Sanford closed down his ice-cream parlor and went to Fayetteville to run a hamburger joint for somebody.

They put a CCC camp out in the woods near Devil's Mountain. Each Saturday night two army trucks would come in with a load of the CCC boys, and they'd get drunk and raise hell in old man Kruppman's beer hall. Archer had left town to join his brother Pug, and it was said that they were both serving time now on a Mississippi chain gang for assorted kinds of mayhem and theft.

Arlene was gone, too, with the money she'd saved working at Sycamore Lodge, headed for the East, she said. But Tooth allowed she likely never got any farther than Tennessee where they were building all those dams.

And in the barbershop, Olie Merton stood each day and watched the town rotting away through his dusty windows, vowing that soon he would take a bucket of soap water out onto the sidewalk and scrub off the filthy panes. But he never did. And the picture from the *Police Gazette* of Jack Sharkey hanging on his wall changed to Primo Carnera, and then to Maxie Baer.

In the spring of 1935, Barton Pay died. Of a second stroke followed by pneumonia and other complications no one could diagnose, or even cared to try.

And on that day, as always in fair weather and foul, the indestructible Mr. Harmon Budd lay drunk under the maple tree at the Frisco depot, his peg leg jutting out before him like a felled hickory sapling.

Duny Gene Pay came back to the hills for the first and last time to see his daddy buried. It was in April, with rain. He and his mother sat in the old living room, the same one from which they'd watched the bank being robbed back in 1925. They did not speak of that. They talked mostly about what Duny Gene was doing in the C's, very little about Barton after the first few moments, when Lydia had explained that Barton seemed to stop living the day they found his fox dog run over by a car on the federal highway.

Eben Pay arrived before noon, and the Ladies' Aid Society had provided a nice dinner of chicken and dumplings, with apple pan pie to top it off. Duny Gene ate very little, and then said he wanted to see about the grave site. He drove the Model A to the Bethel Ford cemetery, in the rain, remembering the day he and Hoadie Renkin had taken the road out of Fayetteville toward Siloam Springs in this same kind of weather. He took a half-pint bottle of whiskey from his coat pocket and sipped it as he drove.

Bethel Ford was an old burial ground, dating back before the Civil War. It was in the broad valley where the federal highway crossed West Fork of

White River north of Weedy Rough. When Duny
Gene got there, he found Tooth Snowdon digging the
grave. As Duny Gene walked to the hole, Tooth
looked up, the rain and tears dripping off his long
nose.

"Hello, Tooth," Duny Gene said.

"I run 'em off. I run 'em all off," Tooth said.
Under a big sycamore nearby were three men, watching them. "I run them funeral-home sons of bitches
off and I dug 'er my ownself. I told your daddy years
ago that when he died I'd do it, and he'd have the
best gawddamn grave in the county. So I run them
sons of bitches off."

Dirt flew out of the hole in furious clots. Tooth
paused again and wiped his nose on his sleeve.

"By Gawd, that's what I done."

"He'd be proud of that," Duny Gene said.

He stood there a long time, watching the old man
shaping the sides of the grave, smoothing the bottom.
Now and again Tooth glanced up, his watery blue
eyes still brimming with tears. Duny Gene could
remember when Tooth once came to the Pay house
for odd jobs, Duny Gene just a boy still, watching
the long, efficient fingers working hammer and saw
and planer. Sometimes, Tooth would have a stick of
chewing gum in his pocket for the boy. Duny Gene
remembered that. And the times around fox-racing
fires, and in the barbershop when he went to get his
hair cut and Tooth would be sitting along the wall,
telling tall tales.

"Well, I better get back to the church for the
services," Duny Gene said. "See you later, Tooth."

It stopped raining and cleared later in the day. By
the time the funeral procession arrived from Weedy
Rough, the cemetery was bright with sunlight. Coming along the federal highway, the procession was
strung out for over a mile.

The family rode in a funeral-home Cadillac, Duny Gene, Lydia, and Eben Pay. When they walked to the grave across the wet grass, Lydia was between the other two, holding herself straight and with a black veil blowing gently around her face. None of them was crying.

Some distance back from the grave, under a still-dripping willow, Tooth Snowdon and Olie Merton stood watching. Tooth was wiping at his eyes and nose, leaning on his shovel. The last of the rain clouds had drifted off to the east, rising now above the wooded hills there, brilliant-white in the afternoon sun. On the far side of the federal highway was a pasture where white-faced cattle grazed, and there were meadowlarks.

Olie and Tooth watched as the service was said and completed, and the people began to move back to their cars parked along the highway. There was a deputy sheriff to see that no fenders were bent as the cars began to unsnarl and head back to Weedy Rough or to the county seat up north.

"Well," Olie said, "he had a peck of friends."

"Yeah. And he had a good funeral, didn't he?"

"I saw people here today I ain't seen in ages," Olie said. "I wonder how old Ike Renkin and his boys got here."

"They come with Homer Gage in his wrecker," Tooth said.

"A lot of those sticks people got here, somehow."

"Yeah," Tooth said, swiping his sleeve along his nose. "It's the biggest gawddamn funeral I ever seen in this part of the country. Except for Pretty Boy Floyd."

A Note About the Author

Douglas C. Jones lives in northwest Arkansas, where he writes and occasionally paints. *Weedy Rough* is his seventh book. His first was a book of nonfiction, *The Treaty of Medicine Lodge*. *The Court-Martial of George Armstrong Custer*, his first novel, was made into a television film. It was followed by *Arrest Sitting Bull* and *A Creek Called Wounded Knee*. His three novels *Winding Stair, Elkhorn Tavern,* and *Weedy Rough* have been set in the South and Southwest, principally in his home state of Arkansas, with a number of common characters and a time span of almost a hundred years. Of *Elkhorn Tavern*, Michael Malone in *The New York Times Book Review* said "[It] has the beauty of *Shane* and the elegiac dignity of *Red River* without the false glamour or sentimentality of those classic Western films." The book received the 1981 award for Best Novel of the Year from the Friends of American Writers.

HISTORICAL NOVELS
OF THE AMERICAN FRONTIERS

MORE
HISTORICAL NOVELS
OF THE AMERICAN FRONTIERS

<u>JOHN BYRNE COOK</u>

THE SNOWBLIND MOON TRILOGY
(Winner of the Golden Spur Award)

☐	58150-4	BETWEEN THE WORLDS	$3.95
☐	58151-2		Canada $4.95
☐	58152-0	THE PIPE CARRIERS	$3.95
☐	58153-9		Canada $4.95
☐	58154-7	HOOP OF THE NATION	$3.95
☐	58155-5		Canada $4.95

<u>W. MICHAEL GEAR</u>

☐	58304-3	LONG RIDE HOME	$3.95
☐	58305-1		Canada $4.95

<u>JOHN A. SANDFORD</u>

☐	58843-6	SONG OF THE MEADOWLARK	$3.95
☐	58844-4		Canada $4.95

<u>JORY SHERMAN</u>

☐	58873-8	SONG OF THE CHEYENNE	$2.95
☐	58874-6		Canada $3.95
☐	58871-1	WINTER OF THE WOLF	$3.95
☐	58872-X		Canada $4.95

Buy them at your local bookstore or use this handy coupon:
Clip and mail this page with your order.

Publishers Book and Audio Mailing Service
P.O. Box 120159, Staten Island, NY 10312-0004

Please send me the book(s) I have checked above. I am enclosing $_____
(please add $1.25 for the first book, and $.25 for each additional book to
cover postage and handling. Send check or money order only—no CODs.)

Name _____

Address _____

City _____ State/Zip _____

Please allow six weeks for delivery. Prices subject to change without notice.

BESTSELLING BOOKS FROM TOR